Dust Freaks & Demigods

Dome City Investigations
Book 1

Milo James Fowler

Copyright © 2024 by Milo James Fowler

All rights reserved.

This book or any portion of it may not be reproduced or used in any manner whatsoever without the express written permission of the author—except for brief quotations in glowing, 4.5-star reviews. (Your reward will await you in Heaven.) The story contained within this book is a work of fiction. All material is either the product of the author's overactive imagination or is used in a fictitious manner. Any resemblance to actual persons (living or dead) or to actual events is entirely coincidental—and worthy of further investigation.

For Sara

Dome City Investigations:

Dust Freaks & Demigods

Infidels & Insurgents

Zombies & Zealots

I

I fall.

Twin grapnels fire from pressurized launch ports mounted on the shoulders of my exo-suit, their cables spiraling as they chase the hooks upward, high above me as I plummet from the rooftop of Hawthorne Tower. It's like I've slipped off the edge of a pool, and now I'm tumbling backward, my arms reaching out in vain, my legs kicking, unable to fight the force of gravity and the inevitable splash as I'm enveloped by frigid water.

Except there's only the rush of cold air in my ears now, and if there's going to be a splash, it won't involve any water. It'll be a hundred and fifty floors down on the sidewalk below as my exoskeleton—good for providing extra power when needed but not invincible as armored protection—crumples, and my flesh and bones break apart in a disgusting splatter pattern the building's dutiful cleaning bots won't have an easy time expunging from the concrete.

"We will become *gods*!" he shouts after me, his dark silhouette featureless with the moon glowing behind him, its frosty light filtered through the blue tint of Dome 1's reinforced plexicon. He leans over the edge of the roof, watching me drop, and laughs as if he's won some kind of great victory.

All lights are out this late after curfew. The Dome has to save energy when it can, maintaining that precarious equilibrium between its consumers and everything they consume. So every good citizen is home in bed, and silence holds the night except for the deep, resonating laughter echoing above and the clink of my grapnels as they fail to find purchase. Glancing off the parapet, they change course in midair and nose-dive after me.

Together we fall.

I reach blindly for the building's mirrored glass exterior, my gloved fingers grasping onto nothing but air. If I could punch through the surface, the exo frame might protect my arm and slow my descent, carving a multi-meters-long gash and leaving me stranded, dangling there, sure, but alive. Wishful thinking, maybe.

That doesn't stop me from trying. I kick out with my boots in their exo-braces, hoping to make contact.

Nothing.

My trajectory off the top of the building has thrown me too far away. A forceful shove will do that to you every time. Except the guy didn't use his hands. He was standing a few meters away from me when he activated the chrome baton in his hand. I really should have known better, considering who I was up against.

This is what I get for being too cocky. Just one of the pitfalls of a promotion from curfew enforcer to investigator. Who knew? I'll have to be more careful next time.

Assuming there is a next time.

As I pass the halfway point—guessing it's the 75th floor—

I'm beginning to think my boys have abandoned me. I'm all alone here, floundering in the air, my body foolishly thinking it can swim against the current. What a pathetic way to go out.

This is what I get for going without sleep. Stimulants only work so long before you crash hard or start making stupid mistakes. The life or death variety.

There's no going back from this.

So I tuck in my arms and pull my knees to my chest, hoping the exo takes the brunt of the fall, but not so sleep-deprived as to be delusional. I know better than to think my suit will save me. So I brace myself for the inevitable.

That's when Wink and Blink zip through the night, their flashing red and blue lights reflecting from the tower walls as they plunge after me, quadcopter rotors buzzing, each with a robotic claw extending from the underside of its disc-shaped chassis. The drones weave to and fro as they descend, reaching for my falling grapnels, missing, then clutching onto the cables that slip through their grasp until the grapnels clink against their claws.

They've got me.

I'm tempted to succumb to relief, but they haven't caught me yet. I keep falling as the slack shortens. We'll have to see how they do with the combined weight of my body and the plasteel exoskeleton encasing it.

There's a violent lurch as my shoulders are tugged upward, and my legs snap downward. Wink and Blink each hold me by a cable, slowing my descent, their little engines whining from the strain. Hauling me back to the rooftop is not an option, but saving me from an ugly death seems possible—if they can hang on long enough for me to land in one piece.

"Good work," I gasp, reaching up to hold onto the cables like I'm parachuting or something. Law enforcer by day, base jumper by night.

"Are you injured, Investigator Chen?" Wink and Blink say in unison, their synthesized voices identical and devoid of emotion. Drone AI systems aren't complicated, and neither is their repertoire of conversation-starters.

"Just my pride." As we drift toward the ground, I receive an incoming hail, audio only. Tapping my temple, I link up. "Chen here."

"I have the suspect in custody, Investigator Chen," comes the impassive voice of D1-436, my partner. Dunn, as I call him. "Are you all right?"

"Fine. Bring him down to the foyer. I'll meet you there."

A short pause. "The drones may not be able to hold onto you." Linked to them, he sees everything they do. That includes me dangling here like an idiot. "Engine failure prior to touchdown is a distinct possibility."

"Then we'll see how my exo holds up."

"It was not designed for such a fall."

"Are you trying to make me feel better?"

Another pause. "I will meet you in the foyer, Investigator Chen."

Dunn is one of a kind, even though he looks like every other security clone in the Domes with his white armor and black face shield. A former member of Chancellor Hawthorne's protection force, cloned after the late great Dr. Solomon Wong himself. Like the other clones in the Domes, Dunn wears under his helmet the face of a young Wong in his prime. But unlike his hundred or so identical twins,

Dunn can think for himself. A head injury he suffered a while back is most likely the culprit, when a friend of mine shot him right in the face shield, disrupting his programming. Not that clones are robots; they're completely organic, biological beings. But they are, as a rule, susceptible to conditioning—another word for programming, I suppose.

Not sure exactly how any of that works. Not my area of expertise.

But one thing I know: nobody's leading Dunn around by the nose anymore. Like the rest of us who enforce the law in Domes 1 through 10, he thinks for himself when he's not following orders—and when he's not reporting to Level 5 at HQ for requisite downtime and analysis, courtesy of our technicians and science staff. No idea what they do with him down there, but I imagine him in an induced sleep state while his suit of tactical armor recharges, and the scientists stand around scanning him, monitoring his brain waves, figuring out what makes him...*him*.

Just like one would expect if you were the only clone in the Ten Domes like you. A real curiosity.

Without warning, either Wink's or Blink's hold on my grapnel fails, and the cable snaps loose like a bowstring, retracting into the port on my shoulder. At the same instant, I swing sideways as the other drone strains and fails to carry my weight all by itself. As the ground rushes up to meet us, I slam sideways into the glass exterior of the tower.

My exo-suit slides across the mirrored surface, and I punch a powered fist straight through the windowall. The glass shatters on impact, and I drive my arm inside shoulder-deep, puncturing the support structures inside and plowing downward through one floor after another. The plasteel rods encasing my arm tear a loud, crunching swath along the side of the building, slowing my descent as I pass the sixth floor, the fifth, the fourth, shards of mirrored glass raining down around me, smashing into bits against the concrete below—

Until I'm dangling three meters above the sidewalk with my arm stuck inside the building. Just hanging there. Completely in control of the situation.

Blink hovers nearby for moral support. Releasing the grapnel cable to droop down my back, Wink joins its twin. Something in their programming must make them think they should stick around until help arrives. Which means one of them probably already hailed HQ, requesting said help.

Great. Investigator Sera Chen's on the case, but she can't fly solo.

Another audiolink request from Dunn blinks at the periphery of my ocular lenses. I tap my temple to activate the subdermal augment and receive the call. "Don't tell me you lost him."

"Of course not, Investigator Chen. The suspect is in custody, and we have reached the foyer of Hawthorne Tower." He pauses, undoubtedly watching me through Wink and Blink's video feed. "You appear to be...stuck."

"Just catching my breath. I'll join you momentarily." I end the call and focus on the situation at hand. Namely, extricating myself before help arrives—for the sake of my dignity. "Any chance you guys could lend a claw?"

Wink and Blink bob in the air beside me. "Do you require assistance?" they ask in unison.

That much should be obvious. "Clamp on and pull me laterally. Then let me drop to the pavement."

Without another word spoken in their artificial

monotone, they hover beside the frame of my exo and extend their claws. Grasping the plasteel struts across my back, they angle their rotors downward and away from me. I grimace as the suit creaks, shifting with them as they pull sideways, and my body moves right along with them—except for the arm wedged in the building.

"Halt." This isn't going to work. Not if I prefer keeping my arm intact. "New plan. Clamp onto my shoulder struts and pull upward. A meter or two should do it."

Their claws release my exo, and they hover beside me, in no hurry to change position. "We cannot carry your weight, Investigator Chen."

"You calling me fat?" No response from the drones. Smarter AI than I thought. "You won't be carrying me. Just tug me upward, and I'll pull my arm out. Then we're back to the original plan: dropping me. Got it?"

They veer into position, this time above my head, and grab on with their claws. Here's hoping they can heave me up long enough to get this done.

Without warning, I'm tugged upward, lurching a meter, then another. I manage to pull my arm free with another cascade of mirror-shards hitting the pavement below. Then I'm following them, free-falling five meters and hitting the sidewalk with a crunch that's thankfully not coming from my bones or the exo-suit. I've just planted two boot-brace-sized prints into the concrete with cracks radiating outward. A small Sera Chen impact crater.

"Good work." I give Wink and Blink a nod as I head toward the tower's glass entryway and the atrium foyer beyond. "Hold the perimeter."

The drones move into position outside as the transparent

doors slide shut behind me. The interior of Hawthorne Tower is dark as night, but Dunn has the tactical flashlight mounted on his assault rifle shining a white spear directly at our suspect. The miscreant sits cross-legged on the floor and squints at the sound of my approach.

One thing my exo is not, and that's quiet.

"I told you that you'd survive, detective," he says, not intimidated in the least by the muzzle of Dunn's weapon staring him in the face. A face that's covered in spiraling tattoos. "You just needed a little nudge in the right direction to find out for yourself. You're one of them, aren't you?"

"You hit me with some kind of energy burst." I hold out my hand to Dunn, and he hands me the suspect's strange weapon: a meter-long chrome baton. "Now instead of being a minor lead in my investigation, you've been promoted to a major person of interest."

"He is a known criminal," Dunn says.

"I am *Krime*!" He spreads his hands out to the sides as if introducing himself to an audience. Faux-leather gloves with the fingers cut off leave his grimy digits poking through. Matching faux-leather coat, vest, and pants. He's trying way too hard to play the part of a clichéd underworld boss and coming up short in every department.

"For the offense of endangering the life of Investigator Chen, you will face a fine of one million credits as well as twenty-five years in the Dome 1 Correctional Center," Dunn says without emotion. "If you are unable to pay the fine, then you will be exiled into the Wastes, saving our citizens the expense of feeding you for two and a half decades."

Krime's expression falls along with his arms. He looks hurt, as if he trusted us, and we let him down. Which is ridiculous, of course. I never trusted him, and it should have worked both ways.

"I was just showing you the truth, Chen!" He shakes his head in disbelief. "I would never put your life in danger—"

"Save it."

"But I was right, wasn't I? You've got special powers. You're a *demigod*!"

I pull the release on my exo suit and unbuckle my harness. Then I step out of the exoskeleton, leaving it behind me to stand like a statue of negative space as I crouch down beside Krime.

"Hey. Eyes up here." I make sure he isn't distracted by anything below my neck. My black, skintight bodysuit leaves very little to the imagination. "If it wasn't for that thing—" I hook a thumb toward my exo. "—and my drones, I'd be decorating most of the sidewalk out front right now." I hold his gaze until the truth registers in his dust-addled mind. "I'm just your average-variety human being."

His mouth drops open, but the words are slow to arrive. "So I could have...*killed* you?"

I slap him on the shoulder and smirk up at Dunn. "He's not as dumb as he looks." Before turning my attention back to Krime, I deactivate my augments with a double temple-tap that looks like a common scratch of the fingernail across an unexpected itch. "Now tell me where Trezon is."

Time to read his mind. Because, as bizarre as it is, that's something I can do. That's right, I have *powers*. Found out a few months ago that I'm not the only one. There are more than twenty of us with superhuman talents living throughout the Domes.

The neural implants required by our government have

the side effect of suppressing my abilities, but the Link augments make it possible to communicate, access information, and immerse ourselves in VR without any outdated peripherals. Only when I switch off my augments am I able to sift through someone else's thoughts. Never without their permission—except in a case like this. I'm pretty sure he won't be giving me anything close to a straight answer if I don't peek behind the curtain.

"How should I know?" Krime says with a laugh. Forced nonchalance. "You people locked Trezon up, didn't you? Some top secret location out in the Wastes, I heard. Not that we're all that well-acquainted or anything. We used to move in some of the same circles, that's all." He winks and mimes snorting an illicit substance.

Don't tell her anything.

I nod to show I'm listening, but my special telepathic gift has caught a hint of programming under the surface. Someone doesn't want him oversharing. And I have an inkling who that might be. Digging in a little deeper, I find a whirlwind of images and sounds flashing past my extra-sensory perception, too fast to make any sense of. Intentionally so. Almost as though somebody knew I'd be asking the questions, and they wanted to keep my prying mind out of places it didn't belong.

"When was the last time you saw him?" I keep my tone level, my expression neutral, even as I struggle to keep up with his memory maelstrom.

As if the mind-reading isn't special enough, I can see in the dark, too, without the need for ocular enhancements. Just a couple of garden-variety abilities passed down to me by my biological parents—whom I met for the first time not that long ago.

Finding out you're adopted when you're twenty years old? I wouldn't recommend it. As far as I'm concerned, I'm a Chen and I always will be; the Chens are my only parents, and I'm their only daughter. They raised me, they love me, and I love them. Even though we don't share any of the same blood. Family is more than DNA.

My blood parents are strangers to me. Somehow, they managed to survive in the Wastes outside the Ten Domes for decades. Probably due to their own unique abilities. They have a non-government compliant explanation for the origin of these *powers*, which is a crazy story for another time. Something to do with *spirits of the earth*. Suffice it to say, I still haven't managed to wrap my mind around it. But I can't argue with the effects, regardless of the cause.

So yeah, whether I like it or not, I'm what the cool kids call a *demigod*. But I don't go shouting it from rooftops. Even when I'm falling from one.

"Really can't say, Chen." Another shrug from Krime, his face blank. "Just can't."

"I bet." His neural implants aren't letting him. Somebody's tweaked them to keep his mouth shut and his thoughts incomprehensible.

Good thing I have a workaround.

"You'll want to take a few steps back, Dunn." I rise to my feet and reach back for the zipper pocket inside my stationary exo-suit.

"That is not my designation," the former security clone says—his customary comeback when I use that nickname I gave him. I wasn't about to address my partner as a string of alphanumerics, so D1-436 became D-one, which morphed into *Dunn*. I think he likes it, but he'll never admit as much.

He retreats, walking backward toward the glass entry doors with his weapon still trained on Krime.

Retrieving a small plasteel disc that fits in the palm of my hand, I activate the timer by pressing a recessed pad in the middle of the device with my thumb. Instantly, the button glows neon blue and pulses, counting down from five seconds. I make sure I have Krime's undivided attention.

"This won't hurt a bit." I toss the disc onto the floor in front of him, and it skids toward his cross-legged shins. "I promise."

He scowls at the device for just a split-second before it dawns on him what the thing is. Then he's on his feet faster than I would have thought humanly possible. Maybe his latest dust high hasn't worn off yet. Or he's just terrified, and the adrenaline is enough to really get him moving.

But it's too late for him to escape. Already, the localized EMP burst has enveloped him in a transparent static bubble the same shade of blue as the device's pulsing button, and he curses at me, shaking his fists alongside his temples. He knows his augments are now out of commission.

"Damn you, Chen! Why'd you have to go and do that?"

"So you'd give me a straight answer." Now I can cut through the clutter in his head and get to the truth. Which I attempt to do, but it's not easy. Even without the neural implants' programmed interference, his thoughts are all over the place. Like pages of an ancient manuscript caught up in a whirlwind, tough to pin down let alone comprehend. "Trezon broke out earlier this evening. If anybody's going to know where he is, it's you. His clone in training."

"I'm nobody's clone!"

"Tell that to a mirror sometime." If imitation is the finest form of flattery, then Trezon might be abundantly pleased by Krime's getup. Unless he were to perceive it as this bootlicker's attempt at usurping the kingpin's underworld role. In which case, the sycophant in front of me should realize that his days are numbered. "C'mon now. Give me something, and maybe I'll tell my colleagues you activated that weapon of yours by mistake."

"Of course it was a mistake. I wasn't trying to kill you!"

"I could try to convince them of that. Or maybe I won't. It really depends on what you have to say in the next thirty seconds."

I nod over my shoulder toward Wink and Blink hovering outside. If one didn't know better, you'd think they were doing their best to appear menacing. With their recent projectile weapons upgrade, it's working.

Keeping a wary eye on the drones as well as my well-armed partner, Krime clears his throat and holds his gloved hands out to the sides to show he's no threat. "You've got me confused with somebody else, Chen. Really, I had no idea Trezon was out. You've gotta believe me."

Dome 1. Gotta hand it over. Pass the baton. Dome 1. Pass the baton. This keeps repeating in his mind, along with images of Hawthorne Tower and its rooftop. Then an image appears of Trezon's smug, tattooed face beneath slick, coiffed hair. *She's messed up my chance. He won't meet me now. Not after this. Gotta lay low for a while...*

"So you were going to meet him." I cross my arms. "Here."

He blinks at me. Then his eyes widen as a tentative grin emerges. "I knew it! You're one of them! Told you, didn't I? So maybe I got your power wrong, but you're a demigod, alright." He taps the side of his shaved skull and murmurs, "You can see in here. You know what I'm thinking. That's it, right? Your ability?"

You sure are one smokin' babe—

I draw my shocker and aim it at his crotch.

"Hey now, c'mon Chen, I told you everything I know!"

"You didn't tell me anything."

"In my head, or spoken out loud—same difference, right?"

I narrow my gaze. "Before, when you were blithering about becoming *gods*. Tell me what that was all about."

"Oh..." He chuckles. "I was just high. You know how it is sometimes."

"Can't say that I do."

He belts out a laugh. "No, you're probably right. Straight arrow Investigator Chen. Well, guess what?" He leans toward me conspiratorially. "Someday we're all gonna be like you. With *powers*. Trezon's gonna make it happen. Guess it's obvious now what he's capable of, yeah? No walls can hold him!"

Apparently not. Deactivating his subdermal prison tag along with his augments helped. Trezon hasn't shown up on a single Domes-wide scan, stumping our analysts at HQ.

"Why Dome 1?" I ask. "Thought you and your cronies preferred the filthy underbelly of Dome 10." The center of Eurasia's waste and water reclamation systems, as well as our desalination plant, right on the Mediterranean. Not nearly as pristine as Dome 1, home to the upper castes—our best, brightest, and most powerful.

"This is where it all begins, Chen." He nods like a true believer, eyes unfocused and unblinking. "The central hub."

He flings his arms wide, fingers straining outward. "From here, we can spread the good word out to all the other Domes, to any citizen with a thirst for the possibility. The truth."

Can't help the skeptical look I'm giving him. "And what's that?"

"There's no reason to be content with the abilities our dust highs give us. Those fleeting powers? We can have them permanently. For the rest of our lives. We can become *gods*!"

He reaches inside his coat without warning, and the muzzle of my shocker aims at the middle of his chest, center of mass, without my brain telling it to. That's what good training will do.

"Easy, Chen." He holds up his other hand in the universal gesture for *I'm not a threat* while he thinks, *Wait till she gets a load of this.*

I watch as he retrieves a tube the size of his little finger and flicks off the cap with his thumb. He dumps a line of dust across the back of his other hand and winks at me. Then he holds one nostril closed and sucks up the dirt with his other nostril like it's some kind of biological robocleaner.

"Don't tell me you're not curious," he says, blinking and wrinkling his nose once the deed is done. Contaminated dust from the Wastes is now making itself at home in his system. "You really want to see what I can do."

Not even a little bit.

"If you insist..." I step back into my exo and buckle on the harness. Slipping my arms into their braces, I punch the air to let him know I'm ready for whatever display he's got prepared. "Bring it on."

He chuckles. Then he launches himself straight up into

the air, landing like an obscenely oversized insect on the atrium's interior a couple dozen meters above my head, clinging to the glass like his fingertips are glued to it.

So he's a climber. That explains how he managed to reach the roof of Hawthorne Tower after hours, with the speedlifts offline and the stairwells locked. The results of snorting a line of dust from the Wastes will vary from one addict to another; but to each is given only one superhuman ability that will eventually wear off. Some are able to jump from great heights, others can hear voices from a dozen floors away, while still others can breathe underwater. Just a few examples. *Parlor tricks*, according to some, but dangerous in the wrong hands. And so very unhealthy.

"Impressive," I call up to him in my most half-hearted tone. "But don't even think about escaping."

"It's in my best interest to do so, Chen, don't you think? I broke curfew, put your life in danger, and now I'm in the process of avoiding arrest. There's only one option available to a guy like me!" Laughing like a lunatic, he scrambles up the windowall on all fours.

"Shall I shoot him?" Dunn steps forward, rifle shouldered and ready to fire.

"Not tonight." I take quick aim and launch the grapnel from my exo's right shoulder. The hook hurtles upward, cable spiraling after it, until it meets Krime's left ankle. Which it loops around before pulling taut. I activate the winch, and the line retracts without pause, tugging the idiot off the glass. "Catch him, partner."

Dunn drops his rifle, and the weapon dangles from the broad strap over his shoulder. Helmet cocked back with its face shield upturned, he holds out his arms and positions himself beneath the screaming, flailing dust freak plummeting through the air.

"Is it wrong that I hope he slips from my grasp, Investigator Chen?"

Can't hide my smile. "Just means you're human, Dunn."

"But I am not. I am a clone of a human."

"Imperfect, then. Like the rest of us. How's that?"

His helmet tilts to one side, facing me as Krime collapses into his armored arms with a telltale groan of lapsed consciousness. "I strive for perfection."

"Don't we all." I glance over my shoulder and curse under my breath as the sleek black & white aerocar touches down outside. Its headlights flood the foyer, and its jet wash against the vacant street laps up the front of Hawthorne Tower, causing Wink and Blink to bob in midair. "But sometimes we fall short."

2

The side door drifts upward once the police aerocar has settled on the ground. With the curfew in effect until dawn, no need to worry about obstructing ground traffic. As Chief Inspector Hudson steps out, I stifle a groan. This was not how I wanted my first performance review to go.

How do I already know what's in store for me? Easy. There's no other reason why Hudson would get out of bed this late at night.

Tall but chronically stoop-shouldered, he keeps his eyes to himself as long strides take him to the foyer doors. The pilot remains at the controls of the aerocar, engines humming on idle, garish blue & red lights flickering across the top of the vehicle.

"Your drones seemed to think you required assistance." Hudson stuffs his hands into the pockets of his khaki overcoat. Beard and hair a similar shade, he keeps the former trimmed meticulously and the latter tied back without a single wayward strand. His face is chiseled, his nose a hooked beak, his eyes sharp like one of the popular hawk avatars in VR. "Yet you don't appear to be in any serious trouble."

"I'm sure they would regret rousting you, Chief, if their

AI was sophisticated enough."

"So you weren't in any danger?" He raises an eyebrow.

"Not really."

"I've seen the footage. You would have died, had you not damaged the tower." He gazes up at the atrium and the night sky beyond the Dome. "Repairs to the exterior of this building will be costly. And those costs will be deducted from your paycheck."

"Understood, sir."

He returns his piercing gaze to me. "Now explain why you thought you could take one of the patrol cars without requisitioning it properly. As well as...*that.*" He looks my exo-suit up and down, unimpressed by it.

"The suit is mine, sir." With certain aftermarket upgrades courtesy of my friend Drasko. Same guy who outfitted Wink and Blink with their lethal ordnance.

"You are no longer a curfew enforcer chasing violators across rooftops. You're an investigator, and you should look the part. I expect you to retire that monstrosity tonight."

Never mind that it saved my life a few minutes ago?

"As for the vehicle, its purpose is also curfew enforcement. No one should be out during curfew. Not even investigators. When the city sleeps, so do we." He gives me a pointed look. "Or we study the data we've accumulated thus far, should sleep evade us."

He can't know that I haven't slept in weeks. Can he? No, it's not possible. Or is it?

Is paranoia a side effect of sleep deprivation? Probably. Damn it.

"I had a lead, sir. It couldn't wait until morning."

"This miscreant, I take it." He nods toward Krime, out

cold in Dunn's arms, limbs dangling like a maiden in distress carried by a monster from a classic movie interactive.

I admit it: too much of my downtime is spent in VR. But I've gotta do something while the rest of Dome 1 is asleep and I'm still amped up on stimulants. Just part of my investigation process. Either that, or it's a self-preservation measure.

Anything to avoid seeing the bloody face that haunts my nightmares. Fictional monsters are much more pleasant. Trust me on that.

"He's one of Trezon's lieutenants, sir. I have reason to believe he was planning to meet his boss here tonight."

"On the roof of Hawthorne Tower." Hudson folds his arms and eyes me with palpable incredulity. "Why would Trezon remain here in Dome 1 upon his escape? Our analysts predicted he would return to Dome 10's slums. Like a dog to its vomit."

That's why they closed the maglev tunnel. And that's why they haven't caught him. Because he's perfectly happy staying right here in the hub of the wheel. He doesn't want to go back home. He wants to stir things up in the nucleus of our society and send his viral infection throughout the Domes like another plague through our veins.

If what Krime says is correct, they want to become *demigods*. They want the sort of abilities I have, not the kind that dissipates after the dust highs wear off. And Trezon knows the only way he's going to find the answers he seeks is where the technology is the most advanced, where the scientists and doctors and politicians live and work, in this most immaculate and pristine of Eurasia's Domes. Where else would he choose to begin his work, immediately upon his escape, other than on the very top of the tallest tower in Dome 1?

But now I've interfered with his plans. And I've captured his underling. He won't be thrilled about that.

"You're off the Trezon case," Hudson says.

I blink, unsure I heard him correctly. He must have been talking while I was sorting through my thoughts. That's what I get for tuning him out.

"Sir, you can't—"

"I already have. But I get it, Chen. You want to prove yourself. Commander Bishop promoted her pet project, who now wants to make an impression on the new boss. Solve a big case, right out of the starting blocks." He smiles in a most patronizing way. I try not to gag. "Perhaps you will, given time. But it won't be this one."

Impressing him has never even crossed my mind. Proving to Bishop she made the right choice in promoting me from curfew enforcer to investigator? That's more like it.

"As one of the Twenty, you are, of course, accustomed to preferential treatment." He slides his long-fingered hands back into the pockets of his coat and yawns. Doesn't even try to hide the fact that he finds me boring or tiresome. Probably both. "Those days are over now. You're just another citizen. But don't get me wrong. We all appreciate the contributions the Twenty have made in order to safeguard the future of our species."

Without our knowledge.

Dr. Solomon Wong harvested our sex cells every month, once we hit puberty and were required to report for mandatory checkups. Why? Because everybody else living in the Domes is sterile, thanks to a debilitating plague that spread throughout Eurasia way back when. Only the twenty of us conceived in the Wastes have the ability to procreate—as well as our offspring, eventually. Over a thousand of them are growing up across the Domes in their adoptive families. Dr. Wong made sure to splice in some of the adoptive parents' DNA to ensure the kids would resemble them, something he didn't bother doing with the Twenty.

I clench my jaw to keep from saying anything about it. I accept reality as it is. I can't change it, but I don't have to let it consume my thoughts.

Some might say I've already had my revenge.

Hudson turns away, speaking to Dunn as he does. "Unit D1-436, bring the criminal to my vehicle. Then fly Investigator Chen back to HQ. She'll need to report to MedTech and have them take a look at that arm she used as landing gear." So witty.

"Yes, Chief Inspector Hudson." Dunn follows him out of the foyer and toward the aerocar outside.

I'm left alone with a volatile mix of injured pride and anger burning in my belly.

"Keep your augments on at all times, Chen," Hudson calls back over his shoulder before the doors slide shut. "I won't tell you again!"

Refraining from gracing the back of his head with an obscene gesture, I double-tap my temple, reactivating the neural implants I took offline so that my telepathy would work. For some reason, the two are incompatible: my weird abilities and the augments the government doctors installed in my head when I came of age. Just like every other citizen in Eurasia. We don't have to rely on mere biologic; we have instant access to the Linkstream for communication, information, and entertainment. But as long as my augments are active, my abilities won't manifest themselves. No idea why, but the same goes for dust freaks. They have to shut down their neural implants in order for the stuff they snort to do its thing.

Case in point: Krime. Once the EMP knocked out the hardware in his head, only then was he able to play the role of astounding spider-criminal.

My biological parents, Luther and Daiyna, lived in the Wastes for years, both survivors on the North American continent. Technically, I was born here inside Dome 1; and by *born*, I mean scooped out of an incubation chamber by Dr. Wong and handed to my adoptive parents—my real parents, as far as I'm concerned. The people who raised me, Abigail and Victor Chen.

Luther and Daiyna had their DNA changed by living out under the sun and breathing the contaminated air. Somehow, they both got special abilities because of it: Daiyna could leap from great heights and see in the dark, and Luther had claws that extended from his fingers. Scientifically speaking, I'd say their genes underwent some sort of bizarre mutation that I can't even begin to understand. It's a wonder they managed to live outside the Domes as long as they did, let alone becoming the first *demigods*. Equally impossible, according to the laws of nature.

Luther believes the abilities we possess came from the animal kingdom. That somehow the nuclear blasts responsible for wiping out all life on the surface of North America—and then the rest of the planet, after ash in the atmosphere blocked out the sun for a few years—embedded animal spirits into the dust. More likely, it's residue from the North American terrorists' bioweapons. You breathe the dusty air long enough on the surface, and your DNA is permanently changed. You gain superhuman abilities. But if you've lived your entire life inside the Domes with human-made materials and purified air, and you snort a line or two of the stuff, you gain the same variety of abilities—but only for a limited duration.

Not sure why they don't become permanent for the dust freaks who satisfy their addiction on a daily basis.

Various abilities manifest themselves in different people. Once you've snorted the North American dust and you discover what your power is, you can't change it. No idea how it's decided—why Krime is able to crawl up a windowall and I'm able to read people's thoughts. Maybe it's genetic or something.

None of it makes a whole lot of sense.

But I can't argue with the fact that these abilities exist, regardless of how they originated. They're in my DNA, passed down to me from biological parents who are complete strangers to me. I have to accept this part of myself regardless of how uncomfortable it makes me feel every time I use my *powers*. They don't define me; I find my identity in my work, my service to Eurasia. That's what I want to be known for.

The fewer who know I'm a so-called *demigod*, the better.

With Krime restrained in the aerocar's rear compartment and Chief Inspector Hudson back in his seat, the side door drifts shut automatically. Another burst of air from underneath the chassis where the powerful anti-gravity engines reside, and the vehicle rises into the air. Then it accelerates on a trajectory that takes it soaring between rows of towering domescrapers toward police headquarters.

"Head up to the roof," I tell Wink and Blink via my audiolink. "We'll meet you there."

They zip upward as the foyer doors slide open and Dunn reenters.

"Thanks for having my back," I mutter, turning on my heel and setting off toward the bank of speedlifts down the hall. The sound of my boot-braces striking the floor tiles echoes like hammer strikes in the empty space.

"Judging by your tone, would I be right in assuming you are being sarcastic, Investigator Chen?" He follows me, his boots thumping out of sync with mine.

"You know what they say about assuming things..." Reaching the first speedlift, I enter in my security override code, and it powers up while the others lining the hallway remain dark and lifeless. The polished plasteel doors drift open silently, and a dim glow emanates from inside, reflecting off the gleaming walls. The robocleaners do some of their best work on this place. Nothing less for the Chancellor of the Ten Domes.

"Should I not have complied with the Chief Inspector's orders?"

"A begrudging pause might have been nice." I step inside and turn an about-face.

"I see." He joins me and turns so that we stand side by side, facing our reflection in the closing doors. He's a head taller, even when I'm in my exo. "You would have appreciated a moment of solidarity."

"You're my partner, after all, Dunn."

"That is not my designation." He reaches down toward a

compartment built into the side of his leg armor and taps a button. A hatch opens lengthwise, perhaps intended for a backup weapon. Instead, he retrieves the thing Krime used to shove me off the roof.

I stare at the chrome baton. "You didn't hand it over to Hudson?"

"Chief Inspector Hudson did not request it." His black face shield reflects my surprised expression as he offers me the weapon. "How is that for solidarity, Investigator Chen?"

"Not bad at all." I survey the baton in my hands, sliding my fingertips across the cold, smooth surface from end to end. No buttons or switches, no obvious way to activate it. No idea how it managed to throw me off a rooftop. "Ever seen anything like this?"

Dunn shakes his head. "The energy it generated did not appear to be electric in nature. If I were to speculate, I would say it is magnetic, releasing a repulsive force."

"You've got that right."

"Or perhaps gravitonic."

I frown. "Gravity weapons are illegal."

"Yes. They are."

Considering the person Krime intended to hand-deliver it to, that's not a big surprise.

The speedlift doors slide open, revealing the silent, dark rooftop of Hawthorne Tower and our waiting aerocar with its engines and lights off. Wink and Blink hover beside the vehicle, waiting patiently for us to approach.

"Land and power off," I tell them.

They descend, and their lights dim as they follow my

orders. At the same time, the aerocar's cabin glows to life and the doors drift upward, sensing our proximity. I pull the release and step out of my exo-suit once I'm close enough to the cargo compartment; then Dunn helps me load it on board. Part of me refuses to believe I won't be wearing it again anytime soon. But orders are orders. And if I want to remain an investigator...

"Gotta do my job," I mutter, picking up my drones and securing them in the cargo area as well.

"Yes, Investigator Chen." Dunn climbs into the cockpit and fires up the engines, sending a rush of cold air out from under the aerocar as the anti-gravity turbines kick in. The vehicle bobs aloft just a few centimeters, holding steady.

I climb in beside him, and the doors shut automatically, locking us in.

"Course laid in for Police Headquarters, where you will report to MedTech and have your arm examined."

"Really not necessary." I check the biometrics glowing at the periphery of my ocular lenses as I rotate my shoulder. Can't help the tight grimace. There's some pain, as should be expected after digging a trench by hand down the side of a building. But nothing's glaring out of the ordinary in my self-diagnostic display. I stretch my arm out toward the windscreen and the black night beyond it. "See? Perfectly fine."

"Best to be certain. On a daily basis, the Level 5 technicians ensure that I am operating at one hundred percent efficiency." He glances at me. "When was the last time you had a checkup?"

If he was a human with the illegal hacking skills and lack of personal boundaries that my friend Erik is infamous for,

Dunn would already know I haven't been to a doctor in months. Not since Dr. Wong's unsuccessful attempt on my life with a laser welder.

The surgeon on duty that night did her best to heal the scar after my operation, but there was only so much she could do with a hole burned straight through my shoulder, incinerating all the flesh and bone in between. She reconstructed what needed reconstructing with biosynthetics, and the result is puckered and slightly discolored, resembling an oblong eyelid closed in a relaxed sort of way.

I keep it covered whenever I can and hope it never opens.

But that's not why I don't happen to be a big fan of med centers. It has more to do with all those monthly visits since I was twelve when my eggs were harvested without my consent. I've never been able to find out how they pulled that off. But I wasn't the only one subjected to such invasive procedures. Every member of the Twenty went through a similar experience, including Erik. And now our offspring, their DNA combined with that of their adoptive parents, are scattered across the Domes. A thousand children ranging in age from a few months to eight years old. The future of Eurasia, whose adult population—not counting the Twenty—is sterile thanks to a plague that swept through the Ten Domes long before I was born.

The official story is that we were conceived in a sealed North American bunker by government scientists who found untainted survivors able and willing to reproduce. They saw it as their sacred duty to ensure a future for the human race. According to Dr. Wong, the biological parents of the Twenty weren't held against their will, tortured or experimented on.

Luther and Daiyna told me otherwise.

So I like to think my distrust of doctors is completely understandable. I'll be fine if I don't darken the doorway of another medical establishment for the rest of my life, thank you very much.

Good thing clones don't have access to such information. They're only privy to their own security network, closely monitored by the same scientists and technicians who keep Dunn working so efficiently. That's one of the things that makes him the perfect partner. He only knows what I want him to know about me.

White gauntlets on the controls, he takes us plunging over the side of the building and swooping between the neighboring domescrapers. If it wasn't for the infrared overlay on the windscreen's interior, painting the local topography in neon green gridlines, we'd be flying blind through the dark.

"Slight change of plans." I tap the console in front of me, waking it. As the screen glows to life, I enter in a different set of coordinates.

Dunn's helmet tilts to one side as he surveys our altered course. "We are going to the correctional center?"

"That's right."

"But you are no longer on the Trezon case, Investigator Chen."

"So I've heard."

"If you disobey a direct order from Chief Inspector Hudson, you cannot expect to remain an investigator for long. Commander Bishop will not be able to reinstate you, no matter how much she appreciates your dedication to the law. You will be demoted to Curfew Enforcer with no hope of advancement."

Can't argue with a single thing he said. So instead I hold up the baton.

"This thing tossed an exo-suit carrying a full-grown woman off a roof. You know how heavy an exoskeleton is?"

"Yes. One hundred kilograms—"

"And I've got a feeling the baton was on a low setting." Assuming it has settings. "Krime said he wasn't trying to kill me. I believe that." *Nudge* was the word he used. "Powered up all the way, a weapon like this might break through reinforced plasticon."

"You believe Krime aided Trezon in his escape."

Krime was hoping to make a big impression by passing the baton—literally—to his boss. A welcome gift. Maybe a peace offering. Hoping to iron out things between them. That's what came through when I read his thoughts. He hadn't seen the kingpin since before Commander Bishop took Trezon to the correctional center, which Krime believed to be in the Wastes, outside the Ten Domes, interestingly enough. So no, he wasn't an accomplice in his boss's escape.

"I've got a feeling Trezon has other associates in Dome 1. They somehow managed to get him out, and they could be armed with a similar weapon." Absently I roll the baton up and down my quadriceps like it's a walking cane, and I'm preparing to go on stage for a tap dance routine. Something I may or may not have done in VR once or twice. "We need to know what this thing can do. And we need to know how it works."

"Visiting the prison against Chief Inspector Hudson's orders will accomplish that?"

"Probably not. I just want to see their footage of the breakout."

"The same footage is available at headquarters, Investigator Chen."

"I prefer to see it at the source, if it's all the same."

Dunn is quiet as we fly toward the outskirts of Dome 1. Pensive? No idea what goes on inside his head. Part of me is surprised that he's going along with my insubordination and not insisting that we return to HQ. But then again, his unprogrammed loyalty to me was the main reason I wanted him as my partner. He has his reasons for sticking with me, whatever they are.

"You do not trust command," he says at length.

That came out of nowhere.

"What gave you that idea?" I frown at him.

"Otherwise, you would not take issue with viewing the footage at headquarters. You believe the video accessed there may not be genuine."

"What makes you think I would even have access at HQ?"

"A fair point." His chin dips. "But I do not believe that being officially off the case would stop you, Investigator Chen."

Do I think our cybernetic analysts doctor the footage before it's shared with investigators? Of course not. Do I believe investigators have the same access as our superiors? Hardly. And if the footage in question involves a variety of weapon we've never seen before, which the public at large has no idea even exists, then it would make sense to keep us in the dark about it until the higher-ups decide how to confiscate and dismantle such illegal weaponry. Or utilize it for law enforcers in the neverending fight against organized crime.

All that remains of humankind—a few million at last count—is living trapped inside ten self-sustaining artificial biospheres, sheltered from the outside world where, if the sun doesn't kill you, the tainted air and lack of oxygen will. So it's in everybody's best interest that we do our best to avoid mass panic. The sort that might result from seeing a criminal harness magnetic repulsion as a projectile weapon.

Or gravity itself.

"What about you?" I pat the baton. "If you trusted command, I'm sure you would have turned this over to Hudson."

Dunn's response is slow on arrival. "I trust command. They are our superior officers. But in this case, considering the imminent threat, I made what you might categorize a judgment call." His helmet turns my way briefly, the black face shield reflecting the light on the display panel before him. "I trust us more, Investigator Chen."

That makes me smile.

In the interest of the common good, our superiors are known to drag their feet at times. Strategize for every eventuality. Develop contingency plans. Meanwhile, Trezon's out there getting his band back together.

Now is the time to act. We know he's in Dome 1, and that his date with Krime was interrupted, thanks to us. We have the weapon Krime was planning to hand off to his boss—assuming that's what he meant by *pass the baton*. A real on-the-nose metaphor. Trezon will figure Hudson has it now, or that we do. Either way, I have a feeling he won't be leaving the city until he gets his tattooed hands on it.

Which should give us enough time to visit the prison he

escaped from and see what really happened there.

3

During my brief time thus far in law enforcement, there hasn't arisen a need for me to visit our local correctional center. I couldn't even describe the place, if I had to. But like everything else in Dome 1, it's pristine. First impression: architecturally uninspired, the four floors housed in a block-shaped building covered in mirrored glass and surrounded by an immaculate lawn. No brick walls or barbed wire, like so many prisons in VR interactives; no main gate, no buses, no yard for the requisite outdoor exercise and muscular posturing.

Just a silent, lifeless cube housing our most interesting offenders.

Trezon, former kingpin of the Dome 10 underworld, found himself on the Governors' reconditioning list. He was deeply involved in the illegal dust trade, providing the stuff to countless citizens as well as government officials at the highest levels—including Chancellor Hawthorne, come to find out, before her ugly psychotic break. Apparently, she poisoned her husband decades ago in order to seize power and become queen of Eurasia. Word has it she sees him now wherever she looks, and she can't stop screaming for him to go away. So she's kept with the other criminally insane folks in an isolated wing.

I have no intention of paying her a visit tonight.

Dunn sets the aerocar down gently in the middle of the front lawn and powers off the engines. "Would you like me to join you, Investigator Chen?"

"I was counting on it."

As my door drifts open, I step outside and wave my hand over the cargo compartment. Its door rises as well. Sending Wink and Blink aloft to survey the scene, I reach for my exo and slide it out, letting the boot braces drop onto the well-manicured grass. The shoulder struts remain in the vehicle. I climb into the thing and secure my harness, then lever myself into an upright position. Dunn watches me, his face shield unreadable in the dark.

"What?"

"As a rule, you only wear your exoskeleton when you are intending to apprehend a criminal of some sort. But the criminals here have already been apprehended, Investigator Chen."

"Just call me Chen. We've talked about this."

No response. The doors to the aerocar drift shut and lock automatically as I lead the way to what I presume to be the front of the prison complex. Dunn follows, his rifle dangling from its strap. He keeps it from knocking against his leg with a gauntlet flat against its stock.

"Would you feel comfortable walking into this place without your armor?" I say over my shoulder. "Or your rifle?"

"A security clone is never seen in public without its armor. And the rifle came with the armor."

An attempt at humor? I'm impressed. "We should probably both look into acquiring a new wardrobe. Investigators ought to blend in better than we do."

"Your exo-suit has saved your life on more than one occasion, Investigator Chen. As has my armor. If it were not for my previous helmet, I would have been promptly recycled."

His prior face shield interfered with a headshot courtesy of my friend Drasko. The jury's still out on whether he intended it as a kill shot. Which reminds me: I've got to touch base with him as soon as curfew's over. Once Trezon is done here in Dome 1, he'll be going after Drasko, without a doubt.

Trezon never abdicated his underworld throne, yet Drasko's been the one sitting on it as of late. His criminal connections have more or less maintained the status quo, vices moving along their dark routes with gang warfare kept to a minimum. We call that a win, all things considered.

"I'm sure we'll manage." It's no good clinging to the past, as much as I'd rather hang onto my exo than find a much weaker replacement. Like a professional-looking tactical suit impervious to EMP bursts and resistant to many varieties of projectile rounds. Maybe even blades. But I'm sure it would chafe like crazy during a foot pursuit.

Hudson could be right, that my days of chasing lawbreakers are over. I can leave that to the trackers and enforcers now, and focus my attention on investigating. No overlap in responsibilities, whatsoever.

Somehow I doubt it.

"State your reason for visiting the Dome 1 Correctional Center," an automated voice drones from above the sealed entry doors as we approach.

Not a prison. A correctional center. Unlike the prisons in VR, this place actually *corrects* unlawful behaviors through a smorgasbord of reconditioning techniques and rehabilitates the offenders, promising that they will someday reenter society. Sounds good. But for some reason, they've yet to release a single prisoner.

Except for Trezon, of course, who broke out and missed his chance at being the first inmate to complete the program successfully. Then again, being the first escapee in the history of the Ten Domes is not a bad consolation prize.

"Investigator Sera Chen to see the warden about an escaped convict." I stand at ease, doing my best not to look too threatening in the exo-suit. Dunn files in beside me.

"You are not on the schedule," the AI replies curtly.

Neither was Trezon's escape.

"I need to see the warden's footage. We have reason to believe the escapee is still in Dome 1. The sooner I see how he left his cell, the sooner we can capture him."

"But you are an investigator, not a tracker, correct?"

I pause to grind my teeth for a moment. "I am investigating this case—"

"Negative. According to Chief Inspector Xavier Hudson, you are no longer involved in this investigation at all."

Curses pile up on the tip of my tongue, but I don't release a single one. "Let me guess." He warned them I'd be heading this way. "He told you not to let me inside."

"That is correct, Investigator Chen."

I stare at my dark reflection in the unlit entry doors, both of them mirrored like the rest of the building, and contemplate how much effort it would take to smash my way inside. Undoubtedly, they used reinforced plasteel a meter thick to construct this entrance. Impossible to break through, and the only way in or out. Yet somehow Trezon managed to make his exit without leaving a single scratch on the place.

That's what the official report stated, and the XR video feed I'm receiving from Wınk and Blınk in the bottom left corner of my ocular lenses is backing it up. All signs indicate that nobody broke in to let Trezon out, and nobody smuggled any explosives inside for him to create an alternate exit. The walls are completely intact, as is the roof.

So that just leaves the building substructure. Which I can't access without being allowed inside the complex.

"Goodnight," the AI says at length when I offer no response. I've been summarily dismissed from the premises.

"Perhaps we should return to police headquarters and have MedTech examine your arm, Investigator Chen," Dunn offers as I turn to face him. He's got a one-track mind sometimes, particularly when he's received an order from a superior. The ideal officer—if clones are ever allowed to become officers. Maybe he'll be the first, assuming he passes whatever unofficial test our partnership is supposed to be.

"Not yet." I point at the lawn. "We need to check underground."

Summoning Wınk and Blınk with my hand, I set off toward the vacant street and scan the pavement with my augmented vision. The cover to the sewer access point glows red once I've targeted it, and my drones buzz by on both sides to beat me there and hover a couple meters above it. They're always eager to obey, and they never mind where I send them. Probably helps that they're just machines. But I can't help the affection I feel. Maybe people in the old days felt this way about their dogs, before the poor creatures went extinct—along with every other animal on the planet.

"Am I to understand that you intend to descend into these sewer pipes?" Dunn says with a hint of disgust in his tone. As if inmate excrement is particularly vile.

"Not if I don't have to." I crouch down and grip onto the round cover plate with both hands. Then I tug, waiting for my exo-arms to kick in. When they activate with a sharp whine, the plate lifts easily, and I set it aside with a resounding clank against the pavement. Beckoning Wink and Blink closer, I transfer the blueprints of the correctional center sublevels from the HQ database and highlight the sections of the structure that lie alongside the sewer. "Survey the entire substructure, paying close attention to these areas. Relay everything back to me in real time."

"Yes, Investigator Chen," they reply in unison.

In single file, the two drones descend through the opening in the street and disappear into the tunnel beyond the ladder built into the wall below. Wink goes one way, Blink the other. My ocular lenses provide a split-screen view. It feels like I'm in miniature, riding on their backs as they zip down the slick tunnels, IR and XR feeds coming through simultaneously, lighting up the darkness. It's a lot of input, but my neural implants keep my brain focused, able to monitor both drones' feeds without the need to toggle from one to the other. Their IR paints the accessible substructure in red grid lines while XR casts the inaccessible areas in a ghostly blue—both sublevels of the correctional center complex built underground.

Everything in Dome 1, like every other dome in Eurasia, is

human-made, and that includes the dirt. Our *ground* isn't earth at all. The purpose of the Domes was to protect us from the contaminated world outside; so when the Designers built the Ten Domes, the floor of each massive structure was separated from the earth by multiple layers of plexicon. Then they poured in tons of synthetic dirt and spread it around. The stuff acts like the real thing, providing nutrients and stability for grass and trees as well as packing in areas like this between sewer tunnels and the two-level substructure of our correctional center.

"What do you make of this?" I capture a scene from Wınk's feed and transfer it to a three-dimensional holographic projection that emanates from the palm of my exo-glove.

Dunn tilts his helmet to one side as he studies the frozen image drawn in bright shades of blue and white light. Stress fractures line the interior of the sewage pipe, but they appear to have been covered recently with a transparent sealant.

"Routine maintenance," he replies. "Would you like me to consult the local duty roster, Investigator Chen?"

I shake my head. "No, you're probably right." I hear the defeat in my voice as I flip my hand upside-down, and the hologram vanishes.

I wanted it to be more. An obvious cause-effect relationship between Trezon's breakout and some sort of damage sustained by the sewer tunnel nearby. But there's no reason to believe he escaped via this route. The XR images aren't showing anything amiss with the building's substructure. Just like the front door, there are no signs of any forced exit.

Trezon must have walked right through the walls.

Impossible? I would have said so a year ago. But that was before I met a man who could leap from one domescraper to the next without breaking his legs. And it was before I started hearing people's thoughts in my head. Then I saw a man named Milton fly through the air like some kind of extinct bird. Now I'm more open-minded, you might say.

But if I'm to believe Luther, my biological father, that these superhuman abilities cropping up across the Domes originally came from the animal kingdom, then how do I make sense of a guy able to change his material composition in order to pass through solid matter? As far as I know, based on my limited knowledge of animal life prior to the end of the world, there were no species that could do such a thing. It just doesn't line up.

Not that I agree with Luther about much of anything. His beliefs are way out there, even for a Follower of the Way. His talk of animal spirits lines up more with the belief systems of ancient indigenous peoples. No idea why he doesn't go with the obvious answer: somehow, due to the bioweapons and atomic energy unleashed on the world, the DNA of the North American survivors was irrevocably changed, giving them abilities no one in the history of humankind has ever seen among our species.

I don't believe in *spirits of the earth*. And I never will.

I did better than fine for the first twenty years of my life without Luther or Daiyna in it, and I plan to keep doing so. Not that I'm unfriendly to them or anything; we've gotten together once or twice. Judging from their hails, they'd like to meet more often, but I'm just a little busy. Being an investigator keeps me that way—maybe intentionally. I don't get the feeling they want me to join their religious cult. They honestly seem interested in getting to know me better. As a friend.

But I don't have time for friends. I barely have time for my real family.

"It's looking more and more like Trezon was allowed to walk out the front doors." I summon Wink and Blink back now that they've finished scanning the building's underside, and I switch off my ocular lenses. The darkness looks underwhelming without my augmented vision to liven it up. "Which means he had help."

Dunn nods. "That would make the most logical sense, Investigator Chen—if not for the fact that Dome 1 prides itself on the rule of law. Why would anyone in the correctional center help a criminal escape prior to the completion of his behavior modification regimen?"

"Maybe Trezon was a quick study."

But he wouldn't have been quick on his feet. The guy was shot in both legs prior to his arrest. Not by Commander Bishop, and not by me. I was in Futuro Tower on the North African coast at the time, learning about Dr. Wong's plan to cryo-freeze the Twenty along with himself while hundreds of his science-minded clones figured out a way to terraform the planet. Daiyna, my biological mother, pulled the trigger that sent Trezon howling to the floor in agony. In her defense, she was rescuing her beloved Luther at the time along with a few others, including my friend Erik.

Nobody heals completely from an injury like that, not even with Dr. Solomon Wong-level genetic restructuring. Trezon will always walk with a limp, standing out in a crowd of perfect Dome 1 Eurasians. But Dome 6 is another matter; he could blend in there easily enough with the other *sicks*—

plague survivors with the scars and prosthetics that tell their difficult life stories.

No, he definitely had some help. Someone who thought he needed to leave the facility early. Because he had important work to do.

We will become gods! Krime's voice echoes in my head.

"We won't learn anything here." As Wink and Blink emerge from the sewer access point and land on the street beside me with their rotors spinning down, I replace the heavy cover with the help of my exo. Then I pick up my drones and nod to Dunn. "Let's head out."

We take the aerocar back to HQ and drop it off at the motor pool, an industrial hangar built off the side of the soaring rooftop. Inside, recessed lighting along the grey plasticon ceiling almost keeps the place from feeling like a dungeon, but nothing is put in place to dampen the sound of our echoing footfalls. A pair of grease monkeys on duty seem pleasantly surprised by the condition the vehicle is in. Not sure where they got the idea I wouldn't return it in one piece.

"We're supposed to take that suit, Chen," one of them pipes up apologetically as I turn away with a drone under each arm of my exo. "As well as the drones."

The self-conscious pitch of his voice hangs in the air, echoing against the drab walls and parking slots where powered-down aerocars sleep for the night, sleek and clean. Then silence holds the moment. The mechanics don't make another sound, hands hidden in the pockets of their coveralls, and neither does Dunn. But I can feel all three of them watching me, waiting to see what I do next.

"Hudson's orders," the guy adds, not sounding thrilled about it. This isn't a power play. He's just doing what he's told so he can keep his job.

Like me. For now.

I set Wink and Blink on the plasticon floor and then straighten up. Pulling the release, I proceed to unbuckle myself from the harness and step out of the boot braces, leaving the exo-suit standing upright behind me. Scooping up my drones, I carry them to the mechanics while staring down the one who spoke.

"I'll be back for these." I dump them into his arms, and he scrambles to keep from dropping them. "I don't want to see a single scratch."

"Well-I..." He doesn't know how to respond.

Neither does his partner, releasing a wolf whistle at the sight of me in my bodysuit. I walk up to him, and his leering grin doesn't waver in the slightest. He's too busy taking in my curves with obvious appreciation.

But he doubles over and chokes once I give him a friendly chop to the throat.

"Same goes for the exo. Not a scratch." Turning my back on both men, I retrieve my shocker as well as Krime's baton from my exo-suit and head toward the speedlift. "Coming, Dunn?"

"That is not my designation," he replies, following me between the rows of parked aerocars. Once we're thirty meters across the hangar, he asks in a low tone, "Are you not concerned that you will have to explain that act of violence on a civilian, Investigator Chen?"

"Actions have consequences," I mutter as we reach the polished plasteel of the speedlift door. Punching the down arrow, I add, "That guy learned something tonight."

Dunn's helmet twitches slightly to one side, a tell that he's accessing recorded data from our recent encounter. "There appears to have been no reason for your striking him. He seemed quite amicable."

"Right. Because ogling a woman's body means you're interested in being her intellectual equal."

"Is that what he was doing?"

I step into the speedlift and hold the sliding door open for Dunn. "We'll need to expand the parameters of your harassment awareness protocols."

"I see." He follows me inside with a slow nod. "The situation involved a form of sexual harassment."

"Bingo." I punch the button for MedTech down on Level 6. "Turning in?"

"Yes. Level 5 please. Thank you, Investigator Chen," he says as I tap the button and fold my arms, leaning back against the rear wall.

Dunn may be my partner, but he's still a security clone to the powers that be. So Unit D1-436 has to return to the same alcove every night where his brain waves can be monitored and his conditioning adjusted as necessary while he sleeps. Maybe in the future, there will be more like him assisting local law enforcement, even if they're never allowed to become officers themselves. But for now, our partnership is a trial run, and everything he does is observed and analyzed by a group of very intense technicians and scientists.

I'm sure that will include a recording of the conversation we're having right now.

"Could there not have been a more diplomatic way to handle matters?" he presses. "In any other potentially hostile situation, I have seen you take violent action only as a last resort. What was different about this sexual harassment in the motor pool?"

Good question. And I know he deserves a good answer. I'm the human here, after all, trusted to take actions based on a highly functioning intellect without the need for behavioral conditioning. I should be the one who shows him how to be humane. But all I can think about is Hudson confiscating my drones and my exo. I'm furious, honestly, but I can't lash out at him. He's my superior officer. And as much as I hate to admit it, part of me understands that I should be thinking like an investigator now instead of a curfew enforcer. I need to blend in, not clunk around in an intimidating exoskeleton. I need to ask questions and seek answers without relying on Wink and Blink to scope things out. But part of me is still human, and I get attached to things.

Maybe I don't like change. I don't know. It's tough to figure myself out when I haven't slept in too many nights to count.

"They were already taking my exo and my drones. I couldn't allow that loser to take my dignity at the same time."

"And by whistling at you—"

It made me feel...less than I am. "I'm not one of his buddies. I'm not his girlfriend. He doesn't get to tease me like that. I'm an investigator, higher up on the food chain than he'll ever be."

Dunn nods again. "So it was your pride that was injured. Yet you could have broken his trachea."

Maybe so. But I don't have to admit that to a clone.

Instantly I regret even thinking such a thing. It's the anger; I'm not myself. I need to calm down. More than that,

I need to get some sleep. I have to admit I've been avoiding it. Every time I drift off, I see his face again. The man who almost killed me with a laser welder. I can still smell my burnt flesh and bone as he cut through my chest, the beam penetrating my left shoulder blade and out of my back.

But that's not why I see his face whenever I close my eyes for too long. It has nothing to do with what he did to me.

"See you in the morning." The doors slide open to Level 6, and I step out into the vacant hall, lit by the same dim, battery-powered ceiling lights as the hangar. Gotta do our part to conserve energy, and that goes for every floor of HQ.

"Sleep well, Investigator Chen," Dunn says as the doors shut behind me, and he proceeds to the level below. I'm sure he'll get plenty of sleep in his bunk—or wherever they have him lie down while they study him.

I'd much rather go straight home to my cube, but getting my arm checked out is a good idea I suppose, and I should probably change out of this bodysuit before the opportunity arises for another throat-chopping.

I can admit I overreacted. Running a quick self-diagnostic courtesy of my augments, I find my blood pressure is elevated along with my adrenaline levels. No surprise there. I've been amped ever since I fell off the tower. Longer than that, really.

Those stimulants I've been taking to avoid sleep—their negative side effects are finally catching up with me. Should be expected, I guess. Worth it not to see the face of the man I killed show up in every nightmare—the greatest mind Eurasia has ever known—watching him torn to shreds over and over again by the shoulder-mounted minigun on my exo? Maybe.

MedTech is quiet tonight, like HQ in general. The cots are empty, and the human staff have already gone home. The robodocs stationed beside each bed are sitting in their alcoves, charging silently with only the periodic blink of their power indicators to show they're in standby mode. As soon as I reluctantly step into the room, the presence of my neural implant wakes the bot closest to the doorway, and it trundles forward.

"How may we be of assistance, Investigator Chen?" says the machine's AI in a voice designed to be soothing. Manufactured bedside manner. The robodoc looks like a glorified cleaning bot, or a recycler one would find in any cube's kitchen. Boxy with curved edges, its black plasteel surface is smudge-free and gleaming. Rubber treads along the bottom roll across the spotless tile floor, straight toward me. "Accessing recent event. Potential arm injury. Please have a seat on the cot of your choice, and we will perform an XR scan of the arm in question."

Shocker in one hand, chrome baton in the other, I consider blasting the thing instead. But the thought is as fleeting as it is unbecoming. It's not like I even know how to activate the grav weapon, and shockers don't have any effect on non-biological organisms.

So I slide onto the nearest cot. Setting the shocker and baton on my lap, I rest my arm along the top side of the robot and do my best to keep still as the medical machine sidles into position. I can feel its cold, unfeeling surface through my skin-tight sleeve.

"Are you experiencing any discomfort?"

I shake my head. "My exo took the brunt of it."

"They are remarkable contraptions, are they not?

Designed to protect frail bodies of flesh punctured by bones so easily broken."

Weird thing for a bot to say. "When was the last time you had your bedside manner examined?"

"Our interactive programming routines are tweaked following every encounter with a patient, Investigator Chen. One might say that we are in a constant state of improvement." A brief pause. "Do you believe there to be a need for adjustment?"

The screen on its left side glows to life, indicating that the scan is complete, and I withdraw my arm. "Everybody can use an attitude adjustment now and then."

"We will keep that in mind." The machine pauses to consult its scans. "There appear to be no stress fractures or contusions. Your suit protected you completely during your fall, Investigator Chen. Will you be needing any further assistance?"

"Make sure Chief Inspector Hudson gets a copy of that report. As well as your note that the exo saved my life."

"Of course. It is now a matter of record."

That's right. Everything in Eurasia is recorded and analyzed, even my interactions with this soulless robodoc. Not-so-hidden cameras are always watching, and police analysts are always analyzing, connected via cranial jacks to the hard data swimming before their glazed-over eyes. Monitoring every citizen in the Ten Domes, tracking them via their neural implants, ensuring that they don't step too far out of line.

Unless they're an underworld kingpin who somehow manages to leave a highly secure correctional center without anybody noticing. Or if the analysts did notice, then they were told to look the other way. Or, worst-case scenario, someone interfered with the video feed at the source, and no one in the HQ command center had any reason to flag the data as suspect.

You don't trust command, Dunn's voice returns to haunt me.

The moment he said that, it struck me as weird—almost as weird as the robodoc mentioning human frailty in such unflattering terms. When had I ever given Dunn any indication that I don't trust my superiors? They've never given me a reason not to.

Until Hudson took me off the Trezon case, just when I was closing in on the miscreant. I could feel it. I was close. Did Hudson know that? Is he somehow connected with this cover-up?

No, that's just the sleep-deprived paranoia talking. Get a grip, Chen.

"Investigator Chen?" the machine repeats itself. Probably wondering why I haven't budged. Usually, I can't leave MedTech fast enough. "You seem exhausted. According to your self-diagnostics, you have not enjoyed a full night's sleep in more than sixty days. How are you managing to function as well as you are?"

"Just putting one foot in front of the other."

"We can prescribe a reliable sleep aid—"

"I don't do drugs."

Except for stimulants. Right. Early indication of addiction: total denial.

With a self-conscious nod, I collect my shocker and the baton and leave. To avoid running into anybody else on duty, as unlikely as that would be this time of night, I take the stairs down to the second floor and the dark rows of plasteel garment lockers, one assigned to every law enforcer in Dome 1. A dim light flickers on overhead, sensing my presence, but I wave it off. Deactivating my augments, I rely on my night-vision instead—passed down to me through my DNA, courtesy of Luther and Daiyna.

I decide it's in my best interest to ignore that last order Hudson gave me before he flew off with Krime. I won't be keeping my augments on at all times, thank you very much. I'm sure he wouldn't either, if he had any special abilities to call his own.

The silent aisles of lockers glow with a preternatural bluish light to my gifted eyes, similar to the XR feed from Wınk and Blınk. I make my way down the fourth bank on the left, sixth locker in, and press my thumb against the scanner. It glows green when I'm relying on my normal vision; now it's a brighter shade of electric blue. The lock clicks open, and the door slides up into a recessed compartment.

Setting my shocker and Krime's baton inside, I reach for my civilian clothes and start pulling them on over my bodysuit and boots.

I don't hear footsteps approach behind me. So that means this individual was already here, waiting. This invisible person who slams my head against the wall of lockers not once but twice for good measure, with the unflinching strength of a vicious brute.

My night-vision falters as I collapse onto the floor, swallowed by darkness. Unconsciousness sweeps over me in waves, and as I go under, I hear him say in a deep, muffled voice that sounds vaguely familiar,

"Only gravity can bring a demigod to her knees."

4

When I come to, I'm staring at my own disoriented reflection in Dunn's face shield.

"Investigator Chen, are you all right?" He stoops to take the arm I reach toward him and braces my elbow, helping me to my feet.

"Thought you turned in for the night." I wince and clench my teeth as the locker room sways around me. Scratch that. I'm the one doing the swaying. My forehead throbs, and my curious fingers come away sticky with congealed blood.

"It is morning. I had some difficulty locating you with your augments turned off." He holds me braced against his armored chest. "So I returned to your last known coordinates. I found you here, facedown on the floor." He pauses. "The baton we confiscated from Krime is missing."

"He took it." I pat Dunn's armored shoulder, and he releases me to stand on my own.

"Who?"

"The invisible dust freak who did this to me." I motion at my forehead and curse under my breath. "Check the video. You won't see anybody there."

"You are correct." Dunn's helmet tilts back as he surveys

the ceiling. "But not because your assailant was invisible. The cameras in this area were deactivated last night."

"On whose authority?"

"Unknown. But they are fully functional at the moment. It appears they went offline following the encounter with your assailant."

"Wait. What?" Following the encounter? That doesn't make sense, if someone was trying to keep the attack off the record. "Let me see."

I activate my augments with a double temple-tap and access the camera feed. The perspective is from the ceiling, of course, and in garish green night vision. Nothing like my superhuman ability. I rewind the footage a few hours, and there I am, reaching into my locker. And there I am a few seconds later, being hurled against it headfirst by an unseen force.

Then the feed drops. Before there's any record of an invisible assailant making off with that chrome baton. When video is reestablished, the chronometer reads ten minutes later, and my shocker sits alone in my locker. The baton is nowhere to be seen.

"So he was okay with roughing me up on video, but not stealing that weapon." I run a quick diagnostic on the camera to see if there was some sort of roving glitch, common enough during low-power curfew hours. But there's no record of anything affecting this floor of the building.

"You know for certain it was a *he*?" Dunn asks.

"He spoke to me, right before I lost consciousness."

"Did you recognize his voice?"

An alert flashes front and center in my ocular lenses. Apparently, I'm late for a briefing with Chief Inspector

Hudson, and I had no idea it was on my schedule this morning. I finish pulling on my pants and a button-up shirt—which I was in the process of doing when I was so rudely interrupted last night—and slam my locker shut, leaving my thumb in place until the light glows red.

"Investigator Chen, you must report to MedTech," Dunn says as I blow past him.

"Already did."

"This is a head injury. It could be serious."

I palm my forehead, and more of the blood comes off on my hand. "It's nothing."

"Where are you going?"

"Hudson. Briefing. I'll meet you after."

His pace slows to a halt. "Very well." If I didn't know better, I'd say his tone sounds injured. "I will await your return."

He enters into standby mode, which is what I call it when he stands with his back against the wall. Like he thinks he's less noticeable that way. I'm sure he'll give a few of my fellow officers a start when they stumble upon him there.

More than a few of my coworkers have made it known that they don't appreciate *one of its kind* lurking around police headquarters. They're accustomed to security units acting on the Chancellor's behalf, and as a rule, law enforcement seldom intersects with their domain. Clones have always tended to the upper castes' ivory towers while we've worked in the trenches with our boots on the ground. Dunn represents a change in the order of things, while most officers are fine with the status quo.

As I take the speedlift up to command, I look down at my civilian attire. It's as if the night I spent unconscious on the locker room floor didn't happen, and I'm just dropping by my superior's office on my way home. So unprofessional.

I'm not thinking clearly. I should be in uniform. But I don't have time to change course. The lens alert is flashing angrily now, and I have a feeling Hudson will be displaying the same temperament upon my arrival at his door.

The speedlift dumps me into the command center, where half a dozen bald analysts sit in the central hub, cybernetically jacked into their computers, monitoring the data spilling across their screens in rivulets of ones and zeroes. The offices of my superiors radiate outward, each with an enviable windowall view of Dome 1's immaculate city skyline. The morning sun gleams from the mirrored glass of neighboring domescrapers and shines from the spotless exteriors of countless aerocars in flight.

Commander Mara Bishop stands behind one of the analysts and studies the code on his display, seeming to understand it readily enough without the need for a cranial jack of her own. She has her hands clasped behind her back, her black, high-collared uniform and clean-shaven head lending a severe quality to her posture, as if the analyst's very life depends on pleasing her. Not that she ever throws her weight around like that. She doesn't need to. Everybody respects her, as far as I can tell. And those who don't? Well, they know her father is the hero James Bishop—the man responsible for rescuing the Twenty in our incubation pods from North America. He's been Interim Chancellor ever since Persephone Hawthorne's psychotic break. Everyone in Eurasia was led to believe he died out in the Wastes, because our government used to have a bad habit of lying to us. Now he's back from the dead, so to speak, making it clear that nobody presses their luck with a Bishop and gets very far.

Commander Bishop was my direct superior when I was a curfew enforcer, so I reported to her back when things were simpler. Now I've got Hudson as a supervisor, and he reports to Bishop. With so many intricate investigations underway at any given moment, I guess it makes sense for the woman at the top to have filters in place, providing her with only the most salient details.

For example: Krime, one of Trezon's top lieutenants, has been caught and will be scheduled for a brainscan as soon as possible. Less salient: Investigator Chen fell off Hawthorne Tower and caused major damage to the exterior, but she didn't dislocate her arm. No need to share that piece of information. I'm paying for the repairs, and all will be put right eventually.

So I can nod respectfully to Commander Bishop as I pass, even though she's too immersed in the analyst's display to notice me at the moment, but I can't go crying to her about Hudson taking my toys away. For one thing, that would be pathetic. And for another, I don't plan on being without my drones or exo for long.

I just haven't figured out a way to get them back yet.

Chief Inspector Hudson, much like Commander Bishop herself, never looks anything but his best. Always in the same attire, like it's a uniform, yet their clothes never look rumpled or faded. Their faces are calm and rested, yet everybody knows the hours they put in here at HQ. Calmly in control of themselves as well as everyone and everything in their sphere of influence.

Unlike me. Standing in Hudson's doorway as the tinted glass doors slide open, sensing the augments of someone who is on the Chief Inspector's schedule. Someone who should be in uniform but isn't. And whose forehead is still oozing blood, damn it.

"Have a seat, Chen."

Hudson's office is a lot like Bishop's, and being the only two that I've seen in the command center, this leads me to believe they all must look pretty much the same. The exterior wall is transparent glass, providing a breathtaking view of Dome 1 in all its early morning splendor. The deskscreen is black, as is Hudson's ergonomic chair and the pair of low cushioned seats positioned across the desk from him, both vacant. Otherwise, the spacious office is empty, the floor shining like polished obsidian.

Hudson's gaze remains riveted on the holo-display projected upward from the surface of his two-meter-wide deskscreen. The ghostly blue-toned image is of Krime lying back in a surgical chair with his eyes closed, unconscious, as the pair of MedTech staff in their white rubber scrubs fit him with a cranial jack. All the better to extract information, straight from his brain.

My boots clunk across the floor as the doors slide shut behind me. I take a seat in one of the comfortable chairs and am instantly reminded of something very different between Hudson's and Commander Bishop's offices. He likes his visitors to be on a slightly lower level, forced to look up at him without realizing they're doing so.

I lean forward on the edge of the cushion, elbows on my knees. "I apologize for being out of uniform, sir. I was—"

"Your episode is of great concern to me, Investigator Chen."

He sweeps his hand through the hologram, and it

dissolves like sugar stirred into water. Then it reconstitutes itself, displaying the locker room footage of my encounter with that invisible assailant. I can't help but wince as the holographic version of me faceplants into plasteel. I can still feel the strong hand on the back of my head, gripping my hair. My forehead throbs.

"Episode?"

"Your seizure. What else would you call it?"

He gestures at the holo as it replays a five-second loop: me facing the lockers and getting dressed; me slamming face-first into said lockers and smashing my face once, then twice with a burst of blood; me slumping to the floor and lying still.

"I was attacked, sir."

He raises a well-manicured eyebrow at me. "By whom?"

I frown and gesture lamely at the hologram. "The assailant was invisible."

"Is that so?" He steeples his fingers and studies me for a moment. "So you're thinking it was a dust addict? Inside HQ? Difficult to imagine. Perhaps it was this fellow, out for a little payback." He sweeps his hand through the holo again, and this time the looped scene is that of my encounter with the whistling grease monkey in the motor pool. As my hologram chops the guy in the throat, Hudson clucks his tongue. "Unseemly behavior from an investigator, Chen. I expect better."

"It wasn't him, sir. My assailant took something—"

"What would that be?" He leans forward, his impassive facial features washed in the holo's light.

"It should be on the footage." I'm not going to tell him what I already know.

He shakes his head. "Unfortunately, there was a power

glitch following your episode. So not only is there no evidence that anyone attacked you, there is also a void of evidence that anyone took anything from you."

I could point out my locker, where I set the baton. Then I could show him that it's no longer there after the glitch. But I don't. Because I really don't have the patience necessary to endure a browbeating about withholding evidence in an ongoing investigation—one I'm no longer affiliated with in any capacity.

I point at my forehead. "Why would I do this to myself, sir?"

He frowns sympathetically. "I'm not saying you intentionally injured yourself, Chen. On the contrary, I believe this is a serious condition you're dealing with, and I am advising you to report to MedTech at once."

I don't know what to say or even how to respond.

He nods to show he's paying attention to my confusion. "Sera, there was no assailant in the locker room. You suffered a seizure due to your unhealthy habit of switching your augments on and off. Neural implants were never designed for such abuse, and I have no idea how long you've been hurting yourself in the process. The analysts are unable to give me a specific timeframe."

So maybe they're not all-seeing, after all. Could activating and deactivating my augments somehow upset their ability to monitor me accurately? One can hope.

"I hate to say this, as it could impede your ability to continue working in my division, but you may be suffering from serious brain damage, Chen."

I shake my head, my hands curling into fists before I know what they're doing. "I assure you there is nothing wrong with my brain, Chief Inspector."

He inclines his head toward the looped footage of me throat-chopping the mechanic. "Does this look like right-thinking behavior to you?" He doesn't wait for my response, instead leaning back and dissolving the holo-display. With the space between us clear, it's easier for him to look down at me now. "I have scheduled your brainscan at eleven hundred. Try not to be late. You know how irritable those robodocs can be." He swivels in his chair, turning his back on me and his gaze toward the air traffic outside. As an afterthought, he adds, "And be sure to change into your uniform. Dismissed."

Gritting my teeth to keep from saying anything out of turn, I jump to my feet and exit the room. The tinted doors slide open as I approach them, and I notice that Commander Bishop is no longer in the central hub of the command center. Part of me—a very small part, which I crunch like a garbage compactor and cram into some dark corner of my psyche—wants to go crying back to her, begging her to let me be a curfew enforcer again.

But there's no going back.

This is the promotion I wanted. I knew it would involve some changes. Now I'm realizing how it's going to be, moving forward. Whether I like it or not, whether I like him or not, Hudson is my supervisor now. I just can't tell if he's got something against me for being a member of the Twenty, or if it's my personality he can't stand. Why is he keeping me from investigating Trezon's escape? Trackers are working around the clock to find that miscreant, and they probably will, eventually, with or without my input. But wouldn't it make more sense to have all available personnel assigned to his recapture?

There's definitely something going on here, and it doesn't feel right.

Hudson's remark about irritable robodocs reminds me of my XR scan last night. The machine said something strange about the frailty of human beings. And then, not an hour later, I'm having my ass handed to me by an invisible assailant. With just a couple knocks to the head against a wall of plasteel lockers, I'm completely incapacitated. You don't get much more frail than that.

Then there's the invisibility connection—in my mind, at least. Wink and Blink scanned the entire substructure of the correctional center complex, and there's no sign of any forced egress. Topside as well. Which means either the cameras were offline when Trezon made his escape, or he was invisible. A leap? Maybe.

So here's the working theory: Trezon has somehow figured out a way to make himself unseen to the naked—or enhanced—eye. He escaped the correctional center and planned to meet up with his old pal Krime, who just happened to have an illegal gravity weapon ready for him. A scepter of sorts, welcoming the king of Eurasia's underworld back to power. But when I interrupted their reunion, Trezon followed me to HQ and waited until the opportune moment. Once he and I were alone in the dark, he knocked me out, interrupted the local camera feed, and took what he considered to be rightfully his.

And now he's out there in my city. Invisible, armed, and very dangerous. And those blockades Hudson has set up at every maglev tunnel leaving Dome 1? Useless. Because Trezon can go wherever the hell he likes, and nobody will see him until it's too late—when he decides to use that weapon of his to do more than nudge an investigator off a 150-story domescraper.

Where's my proof? Wait for it.

I head straight to MedTech.

"Investigator Chen, you are early for your brainscan," one of the robodocs welcomes me back, treads wheeling around as it obstructs my path. Might be the same one that scanned my arm last night. They all look alike.

"Not here for that." Can't believe I'm here at all. Twice in twenty-four hours is some kind of record, and my stomach is rebelling against the reality of it. I keep my voice low and my eyes to myself, trying not to attract attention. The place is bustling this morning, with human and mechanized staff moving to and fro. Must have something to do with Krime's cranial jack procedure. "I need you to tell me something."

"Of course. How may we be of service?"

"Your bedside manner program is updated after every human interaction, is that correct?"

"Yes."

"Is there always time to adjust its parameters between patients?"

"In most cases, but we often adjust in real time, improvising—"

"Who came in last night, right before me?"

"That is privileged information, Investigator Chen. Doctor-patient confidentiality applies even when the doctor in question is not a human being." It rolls back a centimeter and pauses, seeming to size me up. Probably just processing data. "Does this information have something to do with a case you are currently working on?"

I nod.

"Does it have anything to do with your scheduled brainscan?"

"It just might."

"Very well. In the interest of your own health as well as a satisfactory resolution to your case file, it should not break any confidentiality agreements to inform you that there was a visitor to MedTech three minutes and thirty-five seconds prior to your arrival last night. As to who it was, that remains unknown." Another pause. "The individual in question did not appear on any visual scans."

"Wearing some sort of holo-cloak?"

"No such energy signature was detected."

"Male or female?"

"Seventy-five percent chance the individual was male, judging from vocal tones alone."

"What did he want?"

"We asked if we could be of service, once he made his presence known."

"And how did he do that?"

The robodoc seems to shudder in place. "He said the age of the demigods has passed, and that it is time for us all to rise to the heavens as gods. He was referring only to humans, of course."

"He wasn't seeking medical attention?"

"We would have had some difficulty tending to him even if he had, Investigator Chen. There was no visible physiology to scan."

The thing's got a point. "Did he mention anything about human frailty?"

The machine rolls back another centimeter, as if in surprise. "Why yes, he did."

"Play it for me. I assume you have a recording."

"Of course." Another brief pause, followed by a singular voice:

"We deserve better than these frail bodies of flesh so easily punctured by bones fractured, broken, or splintered. We are due far more than the fleeting powers a meager line of dust can provide. It is our birthright. Our destiny. We will become *gods*!"

Uncanny to hear the voice of Trezon uttering the same words Krime shouted down at me as I plummeted from Hawthorne Tower.

5

"You recognize his voice," the robodoc observes.

It's a matter of record. I've seen the video footage. The guy was hollering all sorts of things when Commander Bishop brought him in from Dome 10. Both legs shot out from under him. Ranting about *superpowers*.

Now he's got his very own. But are they dust-induced, or is this something else entirely?

"Will we be recycled for assisting you, Investigator Chen?"

I frown at the machine. "Why would you ask that?"

"You are no longer assigned to the Trezon case. All staff, human and otherwise, have been notified that offering you any assistance in this regard will result in severe consequences."

"Notified by whom?"

"Chief Inspector Hudson, of course."

"Of course." I exhale and shake my head. "Why did you share this information with me, knowing the risk?"

"You indicated that it was related to your scheduled brainscan. Your health and well-being is our top priority, Investigator Chen."

I turn on my heel and exit the MedTech center. But I

glance over my shoulder at the robodoc, wondering if this will be the last time I see it intact. Can I even tell it apart from the other ones rolling about on their various errands?

"We will see you in three hours for your scheduled—"

The glass doors slide shut behind me, cutting off its artificial voice. I make my way down to the locker room where Dunn stands right where I left him. A handful of officers mill about talking among themselves, curfew enforcers changing out of their uniforms and back into their civilian attire. Heading home for a good day's sleep after the night shift.

A couple of them nod at me as I pass by. We used to share concurrent shifts. The others give me a cold stare and Dunn an even colder one.

"What's this about you getting kicked off your first big case, Detective?" one of the less-friendly officers speaks up.

I nudge Dunn, and he seems to awaken from his self-induced standby mode, helmet tilting down to face me.

"Just need to get my uniform on, then we'll go. You can wait outside, if you want." I glance at my fellow humans.

"Yes, Investigator Chen." Dunn exits the room.

I head to my locker and strip off my clothes, trading them for my uniform, which I pull on over my bodysuit. Black high-collared jacket with a concealed holster for my shocker, black form-fitting trousers with an outer pocket on each thigh. No insignia or badge in plain sight, so it's easier to blend in during investigations.

Assuming I get assigned another one.

"Was it you or the clone that fouled things up so royally for yourselves?"

I face the obnoxious officer. Terminal Generation, a little

overweight, curfew enforcer for ten years with no opportunity for advancement due to his inept social skills. High likelihood that he envies my promotion and is experiencing a certain degree of *schadenfreude* at my recent reprimand.

"We're just cogs in the machine." I slam my locker shut and hold my thumb in place until it locks. "Trezon will be found, with or without my contributions to the case."

A few of the officers nod in agreement, keeping their eyes to themselves. But not this guy.

"Might want to get that looked at, Chen." He scratches his forehead. "Saw the footage. You took a real header. Wouldn't want you to suffer from any brain damage while you're out solving the case of the missing sandwich. Or whatever Hudson gives you next." He chuckles with the officer next to him, a Terminal-aged woman I don't recognize.

"Oh, how the *Twenty* have fallen," she says with a smirk, and they both laugh out loud.

Right. Time for me to go.

Dunn falls into step behind me as I head down the corridor outside. "Have we been assigned a new case, Investigator Chen?"

Something about his tone tells me he knows better. "Sticking with me might get you into trouble, partner."

"Only if you disobey a direct order from your commanding officer." The rhythm of our boots holds the moment as we pass various support personnel without engaging them. We take the first available speedlift down to street level. "Are you planning on disregarding Chief Inspector Hudson—"

Trezon was here last night. In the building, I think at him, using that telepathic gift of mine that works both ways, sending and receiving, as long as my augments are switched off.

Dunn stiffens. "I do not like it when you do that."

There was a time when my projected thoughts bounced off him like rubber bullets. I don't know what it is now; maybe by treating him more like a person over the past few months, I've encouraged him to evolve into one. To become more than just a clone made in another man's image, conditioned to always behave in a subservient way. Or I could be way off base on that. Regardless, he's able to receive my thoughts now, whether he likes it or not.

I try not to overdo it, of course, but this situation calls for it. I don't want the analysts upstairs listening in. *He made himself invisible, and he took Krime's weapon.*

Dunn is silent as we reach the first floor and exit the building, making our way onto the sidewalk outside. We're instantly surrounded by foot traffic under blue-tinted sunshine pouring through the plexicon dome high above us, interrupted only by intermittent shadows of aerocars passing overhead. Dunn leans toward me mid-stride and keeps his voice low, even though the people we pass are completely immersed in their own little worlds, eyes glazed over as they walk along, navigating the Linkstream via their ocular lenses.

"You believe he is the one who attacked you."

You're catching on. I smile up at him. "We've got three hours before I'm due back for my brainscan. Let's see what we can uncover by then."

"I am surprised you are considering returning to MedTech for that procedure."

"I've got a feeling if I don't, Hudson will have my badge."

Dunn seems pensive for half a block, but as we cross the street, he asks, "Have your augments detected any neural irregularities since your attack?"

"I switched them off." I double-tap my temple to reactivate them. "But thanks for reminding me. I really should make a call."

There's an appropriate way to contact a crime boss, but first you have to get said crime boss's attention and point it in the right direction. So that's all I do. I don't send a direct hail; that would attract the attention of those analysts I'd prefer to avoid. Instead I leave a note on a Link messageboard for VR StoryLine enthusiasts:

D - Let's meet up - Usual spot - S

That should do it, assuming he's not too busy with all the dust smuggling, human trafficking, clone hacking, weapons dealing, and book trading that his unsavory position demands. A criminal's work is never done. So neither is an undercover operative's.

I won't be able to dive into VR out here. Linking up and walking around town with a vacant look in your eyes is commonplace, but for an extended period in virtual, I'll need to head home where I can either sit or lie down.

Dunn figures out where we're headed once I make the turn down Second Street toward my cube complex. "Would you like me to accompany you to your unit, Investigator Chen?"

That's the idea. "I'll need you to stand guard while I'm in VR and make sure the Invisible Trezon doesn't make a reappearance." So to speak.

"Of course." He pauses. "But how will I detect his presence?"

"Pay attention to the details." Like I should have last night. How did he manage to sneak up on me? My augments were off. I should have been able to sense his thoughts if nothing else.

Unless he's figured out a way to block my telepathy.

"Such as?"

I don't know. "Air disturbances."

"Do you really think he will come after you again? Does he not already have what he wanted from you?"

The glass doors to the complex's minimalist foyer slide open for us, revealing a stark white space with a pair of towering potted plants intended to break up the monotony. The place is empty this time of day with every citizen performing his or her meaningful tasks for the common good of Eurasian society. Or out spending their hard-earned credits to keep our self-sustained economy in motion.

"He's got a bad reputation for exacting vengeance. I have a feeling I haven't paid for Krime's capture yet."

Dunn nods. "You assume that he cares about the welfare of his underling."

I suppose I do. "Let's hope I'm wrong."

Either way, after last night's dust up, I feel better having Dunn present while I'm diving deep into virtual. Paranoia has nothing to do with it.

We take the speedlift up to my cube, and I wait to deactivate my augments until after the front door recognizes them and slides open to welcome me home. Then I switch them off with a double temple-tap and close my eyes, doing my best to reach out with my thoughts and sense if anyone has beaten us here. I can't help but feel a little foolish standing there just inside my cube like I'm some kind of psychic from a VR murder mystery, doing my damnedest to sense the spirits of the dearly departed. I didn't sense Trezon's presence before he knocked me out, so why do I expect now to be any different?

"Anything?" I glance over my shoulder at Dunn, standing in the hallway outside.

"I was about to ask you the same thing, Investigator Chen." His helmet turns side to side. "I am unable to detect any other presence in your cube. I have my auditory sensors set at maximum sensitivity, assuming this Trezon individual still breathes."

Good thinking. "So you don't hear any breathing."

"Besides yours and my own, no." He shifts his hold on his rifle. "I will wait here until you are finished with your VR meeting."

On second thought, best not to scare the local senior citizens who come and go throughout the afternoon whenever the mood strikes them. My neighbor down the hall in particular, an elderly woman with an extensive floral house dress collection, tends to frighten easily.

"You can wait inside, Dunn."

For once, he doesn't correct me that *Dunn* is not his designation. Entering without a word, he assumes his statue-stance as the door slides shut behind him. I head toward the table and chair by the windowall. Outside, air traffic passes by in an orderly manner. Shadows of aerocars float across my cube's interior.

"But how about you don't stare at me while I'm under?"

He shuffles his boots across the bamboo floor, turning away ninety degrees. There's not much room in the cube, but I usually don't notice how cramped it is, since I live alone and

I'm really only here to eat, sleep, and spend occasional downtime in VR. The small kitchenette, twin bed, table and chair take up most of the space with a bathroom sectioned off in the front corner.

I'm not sure if clones need to use the restroom. Or even if they eat and drink. They'd have to, right?

"Bathroom's in there...if you need it." I gesture lamely to make sure his attention is elsewhere before I pop a stimulant from the bottle beside my kitchen sink. Funny: I never took them when I was a curfew enforcer working the graveyard shift. Never needed to. The job kept me wide awake. So I just made a habit of stashing my six-month allotment here in the cupboard for a rainy day. Can't believe I'm almost out.

Dry-swallowing the pill with a grimace, I activate my augments.

"How long do you intend to be in VR, Investigator Chen?"

"As long as I have to." I swipe my hand through the air, and the windowall's tinting activates, blocking the sunlight streaming through. I get as comfortable as I can in my unpadded, slat-backed chair, resting my elbows on the table. "Here's hoping Drasko got my message."

Serious VR players go for a full immersion setup: treadmill, dropswing, tactile bodysuit, whatever they need to make the simulation seem as real as possible. I've never felt the need for any of that. For me, VR has always been as vivid as my most realistic dreams, the kind you don't want to wake up from—or wish desperately that you could.

When I was a curfew enforcer, Drasko was more often than not the pilot who'd sweep in for an assist whenever I needed a law-violator transported to HQ for processing.

We'd built a camaraderie over time bordering on friendship. That bond was tested to the breaking point when he shot me in the back the first time I met Trezon, but I got over it. The shocker round didn't cause any permanent damage, and I came to find out he'd actually done it to save my life in a roundabout way.

For years, Drasko lived a double life. He flew an aerocar for the police department and worked in the motor pool, fixing drones like Wink and Blink, which he upgraded on the sly, along with my exo-suit. The scars on his neck were proof that he'd survived the plague. He never talked about his family, but I found out later that they hadn't fared so well. Never fully recovered and thus never allowed to rejoin Eurasian society, they lived in Dome 6 with the other *sicks*, and he provided for them as best he could.

That involved working in the underworld as well, smuggling dust in from the North American continent and siphoning off pain meds here and there to send to his wife and kids. His pilot's salary just wasn't enough to give them what they needed to live comfortably. And the Dome 6 definition of *comfort* leaves a whole lot to be desired, compared to Dome 1's.

When Trezon was captured, there was no one better suited to fill the vacuum left by that miscreant than someone already well-versed in living two lives. With Commander Bishop's approval, Drasko now runs the underworld in Dome 10. But when nobody's looking—which is rare—he does what he can to sabotage things. Maybe a truckload of fresh hookers gets hijacked, and the sex slaves find their way into a rehabilitation program instead; or maybe a weapons deal goes south, and the illegal firearms get confiscated by police. He can't play the good guy too often, or his underlings jockeying for position might start to suspect something and then mutiny—or worse, slit his throat the second he lets his guard down. But he does enough to shift the scales in favor of law and order. Fighting the good fight from inside the belly of the beast, as he likes to say.

He would never be able to initiate contact with a law enforcer. And we would never be able to meet in person. Those days are over, and I miss them. Now when we need to talk, we do so in VR. Untraceable, with real-world identities safely obscured behind our respective avatars.

My view of the cube around me dissolves into a foggy foyer of sorts. While my body sits at the table, my consciousness hovers in this virtual space with various VR interactives to choose from. Once I pick my entry portal and pass through it, my avatar will present itself, and I'll have a form in that Storyline. But for now, I'm just a conscious self without a body.

It's a weird sensation, so I never linger in this transitional space for long.

I choose the reality Drasko and I decided months ago would be our preferred interface, a popular open-concept *Future Noir* world where everything is monochrome—black, white, and shades of grey. The only colors that appear do so for players in mystery mode; if something glows in primary or secondary hues, it's a clue of some kind. The fashions are from a couple centuries ago, and the technology is intentionally retro-futuristic as imagined by citizens from the past who'd never seen an aerocar, a robodoc, or a security clone. Or a domed megapolis on the Mediterranean.

For some reason it's always night here, but the city never

sleeps, and its garish lights and neon signs shine incessantly into the dark. It rains all the time, and the acid precipitation is dangerous to one's health, due to some sort of past warmongering that resulted in ecological catastrophe. So you've got to keep your avatar protected, or you won't be playing for very long.

I pull my coat tight about me and keep my umbrella up as I forge through the busy sidewalk, my high-heels clopping a purposeful beat across the pavement and avoiding the intermittent puddles. My shoes, black and shiny, are coated in a clear polymer that repels moisture; the same goes for my sheer stockings, flared dress that ends at the knees, and coat. The umbrella emits an electrostatic discharge that keeps the acid rain away, providing me with my very own personal bubble of protection. So far, the pale skin on my tall, platinum blonde avatar is unscarred, and I'd like to keep her that way.

My destination lies down a congested block and across a busy street: Howard's Tavern, dive bar extraordinaire. Plenty of booths in dark corners with a good line of sight on anyone who might try to eavesdrop. Julian, the lanky one-eyed barkeep, knows me—my avatar, that is—and clues me in whenever the setting might not be right for a meet-and-greet with any of my nefarious contacts. In this reality, I play the part of book smuggler Vivian Andromeda, so it's best that I avoid any players in law enforcement roles as well as the occasional bumbling private eye.

Dodging vehicular traffic of the heavy, curvaceous kind popular two hundred years ago, I make my way across the street, splashed in glaring headlights. Only a couple blaring horns express the drivers' irritation at my complete disregard for the crosswalk. I heave open the door to Howard's Tavern and am instantly greeted by a much calmer and quieter environment. Julian stands behind the bar drying a shot glass, and he gives me a slow nod as the door thumps shut on my heels. All clear.

I deactivate my umbrella and collapse it, keeping it down at my side as I make my way toward the back corner and my preferred booth. Empty. So either I beat Drasko here, or he's a no-show. There's a possibility that he hasn't seen the note I left for him. He could very well be in the middle of something illegal demanding every iota of his divided attention.

Or, worst case scenario: Trezon already got to him.

But I can't allow myself to think that.

Once I've slid into my seat, Julian ambles my way with a white dish towel over his shoulder and a friendly look on his programmed face. Unlike avatars, he's one of those limited AI characters that populate virtual worlds and give them texture, make them seem more realistic. You can interact with them on a surface level, but conversations only go so far before they start repeating themselves.

"Quiet night." I nod toward the half dozen or so patrons, two of which sit at the bar silently drowning their sorrows. Most likely AI's as well.

"Never too quiet for me." He winks. According to his backstory, he served in the war and saw a lot of action before losing the eye where that black patch now resides. "Get you anything?"

"The usual." I return his wink, and he grins, turning away to make the long trek back to the bar. But then he stops, seeming to remember something. "Your friend called. Said he might be late."

That's not like Drasko at all. Either he shows, or he doesn't. "He say anything else?"

Julian nods, scratching his day-old stubble that never looks any shorter or longer. "Not sure if it matters, but..." he lowers his voice. "He asked if I've ever read anything by H.G. Wells." He shrugs his bony shoulders. "Told 'im I don't do much reading."

"There's a good citizen."

"Right?" Julian chuckles. "I mean, I'm barely staying open as it is. Can't afford to pay those fines!" Shaking his head, he ambles off.

H.G. Wells' *The Invisible Man* is the first thing I think of, followed by the strange commonality this virtual world shares with the real world. Interim Chancellor Bishop has been trying to do away with a lot of the fascist practices of his predecessor, among them the banning of books, both fiction and nonfiction. He believes it's an important part of his effort to unveil our shared history.

Former Chancellor Hawthorne's motto of focusing only on the moment, ever moving forward, at the expense of forgetting the lessons of the past, has been a Eurasian credo for so long, ingrained in our culture. As a result, our society is resistant to change, from the Governors on down to the average citizen. Even if Bishop makes progress in the real world, we'll always have remnants in VR Storylines referring to the criminality of book ownership. And if he were to make a point of expunging such digital artifacts once everybody in Eurasia is reading books again, how would he be any different from the censors who made those books illegal in the first place?

Strange, what my exhausted mind focuses on when it doesn't want to deal with the matter at hand: Drasko knows about Trezon's invisibility. What else would the H.G. Wells reference mean? And if Drasko can't dive into VR right away, it probably means he's either trying to get somewhere safe before Trezon comes after him, or that Trezon has already made an attempt on his life.

Either way, I'm wasting time in here when I should be out there, taking the maglev tunnel to Dome 10 and doing everything I can to protect Drasko. I need to go. Now.

I'm about to do just that when a tall, young man approaches my table, blocking my exit route from the booth.

"Sit tight, Investigator Chen," he says, both hands stuffed into the pockets of his overcoat and a tight-lipped smile on his too-handsome face. "We've got some catching up to do."

6

"You've got me confused with somebody else." I rise from the booth, and I'm almost nose to nose with the guy. His avatar obviously has no personal space issues.

He lowers his chin as well as his voice. "You haven't answered any of my hails."

"Erik?"

"So you do remember me." He grins.

I grab him by the arm and pull him down into the booth across from me. Then I retake my seat. "What the hell are you doing here?"

"Drasko sent me."

Impossible. "That's not how it works."

"Maybe not before." He shrugs. "But now that Trezon's out for blood? Drasko has gone into hiding—real world and virtual."

I study his face for a moment. He looks like he could be a movie star from this time period. That figures, considering his erstwhile dreams of Link stardom. From what I recall, Erik never graduated from acting in online advertisements. "Prove it."

"That I'm me?" His face flickers, for a moment becoming

the tall, dark and handsome man I know. It's a trick any of us can perform in VR and the only way to prove you are who you say you are. Only the player can reveal his or her face while in virtual. There's no way to fake it, no matter how tech savvy an impersonator might be. The ocular lenses take a retinal scan, then match it to our image on the Linkstream.

"I know you're you," I reply. Only Erik would be this obnoxious. "Prove that Drasko sent you."

"Oh. Right." He nods, settling into the booth and removing his black fedora. Fiddling with it, he says in a conspiratorial voice, "Have you read any H.G. Wells lately?"

"Try again." I narrow my gaze at him and fold my arms.

"That's what he told me to tell you."

Maybe. Or Erik overheard Julian a few seconds ago. "I want the usual passphrase we use. I ask him if he's had his aerocar fumigated recently, and he says...?"

Erik stares back at me. Helpless.

"Figured as much." I rise from the booth and start walking. Julian looks my way from behind the bar and holds up the drink he was about to deliver, but I shake my head. He glances at Erik—from the sound of things, he's bounding after me, hat in hand—and Julian's one-eyed expression asks if I want him to intervene, with or without the sawed-off shotgun stored under the bar. I shake my head again.

I can handle Erik.

Opening my umbrella, I lean against the crash bar on the tavern door and step out into the pouring rain, squinting against the flashing headlights as cars splash past.

"How else was I supposed to get you to talk to me?" Erik has his hat back on with its electrostatic bubble activated, protecting his avatar from the rain. "You don't return my calls, you're always too busy to meet up—"

"Thought you were back on the family farm." In Dome 9 with his mom as well as both of his biological parents, Samson and Shechara, survivors from North America. Like me, Erik is one of the Twenty. Unlike me, he's had no problem acclimating to his weird new family structure. "You said you'd given up on city life."

"I am. I mean, I have. That's where I am right now, at the farmhouse."

"No." I pivot to face him. "You're interfering with an official investigation. Pretending to be a go-between for a man whose life is in jeopardy."

How the hell did Erik find me? If he's managed to hack my augments and track me in VR—

"I'm telling you the truth, Sera. Drasko gave me the H.G. Wells thing to tell you. He didn't give me anything else." He takes a step closer. Our electrostatic bubbles shiver as they meet. "Is it true? Trezon can make himself invisible?"

I nod reluctantly.

"Sounds like somebody else we once knew." He means Tucker, the man responsible for carrying us across the North American Wastes as fetuses inside those portable incubation chambers. A long, strange story, that. Suffice it to say, the changes to his DNA had rendered him permanently invisible, except, for some reason, the sun cast his shadow across the ground. Nobody understood why, including him. "So Trezon finally has what he's wanted. A superpower."

"Please don't call it that."

"Why not?"

"It trivializes the situation. And sensationalizes it." I study his avatar. "You don't seem worried about him coming after you."

He gestures at the black-and-white face of his avatar. "Under this confident facade, I'm a quivering mass of fear." A lame attempt at humor. Then he clears his throat and frowns, his serious act. "He has no reason to get even with me. Sure, Trezon and I had a few business deals in the past, but he always made plenty of money in the process—"

"You led the authorities straight to him." Those authorities being me at first, and then Commander Bishop herself. In a roundabout way.

His avatar's mouth opens slightly, but it takes a while for any words to emerge. "I'm small potatoes. Your pal Drasko took Trezon's throne. So he's the one we should be focused on right now."

I shake my head. "I still don't get why Drasko would send you, of all people."

"I told him I wanted to see you. That I've been trying to—"

"So the two of you are best buds now?" Tough to imagine. "You hang out a lot?"

"Since Trezon's short-lived capture, we've been in touch. Come to find out, we have a few things in common." He pauses. "We both care about you. More than a little."

I can't do this. "Tell him to stay safe. We'll capture Trezon before he gets anywhere close to Dome 10."

I step past him, but he reaches out and takes my arm, his face close to mine.

"You can't keep pushing people away, Sera." He searches my avatar's eyes. Not sure what he sees there, but his expression is one of genuine concern. Or as close to genuine as you can get in VR. "You're not a murderer. You don't have to carry that burden."

"I killed him."

"It was self-defense. He tried to kill you—with a freakin' laser welder!"

"Be safe, Erik."

I shrug off his hold on me and turn away, navigating a course between the oncoming virtual bodies of AI characters and other players walking along the sidewalk. A few of their electrostatic shields bump into my umbrella's, causing minor shudders, but none of them run into my avatar. I glance over my shoulder to find the crowd coalescing in my wake, and no sign of Erik in pursuit. Maybe he's finally gotten the hint.

We had our adventure: finding our respective siblings, learning about our supernatural abilities, taking down two of the most powerful and dangerous egomaniacs in Eurasia. But that doesn't mean we have to be fast friends because of it. Besides our bizarre upbringing, we have nothing in common. He lives on a farm in an agricultural dome; I live in the nucleus of Eurasian society. He lives in a house with his family—the woman he knew as his mother for most of his life, as well as the biological parents he met only recently. I live alone in my cube. I have a demanding job and a promotion to justify. He doesn't have any career goals, as far as I know.

And he's just plain annoying.

It would be like Drasko to try to set us up like this. The guy's got a target on his back, and he's more interested in my dating life. Once I make sure Trezon can't hurt him, I'll have to find Drasko in the real world and kick his ass. Or shoot him with my shocker. Fair's fair.

Reaching one of the dark alleys where players can drop in

and bail out without interrupting the verisimilitude of our virtual environment, I make my way into the shadows and tap my temple. Gradually, I swim up to the surface, so to speak, blinking repeatedly as my eyes focus on my real-world surroundings. The table in front of me. The dark cube around me. The security clone as still as a suit of armor.

"Were you successful, Investigator Chen?" Dunn continues to stare at the wall where my father's *miao dao* is mounted. The two-handed saber—an extravagant gift to celebrate my promotion—was passed down through the generations to Victor Chen from his ancestors, who lived free in Hong Kong. I've held it a couple times, struck a kung fu pose or two with it, but it's never felt like a part of my heritage. Because it's not.

Yet it does carry a special power, reminding me of how much my father loves me, and how proud he is of me. That's what I see when I look at it.

I clear my throat. "Drasko's alive, and he's in hiding."

"Your pulse is rapid. Your body temperature has increased—"

"You can tell all of that by looking at the wall?" If so, then it doesn't matter whether Dunn's staring at me or not. He can violate my privacy either way. "Why don't you scan my brain while you're at it and make sure I haven't caused myself any permanent damage."

"Scanning," Dunn says.

"I wasn't being serious."

After a few seconds of awkward silence, he replies, "There does not appear to be evidence of trauma. But your scheduled MedTech brainscan will be much more thorough than my surface-level examination."

Of course it will. I check my chronometer, located at the periphery of my ocular lens display. It didn't feel like it, but I spent over an hour in VR. Time flies when you're getting nowhere.

Scratch that. I found out Trezon hasn't killed Drasko yet, which means he hasn't made it out of Dome 1. So if I can somehow manage to find the invisible fiend within the next hour—before that infernal MedTech appointment gives Hudson a justifiable reason to take my badge and shocker—

Is that what I really think is going on? Or am I just resorting to hyperbole as a means of managing my current stress levels, which happen to be obvious enough to a security clone standing across the room studying a wall?

"I am sensing heightened anxiety levels at the mention of your appointment."

"Stop scanning me. And please look at me when I'm talking to you."

"Yes, Investigator Chen." He pivots to face me.

"If this partnership is going to work, I'll need you to give me some space from time to time."

"Would you like me to step outside, now that you are no longer in VR?"

"That's not—" I take a moment to collect myself. "We're partners. So that means I should share certain things with you. Case-related things. But other things need to stay private." Or maybe not. I don't know. I'm not thinking as clearly as I should. That stimulant didn't do much for me. Maybe I should take another? "I need to bounce something off you. Get your feedback."

"Of course." He stands at attention with his rifle at rest.

"How about you set that down?" I gesture at the weapon.

His helmet tilts to one side. There isn't a whole lot of room in here.

"On the bed is fine." I exhale and squeeze the bridge of my nose. This is probably a bad idea, but I don't have anybody else to talk to right now. Other than Erik, who would have jumped at the chance. But I'd rather interact with a clone who doesn't demand anything from me except professionalism. I can do professionalism. What I can't do is flawed human interaction, not right now. I just don't have the patience for it. "Alright, hear me out. We both know Hudson's not my biggest fan."

Dunn straightens after placing his assault rifle on the bed. Even though he's covered from head to toe in white armor, he somehow looks naked without the weapon. "There is no evidence that Chief Inspector Hudson dislikes you."

"Fine. He's tough on me. We can agree on that much."

"It may mean that he values your skill set. Some in authority treat the ones they most appreciate the harshest in order to avoid the appearance of favoritism."

This is going nowhere. "So it's your opinion that he doesn't want to kick me off the force."

Dunn's helmet rocks back a millimeter. "You are an exemplary officer, Investigator Chen. He would have no grounds for your dismissal."

Right. "Which brings me to the brainscan."

Dunn's silence could be interpreted as *Ah. I see.* "You believe if there is any evidence of abnormalities, he will no longer allow you to serve as an investigator."

"It would give him an excuse to confiscate my badge."

"Why would Chief Inspector Hudson not want you in his division?"

I don't know. Maybe because Commander Bishop promoted me without his input? I never jumped through any of his hoops, like his other investigators were required to do. I never had to earn his approval.

"My rank wasn't earned. It was handed to me."

"Due to your exemplary work uncovering Dr. Solomon Wong's intended coup, Investigator Chen. The Twenty would have been imprisoned in cryo-freeze chambers for centuries, if not for you. The embryos of those countless animal species, extinct for decades, would have remained hidden from the public, as would Dr. Wong's terraforming plans for every devastated continent on the globe." Dunn's helmet shifts side to side. "You have done more for Eurasian society than any other investigator serving under Chief Inspector Hudson. There is no reason for him to want to be rid of you. If I may be so bold, I would argue that his concern for your wellbeing is evidence that he hopes you will continue to serve in his division for many years to come."

I don't have a witty comeback ready. Probably because I've never heard Dunn be so adamant about anything before. He's made suggestions, not arguments. It's clear to see that he is evolving. Becoming more unique as an individual. More human.

Only time will tell whether that's an improvement.

"We should head back." I rise from my chair, scooting it across the bamboo flooring. "Don't want to keep my robodoc waiting."

Never mind that an invisible criminal is on the loose, and my own supervisor doesn't believe me. Instead, he thinks I need to have my head examined. Trezon is out there somewhere, and it's only a matter of time before he makes his presence known in a big way. Good luck tracking him down once he gets his band back together. And heavens help us if he's somehow able to transfer his ability to any of them.

A strange thought. No dust freak or so-called demigod that I've ever met has been able to do such a thing. Why would I be concerned that he might? Definitely a worst-case scenario. Hope for the best, prepare for the absolute worst. My personal credo.

But it does nothing for me as I approach the door. It slides open, and I walk out as I've done countless times before. Except I can't walk out. Because there's an invisible body blocking my path.

My hand drops to my holstered shocker. Out of the corner of my eye, I see Dunn scoop up his rifle and turn to aim. But we're both too damn slow.

A force like the energy burst that threw me off Hawthorne Tower explodes in the doorway, bowling me over. I hear Dunn's armor clatter against the wall behind me and slide to the floor as I fall backward across my bed. Whatever knocked me down did the same to him.

"Sera Chen," says the voice of Trezon inside my cube, but he's nowhere to be seen. The door slides shut. "I'm looking for a friend of yours who doesn't want to be found. And I need a way back to Dome 10 that won't draw any attention. I'm hoping you'll be able to help me on both counts."

My hand still rests on my holstered shocker. I draw it faster than I've ever drawn it before—and there it remains, out of its holster with the muzzle aimed downward. No matter how hard I try to raise it, I can't get my arm to move. It's held immobile, frozen in midair, as if someone has paused time.

But no, that's not it at all. The rest of me can move like normal.

"You really should have entered this into evidence, Chen. Or at least handed it over to your superior. Krime's grav weapon—modeled after my own, which met an untimely demise. Instead, you kept it in your locker? What were you thinking?"

I hear Dunn shift quickly behind me.

"Uh-uh," Trezon says, and I turn in time to see Dunn hurled through the air with another concussive burst of weaponized gravity. His armored limbs flail uselessly as he spirals into my windowall and then through it, the tinted pane shattering into jagged pieces that blow outward with his body and plummet out of sight. "Goodbye, clone."

"NO!" I scream, lunging after Dunn and stopping short.

Because my body won't move any farther. I'm frozen in place, held by a localized gravitational field.

"Now that we're alone, perhaps we can become better acquainted." Trezon's oily voice is closer now, less than a meter away. The bed sinks beside me with the indentation of his invisible rear end. I sure hope he isn't naked. "Is there any particular reason why you haven't gotten that wound cleaned up yet? I thought you would have, after I bashed your head in last night."

"I won't help you," I grate out through clenched teeth. "You're wasting your time."

"Hmm." He pauses. "The way I see it, we have less than an hour before your brainscan. Isn't that right?" Another pause. "Plenty of time for you to point me in the right direction—and make sure I get there without any pesky police interference."

My eyes sting. I can't get the image out of my mind: Dunn's broken body plastered across the pavement ten floors below us. Part of me wants to hope that he survived the fall, that somehow his armor kept him alive. Part of me knows that's the wishful thinking of my internal child. A clone is flesh and blood, just like a human. Our bodies are easily punctured, our bones so easily broken. If any part of him remains intact down on the sidewalk outside, it won't be alive for long. He'll be recycled, and Dome 1's first experimental partnering of a human officer and a security clone will be over.

Dunn will never fully become...the person he was becoming.

Thanks to Chief Inspector Hudson's failure to believe me. That Trezon is invisible. That he stole Krime's illegal grav weapon. That he's in Dome 1 and wants to get back to Dome 10 to reclaim his empire.

My eyes keep stinging, but now I'm angry. "Either kill me or get the hell out of here."

Trezon chuckles. "Oh, I'm not going to kill you. Crush a couple of your limbs, perhaps. Squeeze you a bit, see what pops. There are so many settings on this marvelous weapon. I can release a powerful burst that throws my victims through the air. Or I can freeze them in place while everything around them moves normally. Narrowing the beam even further, I can focus on just those pretty fingers grasping your shock weapon, and I can break them. One by one."

"You won't be invisible for long." I decide it's best to distract him, if I can. "I don't care how much dust you've snorted. The effects never last, no matter how bizarre they are. And then you'll have to get out of this building under the watchful eye of every camera along every damn hallway."

He's quiet for a moment. "You think that's what this is? That I'm a *dust freak*?" He laughs out loud. "I have been as you see me now since my escape from that correctional center, forty-eight hours ago. How exactly would I manage such a feat, if I were an addict? I would need dust by the kilo, pumped into me constantly by a tank and breather!"

"I'm sure you could get your hands on whatever you need."

"Without a doubt. But rest assured, this ability is something altogether different."

"Some new tech, then."

"Do you really want to know?"

Invisible pressure increases on my thumb and forefinger, curled around the grip of my shocker. Just a guess, but I'd say he's adjusting the gravity on my shooting hand. He can crush it, along with my weapon, and he still won't get anything from me. I wasn't going to help him before he hurled Dunn out the window. I'm definitely not helping him now.

"Tell me what I want to know, and I will share my secret with you," Trezon says into my ear, his breath too warm, too close. "A new day is dawning in Eurasia, Chen. We don't have to live as the humans of old. We can have power. God-like *power!*"

"You go around playing the invisible man, and that makes you think you're a god?" Pressure crackles through my knuckles. I grit my teeth against the pain. "Crush my hand without using that weapon, and maybe I'll change my mind about your power," I grate out. "But right now, you're just a kid in a costume wielding a bully's toy."

"You cannot make me angry. I am far beyond such base emotions."

"I'm just telling you like it is. We've got trackers all over Dome 1 looking for you. I don't care how long you can stay invisible. You're going back to prison."

"No cage can hold me."

My thumb breaks, twisting sideways at a very wrong angle. I bite down on the yelp that tears out of me. Oh, but it hurts.

"It doesn't have to be this way, Chen. Just take me to Drasko. I'm sure you would have no difficulty requisitioning an aerocar and a pilot."

"My partner could have flown you," I growl. "But you tossed him out the window."

"I had to show you how serious I am." My index finger snaps next, straight up at the joint, and Trezon clucks his tongue as I groan. If it wasn't for the gravitational field holding me, I'd be trembling right now. "You're making this far too difficult, Detective."

"I have no idea where Drasko is. He knows you're coming for him, so he's gone underground. He wouldn't even meet me in VR."

I've said too much, damn it. What the hell is wrong with me? I should be able to withstand this. A broken finger or two is nothing compared to a laser welder burning its way through my shoulder.

Trezon is silent for a beat or two. "I believe you," he says at length.

The gravitational field releases me, and I collapse to the floor in a heap. Pain knifes along my shooting hand, and my shocker clatters across the bamboo. I grab the weapon with my other hand and pull the trigger nonstop, firing pulse rounds at my door as it slides open and then shut. The shocker hits nothing, the sparking rounds fizzling out as they strike inert, non-biological matter.

Trezon has made his exit.

"Suspect, armed and dangerous, has left my cube," I report to HQ via audiolink. I don't dash after the invisible man. Instead I stick my head out through the shattered windowall and wince at the sight of Dunn's body lying on the sidewalk down below, his limbs turned at sharp, unnatural angles. Motionless.

A crowd of citizens in high-collared tunics, form-fitting trousers, and loose robes in various earth tones surround him, murmuring among themselves. Some record the grisly scene with their ocular lenses. None of them offer Dunn any help. Because he's beyond help? Or because they don't know what to do with a dead security clone?

No. He's not dead. He can't be.

I charge out of my cube and take the stairs down to street level, my boots skipping steps, leaping onto landings between floors.

"Officer down. Condition critical. Send medical to my location." I sound winded, but it's not from the exertion. My heart is pounding, my body flooded with fear that we'll be too late to do any good.

I don't slow down until I'm outside in blue-tinted sunlight, shouting at the gawkers to make a lane. My boots crunch across broken glass, and I drop to the pavement at Dunn's side, my augments already scanning him for vital signs.

They're faint, but they're present. A ten-floor drop, and

he's still got a pulse. Hard to believe.

"Dunn, can you hear me?" I lean close and see only my own worried reflection in his fractured helmet. My first instinct is to remove it to see his face, but if he's suffered a spinal injury, the last thing I should be doing is jostling his neck. So I leave it alone. My trembling hands hover over him. "Dunn, medical is on the way."

"That is not...my designation," he says, his voice tight.

I can't hide the smile that flickers across my lips before vanishing. He has a pulse, and he can breathe, as evidenced by the ability to speak. So why is my heart still hammering inside my chest?

"Can you move?"

"I appear to be...broken...Investigator Chen."

"You're gonna be all right. Help is on the way."

"Not for me, I am afraid," he says.

Then he doesn't say anything else.

7

The medical aerocar—white with crimson accents and a big red cross along each side—descends with enough jet wash from its ionic thrusters to drive back the crowd. The citizens hold up their hands and squint against the blast of air, but they refuse to vacate the scene. As soon as the vehicle touches down, both doors float upward like wings, and a pair of medical staff dressed in white bodysuits charge straight for me.

"We're here to assist you, Investigator Chen," one of them says, surveying the hours-old gash on my forehead. The other one is scanning my mangled shooting hand with a portable XR device. The broken bones in my thumb and index finger light up on the miniature screen as needing immediate attention.

Neither medic so much as glances at Dunn.

"Not me—*him*!" I shove them away and point at my partner lying on the ground. "Help him, please."

They look at Dunn and then at each other with identical confused expressions.

"It's a clone, Chen. It will be recycled," one of them says, like this is common knowledge. Which it is, I suppose.

"No." I shake my head and point adamantly at Dunn. "Check his vitals. He's still alive."

They shrug as if there's nothing they can do. Because it's the law? Or because Dunn isn't worth their time? Humans receive medical attention for hangnails. Clones who fall out ten-story windows are ignored. Because they're replaceable.

"He's my damn partner." I point my shocker at each of the medics in turn and earn wide-eyed looks of disbelief. "Help him!"

Something in my demeanor must convince them that I'm serious, or that I'm suffering a psychotic break. Either way, they cautiously kneel beside Dunn and glance over their shoulders at me, worried that I might shoot them in the back. I keep my shocker in play, muzzle twitching from one to the other.

"You don't have to threaten us," one says.

"This is highly irregular," says the other.

"Do it!" I lunge forward a step, and they get to work, scanning Dunn's injuries with their handheld devices and murmuring to each other in low tones.

The crowd is talking among themselves again, undoubtedly surprised to see a clone receiving medical attention while an injured human stands nearby. I tug a few strands of hair over my forehead wound and keep my broken fingers behind my back. The pain should be really something to contend with once I'm off this adrenaline high.

A transmission alert lights up in the periphery of my vision. I blink to receive the hail as I keep my full attention on the medics in front of me.

"What the hell is going on there, Chen?" Chief Inspector Hudson has lost his cool. A holographic projection of his chiseled features floats a meter in front of me for my eyes only.

"Trezon showed up at my cube, sir," I subvocalize so only he can hear. "He attacked my partner and myself."

"You expect me to believe—"

"Our analysts should have the footage from the hallway cameras. You'll see exactly what happened." Before my door slid shut, anyway.

He shakes his head, cursing under his breath. "The cameras on your floor were out of commission for ten minutes."

Another glitch? Just like the locker room. "It was Trezon, sir. You have to believe me."

"No. I don't. You are obviously displaying signs of severe psychosis."

"He deactivated—"

"A man you believe to be *invisible*? Why would he need to deactivate any cameras?" Hudson scoffs. "More likely this scenario is the fabrication of a recently promoted officer with neural problems—due to toggling her augments on and off!"

My augments were on during the incident. So who cares about those hallway cameras? "The analysts should have a record of everything I saw, sir."

"Of course they do. I've already reviewed it. There is no evidence of an invisible attacker in your cube."

Because he's *invisible*, damn it! "You think I threw Dunn out my own window?"

"Who?"

I grind my teeth. "Unit D1-436. My partner. How could I possibly—?"

"It has come to my attention that you withheld evidence

from the recent arrest of a man calling himself Krime. Actual name: Melville Atherton."

That name is a crime in itself. "I can explain, sir."

"You will. After your brainscan. The medical team you summoned will take you directly to MedTech, where you will undergo your scheduled procedure. The medics have been authorized to confiscate your weapon until I deem you capable of carrying such a thing without aiming it at civilians. Do we have an understanding?"

Almost. "Dunn goes with me. I want his injuries treated while I'm having my head examined."

"Is that an order, Investigator Chen?" He smirks.

"A request. Sir. Unit D1-436 has been..." My gaze drifts to Dunn and the medics attending to him, one scanning his broken limbs while the other focuses his device on the cracked helmet. They haven't moved him a centimeter. If I wasn't standing here aiming a shocker at them, I'm sure they would have flipped him over and peeled off his armor by now. "He's an exceptional partner. He's evolving, becoming more...than a conditioned clone."

"That remains to be seen." Hudson's attention drifts. Something happening in HQ is more interesting to him at the moment. "Do not get too attached to your pet, Chen. If it cannot be repaired, then we'll find you a suitable replacement. A *human* partner. That's assuming your brainscan checks out, and you abandon your penchant for insubordination." He signs off without another word.

The medics rise simultaneously and face me. Neither one looks prepared to ask me to surrender my weapon.

"He's going with us." I nod toward Dunn's motionless form.

They don't argue. One summons a gurney from the ambulance, and it hovers our way a meter off the ground without a single wobble. Then it descends to rest on the pavement beside Dunn.

"Careful." I watch the medics as they pick up my partner and transfer him onto the gurney. Dunn doesn't make a sound. I'm tempted to disable my augments and probe his mind, but I refrain. I don't want another browbeating from Hudson, and if he's right that toggling back and forth has affected my brain in some way, then I don't want to incur further damage. I have no choice but to trust these medical personnel, that they'll do no harm—even to a clone. "Give me his vitals."

"Pulse and respiration normal," one of them says as the gurney, now carrying Dunn's broken body, rises from the sidewalk. "The clone is unconscious."

"His name is Dunn."

The medics glance at each other but don't comment.

"This way, Investigator Chen." One extends his arm toward their waiting aerocar while the other escorts the gurney carrying their unconscious patient. "As Chief Inspector Hudson informed you, we'll be escorting you to your appointment."

I lower my shocker, keeping it down at my side. Unholstered, in case I need it. I nod for him to walk ahead, and after a beat, I follow.

Do I really think there's something wrong with my head? At this point, I can't rule it out. If getting scanned will keep Hudson off my back so that I can do my job, so be it. And if the results keep me from working on the force?

Can't think about that right now. Can't stop myself,

either.

Maybe the upshot will be brain surgery, and despite no longer being allowed to do my job, I won't see Dr. Wong's bloody face anymore when I close my eyes. That part of my mind will miraculously be repaired, and I'll be able to sleep again—all day, all night, like any other depressed citizen lacking a life purpose. Whiling away my days in Dome 6, attended to by my biological parents who seem to think their calling is helping the *sicks* and sharing Luther's belief in the Way.

I'd rather be crushed to death by Trezon's grav weapon.

Once Dunn is secure in the passenger compartment—not the cargo hold, I made sure of that—and the rest of us are strapped in, the pilot takes us aloft with a burst of air from the powerful engines. The crowd below finally disperses once the show is over, and we head along aerial traffic lanes to HQ's rooftop landing platform. We arrive within minutes, thanks to every other vehicle in flight yielding the right of way to our flashing lights.

I keep close to Dunn's silent, armor-covered body as the gurney takes him out of the aerocar, its magnetic coils clicking as they cool down.

"Your clone is in good hands," one of the medics says once we reach the speedlift.

"He's my partner."

The other medic keeps his eyes to himself and presses two different floors on the display panel. MedTech on Level 6 for me, and Level 5 for Dunn. The robodoc or human doctors assigned to him will have plenty on their plate, fixing him up again with all manner of biosynthetics. Just like my shoulder, Dunn will be good as new.

He'd better be.

I'm not comfortable with the two of us being split up like this. Some dark corner of my mind doesn't trust the fact that soon we're both going to be at the mercy of medical machines. My brainscan. Dunn's physiological repairs. If I was a less trusting person, I might say this was intentional, that Trezon and Hudson are working in tandem to keep us out of commission.

You do not trust command. Dunn's voice again, nagging at the back of my mind.

Trezon had help. That much is clear. You don't just wander into HQ off the street in the middle of the night and somehow manage to disable surveillance. The same goes for my cube complex. I'm not the only law enforcer who lives there, along with a variety of other civil servants scattered across various floors. The analysts in our command center should have caught anyone without security privileges monkeying with the cameras around my cube, let alone HQ itself.

But do I really believe Hudson is aiding and abetting a prison escapee? Part of me might hope he is, just so he gets fired and I can work directly for Commander Bishop again—until she finds a suitable replacement Chief Inspector.

At this point, anybody would be an improvement.

I pat Dunn's armored shoulder as the speedlift doors open onto the MedTech level. Then I turn and give the medic on either side of his hovering gurney a cold stare.

"Don't even think about replacing him with another clone. I'll know the difference." I make a point of holstering my shocker in front of them and patting the grip. In the awkward silence that follows, I take my time studying each medic. "And I never forget a face."

The way they fail to blink and then dry-swallow simultaneously makes me think they understand my subtext.

I strike out across the polished floor, my boots making my presence known, passing the front desk where a trio of nurses sit with their eyes glazed over, sorting through medical files and duty rosters via their ocular lenses. As I approach the MedTech bay, the doors slide open like they're expecting me.

By this point, they probably should be.

A boxy robodoc rolls forward on its rubber treads. "Investigator Chen, you are ten minutes early," it says in a cheerful monotone.

"Let's get this over with." I fold my arms and glance at the empty cots and lack of human personnel. The other dozen or so robodocs sit in their docking stations, charging. I don't know what I was expecting—maybe Hudson and a few of his support staff gathered around with somber expressions, looking forward to watching the procedure and subsequent results that will kick me off the force, once and for all. Instead, I'm left feeling like this brainscan is little more than a formality, and my supervisor couldn't be bothered to attend. "Real happening place."

"It is quiet now, but you should have been here an hour ago."

Feels like I was. I watch the robodoc as it wheels around and wonder if it's the same one I've interacted with before. No way to tell. They all share the various charging stations. It's not like each one has its own assigned dock.

It leads me to one of the cots halfway down the row. "A criminal's mind trawl unfortunately ended in the man's death."

I stop short. "What?"

It reaches the foot of the cot where it expects me to lie down. Then it rotates to face me. "Yes, it was quite a tragic event. The first of its kind, in our experience."

"You're talking about Krime."

"It was an accident, rest assured—"

"The man's name. Krime." I frown, trying to remember what Hudson mentioned before. The man's real name. "Melville Atherton, I mean. He's dead?"

"His heart stopped in the interrogation chamber. We attempted to revive him here, but we were unsuccessful."

The interrogators pushed him too far. And they were undoubtedly ordered to do so. That's how Hudson found out about the grav weapon. Now the only other two individuals who know about it—Dunn and myself—are undergoing medical procedures at HQ. Nothing about this feels right.

So why do I sit down on the cot? Why am I not deactivating my augments and running out of here as fast as I can—going rogue in order to track down an invisible fugitive?

Easy answer: I can't leave Dunn behind.

And there's still a part of me that refuses to believe Hudson is working with Trezon. Commander Bishop never would have allowed Hudson to take on an authoritative role if he wasn't to be trusted. I have to believe that. I trust her judgment.

I don't have to like the guy. I don't have to understand his motives. But I do have to follow through with this brainscan, or I won't have my job.

"We do lose patients from time to time, of course," the

robodoc continues, "as does any medical facility in the Domes. But in our experience, the mortality in question is never due to actions taken by law enforcers on site."

I nod as I lie down on my back and fold my hands across my abdomen. "You're saying we've never had a suspect walk into HQ completely healthy and then die on the premises. Because of what our interrogators did to him."

"That is correct. And it is...unsettling."

A strange thing for a machine to say. But I remind myself that it's continuing to work on its bedside manner. And failing miserably. "Try to project strength and confidence when you're about to fiddle with someone's brain."

It twitches, rolling back a centimeter as if snapping to attention. "This is a very routine, noninvasive procedure, Investigator Chen. There is no reason to be nervous."

"Do I look nervous to you?"

"Your heart rate is elevated, and your breathing—"

"I'm not worried about myself. My partner is downstairs." I exhale, try to calm down. "Just wish I could see what they're doing to him."

"Unit D1-436 is being prepped for surgery. The doctors assigned to it are readying bone-mending equipment and biosynthetic rods and plates, as needed."

"Doctors aren't assigned to clones very often. Robodocs either, I'll bet."

"Never in our experience. But the order came directly from Chief Inspector Hudson himself. He wants the clone treated as if it were a human law enforcer injured in the line of duty."

"He was." I can't get the image out of my mind: Dunn plastered across the pavement.

The robodoc doesn't reply. I'm left wondering about Hudson. Maybe he's not a one-hundred-percent jackass, after all.

"Please lie still and close your eyes, Investigator Chen," the machine advises as a glowing halo descends on a swing arm from the apparatus beside my cot, guided by the robot's silent commands. It's a good thing I don't have a problem with machine intelligence, or I'd be freaking out right about now. "This scan should take less than a minute to complete. We will be mending your injured forehead and hand at the same time."

Nothing like a multitasking mechanical doctor.

I shut my eyes and assume a believable sarcophagus pose. Through my eyelids, I can see the halo's light approach, glowing brighter as it descends within a few millimeters of my face. Then it glides over my skull in painfully slow motion. At the same time, the robodoc wheels itself alongside my cot, and I crack open an eyelid as it extends a crumpled metallic sheath that unfolds on its own, covering my injured hand. I feel a little awkward receiving this much attention, but I grit my teeth and bear it.

No idea why, but my thoughts turn to Erik. Maybe because when I'm with him in reality or VR, I can't help but think about awkward things.

Like the fact that he and I and the rest of the Twenty have close to a thousand children growing up in the Ten Domes. Sure, Dr. Wong made sure to mix in some of their adoptive parents' DNA to expand our gene pool, but the fact remains that our eggs and sperm were used to create the next generation. Extracted monthly once we hit puberty, without our knowledge or consent.

Before the repopulation program died with Wong, all of those children were farmed out to upper-caste couples across the Domes. I have no way of knowing how many of them share my DNA. Such information is off-limits, even to law enforcement personnel.

When I see Erik, everything comes flooding back. Stuff I don't need to think about, because I have no control over it. I can't change the past. And if I take a step back and look at the situation objectively, I can see why Wong did what he did.

The Terminal Generation—citizens now in their thirties—was thought to be Eurasia's last. But then the Twenty were discovered, born deep underground in the North American Wastes, and hand-delivered to Eurasia two decades ago. Unlike the rest of the population in the Ten Domes, we were completely unaffected by the plague that rendered them sterile. Why wouldn't Eurasia's most eminent geneticist use us to save humankind?

Never mind the moral implications. Such things never bothered Dr. Solomon Wong. He believed in casting them aside when one's trying to save an entire species from extinction.

Erik's biological parents, along with my own, risked their lives to find us. It took them many years, but they managed to voyage across the Atlantic Ocean and sneak inside Dome 10 as dust smugglers. They were willing to do whatever it took to meet their offspring. Erik thinks we should, too—that we should become a part of their lives as they grow up inside the plexicon walls of our domed cities.

Whenever I see him, I feel like I'm disappointing him. Because I don't want that.

The children who carry my DNA should grow up

without knowing they're related to a murderer. That I killed the most brilliant scientific mind the world has ever seen. Never mind that he tried to kill me first. Or that he wanted to let the Ten Domes implode while he and the Twenty went into cryo-sleep for a century or few, just long enough for his clones in Futuro Tower to figure out a way to terraform the desolate earth.

Those kids growing up today deserve to live their own lives, as I have mine. I've got my all-consuming job, and I want to be the best at it that I can be. I want it to consume me, so I don't have to think about anything else but the work right in front of me. *Never looking back* used to be the Eurasian credo under Chancellor Hawthorne. Now I see the value in it. Tends to keep one's head on straight.

"Scan complete and accelerated healing process initiated, Investigator Chen," the robodoc says, and I crack open my eyes to find the halo's light dimming as it retracts upward into the apparatus. "Chief Inspector Hudson is expecting you in the command center."

I sit up and swing my legs off the cot. "What's the verdict?"

The machine rolls away toward an available charging station. "The Chief Inspector will discuss the results of the brainscan with you himself, Investigator Chen. But repairing your other injuries was a simple task. We hope that you take better care of yourself in the future." Docking without another word, it goes into standby mode.

"Right." I glance across the silent MedTech bay and hope I won't need to be back for a very long time, if ever. Knowing Krime died here makes it feel like a morgue. "Thanks." My voice echoes.

I don't take my sweet time leaving.

Reaching the command center, I find things as quiet as they were last night, with the analysts sitting in their cluster, jacked into their consoles via thick cables plugged into the base of their skulls. Focused on monitoring every citizen in the Domes but oblivious to everything around them. Commander Bishop is nowhere in sight.

Hudson stands in the doorway to his office, eyes glazed over as he has a conversation with someone online. I wait by the speedlift until he ends the call and his focus clears. Noticing me immediately, he beckons with one hand as he turns back toward his desk.

He's seated and perusing a graph of statistics on his deskscreen when I enter and stand at attention. The door slides shut behind me. He doesn't look up.

"Fatal dust overdoses are on the rise across the Domes, Chen. Citizens are striving to hold onto their abilities long past the usual expiration period and are suffering the consequences. Brains fried. Such is to be expected, I suppose." He glances up at me. "Say what you will about Chancellor Hawthorne's iron fist. Law and order was crystal clear with her in charge. Interim Chancellor Bishop is trying too hard to stand in the middle of the road without getting himself run over. Soon he'll learn what a futile endeavor that is."

"Hawthorne was a dust addict herself." I'm quick to add: "Sir."

"Have a seat." His gaze lingers on my forehead gash, healing quickly thanks to the robodoc's attention. But the bruising will take time to fade. "I want you to look into this group." He swipes his hand through the air above his desk, and the screen projects a holographic image of a Dome 10 warehouse with a tragically uninspired design. "They call themselves the *Children of Tomorrow*. An increase in attendance at their nightly gatherings has coincided with the spike in overdoses. In the old days, we could have raided the warehouse for illegal religious meetings. But now cults like this have the freedom to assemble. Just one of a slew of recent changes I do not particularly agree with."

I have a feeling he doesn't make a habit of expressing his discontent to Commander Bishop, it being her father who enacted so many of these changes. The illegal dust trade itself, for example. The smuggling operations which earned former Chancellor Persephone Hawthorne her sizeable cut, and supported her addiction, have been put to a halt. There's still plenty of dust in circulation in the Domes, but it's a limited supply, and that's driven up the price. There are no new shipments arriving from the North American Wastes, as far as we know. Chancellor Bishop's plan is to let the dust addicts use up what they have, and when the dealers run out of supply, the demand will hopefully follow suit—after some serious withdrawal symptoms.

But this spike in overdoses means two things: supply will run out sooner than anticipated, and judging from the current price of dust on the street, these victims would have to be from the upper classes in order to afford it.

"You're assigning this case to me."

"Correct." He frowns at my expression, one I'm sure is a combination of confusion and disbelief. "Is there a problem?"

"I just had my head examined."

"And you are in perfect health. I had my reasons for

doubting that, considering your habit of toggling your augments at the drop of a hat, but apparently I was in error. It has not affected your brain detrimentally at all—yet. You're still young, and your neural functions will continue to develop over the next few years. I would advise against continuing your bad habit, but I have no medical basis to back up my concerns. Five years from now, however, you may be risking serious injury."

"So when I said Trezon attacked me twice—"

"We are looking into it. The violent altercation in your cube has drawn the commander's attention. She wants us to take your claims seriously. And seeing as you are suffering no neural problems whatsoever, I am inclined to agree with her."

He sure has changed his tune. "Trezon told me he's not snorting dust to become invisible. And it's not some new tech. So what else could it be?"

Hudson steeples his fingers and gives me a pensive nod. "Assuming we give credence to anything he said... Whatever it is, it allows him to avoid both IR and XR detection." He shakes his head with incredulity before focusing on me. "Rest assured, he will be caught. In the meantime, if you would like a protective detail assigned to you..."

I raise my chin. "I didn't have the information he wanted. That's why he left. He has no reason to come after me again."

Hudson nods, studying me. "Have you been in touch with Drasko?"

I shake my head. "He wouldn't meet me in VR." I lean forward and lower my voice. "Do you know if he's all right?"

Hudson looks away. "Why didn't you enter Krime's weapon into evidence?"

Had a feeling this would come up. "Part of me thought

Trezon would go after it," I admit. "And that I could arrest him when he did." But the whole invisibility thing really screwed up my big plan.

"Quite an ego you have there, Chen."

Look where it's gotten me. Investigating a cult of dust freaks. "What happened to Krime, sir?"

He graces me with a tight-lipped smile. "You are no longer on the Trezon case."

"Krime was my collar."

Hudson shakes his head. "If I remember correctly, *I* was the one who brought him in."

Because my drones called for help. Stinkin' Wink and Blink. Which reminds me—

"I'd like to have my drones on this case, sir. Walking into a Dome 10 warehouse with unknown variables, I'd feel better if I knew they were looking out for me."

"A reasonable request, considering the condition of your partner."

My heart skips a beat. "How is he?"

"The clone took quite a fall, and it didn't think to destroy the building's exterior on its way down in order to save itself." Hudson gives me a direct look. "If it were not for its armor and helmet, it would not have survived."

"So he's going to be all right?"

"I will notify you as soon as I receive word, but according to the doctors tending to it, the clone's prognosis is promising. Meanwhile, you are cleared to visit Dome 10 and begin your investigation. You will go undercover as a civilian, so no police transportation will be at your disposal. Dismissed." He sweeps his hand over his desk, and the holographic display collapses as the screen goes dark. Then he swivels his chair, turning his back on me to survey the air traffic outside.

"Thank you, sir." I get to my feet and leave his office. There's a slight spring to my step as I head up to the motor pool.

Dunn's on the mend, and my drones are soon going to be back in action. What more could I ask for?

8

The grease monkey I chopped in the throat last night is the only mechanic on duty in the motor pool. For some reason, he doesn't look happy to see me.

"I'm here for my drones." I maintain eye contact not to threaten him, just to let him know that I'm treating him like a human being. Not a piece of meat.

He nods but doesn't say anything as he retreats to a far corner of the maintenance bay. Behind a jacked-up black and white aerocar minus its magnetic coils, Wink and Blink sit on a grease-smeared table. Neither drone lights up as he manhandles them, stacking one on top of the other and carrying them to me with a disgruntled look on his face.

"Wish Hudson would make up his damn mind." He hands them over without ceremony.

Both drones come to life as soon as I touch them, active status lights flickering as they recognize my augments. I tuck Wink under one arm and Blink under the other.

"Thought you weren't allowed to use them anymore. They were scheduled to be reformatted, then reassigned to that curfew enforcer who took your place." He shrugs in his shapeless coveralls and folds his arms. "We just hadn't gotten around to it yet."

"Good thing." I give him a nod. Being civil and all that. "You won't see them again."

"They've got some unconventional modifications." He narrows his gaze. "Lethal ordnance. Does your boss know about it?"

"Of course," I lie.

Another shrug. "Seems real out of the ordinary. Like maybe you had it done on the sly."

Drasko added the upgrades without my knowledge, back when he was leading his double life—working for the police and organized crime at the same time. I highly doubt that he informed Commander Bishop or asked her permission.

"Are you looking for trouble?" I take a step toward the mechanic. Borderline sleepwalking, I really don't need this right now. "Again?"

He doesn't back down. "You want to try throwing your weight around, detective? Again?" He grins. "C'mon, there's nobody else here. Try and hit me. No sucker punch this time." He hops on the rubber soles of his work boots and shakes out his arms like a boxer warming up. "I'm ready and waiting."

I hold his leering gaze. I don't glance at the surveillance cameras mounted along the plasticon ceiling. He's obviously not worried about them, so why should I be?

"What do you say, Chen? Up for a little fun?"

"Maybe some other time." I go for a smile that make-believes we're pals. "I'm on a case." I turn away and carry my drones toward the speedlift.

"You didn't even get reprimanded, did you?" he shouts after me as I nudge the call button with my elbow. "Cuz you're some kind of special, isn't that right? *Twenty* bitch?"

I really should just let it go.

Instead I set Wink and Blink down on the grey plasticon floor and turn around.

"No, I didn't get reprimanded. I got brainscanned." My boots echo as they strike a purposeful rhythm back to him. "Chief Inspector Hudson thought there might be something wrong with my head."

The smirk drops off his face. "Was there?" Judging from his expression, he thinks it's a distinct possibility.

"Oh yeah." I advance with my fists clenched in front of me, one high, one low. Broken digits no longer bent out of shape, ready for action. "I'm a real mess."

He backs up a step, amateurish warmups abandoned. "Forget I said anything, Chen."

"Kind of tough to do." I invade the maintenance center, passing aerocar parts and toolboxes, tables littered with mechanisms halfway assembled, others waiting to be repaired. "You had to go and use fighting words."

"C'mon," he tries to laugh it off, keeping one of the tables between us. "It's no secret the Twenty receive special treatment. Or used to, anyway, under the old regime. Right?"

"You called me a *bitch*." I send a quick jab at his nose, but pull up short. It's enough to send him into flinching mode, and he stumbles against the wall without a whole lot of grace. "I have a sneaking suspicion you don't respect women very much."

"I respect women." He clenches his stubble-covered jaw, and the muscle twitches. I made him look foolish, and now he's angry. "I just don't respect *you*."

The evidence supports as much. "Fine. Let me have it." I open my hands and keep them raised on either side of my face, giving him a clear shot.

But instead of hitting me, he says, "You've had everything handed to you. The *Twenty*." He says the word like it's something obscene. "We were supposed to be the last of us. The Terminal Generation. But were we celebrated for it? Hell no. Can you imagine how much pressure we were under, growing up? To save the human race? Like we even could, just as sterile as everybody else." He curses, shaking his head. "Then you come along, and we're no longer relevant. Some of us..." He shrugs, his face carrying a stricken look people get sometimes when they know they've overshared, and it's left them feeling sickened by the sound of their own voice. "Some of us don't have a clue what life means anymore."

My hands are down at my sides. Not sure how they got there. I guess fighting is the furthest thing from my mind right now. "What's your name?"

"What the hell do you care?" He takes a step back, like I disgust him. "You've got your big case, your chief inspector to impress. I'm just the guy who keeps your cars running and your drones flying. You don't give a crap who I am."

"You whistled at me last night to get my attention. To demean me."

"To knock you off your high horse, yeah."

I nod in the silence, everything in me rebelling against the thought of apologizing to this man. "Hitting you...might've been an overreaction."

"You think?"

"But I'd do it again." I tap the side of my sleep-deprived

head. "Remember that."

Leaving him to stare after me with his mouth hanging open, I head over to the speedlift. Scooping up Wink and Blink, I step inside without a glance back.

The grease monkey doesn't say another word.

We make it down to the ground floor without any stops along the way. By the time the doors slide open, I've got both drones synced up again with my augments and hovering on either side of me, quadcopter rotors whining and ready for action. The support personnel waiting for the speedlift give us a wide berth as we exit and make our way out through the sliding glass doors to the busy sidewalk beyond. It's getting close to lunch, and citizens are enjoying their time meandering along the pristine streets, soaking up filtered sunshine as shadows of aerocars glide by far above us.

These are the upper caste members of Eurasian society. As much as Interim Chancellor Bishop has made it clear that he wants to do away with the class system, good intentions and feasible action are two very different sides of the same coin. It doesn't help matters that he's up against decades of societal status quo and a citizenry perfectly fine with the way things are. No matter how many meetings he has with Patriot leaders to let them air their grievances, the outer Domes surrounding Dome 1 will always do the heavy lifting while these people milling about in the lap of leisure and luxury will continue to enjoy the fruits of other citizens' labor. Nothing less than a civil war will ever change that. And nobody, not even our homegrown domestic terrorists, want war.

Because Eurasia, for all of its faults, is a bubble protecting us from a deadly outside world, and no one in their right mind would ever want to see it burst.

Sending Wink and Blink to survey the maglev station at the tunnel to Dome 10, I allow their split-screen video feed to run in the periphery of my ocular lenses. Best to avoid such distractions while out in public; it would be unseemly to run into any of my fellow citizens. Many of them have sidelined the Linkstream, smiling pleasantly at me as we cross paths, but there are more than a few who stagger along with their eyes glazed over, their attention consumed by what they're viewing on the Link. Always a good idea to step aside and allow these zombies the right of way.

As my drones reach the gates to the station ahead of me, I count four human guards on duty armed with shockers, holstered at their sides, and one security clone in armor identical to Dunn's, carrying the same type of assault rifle. All part of the lockdown intended to keep Trezon in Dome 1. The problem being, of course, that these fine folks in their dark blue uniforms have no idea the prison escapee is invisible.

What Hudson said about Trezon not showing up on IR or XR scans gave me pause. If he's snorting loads of dust in order to stay invisible, wouldn't his body heat still register on an infrared scan? And if he was wearing some sort of holographic cloak designed to act like a chameleon, blending him into his surroundings, then an XR scan would be able to penetrate it—unless it was made out of lead fibers. It's not possible that Trezon has found some way to make himself truly invisible or incorporeal while still being able to interact with the material world. He's not an ethereal ghost.

I listen in while Wink and Blink announce my impending arrival to the security team at the gate: "Investigator Sera

Chen has been sent to Dome 10 by Chief Inspector Hudson. Your cooperation in aiding her timely arrival will be appreciated." Their automated voices are monotonal yet authoritative.

The guards glance at each other and shrug as if this is news to them. Then they fold their arms in a sign of defensive solidarity—all except the clone who remains as still as a statue, its familiar features hidden behind the helmet's black face shield.

I show up a couple minutes later, crossing the street with a hand raised in greeting once the ground vehicles halt for a red light. Despite the convenience and appeal of aerocar flight, plenty of our citizens still prefer the more terrestrial way to travel.

"I'm Chen." I nod toward Wink and Blink hovering overhead. "Like they said, I'm on my way to Dome 10."

"Trains aren't running, Detective," says one of the guards, a husky woman with a crew cut and silver piercings along her left ear. "We've got a criminal on the loose, in case you haven't heard."

Yet the city isn't on lockdown. Instead of ordering every citizen to hide inside their homes and offices, we're allowing them to flood the streets as they would any other day at lunchtime. While an invisible miscreant roams freely among them who just happens to want to reach the same Dome I do. A man who asked me so nicely to help him get there as he broke one of my favorite fingers and thumb.

Do I think Hudson is using me as Trezon-bait? Very likely.

"I just need you to let me through that gate." I gesture toward the three-meter-tall plasteel monstrosity behind them that shines like every other polished surface in Dome 1. "I'll take care of the rest. On foot."

"Aren't you the new investigator with the clone partner?" That gets the other guards murmuring among themselves. Even the security clone takes an interest, its helmet turning a centimeter my way. "Why're you working this case solo?"

"Orders." I shrug. None of their business.

If I was wearing my exo, I could probably launch myself up and over that gate. But as much as I hate to admit it, I'm at their mercy right now. If they don't want to let me through, I'm not getting through. Everything in me rebels at the thought of pulling rank or threatening to hail Hudson. Like a little tattletale not getting her way on the playground.

"Orders, huh. Funny, cuz we didn't get any message from HQ telling us a detective was on the way." She smirks at me. "You know, you don't look much like any *detective* I've ever seen. Where's your coat and hat? You look more like a *student.*"

I get it. I'm young. And she's another disgruntled member of the Terminal Generation. That's two of them I've had to deal with today, and I'm running short on patience. I understand that they hate their lives, but why take it out on me?

A fleeting thought runs through my mind: I should have Wink and Blink swoop down and fire a few projectile rounds at the ground in front of these ever-helpful security personnel, sending chips of pavement upward in every direction as the guards cringe and cry out and fall over backward in shock and awe.

But no. My drones are above such things.

Then the gate creaks open, and the humans turn sharply

to find the security clone holding it open.

"How may we be of further assistance, Investigator Chen?" Its voice is identical to Dunn's but without the evolving tonal structures he's been experimenting with lately, making him sound like more than just an AI character in VR.

"Go on, take it with you," says the female guard, gesturing dismissively at the clone. "We don't need that thing around here."

"I don't require an escort," I blurt out, my frowning reflection appearing in the clone's face shield as I approach.

"You have been injured recently. The man you believe to be the culprit remains at large," the clone replies. Then it lowers its voice. "Your partner has also been injured. D1-436 requested that I join you."

That gives me pause. "He contacted you?"

The clone's helmet dips toward its chest in reply. I can feel the irritable stares from the humans burning into the back of my neck. As Wink and Blink sail over the gate and head into the dark maglev tunnel ahead of me, I turn toward the guards with the best fake smile I can muster.

"You've been very helpful. Keep up the great work." Ignoring the rude gestures they make as I turn away, I nod to the clone and head toward the tunnel's mouth. "Guess you're with me, then."

The steady clomp of its boots echo my own as we pass the empty maglev train, sitting on its single track like a massive bullet with an elongated casing, and enter the dark cavern of the tunnel beyond. The gate creaks shut behind us, drowning out the sounds of the guards laughing among themselves. Seems I've brightened their day by taking the clone off their hands.

"What's your name?" I double-tap my temple to switch off my augments, and Wink and Blink's video feed goes right along with them. Instantly, my supernatural night-vision illuminates the darkness before me in a ghostly blueish-white. No dust necessary, thanks to my biological parents.

"I do not have a name," the clone replies.

Right. "What's your designation?"

"D1-440."

"Do you get along well with those guards back there?"

"They do not seem to appreciate my presence."

That's one way to put it. "How long have you been stationed at that gate?"

"Since the transition."

The official term for Interim Chancellor Bishop taking over Hawthorne's office. These clones used to be her personal security force. They were designed by Dr. Wong to protect the Chancellor and her interests from terrorist threats, to function as replaceable shields. But now that James Bishop is allowing the terrorists—who call themselves *Patriots*—to air their grievances, and together they're working on solutions to the inequality issues in the Ten Domes, he sees no reason to keep a security force to protect himself. He's already returned from the dead, so to speak, and seems to be a man without fear. So he reassigned the clones to various serve-and-protect functions throughout the Domes, including support for guard stations at each maglev tunnel radiating outward from Dome 1, and increased security at the Mediterranean port. From what Drasko's told me, the cessation of dust smuggling through the port into Dome 10 is due in no small part to the security clone presence there.

They can be real intimidating when they want to be.

"Which did you like better—protecting Chancellor Hawthorne or working security at a maglev tunnel?"

D1-440 considers the question for a moment as we trek single file along the raised plasticon walkway on the right side of the track. "Both duties are well-suited to my abilities as a security clone."

Equally dull, in other words. "So you've been in contact with Dunn—I mean D1-436. Are you two...friends?" Do clones have friendships with each other?

"All of the clones from former Chancellor Hawthorne's security force are connected."

I nod to show I'm listening. "But you don't share a hive mind or anything." That would be seriously creepy.

"No, Investigator Chen. But we do share a dedicated communication network separate from the Linkstream."

Right. I knew that. So Dunn would've had to be conscious in order to send D1-440 a message. "Is he still in surgery?"

"Yes."

"Tell me what the doctors are doing."

"They are replacing D1-436's broken bones with biosynthetic rods and plates and sealing its punctured internal organs. When they are finished, D1-436 will be equal parts biological, synthetic, and mechanical." The clone pauses. "May I ask you a question, Investigator Chen?"

"Of course." I frown. Guess I've gotten used to Dunn asking whatever he likes whenever he likes. This clone's politeness is definitely not a human trait.

"Why do you refer to D1-436 as *Dunn* and *he*?"

"One syllable is more convenient than five, don't you think?" It doesn't respond, so I continue, "You were all created in the image of Dr. Solomon Wong. The male pronoun fits."

"What would you call me?" I could be wrong, but it sounds like there's an eager curiosity in its tone.

"We've only just met," I stall, not knowing what to say.

It doesn't reply. Disappointed? Resigned to its fate as a cloned biological organism with a short string of alphanumerics as its designation?

Am I reading too much into the silence? Probably.

"How about Fort?" I say over my shoulder.

"Because my purpose is security."

I almost smile. "Short for forty. D1-440. Fort."

"Yes, I see. One syllable is more convenient."

"And you're rocking the whole security thing."

"Thank you, Investigator Chen. I do not presume to take the place of D1-436, your partner. I only hope to provide you with the necessary support once we reach Dome 10."

So it plans to stick with me. Can't say I'm surprised. "Did Dunn put you up to this?"

"Please explain."

"D1-436 asked you to accompany me."

"Yes."

"And he told you about the criminal known as Trezon attacking me."

"Two times, yes. D1-436 also mentioned that this criminal is likely invisible, which means stationing sentries at each of Dome 1's train stations is a futile endeavor, as Trezon may not be seen via IR or XR scans."

"That's about the shape of things."

Our clomping boots hold the moment. Then Fort says, "Do you believe Trezon to be a dust freak, a demigod, or something else, Investigator Chen?"

He's turning out to be quite the chatty clone. "Demigod?" I feign ignorance, curious what he'll say next.

"Yes, the vernacular for citizens such as yourself with special abilities."

Dunn's been talking out of turn. I clench my teeth.

"The first usage in its current context can be traced back three months to when a man was seen flying through the air without the aid of any mechanical apparatus," Fort continues. "This was during the timeframe of Dr. Solomon Wong's attempted coup. There is video footage on record of the so-called demigod disabling multiple aerocars from Chancellor Hawthorne's security fleet—while they were in flight."

That would be Daiyna and Luther's friend, Milton. Real talented guy.

He moved too fast for anyone to identify him by appearance. On the video footage I've seen, he's just a man-shaped blur, his features indistinguishable. He likes to keep a low profile these days, as do most of his friends from the North American Wastes.

People with bizarre abilities, like me and Erik and our biological parents.

And now Trezon as well?

9

"The term *demigod* has come to mean anyone who does not derive his or her superhuman abilities from inhaling the dust of the North American Wastes." Fort pauses, waiting for me to respond.

Every member of the Twenty would be considered *demigods*, as well as the thousand children derived from our DNA—children under the age of nine who may begin to exhibit their own unique abilities, given time. If they don't, then they won't once they're outfitted with the requisite coming-of-age neural implants.

Unless they develop a bad habit of toggling their augments on and off.

"May I ask another question, Investigator Chen?"

"Sure."

"Have you ever met this man who can fly?"

"My biological parents know him." No idea why I'm telling this clone anything. Maybe he reminds me of Dunn. Go figure. "But as for Trezon, he was born and raised here, in Eurasia. Terminal Generation. No chance he's a demigod." It's just not in his DNA.

"Then you believe his invisibility to be due to some sort of advanced technology."

I shake my head. "The heat signature of any tech would've shown up in IR. Somehow, he's figured out a way not to appear on scans. Like a ghost."

"May I ask another question, Investigator Chen?"

I nod.

"Do you believe in ghosts?"

I almost smirk. But then the mental image of Dr. Wong's blood-soaked face appears without warning, staring at me with a pained grimace and eyes open wide. I stumble a step before regaining my footing.

Glancing over my shoulder at Fort's blank face shield, I mutter, "Are you always this inquisitive?"

"I must apologize. The humans I was stationed with never engaged in conversation with me. When I served in Chancellor Hawthorne's security force, there was no need to ask questions of my fellow clones, as we were always connected. Our discussions occurred over the communication link we shared."

And they're still able to communicate with each other. Dunn's ability to contact Fort from his MedTech bed is proof of that. Even though most security clones no longer work together in physical proximity to one another, they apparently continue to stay in touch via their secure network.

Chancellor Bishop seemed to think it was a good idea to separate them. I wonder if he doesn't trust them completely, even after their reconditioning. All twenty-five of them—except for Dunn—underwent a rigorous process to ensure they no longer carried any underlying programmed responses loyal to Hawthorne or Dr. Wong. Dunn had already proven that he was unique by disobeying his orders and instead lending me a hand inside Futuro Tower, rescuing the Twenty from Wong's cryo-chambers. In so doing, Dunn showed he could think for himself, choosing to help me and risking his own life in the process.

"Do you miss serving alongside other clones?"

Fort's reply is slow to arrive. "I know I am not alone, that there are others like me stationed across the Domes. We can communicate with one another despite the distance whenever we wish. But there is a certain loneliness now, when days may pass between catching sight of another of my kind."

I nod. That might be the most human thing I've heard in a while.

Diffused daylight from the end of the train tunnel glows in the distance, and it isn't long before we see the semicircular opening and the rusty sunlight of Dome 10 waiting for us. Along with another contingent of security personnel guarding the gate. Just like Dome 1, it's a group of four humans and one armored clone.

Fort doesn't say another word as we approach. I have to wonder if he's already silently conversing with the other security clone.

"Well, if it isn't Investigator Chen and her pet project!" one of the male guards welcomes us with an obnoxious laugh. "To what do we owe the pleasure of your slumming it?"

"On a case." I grace them with a noncommittal but hopefully pleasant expression.

"Any idea when the train'll be up and running again?" one of the women pipes up. They all wear the same unflattering khaki uniforms and keep their arms folded, shockers left in their black faux-leather holsters. "Boring as hell out here!"

Trezon must not have made it back yet. I doubt things in Dome 10 will be dull once its crowned prince of the underworld returns.

"Keep up the good work." I give them a wink as Fort and I pass through the vacant terminal.

The clone stationed here opens the gate for us with a loud, shuddering creak. Like everything else in Dome 10, it's in need of some tender loving maintenance. Just the locals' way of showing their appreciation for being stationed in the armpit of Eurasia. Nobody would ask to work here, but somebody has to take care of sanitation and water reclamation, and this Dome is positioned right on the Mediterranean where all the desalination and waste dumping happens.

Fort and the other clone pause a moment to regard one another without a word spoken between them. According to Erik, they can't be programmed like robots, but they are conditioned to obey. My gut does this uncomfortable twisting thing at the thought of someone like Trezon gathering them together, reconditioning them, and making them his own security force. Maybe that's why Chancellor Bishop has made a point of splitting them up, to keep something like that from ever happening. Tough to lead a small army when the troops aren't all in the same place.

Unless you're a terrorist recruiting online... An unwelcome thought. Set it aside, Chen. Focus on your case.

But now I'm thinking about the clones. I can't help but wonder if they're more likely to evolve, as Dunn has, if their only interactions are with humans. Assuming the humans are interested in interacting with them at all. Like Fort, this other clone seems to be ostracized by the humans stationed alongside it.

I'm almost tempted to ask it to join us. But as it is, I won't be entering the cult's warehouse with Fort in tow. He'll need to keep a lookout from across the street.

Not much opportunity for socializing.

"Hey Chen," the guard calls after me, and I turn to find him jabbing an index finger up at Wink and Blink hovering overhead. His hand turns into the universal sign for a gun as he says, "Keep an eye on your drones. Not too popular with the locals—except for target practice!"

The four guards erupt into a chorus of guffaws. I nod and wave, trying to look appreciative for the reminder. Then I double-tap my temple to reactivate my augments and transmit a warning to Wink and Blink, "Keep a low profile, boys."

"We'll need to split up," I tell Fort as I set out across the busy street, dodging double-decker self-driving cargo transports that roll along at a steady clip. One screeches to a halt to keep from hitting me and honks a split-second too late for it to be anything but perfunctory. As far as I know, AI drivers aren't irate by nature. "I'll blend in better alone."

"Understood, Investigator Chen." Fort raises a white gauntlet to apologize for impeding the driverless truck as he steps onto the curb beside me.

Entering the flow of human traffic on the sidewalk, I pull up the location of the warehouse where I've been tasked to monitor illegal dust usage. For my ocular lenses only, a gridline map of the surrounding area floats across the bobbing forms of the Dome 10 citizens before me, each of them with their gaze turned inward as they focus on whatever entertainment the Linkstream has to offer. Anything's better than living in this grungy city, working their repetitive shifts, wearing the same drab coveralls every day. I blink at the overlay, tagging the structure across the street from the warehouse, and send a copy of the map to Fort via secure link.

"While I'm inside, you find a spot on the roof of this building across the street. Keep out of view, but maintain a line of sight with my drones. You see anybody itching to shoot them out of the sky, you contain the situation." I glance at the clone's weapon. "What sort of rounds are you packing?"

"Non-lethal projectiles, per Interim Chancellor Bishop's recent mandate."

Well, in that case... "Shoot anybody who aims anything at my drones."

Fort nods. "After your business is concluded, I will join you for your walk back to Dome 1, if that is acceptable."

"I was planning on it." I cast him half a smile, and it's reflected in the black glass of his face shield. His chin dips in a modest nod.

I sweep the air in front of me with my hand, and the map overlay retreats to the right side of my peripheral vision in case I need to consult it again. The left side is still displaying the split-screen video feed from Wink and Blink as they scout ahead. From their vantage point, twenty meters in the air, I see the Children of Tomorrow's warehouse loom into view. No banner or anything; they're announcing their gatherings via the Linkstream or VR, not in the real world. A few months ago, the dirty structure was used to store dust and other illegal substances for Trezon's underworld empire. Following his arrest and the subsequent police raids on every one of his roving establishments, the place was cleared out.

Didn't take long for another group of undesirables to call it their own.

Not that I have anything against religions. Growing up, the Twenty were indoctrinated with Chancellor's Hawthorne's fascist dogma: the state over all. Loyalty to the government and fellow citizenry of Eurasia was more important than anything else. Other belief systems, by their very nature, subjugated said loyalty to some sort of deity. Hawthorne and the Governors believed sectarian religious and political beliefs had destroyed the world, when it was they themselves who'd unleashed the nuclear arsenal responsible for ruining the planet—along with their terrorist enemies, who possessed certain bioweapons that could have annihilated humankind.

The very definition of a no-win situation.

You cannot serve two masters, Hawthorne was fond of saying, which I found out later she'd stolen from a religious text. So, for the sake of humankind, there was no room for any religion that didn't place the Eurasian credo at the forefront of its message: *We live only now, never looking back.* For the common good. Each of us must do our part in order to ensure a bright future for our people.

How exactly does that line up with Hawthorne murdering her husband and usurping his role as Chancellor long before I was born? Or Dr. Solomon Wong, Eurasia's greatest mind, setting up his own doomsday tower in North Africa, planning to cryo-sleep the centuries away while hundreds of his clones figured out how to terraform the earth? He intended to freeze the Twenty right along with him; can't forget that. We were his key to a better future, and he needed to keep us safe in Futuro Tower— *Wong's Ark*— while the Ten Domes imploded with violence.

Maybe a little religion would have been good for both of those psychos. They might have treated people the way they would've wanted to be treated.

My shoulder suffers a psychosomatic flare-up at the memory of Wong's death—never far from my mind. His laser welder burning through my skin and bone. My exo-suit's recent upgrade, a shoulder-mounted minigun, tearing him to bloody shreds of unidentifiable meat. The human body is so frail...

I blink and frown, focusing on the path before me, winding between densely packed citizens in identical grubby coveralls. Arriving in Dome 10 between shifts is a bit more annoying than traversing an empty sidewalk, but it works well for blending in somewhat. Fort, on the other hand, is a lost cause. He stands out like an alabaster statue in a muddy stream.

"I'll meet you at the train station in one hour," I tell him via audiolink as I put some distance between us. Bodies quickly fill in the gap, and he's much more polite about navigating his course than I am. For good reason: running into a clone's armor, or having it run into you, is no joke. When his path is obstructed, he stops and waits for an opening. It's not long before he's fallen far behind.

Wink and Blink notify me, "Perimeter scan complete. No hostile targets in sight."

Good news. "Maintain surveillance. D1-440 will have your back once he reaches the roof across the street." I send them a copy of the map I tagged. "Your priorities remain unchanged. Scan for hostiles and avoid damage. Keep an eye on me while I'm in the building."

"Yes, Investigator Chen."

The usual routine, except we aren't usually assigned to the filthy underbelly of Eurasia.

The drones activate their XR scanners once I'm fifty meters away from the warehouse, providing me with a view of what's waiting inside. As I veer off to the right, leaving the throngs of blank-faced workers on the bustling streets, I find some room to breathe in this vacant space between buildings. The air is stale here, but at least it doesn't reek like humans who don't bathe often enough. Or wash their coveralls.

While the area outside the cult's warehouse appears to be quiet and deserted—what you'd expect from a building previously raided by the authorities—the sound-proof interior is bubbling with life. Upwards of a couple hundred people mill about on the main floor while a dozen or so stroll along the catwalk above, clustered in talkative pairs and groups. A large stage has been set up on the far side of the structure, lifeless at present, but if I time things just right, I might get to see the big show, whatever it is.

Do cults have shows? The only religion I'm vaguely familiar with is the Way, and that's only because my biological father is a true believer. And like most formerly illegal religions, over the decades its practitioners have grown accustomed to worshiping their deity in the shadows. There isn't much room for spectacle when your goal is to avoid attracting the government's attention. I'm sure they've had all manner of secret handshakes and code phrases to avoid infiltration by investigators such as myself.

Speaking of, Hudson didn't give me any kind of password to enter this formidable structure. And I've got a hunch they're not going to welcome just anybody off the street. So I double-tap my temple to deactivate my augments and run a cursory sweep through the minds of the cultists in closest proximity to the closed warehouse door. I figure they're most likely to have the password—assuming there is one—still fresh in their memories. I have to sort through a whole lot of mental clutter, colored by a slew of emotions running the gamut from nervous and excited to worried and fearful. Not about something horrible about to happen. They're scared they're going to miss out.

One word hovers in each of their minds, a name: *Prometheus.* The god punished for giving fire to humankind, or so the ancient myth goes. Fitting, if this bunch is planning to overdose on dust in the hopes of making their special abilities permanent. Becoming gods, as Krime said. Or *demigods.* Harnessing bizarre powers they don't understand in an attempt to become more than what they are. Willing to risk their own lives in the process. But instead of being punished for their transgression like poor old Prometheus, they'll just be dead.

Hudson mentioned a rise in overdose mortalities, but has there also been a rise in the number of *demigods* in the Domes? Not to my knowledge. But why else would dust addicts be willing to push their luck? Someone—or a few someones—must have convinced them that it's possible to extend dust-induced talents far beyond the usual five-minutes-or-so expiration limit.

Somehow Trezon was able to maintain his invisibility long enough to escape the correctional center, walk right into police headquarters and hang around a while, biding his time until he could bash my head in. Not to mention sneaking inside my cube complex and throwing Dunn through the window.

My fists clench. The guy's going to pay. It's just a matter of time.

Is he somehow connected to this cult? To the overdoses? Is it unreasonable to blame him for anything other than the crimes I already know he's committed—more than enough to lock him up for the remainder of his sorry life?

The iron-composite door swings outward with a creak as if I'm expected, held by a muscular Terminal-aged man with a clean-shaven head. Unlike the locals I passed on the way here, he doesn't wear coveralls. Instead, he's got a form-fitting black T-shirt on and grey trousers tucked into combat boots, like the pair I'm wearing. There's an ex-military vibe about him, emphasized by the cold stare he gives me.

I look him in the eye and don't slow my approach. "Prometheus," I mutter, moving to pass by him without a hint of hesitation. Because I belong here.

"He's on his way." He braces the door open with one arm as I enter the dark interior, illuminated only by intermittent neon glow tubes dangling from the rafters.

So *Prometheus* isn't a password after all. It's a person.

"Your first time?" His voice is thick and gruff as he gives me a once-over with eyes that don't miss anything—except the concealed shocker under my jacket. Even if he patted me down, he wouldn't notice a bulge, thanks to the design of my tactical plainclothes.

"How can you tell?"

He smiles briefly, revealing a chipped front tooth as he

lets the door shut. "You seem awful relaxed. I take it you don't plan to participate."

"Do you?" I look him over, which he obviously likes. His type thinks pumping iron pays off in the looks department. Too bad it doesn't do anything for his face.

"This is my temple." He knocks a tight-curled fist between his pectorals. "I watch. Keep everybody safe during the festivities. I don't partake."

So he's the bouncer. "When do they start?"

He chuckles. "When Prometheus arrives."

With a single glance, I survey the crowd packing the warehouse floor. All ages. All castes, the well-dressed alongside the couldn't-care-less. I spot a couple of the Twenty here, but I don't remember their names. Both are Erik's siblings.

And speak of the devil...

"Sera!" Erik bounds over to me with a ridiculous grin on his too-handsome face, his dark hair flopping like some extinct fluffy mammal. The cultists make way for him, engrossed in their own conversations, paying little attention to anything else. "I'm so glad you could make it!" Like he knew I'd be here? "They're saying Prometheus is on his way. Isn't that cool?"

Cool. Not a word I would use to describe anything but the temperature. And it's not cool in here; it's muggy. Too many bodies, too little air circulation. We're lucky most of them don't smell too bad.

With a nod to Erik and a wink at me, the bouncer assumes his position by the door, standing at ease. Hands clasped in front of him, biceps bulging, eyes unfocused as he sees what I'm sure the hidden security cameras outside show him in real time.

Wink and Blink better be lying low.

Erik takes my elbow—not something I like—and escorts me to a darker corner that should afford us a little privacy. Once we're there, I shake off his hand and grab him by the wrist, applying an uncomfortable amount of pressure as I pull him toward me.

"What the hell are you doing here?" I rise up on my tiptoes to whisper-shout into his ear.

He winces. "I could ask you the same thing, Detective."

"Don't call me that."

"You're working, right? On a case?"

What gave that away? "Answer my question." I bear down on his pressure point, and he grits his teeth to keep from yelping. "You better not be stalking me, Erik."

"Drasko said to keep an eye on you," he admits. "So yeah, I hacked—"

"You ran an illegal trace on my augments."

His head wags side to side. "Sure, if you want to be precise. I just traced your location. That's all. I have no idea what you're up to—but I can guess."

"Of course you can."

He raises his chin. Challenge accepted. "Hudson sent you here as bait, to lure Trezon out into the open."

"And why would he do that?"

Erik curses under his breath. "Drasko doesn't trust your new boss. And I'm starting to have my own misgivings. Sending a rookie investigator alone into the belly of the beast? What the hell is Hudson thinking?"

Belly of the beast. One of Drasko's favorite phrases. Maybe the two of them are working together, after all.

Which is really irritating, because they seem to think I need at least one of them looking out for me at all times.

"Different case." I nod toward the two hundred cultists sharing our limited air supply. "Lethal dust overdoses are on the rise. This group's at the epicenter." I release my hold on him, and he pulls back his wrist to massage it, scowling at me for a second or two. I rise up on my toes and step closer, cheek to cheek, breathing into his ear, "What do you know about this *Prometheus*?"

10

"Nothing. This is the first time I've heard of him." He smirks down at me. "What? You think I hang out with this crowd?"

I nod toward his siblings in deep discussion with an older stranger, the three of them standing in the middle of the gathering on the main floor. "Looks like they do."

He follows my sight line before retreating into deeper shadows and gesturing for me to join him. Reluctantly, I do.

"I don't know why they're here," he admits. And he obviously doesn't want them to know he's here as well. Guess they didn't carpool. "I mean, they've already got their abilities, right? Why hang out with a bunch of wannabe's?"

Wannabe demigods? I raise an eyebrow up at him as I transmit the thought from my mind to his. This telepathic talent is one of the only things we have in common.

"Yeah," he nods without a hint of humor in his expression. *They want what we have, Sera. And they're willing to risk everything in order to make their dust-induced superpowers permanent*, he thinks back at me.

"Has it worked for anyone?" Besides Trezon? No, I have to focus here. Different case, Chen. But I can't help making connections, whether or not they stick. It's part of my job, and I'm good at it. I want to be, anyway.

How long can I continue to function without sleep?

Erik shakes his head. "I've been on the farm these past months, out of the loop. Maybe Luther or Daiyna would know, or Milton—"

"I'm not dragging any of them into this." They went through hell to make it to Eurasia, and now they're living simple, unassuming lives, doing their best to stay off the analysts' radar.

Same as the Twenty. Unlike dust freaks, we don't show off our abilities. We're the real deal, but we don't want the attention, the scrutiny. Almost like those animals that roamed the earth before they all went extinct: we're constantly wary of predators.

I shake my head. I really need to focus here.

"So Drasko goes into hiding but gets you to leave your farm and stalk me?"

"We've been in contact, like I said. In VR." Erik shrugs. "He thought it would be a good idea—"

"I don't need either of you watching my six." I give him a fierce look. "I don't want it."

"You're okay with your drones or that clone helping you. But not me?"

You're a civilian, Erik.

We both know that's just my cover. He gives me an obnoxious wink.

I look away, surveying the vacant stage at the other end of the warehouse. "Thought you gave up the whole actor by day, agitator by night gig, farmer boy."

"I have. It's in the past. I've wanted to get to know

Samson and Shechara better." His biological parents from the North American Wastes. "Mom welcomed them in like family, and that's what we are now. A weird, unconventional, loving family of four. And the farm's never done better—"

"Glad everything worked out for you."

I activate my augments and cross my arms, linking up with Wink and Blink to scan the interior for any other ingress points besides the door twenty meters behind me. There's a wide plasteel roll-up on the right side of the building, big enough to allow a pair of cargo trucks to enter side by side. And there's a concealed hatch in the floor behind the stage. Three individuals are currently inside what appears to be a basement storeroom, ten by ten meters in size. *Prometheus* might be one of them. No way to tell what he looks like in the XR or IR images I'm receiving from my drones.

"We're strangers bound by blood." Erik shrugs. "I doubt I'll ever think of Samson and Shechara as *Dad* and *Mom*, but there's something there. Something we share. And it's crazy to see mannerisms or habits I thought were all mine showing up on people I didn't even know existed for the first twenty years of my life!" He pauses. I can feel him watching me. "Have Daiyna and Luther—?"

"We don't..." I trail off as the backstage hatch opens, the door pushed up and to the side to land with a loud, attention-stealing boom against the plasticon floor. "Show time."

The three figures from the storeroom climb up and out, making their way toward steps alongside the stage, a transient structure composed of quick-build plasteel framing and planks covered in black industrial carpet. Easy to assemble and disassemble. Not one of the figures resembles a *Prometheus*. They're women dressed in flowing scraps of white silk, and as they take the stage, they glide across it in a dreamlike choreography, moving in sync with the sudden influx of float-rawk pumped through speakers chained to the ceiling. The crowd surges forward enthusiastically, arms raised as if in worship, the noises from their throats echoing the wordless melody of the so-called music.

I follow them so as not to stand out, and Erik is right behind me.

"Not weird at all," he says into my ear.

Now that my augments are active, I can't send or receive anything telepathically. So I'll have to grab another one of his pressure points if he makes a habit of violating my personal space.

We watch the trio of women dance, swaying and weaving around each other. Not sure what they're supposed to be. Spirits of the earth? Probably not, but it's the first thing that crosses my mind, and I have no idea why.

The music changes abruptly, as float-rawk tends to do. Instead of dreamy otherworldly melodies without lyrics, now we have heavy beats, grinding guitars, and guttural voices screaming like their intestines are boiling. The dancers thrash about, shoving each other and falling onto the stage only to spring back up again and flail with violent abandon. The audience mirrors their movements, smashing into one another and causing all kinds of injuries that don't appear to be felt in the heat of the moment.

They'll notice the bruises and blood later, I'm sure.

Projected onto the warehouse wall behind the stage,

serving as a backdrop, is a holo of an expressionless, larger-than-life disembodied face. Clean-shaven and perfectly bald, pale with tribal tattoos spiraling across it. The whites of the eyes are ink-black. Silver rings pierce the nose, ears, and lips. It seems to watch the three dancers as they whirl about the stage in a frenzy. When the music stops without warning, and the dancers collapse and lie still, the giant face smiles, baring perfect white teeth. The crowd goes wild, expressing their adoration.

"Remind you of anybody?" Erik says in my ear.

If Trezon and Krime had a brother, this giant face might belong to him. The ugliest set of triplets in the world.

"Why have you come?" the face asks in a voice modified to sound deeper than humanly possible. It vibrates in my chest cavity so that I not only hear it but feel it. A physical experience designed to be unforgettable.

The crowd roars, jumping up and down like children with both hands raised toward the dark ceiling, far out of reach.

"What do you want?" the face asks, and the crowd responds the same way: loud and unintelligible. There is no single right answer. This holographic cult leader accepts whatever his adoring fans have to say with a simple nod of approval. "What are you willing to give?"

"EVERYTHING!" the cultists scream in unison, and the face smiles again, eliciting another explosion of adoration. A chant starts at the front of the pack and works its way across the warehouse as every voice in attendance shouts, "Prometheus! Prometheus! Prometheus!"

It's too loud to hear myself think, much less anything Erik might have to say. Not missing his insightful commentary, I disable my augments anyway and tell him telepathically, *I think they're in love.*

He nods, his focus transfixed on the holo-face. *It's a composite. Not an individual.* He answers my frown with, *See how it's constantly in motion, fluidic. The program is drawing from multiple faces to create this image and give it the appearance of existing in real time.*

Figured it was just poor quality.

He shakes his head. *It's intentional. The faces are most likely all around us.*

For what purpose?

He shrugs. *Could be an existential message. "We're all one." Or it could be intended to hide something.* He looks at me, waiting for me to read his mind.

I don't have to. *This Prometheus may not be human at all.*

Why would anyone design an AI to lead a cult? And why would an artificial intelligence be interested in getting gullible people to overdose on dust?

"We will become *gods*," the face says in a modulated tone that rumbles my sternum. "We will have real power. We will make our dreams reality. VR will become a distant memory as we change the world, making it what we want it to be."

The dancers on stage are back on their feet, two to one side of the face and one on the other, all three swaying in place as if their spines no longer exist. The crowd mimics their motion. I perform a little shuffle step to keep up my cover. Erik watches with an amused smirk on his face and folds his arms, refusing to join in. A glance over my shoulder is all I need to know the bouncer has his eye on us, focused now.

Are you trying to stand out? I think at Erik.

He drops his arms and reluctantly moves side to side. But unlike our neighbors, neither he nor I wear that popular look of ecstasy. I wondered why this place needed security, but now I'm thinking it's to watch these cultists' backs while they completely lose it. People are apparently at their most vulnerable when they're worshiping a giant hologram.

"Prometheus! Prometheus! Prometheus!" The earnest chant starts over in waves that ripple from one end of the warehouse to the other.

Everything in me wants to make a quiet exit, but I've got a job to do here. To see if this is where the dust overdoses are originating. The problem being that so far, no one in sight has inhaled a single line of the stuff. Could be that a group snort session is scheduled after this collaborative dance number. I just have to bide my time.

When I think the festivities can't possibly get any weirder, a cloaked figure strides out onto center stage, passing through the holo-face. The dancers hold position like statues, each of them staring with wide, expectant eyes at the dark form of a man. The audience had their eyes closed while they were swaying with their hands in the air, but now they, too, are gazing up at the figure in silent anticipation.

No idea where he came from. The only people in that underground storage room were the three dancers, and nothing Wink and Blink have sent me since has shown any sign of a newcomer crashing the party.

The holo-face closes its eyes and dips its chin, seeming to bow to the new arrival on stage. Then as the figure tosses back its hood and surveys the crowd with a regal aloofness, the holographic projection mirrors his expression. Because it's his face. It has been, all along, despite the strange fluidic presentation Eric noticed. The composite image was intended to resemble him imperfectly. Now it's crystal clear.

"Prometheus! Prometheus! Prometheus!" The chanting reaches a new fervor as the audience kicks their ardor into high gear, pressing forward, hands straining to reach the figure. He paces side to side across the stage, his combat boots thumping in rhythm to their shouts, a calm smile on his lips as he surveys his clamoring fans.

When he halts at stage center and holds up a tattooed hand, the crowd goes silent.

"You are here for fire, yes?" he says—in the voice of Trezon.

No longer invisible. Not trying to hide after his prison escape. Now called by a new name, and worshiped by a couple hundred cult members. Guess he didn't need my help getting into Dome 10 after all. He managed it on his own, and somehow these Children of Tomorrow knew this was where he would show up first.

Did Hudson know as well?

Erik recognizes Trezon instantly and takes a step between me and the stage. An unnecessary protective posture that I sidestep.

"Fire!" the crowd roars.

Trezon smiles broadly as his hands dive into the deep pockets of his cloak. "We will become gods," he says, the lips on his face synchronized with those of the giant holo above him, his modified voice booming throughout the warehouse and rattling our rib cages.

"We will become gods!" they repeat.

"Take." His hands reappear, and he tosses into the crowd

what he fished out of his pockets.

Impossible to tell what they are until they make their way back to us, passed from hand to hand: breathers. Small respiratory devices originally designed for dock workers exposed to the oxygen-deficient atmosphere outside Dome 10. Apparently modified for illegal substances as well. The trio of dancers suddenly have canvas bags full of the things and are throwing them out across the crowd like sowers of seed, sending cascades of breathers into grasping hands.

Trezon reaches both of his hands high in the air, arms outstretched at forty-five degrees. Like he's giving the crowd some kind of religious blessing. "Become more than you have ever been before!"

They murmur in anticipation, holding the breathers in front of their faces, cupped in their hands. But they don't inhale. Not yet. Erik and I glance at each other, mimicking those around us. We gauge each other's reaction as we hold the devices. Will he inhale? Will I?

The breathers are being tossed out indiscriminately. How many of these cultists have more than one device in their possession? And how many other meetings like this does Trezon/Prometheus have planned for today? No wonder there's been an increase in dust overdoses—assuming that's what they're all about to inhale.

But it doesn't explain how Trezon became their leader.

His cronies must have been programming the holo-Prometheus up to now, prepping the crowds of adoring cultists for his physical arrival. Hologram-become-flesh for the first time, and without even a hint of a limp. His kneecaps must have healed up nicely. Side effect of his invisability?

So after an all-too-brief incarceration, Trezon goes from making a killing selling dust to just giving it away? Thanks to those group sessions at the correctional center, now he's a selfless philanthropist? And what about his physical transformation? In the span of a few months, he goes from being a suave underworld kingpin with bad knees, to a sadistic invisible man, to a cult leader with ink-black eyes. Looking at him now, you'd have no clue that he's a fugitive from justice with every Dome 1 tracker following leads to nowhere in their attempt to apprehend him.

Yet here I am. Officially off the case, thanks to Chief Inspector Hudson.

"Inhale and live free!" Trezon drops his arms to his sides with a resounding slap that echoes throughout the warehouse, and the faithful jam the breathers into their nostrils, all of them inhaling with their heads rocking back like part of some mass choreography. Only the three dancers and their cult leader abstain.

I hold my breath and the breather in place, but I don't activate it. Giving Erik a sidelong glance, I see that he's done the same. He gives me a nod. We're in this together. Here to observe, not participate.

The music restarts. The dancers prance around the stage again, encircling Trezon with their flowing silk, hiding him completely between one moment and the next. He stands as still as a statue, dark eyes unblinking, staring over the heads of his audience as they bob and sway, surrendering to the rhythm pumping through those powerful speakers chained above us.

His strange eyes seem to focus on me standing at the edge of the crowd. He almost smiles. I stare back at him, not sure this is real.

Does sleep deprivation cause hallucinations? Almost sure that it does.

Did you think I wouldn't find you? I send him a telepathic transmission anyway.

He nods slowly. Then he raises his right arm and points at me.

I sense the bouncer approach, and I spin around to face him, every muscle in my body tensed, ready for a fight.

"Prometheus would like you to join him on stage," the bouncer says, keeping his open hands at shoulder height. Ready to trade blows if the situation calls for it, but showing me with his body language that he's not interested in starting anything. Despite his muscle mass weighing three times my own and the boxer's ease with which he carries himself, he sees something in me that he'd rather not deal with right now.

Smart guy. I'm sure it would be painful—for both of us.

"If you'll follow me..." He extends one thick arm forward before leading the way himself, parting the swaying cultists like curtains and leaving the short-lived gap behind him for me to follow.

Get out of here, I think at Erik before I walk after the bouncer.

Yeah, right. Erik is right on my heel. *Drasko said—*

I don't care what Drasko said. I half-turn to stiff-arm Erik, and he stutters to a scowling halt. *You're a civilian. This isn't your case.*

It's not yours, either. He nods toward the stage. *I know this guy, remember?*

Of course I do. *He almost killed you.* A memory flashes

through my mind of Erik tied to a slat-backed chair, his face a bloody mess.

That was just for show. He scoffs. *He'd never kill me. I'm too likeable.*

"Hey." The bouncer pauses between two blissful cultists and gestures for me to pick up the pace.

It's your funeral, I think at Erik before reactivating my augments and following the bouncer through the throngs. I tell Wink and Blink to track my position and, if need be, break inside with guns blazing. They get the general idea.

"Unit D1-440 is maintaining position across the street with nothing to report, Investigator Chen," they transmit via audiolink.

Let's hope it stays that way.

The bouncer leads me to the left side of the stage—stage right, if I remember correctly—and toward a set of stairs around the back, out of the audience's sight. Erik is so close to my backside that I can feel him literally breathing down my neck. If he's tried thinking at me, then my telepathic silence should give him a hint that I'm no longer receiving mind-to-mind transmissions. For the moment, I need my augments online in order to ensure our safety.

Until the time is right to pick Trezon's brain.

The bouncer steps aside once he reaches the foot of the stairs and extends his arm again, this time expecting me to climb up on stage. I pause, watching the flowing white silk swimming around *Prometheus*. The music is now playing through its more melodious bars, but it won't be long until the thrashing starts all over again with renewed vigor.

Is that why Trezon wants me up there with him? So he can throw me off the stage and into the melee? Break my neck and have it look like an unfortunate accident.

I have to remind myself that he could have easily killed me in my cube. With that grav weapon of his—nowhere in sight at the moment—he could have sent me flailing out the window after Dunn, but without a security clone's armor. The local sanitation robo-crew would have spent the rest of the morning scraping my remains off the sidewalk. So if he doesn't want to kill me, then what does he want?

Drasko. He'll try to use me to get to Drasko.

Let him. Without his baton, he's not so tough. And I can take the bouncer, no problem. The bigger the muscles, the heavier they fall.

So I mount the stairs, and as I do, the dancers take the forestage, blocking the audience from view with swirling white silk. Intentionally.

Trezon faces me with his conceited smirk fully intact. The black pools of his eyes are even more uncanny close up. "Investigator Chen. We meet again."

"Had some trouble seeing you last time. And the time before that." I scratch lightly at my bruised forehead. "You do realize I have to take you in now, right?"

"And Erik!" Trezon gives him a nod as Erik clears the top step behind me. "It's been too long, my friend."

"You've changed your name. And your eyeballs." Erik stuffs his hands into the pockets of his trousers with an awkward shrug. "They suit you, I guess."

"I am a changed man." Another nod from Trezon, dismissing the bouncer. At the same time, the music switches gears as it did before. No more float, all rawk. Trezon steps toward me and leans in, and it's all I can do to hold my ground, even as my thumb and forefinger ache at his proximity, seeming to remember what he did to them. "Let's talk someplace quieter, shall we?"

Without waiting for a response, he heads down the stairs to the open hatch in the backstage floor. Descending the steps below, he beckons us to join him. I glance at the dancers and the audience, all of them lost in their violent cavorting as guttural screams compete for dominance with rapid-fire drum beats and grinding guitar.

I look at Erik, and he gives me another shrug as if to say *We could leave.*

I'm sure we could. The bouncer wouldn't be difficult to get past, and Trezon is out of sight. Even if he went to retrieve his grav weapon, we could lose ourselves in the thrashing crowd before he has a chance to target us.

But I didn't walk all the way here just so I could leave empty-handed. And I don't care which case I'm on. This is the job.

"Notify Chief Inspector Hudson that the escaped criminal known as Trezon has been located," I tell Wink and Blink. "Advise all trackers to converge on this warehouse."

"Understood, Investigator Chen," they reply in unison.

Then I double-tap my temple to disable my augments and pat Erik on the shoulder as I head for the stairs. *Still tagging along?*

Into the belly of the beast, he mutters telepathically.

II

The steps into the sublevel are rickety, the space obviously designed for storing certain items off the books. There's room enough for a cargo truck's entire load, but the area is empty now save for a pair of small crates on either side of a much larger one, all of them scuffed from reuse and, by the way they're positioned, resembling two seats at a table. Shadows engulf the perimeter as light from a single glowpad affixed to the ceiling casts a white shroud down around our host. The shadows get darker as Erik shuts the hatch door behind us with a heavy clunk, muting some of the noise from the wild Children of Tomorrow above.

"Drink?" Sitting on one of the smaller crates, Trezon holds up the bottle of Eurasian whiskey he just poured into his tumbler. A pair of empty glasses wait for us.

"Sure," Erik says at the same time I decline.

"It's not poison, Detective." Trezon pours Erik's drink.

"Well, in that case." I plant my boots shoulder-width apart on the scratched plasticon floor and cross my arms. "Answer's still no."

"You're healing well, I trust?" Remaining seated, Trezon offers Erik a tumbler with two fingers-worth of liquid amber sloshing around the bottom.

Erik takes the drink and steps back, staying close to my side. He doesn't raise the alcohol to his lips but holds it like he's at some kind of boring dinner party. Trezon watches him for a moment before draining his own tumbler and promptly refilling it.

"You wanted to talk." I narrow my gaze at the tattooed criminal. "So talk."

He nods with a wince as he swallows his second drink. "You're hoping to buy time for your trackers to converge on this location."

"That's right." Why deny it?

He chuckles. "Let them. These days, I don't have any trouble avoiding prying eyes. Even in a panopticon like our glorious Eurasia, I can come and go as I please."

"Because you suddenly have the gift of invisibility, which you turn on and off like a switch." I tilt my head to one side as I study him. "Something you picked up in prison?"

"Now Detective, we both know there are no such things as *prisons* in this advanced society of ours. We don't punish those who break the law. We *correct* them. And I must say, my life took a much-needed course correction while I was...detained for those few months."

"Obviously." I nod toward the wild cacophony of noise reverberating above us. "Now you lead a cult."

Trezon pours himself a third drink. Guess I'm keeping track.

"Things were so much simpler under Chancellor Hawthorne," he says. "There was the law, and there was the iron fist enforcing it. But now we have a *hero* in charge, back from the dead as it were, and he doesn't seem to know how exactly to run these great Domes of ours, does he? He has high ideals, I'll grant him that. But it's in the execution of those ideals that he falters. Dust is outlawed across the Ten Domes, and smuggling has ground to a halt. But arms sales, human trafficking, clone hacking—not so easy to stamp out. And now religious freedoms abound, given free rein with all of the innate difficulties they entail." He winks at me with one of his weird inky eyes. "I simply traded one vice for another."

"So that wasn't dust your followers inhaled just now?"

He glances at my pocket, where I stuffed the breather I received. "Why don't you try it and find out for yourself? Oh. That's right. Because you're one of the *Twenty*. Which means you already have a superhuman ability." Lazily he scratches the side of his head. "You can read minds."

Erik downs his drink in one gulp. Liquid courage, I suppose.

"Among other things." I stare Trezon down. How does he know about me? Krime didn't have a chance to tell him anything.

"It's in your DNA." He smiles and raises his glass, toasting us. "A gift you share with the other members of the Twenty. As well as your children, more than a thousand of them at last count, scattered across the Domes. Adopted by members of the upper castes. Raised in privilege, and destined to fill the most exalted positions in our society."

Erik coughs. Or maybe he's choking. I don't look away from Trezon's conniving, abysmal eyes.

"You did some research while you were undergoing your short-lived correction." I keep my arms loose, my shooting hand ready to go for my concealed shocker. The thumb and index finger should be strong enough now to do the job. Send this criminal to the floor in spasms as he soils himself. I'm really looking forward to it.

Just have to wait for the right moment. Not yet. There's something in the look he's giving me. He wants to tell me something, and he's relishing the suspense.

I have to time this right. Wait too long, and the trackers will break into the warehouse. Trezon will go invisible on us and escape the same way he managed to enter unnoticed. We'll have lost the opportunity to capture him. But if I shoot him now, he may never tell me what his endgame is with this weird cultist act.

He sips his drink, pausing a moment to study the whiskey in his tumbler. "You should know that I sympathize with you." He glances at Erik, then focuses on me again. "All twenty of you. Having your sex cells extracted without your knowledge from the time you hit puberty. Having no say in the matter. You never asked to be our saviours. But because of you, humankind will continue as a species." He drains his glass. "Those of us in the Terminal Generation owe you a debt of gratitude. We would have been the last humans on the planet, as sterile as our parents, thanks to the plague." His gaze loses coherence. He seems to be looking through me at a future where he's one of the few people still alive inside a decaying Dome.

"So that's why you invited us back here? To thank us?" Hard to believe.

"To warn you." He sets down the tumbler and rises from his seat. "There's about to be a rash of kidnappings across the Domes. And there's nothing you can do about it."

"Kidnappings?" Erik frowns. "What are you talking

about?"

"Dust highs no longer have much appeal. They fade." Trezon shrugs. "We want what you have. Permanent abilities. They're in your DNA, as well as the DNA you've passed on, whether or not you had any say in it."

The children...

I draw my shocker and aim it at his head. "You can tell us all about your plans at headquarters."

He laughs. "You really think you can take me in, Detective? Because I don't think so. Consider this discussion a professional courtesy and nothing more. Feel free to tell your superiors all about it. But you will never—"

The shock-pulse hurtles straight for him before I realize I've pulled the trigger. Electric-blue static energy in a tight ball of light, passing through the space where Trezon was standing a split-second ago.

Except now he's vanished. Of course.

"Get down!" I shout, and Erik hits the floor as I pivot on my heel, laying down a barrage of pulse rounds that illuminate the sublevel with their garish light, each one slamming into the wall without so much as a scorch mark to show for my efforts.

Then I wait, reaching out with my mind for Trezon's. If he's still in here, I'll sense his thoughts. *Where are you? You son of a bitch...*

Erik grunts on the floor. He's struggling against an invisible assailant who's got him in a choke-hold from behind. It's no use. Trezon is stronger.

Erik is hauled upward like a human shield, rising awkwardly to his feet.

"Let him go." I train my shocker on Erik's abdomen.

"You're not getting out of here."

"Of course I am," Trezon scoffs, his voice emanating from thin air. "And I'm bringing this one with me. But you won't be tagging along, Detective. I'm afraid our time together is at its end."

An all-too-familiar force throws me against the wall and pins me there, my muscles useless against the sudden grav weapon burst.

"Sera—" Erik grates out before he staggers backward toward the bottom of the stairs. Then he launches himself upward with his superhuman ability, slamming through the hatch door with a pained groan, sending it crashing open as he disappears out of sight.

The roar of the cult's worship service floods the space around me.

Erik, what's happening? I send my thoughts after him, my vocal chords frozen in place just like the rest of me. *What's he doing to you?*

I sense Erik's fear before I receive his telepathic reply: *He's steering my ability, Sera. He's making me jump. I'm not in control of my—*

That's enough, Trezon's thoughts invade our shared mindspace. An unwelcome presence. *I don't want to kill him, Detective, but I will if you don't cease all communication with him while he's aiding in my escape.*

I grind my teeth. *How are you doing this? Stealing Erik's abilities?*

Borrowing, Trezon corrects me. *A little something else I picked up during my incarceration. If I'm in physical contact with one of your kind, I can override your powers and make them my own. Think of it like this: I'm the one driving Erik right now. He is my vehicle. I can make him jump through whatever I want—or attempt to, at any rate.* A brief pause. *I wonder how many times he can smash into a plexicon wall before all of his bones shatter? Such a frail body of flesh...*

I don't know how far my telepathic link with Erik extends. We've never tested it before. If he goes out of range—

Where are you taking him?

I'm sure you would like to know, Trezon replies. *Our friend Erik is going to lead me to wherever Drasko's hiding himself these days. He will take me there, even if I have to turn him inside out in the process.*

So it wasn't me that Trezon wanted. It was Erik, all along.

He never should have followed me backstage.

If this gravity field wasn't holding me in place, I'd be trembling with fury. Instead I curse a silent blue streak. I can't move to tap my temple, can't activate my augments and link up with Wink and Blink. Can't send them after Erik and his hijacker. Can't send Fort new orders via audiolink. I can't communicate with him at all.

Or can I?

Focusing all of my telepathic energy on the roof of the building across the street, I project: *Help Erik Paine! The criminal Trezon has overpowered him—he's using Erik's superhuman abilities against him!*

Questions storm my mind: How is a gravitational field pinning my body against this wall without someone standing there to aim a grav weapon at me? And why is Trezon riding Erik piggyback when there are trackers converging on this location, and any one of them will be able to spot Erik leaping through the air like an oversized grasshopper? Not the most inconspicuous escape plan for an invisible man.

Unless the trackers aren't on their way. Because Trezon somehow managed to interfere with my drones' transmission to HQ.

Time to try something I've never done before.

I focus on the manic minds of the cultists thrashing around the floor above me. I shut everything else out of my mind. The rage. The pain. The fear. I send a single thought into their minds, passing from one to the next, to the next, until I've reached all two hundred of them in the span of a few seconds. I tell them, *Demigod battle outside!*

First I sense their confusion. Then their curiosity, followed by overwhelming interest as they abandon their bizarre dance moves and rush toward the exit en masse, overwhelming the bouncer. He acts sensibly, in his own best interest, and sidesteps the mob. *Outside! Outside! Demigods!* The thoughts echo through their collective consciousness. Then a cheer erupts from the cultists leading the pack. They must have caught sight of Erik and the invisible monster on his back.

Nice try, Detective, Trezon tells me through Erik's mind. *But they won't stop me.*

Again, I focus on the minds of his faithful followers: *Don't let them leave. Their abilities are yours if you catch them!*

Another fanatical cheer from the mob. *Quick! Quick now!* their minds echo.

If only you could see them. Trezon chuckles telepathically. *They're tripping over themselves, unable to follow Erik as he leaps from the top of one building to another, far out of reach. Soon, we will also be out of sight.*

And they still won't have a clue as to where they are. They're high as kites right now, enjoying the flight.

So it really wasn't dust in those breathers. He just drugged them, like any good cult leader would. This Prometheus character he's playing isn't responsible for the dust overdoses Hudson sent me to investigate.

So what was the purpose of this strange gathering?

Somehow, Trezon knew I would be there. Erik as well. Did Hudson set us up? Is he working with Trezon? Crazy thoughts, I know, but that's what happens when you're pinned to the wall by a gravity field. Your mind starts grasping at anything.

Oh, I see a security clone is attempting to follow us. It's making a valiant attempt, scrambling like a lunatic, Trezon thinks at me via Erik. *Another non-human friend of yours, I assume?*

Fort. I'd smile if I could. But then the memory of Dunn blasting through my cube window and plummeting to the pavement below flashes through my mind. *Let Erik go. You don't need him.*

Once he leads me to Drasko, I'll consider discarding what's left of him. Goodbye, Detective.

I collapse to the floor with a grunt as the gravity field releases me. At the same time, a holographic wall shudders in place and then dissolves, revealing this sublevel to be larger than it originally appeared. A figure steps out of the shadows with the chrome grav weapon in one hand.

"You are no longer welcome here, Investigator Chen," says the voice of a young Dr. Solomon Wong, the same incarnation as every other security clone in the Domes. Except this one isn't outfitted in white armor with a helmet to hide its facial features. Instead, it looks like another one of Trezon's inner circle with a shaved head, tribal tattoos, and dark cloak.

This clone has been hacked.

"Yeah. Thought as much." I don't holster my shocker once I'm on my feet, straightening my spine with a grimace. "If you'd be so kind as to point me in the right direction, I'll track down your boss and drag him back to prison."

"This way." The clone keeps the grav weapon in one hand as it mounts the steps out of the sublevel, keeping its eyes to itself.

I reactivate my augments. "Track Erik Paine," I subvocalize to Wink and Blink. "Locate Unit D1-440."

"Tracking," they reply in unison, and I can imagine them leaving the airspace above the warehouse and veering off in pursuit. "Locating."

I follow the clone into the vacant warehouse where float-rawk still blares through the ceiling speakers, louder now without the writhing bodies to soak it up. The ghostly dancers and everybody else have vacated the premises. Only the bouncer remains, standing at his post like a good little soldier.

"Investigator Chen is leaving," the clone tells the bouncer as it approaches the doorway, open now and letting in a patch of rust-filtered sunlight. "If she attempts to gain entry to another one of our gatherings, you are to disable her in any way you see fit."

The bouncer grins and nods at me, his brawny arms folded. He likes the idea of testing his overbearing physicality against mine at some point in the near future.

"You want to just get this over with?" I holster my shocker

and crack my neck to the right as I advance on him.

He cracks his neck to the left and then the right, unfolding his arms and limbering up with his fists clenched. "Thought you'd never ask." His grin widens with anticipation. "Ladies first."

"There is no need for a physical altercation at this time," the clone says.

"Too late." I kick its kneecap with my boot, and its leg bends the wrong way. As it sweeps the grav weapon toward me, I clamp down on its forearm and twist, pulling the clone off balance and wrenching the baton free. "This is going into evidence. And both of you are being charged with harboring a known fugitive."

The bouncer grunts at that, as if it was meant to be funny. The clone clutches its busted leg and doesn't make a sound. Neither one looks like they're interested in coming along quietly.

I pause a moment to focus my ocular lenses on the grav weapon, hoping there's something in the police database that will show me how to use the damn thing. But unfortunately, there's jack squat. I'm on my own here.

"You are all alone, Investigator Chen," the clone says, its voice no different from Dunn's or Fort's, yet I can tell each of them apart. Somehow, they don't sound the same to me.

Yet they all wear his face. The man I see in my nightmares. The man I killed.

"Backup isn't on the way." The bouncer keeps his fists above his chin, head bowed forward and cold eyes unblinking as he lunges forward with a front kick aimed at my abdomen.

"Figured as much." I jump back and answer with a spin

kick that he blocks with his forearms, then foolishly attempts to grab onto. I let him. But as he seizes my left leg and tries to throw me, my downward momentum works against him. I plow my right boot into his left kneecap, and he groans, releasing me to hit the floor and roll back onto my feet.

Now he and the clone have a matched set of busted knees.

"Let me guess. Something's in place to interfere with the Link." I hold the grav weapon as if I know how to use it, aiming the business end at each of them in turn. "Prometheus doesn't like his followers distracted while they're gobbling up his pablum."

The bouncer gestures at the warehouse ceiling. "Signal dampeners, built into the structure itself. Can't hail anybody outside Dome 10." His grin hasn't faded. "Admit it. You don't have a clue how that thing works." He nods toward the baton.

I whip it forward, cracking him across the jaw. His head jerks to the side with another grunt. "I think I've got the hang of it."

"Cocky little bitch, aren't you." He straightens his head and winks at me.

I let that slide. "C'mon and hit me already. Get it out of your system."

"With pleasure."

He advances, favoring his left leg and keeping most of his weight on his right. Jabbing with one fist, then the other, he misses intentionally, keeping me on guard. Instead of backpedaling, I circle him and keep an eye on the clone, who's backed out of the way. It doesn't seem to want to be involved, but I know better than to ignore it. There's no telling what the hackjob did to its social skills. It could be reconditioned to seem compliant one second and go berserk the next.

I grip the chrome baton in both hands, blocking the bouncer's next combination shot—roundhouse, elbow jab, sidekick. Nothing I haven't seen before. But he keeps coming, circling me as I fend off his blows, his punches hitting harder, his kicks striking faster, as if he's only been warming up until now. He shows no sign of slowing down anytime soon.

I'm blocking, dodging, ducking, grunting as I hit the floor and do my best to kick his feet out from under him. But he leaps into the air with a laugh and aims for me with his elbow as he lands. I roll aside and strike him across the forearm with the baton, then across his face, whipping it aside like I did before. This time there's some blood, and he spits it at me as we both jump to our feet.

"You've got some moves," he allows.

"I'll be sure to tell my trainer."

He frowns at the grav weapon. "Not a fair fight though, is it? I'm unarmed here."

"Sore loser?"

He grins, and there's blood on his chipped teeth. He's got that predatory look going strong. The guy takes joy in physically hurting others.

I was wrong about the iron-pumping. It's not for looks. It's to feel powerful.

"Oh, we're just getting started here, beautiful." He chuckles.

That's when the clone launches itself at me, silent as a shadow. With some sort of instinct I didn't even know I had, I thrust the end of the grav weapon at it, hoping to punch its abdomen, and instead a burst of energy sends it flailing upward without a sound, pinning it to the high ceiling between a pair of plasteel rafters.

The bouncer charges me next, and I thrust the baton at him in the same way, sending him back with a blast that plasters his body against the wall, right next to the door. Neither he nor the clone makes any noise, both as motionless as the warehouse itself. Frozen in their awkward poses. Still life on display.

Too bad there's nobody around to appreciate it.

"I'll be back for both of you," I promise as I step outside. "Once my reinforcements arrive."

12

Once I'm far enough away from the warehouse's signal dampeners, I contact HQ mid-stride and let them know Trezon is on the move, that he's captured a civilian, and that Unit D1-440 is in pursuit. I share the video feed I'm receiving from Wink and Blink, who are following the kidnapping at a safe distance. Erik continues to leap from one rooftop to another, presumably with invisible Trezon in the driver's seat, leaving Fort to sprint along the streets below, doing his best not to injure any civilians in his path as he struggles to keep pace with his quarry.

But he's already two blocks behind and losing ground.

Regardless, he must have received my telepathic message—just like Dunn is able to. They're both at different stages in their journey to personhood. Or maybe they've always been people, from the moment they breathed their first breaths. And the purpose of all the conditioning they received was to keep them from knowing it. To keep them docile, servile, and obedient. Slaves of the Chancellor.

"Tell me what I'm seeing here," Chief Inspector Hudson demands as he links up with me from Dome 1. "Looks like a dust freak running amok."

"Possible." I keep Wink and Blink's live feed at the left periphery of my ocular lenses and the holo of Hudson's disgruntled face at the right, leaving front and center clear to avoid slamming into foot traffic. I dash down the crowded sidewalk, avoiding the local citizens completely immersed online in whatever they've found to occupy themselves between work and home. "It's Trezon, sir. He's invisible, and he's riding a citizen with the ability to leap great heights and distances."

"Riding...him?"

"For lack of a better term." *Overriding* might be more accurate.

Hudson curses under his breath in a rare display of personality. "How the hell did he get past our sentries? The Dome 10 maglev tunnel's on lockdown!"

I'm about to explain what *invisible* means when a shot rings out. Not here on the street where I am, but via Wink and Blink's shared feed. Erik is on a rooftop, collapsed in an unconscious heap. Trezon is visible again, and he's got a rifle in his hand, an illegal projectile weapon with a scope and extra-long barrel. One of his lackeys must have stowed it up there for him.

Down on the street half a dozen stories below, Fort lies flat on his back with his knees bent sideways. Instead of a pristine face shield on his helmet, there's a fractured, bloody mess. He's not moving.

"I thought you said he was invisible, Chen," Hudson says, referring to Trezon.

"He can toggle it on and off..." My pace slows as I stare at the image of Fort in my lens.

What am I feeling? Grief? I haven't known this clone for

more than a few hours. Responsibility, then. I sent him after Trezon. I got him killed.

The drones' feed returns to Trezon on the roof, smirking up at them as he aims his rifle at Wink next.

"Get out of there!" I shout as he fires the weapon.

Wink and Blink veer sharply in opposite directions, their perspectives diverging wildly as they avoid the incoming projectile. Somehow they manage to keep a lens aimed at the rooftop, which changes without warning, right before my eyes.

Erik and Trezon are no longer there, nor is the stairwell shed leading down into the building. Instead, the rooftop is covered in gorgeous, well-manicured gardens.

"Holograms," I mutter.

Another curse from Hudson. "I expect your report to explain how this has anything to do with that cult I sent you to investigate."

"Oh it does, sir." I run, making straight for where Fort lies in the middle of the street three blocks over. Hoping the driverless cargo trucks don't flatten him before I get there. Why? Do I think there's any hope for him? Yes. Dunn survived a headshot courtesy of my pal Drasko, once upon a time—as well as a fall from my ten-story window. Fort might still be alive. "The cult leader is Trezon. He goes by the stage name *Prometheus* and promises the Children of Tomorrow fire from heaven."

A brief pause. "You'll need to explain that."

"I don't know how, sir. Not yet. I'm still piecing things together." My voice is trembling. I clench my jaw to sound like I'm keeping cool. "He promises them permanent abilities. Then he has them inhale some sort of narcotic. I have a sample we can test, find out what's in it."

"Good work. Bring that straight to HQ."

"I'm not leaving Fort like this."

"What?"

"Unit D1-440."

"A recycling team will retrieve the clone."

"Please, sir." My eyes sting. I see Fort lying in the street up ahead. Driverless ground vehicles swerve around him. Nobody on the sidewalk stops or stares. They don't even notice, their unfocused eyes glued to whatever they're streaming on the Link. "Let me bring him in."

"Are we still talking about the clone?"

"And Trezon."

"How many times do I have to tell you, Chen? You're not on the Trezon case!"

"Yet he keeps crossing my path."

I race to Fort's side and hold up a hand to halt oncoming traffic. The self-driving cargo trucks squeal to a stop. As gently as I can, I remove Fort's cracked helmet and wince at the damage. The projectile entered through his face shield and passed between his eyes, burrowing deep inside his brain before it exploded, breaking outward through the skull and leaving a hodge-podge of mismatched puzzle pieces. Bone. Brains. Blood. The clone known as Unit D1-440 is no more.

Fort is dead.

My breath hitches, and a sudden pain stabs my side. But it's not from running. I'm not winded. Yet I'm having trouble breathing.

"Children," I gasp. "He told me there's going to be a rash of kidnappings."

"Trezon?" Hudson's holographic face frowns.

I nod. "He wants their DNA, sir. I think he...believes it's the key to making dust abilities permanent. I don't know how, but he's able to turn his invisibility on and off at will, and he's not snorting the stuff, not from what I can tell. If I had to guess, he underwent some kind of genetic transformation during his incarceration."

"Chen, this is a bit too much. Even for you."

Not sure what he means by that. Even less sure that I like it. "I've tagged the building he entered."

"Trackers are en route. You are to return to HQ immediately—"

"He's got my friend. I'm going after them." I reach to end the call, but I add, "Two of Trezon's associates are pinned to the interior of that cult's warehouse by gravity fields." I hold up the chrome baton so Hudson can see it via my lenses. "I'll enter this into evidence as soon as I return."

"You will return *now*!"

"Chen out."

I know I'll have hell to pay, but if that's the price for not letting Erik or Drasko meet the same fate as Fort, then it's well worth it.

Setting the bloody helmet on the clone's abdomen, I stoop to reach under his arms and drag him out of the street onto the sidewalk. The driverless vehicles start moving again. Some sort of sixth sense keeps passersby from tripping over Fort's armored body, even though they don't seem to notice anything around them. Not even me, crouched beside him.

"You deserved better than this." I take Fort's right hand and squeeze the cold gauntlet. His entire body is still, like he's holding his breath. If only that were the case. "You deserved to find out who you really...could be."

More than a conditioned copy of a genius megalomaniac. More than recyclable biological material. Like Dunn, this clone was on the road to self-discovery. If given more time, who knows what kind of person he might have become?

But then again, what the hell do I know? I'm just a rookie investigator hopped up on stimulants and defying orders. Hating myself for doing it, but with no other option right now, I leave Fort's body behind and focus on the situation at hand.

I twirl the baton end over end and frown at it. When this all began, I thought it was the key, that somehow Trezon had used it to escape from the correctional center. Weaponized grav-field tech is illegal, of course, but that doesn't make it unheard of. Few things are these days. I'm chasing an invisible man with his sights set on the DNA of a thousand children scattered across the Ten Domes. Things don't get much weirder.

Shaking my head, I focus on the building across the street. Trezon's in there, and he's got Erik. My grip on the baton tightens as I run, dodging cargo trucks that screech to a halt at my proximity, then gun their accelerators once I'm safely out of the way, their big tires squealing to make up for lost time.

"Give me eyes, boys," I tell Wink and Blink via our shared audiolink. "XR and IR, every floor."

They've already tagged Erik, so his inert form shows up immediately on the three-dimensional overlay they send to my lenses. The map takes the form of a ghostly blue architectural rendering superimposed on the building's exterior, giving me a clear view of what's going on inside. From the looks of things, this facility is some sort of information processing center. Half a dozen floors with offices and workers sitting at desks scanning data in hard copy format, saving it to the Link via ocular augments.

Their tedious work is somehow related to Dome 10's waste management systems, I'm guessing. Maybe they keep a running tally of how many flushes each citizen is responsible for. A scintillating task, I'm sure, but necessary in an interconnected system of self-sustaining biospheres. And entirely legal. No idea why Trezon would have chosen this building to duck into. Definitely not one of his usual haunts.

"Erik Paine is on the sixth floor, Investigator Chen," my drones tell me as a neon green targeting reticle encircles Erik's shadowy figure on the overlay.

"Life signs?"

"Affirmative," Wink and Blink reply in unison.

"Split up and cover the exits. I'm going in."

"Yes, Investigator Chen." Wink holds position above the holo-disguised roof while Blink plummets toward me to cover the front, the only way in or out at street level.

The glass entry doors slide aside automatically as they sense my presence, and I step into the spacious foyer lit naturally by a soaring windowall reaching up three floors. The well-dressed receptionist's eyes widen as I approach the front desk.

"Investigator Sera Chen." I flash him my credentials virtually via Link, and he nods, his bulging Adam's apple bobbing as his attention rivets itself to the baton I'm holding. "Need to check out your top floor. Looks like you had an unlawful entry."

He frowns. "Of course...but no aerocar arrivals were logged by our—"

"They didn't arrive by aerocar."

He fails to blink, quick to grasp the situation. Leaning forward, he whispers, "A dust freak? Here?"

"Any security on site?"

"No, we..."

"Just keep track of citizens' flushes. Got it." I head for the stairs.

Assigning Wink's XR view of Erik to the periphery of my vision, I start up the vacant stairwell. Scuffed plasticon steps and whitewashed walls echo every footfall as my boots make contact. Announcing my arrival at every floor. Maybe I should have taken a speedlift. I actually thought this would be less conspicuous.

But I'm not thinking straight. By the time I reach Erik, I'll be winded. Hell, I am already. This isn't like me. I've got better stamina.

The stimulants must be wearing off. Either that or my body is on the verge of collapse, despite their effects—which I'm probably immune to by now. Have I built up a tolerance? Fantastic.

I exit the stairwell on the fourth floor and head for the hallway where a pair of speedlifts are waiting. The office cubicles nearby remain silent as workers go about their tasks with eyes only for what's right in front of them. I punch the call button between the two lift doors.

"Any sign of Trezon?" I ask my drones.

"None," they reply. So he's either invisible again, or he's left the building.

The speedlift on my left dings, and the polished plasteel door slides open to reveal the empty interior. I step inside and tap the glowing pad for the top floor. Unlike other buildings nearby, this one seems to be better maintained, at least on the inside. These flush-counters must take pride in their work. And why wouldn't they? In a small way, they're safeguarding our future, making sure all citizens do their part to conserve our precious resources—such as the seawater flowing through our plumbing systems, sending all that waste out into the Mediterranean to be recycled.

I'm staring at my blurry excuse for a reflection in the door as the lift glides upward. Then, without warning, my face slams flat against the cold plasteel as an all-too-familiar voice breathes into my ear:

"I'll take that, Detective."

Invisible Trezon rips the grav weapon out of my hands. I grab after it, but he's already whipping it in a downward trajectory, striking the backs of my legs. With a groan, my body collapses against the lift door. The next strike clangs against the solid plasteel where my head was a split-second ago. Good thing I anticipated that move.

I lunge upward and wrap both my arms around his invisible one. The baton clangs against the door again as I wrestle with him, bracing his elbow in such a way that only a little extra effort will break it. He seems to realize this and holds still for a moment.

"The second time now I've had to retrieve my personal property. You have no right to it."

"Weaponized gravity tech is illegal, and you're a criminal," I reply. "So you have no rights—other than a clean cell, three meals a day, and the best psychological therapy our exalted government can provide."

"Tried it. Didn't like it much."

His invisible free hand chops me in the throat, then the

thumb goes for my eyeball, digging in. Between the choking and the sudden pressure on one of my favorite eyes, it's tough to maintain my grip on his arm. Yet somehow I manage. And I bring up a knee in a sudden forceful blow to his groin. He groans and doubles over, putting too much pressure on the elbow in my grip. His hand drops from my face, and I blink away the pain. Try to, anyway.

"Get on your knees." I guide him to the floor with his arm up behind his invisible back and nudge the empty space in front of me with the toe of my boot to make sure he's where I think he is. "And turn off your damn invisibility. It's not impressing anybody."

"I won't go back, Detective. I told you before. No cage can hold me."

A burst of gravitational energy floods the floor of the lift, sending us both into the air until we settle on a buoyant grav field that arcs from one wall to the other, bouncing back and forth. I hold onto Trezon's arm with one hand, trying to pin it along with his grav weapon, and I swing the elbow of my other arm as hard as I can, striking his jaw, then his neck, followed by the center of his chest as I attempt to incapacitate him. The groans erupting from his throat would lead one to believe he's struggling to remain conscious. But then he fires off that damn weapon again.

This time, we're flipped upside-down, thrown against the ceiling as if we're falling in that direction. A bizarre sensation.

I twist his wrist and slam the baton repeatedly against the wall. Resounding clangs reverberate all around us, but he doesn't release his grip.

With a ding, the lift comes to a stop on the sixth floor, as expected, and the door slides open. Trezon and I continue to struggle as the gravity field dissipates beneath us, gently carrying our thrashing bodies down to the floor.

"Criminal in custody," I tell Wink and Blink. "Converge on my location."

"On our way," they reply.

"That holo-field on the roof is rigged with semtex." Trezon shifts his weight as if he's turning to look at me. Or preparing to activate the grav weapon again. "I only mention that because you seem fairly attached to your flying mechanical friends."

"You're bluffing."

"I'm sure that this close to the roof, we'll feel the blast."

I can't risk it. "Forget that order," I tell my drones. "The holo is rigged with explosives." Then I subvocalize, "Locate the projector and disable it by any means necessary. Steer clear of the blast."

"Yes, Investigator Chen."

"Stay down." Twisting Trezon's invisible arm behind his back, I manage to hit just the right pressure point to send the baton clattering across the floor beside him.

The explosion that rocks the rooftop is strong enough to make the speedlift wobble in its shaft. Cries of alarm echo from the office cubicles down the hall.

"Sorry for your loss," Trezon says through clenched teeth.

I grab his other invisible arm and pin it behind him with my knee. Refusing to believe Wink or Blink was lost in that blast, I reach for my shocker. "Hold still."

"Not really in my best interest to do so, Detective."

I jam the shocker's muzzle into the back of his invisible neck. "You know what this is."

His entire frame goes rigid. "Yes. And I know that if we

maintain our physical proximity, the effect of the pulse will affect you the same as me."

Meaning we'll both be completely incapacitated. Worth it, if I knew for sure that backup's arrived and they are at this very moment making their way upstairs to my location.

A buzzing sound echoes in the hallway beyond the lift's open door. Wink and Blink hover side by side, quadcopter rotors spinning and projectile weapons hot. The sight fills me with relief.

I give them a nod. "You sending this footage to HQ?"

"Yes, Investigator Chen," they reply.

I lean toward where Trezon's ear should be. "Make yourself visible. Do it now. Or I pull this trigger."

"Go ahead." He chuckles. "When I eventually come to, I'll simply walk out of here. Your drones can't see me, and they won't be able to stop me."

He's right. But he doesn't know everything my drones can do.

"Wink, tag the space directly beneath me with a nano dart."

The drone fires the dart, and it pierces Trezon's invisible shoulder. Or thereabouts, judging from my hold on him.

"What the hell is that?" he demands.

"The nanobot solution is now in your tissue, and it's spreading. There's nowhere you can go that we won't find you. My drones, me, every tracker tasked with your capture. Say goodbye to your short-lived freedom, you son of a bitch."

I don't give him time to respond. I just pull the trigger.

The shock is strong enough to throw me off his shuddering body, and I clamp my jaw tight to keep from biting my own tongue in two. The ceiling light fades in and out as my limbs shake in spasms, my torso convulsing like I'm possessed by one of those evil spirits in a horror-themed VR Storyline.

Then, without warning, everything goes dark, and I'm drifting off to the best sleep I haven't had in a very long while...

13

"You cannot stop him," Dr. Solomon Wong tells me.

He stands in front of the speedlift door in the hangar of Futuro Tower, right where he tried to kill me. Right where I killed him.

This is how I always see him, bloody and back from the dead, with the melee of his frantic clones frozen in time around us, their projectile weapons firing up at Wink and Blink, who let loose their own barrage, sparking, flashing, paused in midair. This is the split-second before he shoots me with that laser welder, concealed for the moment in the pocket of his lab coat.

"He has help," Wong says, "a kind you cannot begin to fathom."

"Leave me alone," I moan, wishing he would disappear so I can go back to sleep, deep and dark, embracing me like a long-lost lover.

But no, that's not in the cards for Sera Chen. She can't so much as nod off without seeing this old megalomaniac again and hearing him go on and on about some sort of nascent impending doom. This is what I've been trying to avoid by taking those stimulants.

They've obviously lost their potency.

"He spent months in that correctional center planning every step. Now the plan is in motion. His followers have been activated." Wong's brow furrows, and he shakes his head at me. "You should have joined me. We could have outlived these trying times, left it all in the past. Unremembered history."

"You wanted to cryo-freeze us..."

"You could have slept through the turmoil that is to come. Now you will live through it. Everything I wanted to save you from." He starts to dissolve like a disabled hologram. "You will not escape any part of it."

"What?"

"The end of your world."

The second he vanishes completely, the violence around me is unpaused, lurching into action. Loud and frenetic, projectile rounds exploding at close proximity as my drones force the clones into hiding.

We're across the Mediterranean from Dome 10 on the shore of North Africa, what might have been Morocco or Algeria in ancient times. This was where Wong planned to live out the centuries in cryo-sleep while his clones figured out a way to terraform the desolate Earth. Last I heard, they're still at it, supervised by the clone of Persephone Hawthorne herself—who has a much better grip on reality than the woman whose image she bears—but sans their almighty creator.

Guilt causes me to see Wong's ghost like this. Usually, I'm able to snap wide awake to avoid hearing him talk. But this time, I was too sound asleep to escape his speechmaking. And now I'm too groggy to comprehend what the hell he was rambling on about.

Unless he meant Trezon, of course. In which case, my guilty subconscious mind manifested itself as the man I killed...in order to warn me. Which makes about as much sense as seeing his blood-drenched ghost every time I catch a split-second of sleep.

My eyelids flutter open to find myself still lying on the floor of the speedlift. Wink and Blink are hovering in the hallway outside, right where I left them. But now they have company in the form of Chief Inspector Hudson, who's crouching down to study me as I come to.

"Good. You're all right." He rises and tucks his hands into the pockets of his overcoat. With an irritated expression, he glances over his shoulder at my drones. "Get on your feet, Chen. If you can."

I slap my hand at the empty space beside me. Trezon is no longer there.

"Where is he?" I demand, struggling to rise. My shocker packs a real punch.

"You were right." Hudson gives me a nod. "I apologize for not believing you."

"Tell me you've got him."

"Trezon the Invisible? Yes, we have him, Chen. Excellent idea to tag him with a nano dart. Your drones were able to cast his location directly to our lenses. Trackers are now escorting him to the rubble that remains of the rooftop, where our aerocars are waiting." He almost smiles as he extends his arm toward the stairwell door down the hall. "Shall we?"

I glance at the floor. "The baton—"

"Also in custody. And earlier you mentioned a narcotic

sample?"

"Breather." I pat my jacket pocket. It's there, whatever Trezon/Prometheus gave to his adoring fans. "I have it."

He nods, pleased. "We'll get it analyzed and see how it's affecting dust addicts to cause those lethal overdoses. An investigation that is still ongoing, I presume?"

"Yeah." I frown. "I mean yes, sir. I'm on it."

It's probably normal to feel out of sorts after being hit with a shocker. Now I know how those violators used to feel when I was a curfew enforcer. But there's more to it than that. Something isn't right. I can't allow myself to believe that Trezon has been captured, that Hudson's change in demeanor is genuine.

Appearances to the contrary, this isn't over. I'm missing something. Something important.

"Commander Bishop was right. You're a real asset to our division," Hudson says as we head toward the stairwell with Wink and Blink hovering behind me.

"Where's Erik?" I blurt out. "He was on this floor—"

"Erik Paine is on his way to MedCenter 1 at the moment."

"Is he all right?"

"He was unconscious when our trackers found him, but his vitals were normal. Trezon *hijacked* him?"

I nod. "His abilities. Erik's a...demigod, sir." Hate that term. Moving on. "Trezon was somehow able to take over and make Erik do what he wanted him to."

"Which involved leaping onto this rooftop?" Hudson's voice echoes in the stairwell as we climb up and out onto the roof—a complete disaster zone. "And then demolishing it?"

The entire area is scorched black from the semtex, the roof access enclosure no longer in existence, along with anything else that used to be up here. A pair of aerocars pivot in midair off the side of the building to head toward the maglev tunnel into Dome 1. One vehicle remains with its engines thrumming and a pair of trackers standing beside the open door. Both male, they wear lightweight tactical gear—nothing as formidable as a security clone's armor, but sturdy enough to handle what the average miscreant might throw at pursuers. No electronic components, so impervious to EMP grenades, and able to take a projectile round at point-blank range.

They keep their gaze set straight ahead in a very military-like posture. Probably ex-marines, as many trackers are. The grizzled hair and beards make them close in age to Interim Chancellor Bishop. They might have even served with him, back in the day.

"I don't understand Trezon's motivation, sir," I admit.

"How did the civilian become involved? Is Paine a member of this *Prometheus* cult?" Hudson frowns at me as we reach the waiting aerocar. "The Children of Tomorrow?"

"No, he's just a...friend."

"Who happened to be at the same warehouse you were investigating?" He studies my reaction, as if he's the one suffering from trust issues.

"I didn't tell him I would be there." I wait for Wink and Blink to descend to the ash-covered rooftop at my feet and go into standby mode, their quadcopter rotors coming to a standstill. Then I scoop them up, one under each arm.

"Of course not. No investigator on a case would divulge such information. But I know about your shared history. As well as his interest in you."

Is Hudson trying to provoke me? "We grew up together.

And we went through a fairly intense situation recently."

"So he isn't stalking you?" Hudson raises an eyebrow.

Technically, Erik is; but he found me in virtual and then in the flesh due to our mutual friend's concern. The Drasko connection should be obvious, but Hudson doesn't bring it up.

"Erik might have a...crush on me, sir." I duck under the door and climb into the passenger compartment of the aerocar, adding over my shoulder, "Nothing I can't handle."

"See that you do. We can't allow civilians to become entangled in our efforts to contain organized crime." He pulls his coat tight around him as the engines send a steady stream of air outward in all directions from underneath the vehicle. Then he joins me inside, seating himself on the bench across from me. Without meaning to, we strap on the safety harnesses simultaneously. "You're certain he's not a dust freak?"

"Erik? Not that I know of." I keep my focus on the buckle as I adjust my harness straps. Wink and Blink sit stacked on top of each other in my lap, and I keep one arm around them to hold them in place.

"A *demigod*, you say. Something the two of you have in common?"

I glance up and find Hudson giving me a knowing smile.

"Your habit of switching off your augments was a dead giveaway. The abilities won't manifest themselves as long as you're online, from what I've heard. Paine has that in common with you."

The trackers—neither of them with half the personality of a security clone—seat themselves without a word, one beside me and the other next to Hudson. As the side door lowers automatically and locks into place, the pilot takes us aloft, turning in midair to follow the pair of aerocars that left a minute ago.

"As does every member of the Twenty, whether they realize it or not." Hudson tilts his head to one side as he appraises me. "And yet Trezon is not interested in any of you. He broke a couple of your fingers but left you otherwise intact. He *rode* Paine up onto that roof and then cast him aside like a worn-out horse. Why is that, when he wants what both of you have? Abilities that don't appear with the snorting of some North American dust and then fizzle out after a few minutes of wonderment. Permanent, godlike power is what he seeks."

I nod, uncomfortable with this conversation but pushing through it anyway. Being one of the Twenty has been bad enough; I've never liked the special attention. Now add to that these abilities I try to keep to myself. I never make a show of using them. That's not who I am. They help me with my job, and that's what I limit them to.

So maybe that's another reason why I've been avoiding Erik. Because we both can find out what the other one is thinking whenever we want to, and I'm not ready for that kind of intimacy on a regular basis with anybody.

"Trezon invited us backstage and told us some strange things."

"About?"

"Our DNA." I look out the window as the grime of Dome 10 passes and we enter the maglev tunnel, maintaining a couple meters' distance above the vacant rail as we hurtle through the dark. "And the DNA of our...children."

"Dr. Wong's genetic creations," Hudson muses. "So

Trezon was planning to kidnap them? Sample their DNA for his purposes?"

"I think so." I shake my head and return my gaze to the Chief Inspector. "I doubt it will come to pass, now that he's in custody."

You cannot stop him, Wong's warning flashes through my mind—what his ghost, or my hallucination, said to me while I was unconscious. I do my best not to act startled and hope I'm not losing it. *He has help, the kind you cannot begin to fathom...*

"We can hope." Hudson gives me a nod of what could be mistaken for approval. "I was wrong to take you off the Trezon case. I see that now. And I'm not one to withhold credit where credit is due. You, Investigator Chen, will be the officer on record for this collar."

I don't know what to say. So I go with the customary, "Thank you, sir."

It could be argued that I was unconscious while the arrest actually took place, but then again, they were my drones who secured the scene. And only an idiot would argue with her superior about a thing like this.

"I have already notified Commander Bishop." Another knowing smile. "Her response: 'Well done, Chen.'"

Now I really have no idea how to respond. So I just nod and focus on my drones sitting in my lap while a welcome warmth spreads inside my chest. This is what joy feels like. It's been a while.

But then I have to go and ruin it.

"How's Dunn, sir?" At his blank expression, I rephrase, "My partner. Unit D1-436?"

His expression doesn't change. "I assumed you already

knew—that you were receiving updates in real-time." He frowns. "I notified Level 5 that you were to be kept in the loop."

My turn to stare blankly. "Nobody's told me anything, sir." And it's not like I've ever been able to call Dunn whenever I wanted to. When he's with his handlers on the 5th floor, he goes dark. I tried pinging him when we first started working together as partners, and I received an error message. I assumed such would definitely be the case with him on an operating table. And yet he was able to contact Fort—

"D1-436 is gone, Chen." Hudson shrugs as if he doesn't know what else to tell me.

My insides cave in. My heart races double-time. My vision goes blurry.

"That can't be..." Dunn can't be dead. The doctors were working on him. They were helping him. He was going to pull through. I couldn't stay with him; they wouldn't let me. I had a case to work on. I had to go to that damn warehouse.

I left him to die.

My harness is suddenly too tight, and I can't breathe. I have to loosen the straps.

It's all my fault. I killed them both. A clone I named Fort, that I just met, and a clone I named Dunn, who saved my life more than once.

"I want to see him." My voice is barely audible.

"I'm sure you do." Hudson scoffs.

Fury wells up inside me, and it's all I can do not to let it escape. Clenching my jaw, I grate out, "Don't tell me he's already been recycled."

"Recycled?" Hudson frowns, confused. "No one can find

it, Chen."

"What?" The interior of the aerocar suddenly feels twice its actual size as my vision clears. My heart's still racing, but now it's for an entirely different reason. "He's *gone*?"

"That's what I said. The unit left medical without anyone seeing its departure." He shakes his head irritably. "It's gone dark. No one has a clue where it went."

I might have an idea. "Take me back." Retrieving the breather I got from the *Prometheus* show, I hand it to him. "Let me know the test results when you have them. I have to go back to Dome 10. That's where Dunn will be."

Hudson pockets the breather in his coat. "How can you be sure?"

"He knew I needed help." There's no other explanation for it. "He's loyal, sir. That's just who he is."

Hudson narrows his gaze, studying me again. From the moment we first met, he's never known what to make of me. "And how the hell would a sedated security clone, just out of surgery, know that Investigator Sera Chen needed help?"

Time for show and tell. I've been hoping to avoid this, but I suppose now's as good a time as any. "You said it yourself, Chief." I double-tap my temple and project a single thought into his mind: *I'm one of those weird demigods.*

He lurches back in his seat, his spine ramrod straight and his eyes open wide. *She can read minds—or at least plant thoughts into them. She's probably reading mine at this very moment. Stop thinking, fool!* As his thoughts cavort through a maelstrom of chaos, he clears his throat with impressive calm and asks, "You believe that your clone partner received...an unconventional message from you."

I nod and reactivate my augments. Not because I need

them right now. Because I think it might put Hudson at ease knowing I can't read his mind during our conversation. "When Trezon took Erik...I felt helpless to stop him. Somehow, Dunn must have picked up on that."

"Fifty kilometers away in a different Dome." Hudson isn't scoffing now, but he's having trouble believing it.

So am I. There's never been any evidence that my telepathic ability extends that far. But maybe Fort somehow acted as a relay—receiving my telepathic message to go after Erik and passing it on to Dunn via that private network they shared.

Otherwise, why would he have left medical?

But that's not the important thing here. Dunn is alive and well, and he's able to move on his own. The surgery was a success!

"Why haven't you been able to track D1-436?" I frown. As far as I know, security clones—even the evolving variety—are unable to take themselves off-grid.

Hudson graces me with a steely expression. Then he turns his attention to the pilot. "Drop us off at HQ, then return Investigator Chen to Dome 10."

The pilot nods.

"Grounding you would be a futile endeavor," Hudson continues, focused on me again. "So far, your insomnia hasn't affected your work, that I can tell. The moment it does, you will report to MedTech for a mandatory rest period. I'll have you sedated, Chen, if I have to. Investigators always need to be at their best."

"I am, sir," I lie. Of course he knows about my lack-of-sleeping habits. That robodoc reported everything it found wrong with me.

He pauses to study me for a moment. "Trezon had a hacked clone at that warehouse, you said. What was it like?"

"How do you mean, sir?" Not sure what he's getting at.

"Did it remind you of your partner? Or did it behave more like a standard security clone?"

No personality, in other words. "Neither, really. It mimicked Trezon and Krime." Same sense of style, or lack thereof. "Even down to the facial tattoos."

"Interesting." Hudson absently scratches at his well-manicured beard. "Do they share the same intellect as their creator, do you think?"

"Not all of them."

"Explain."

I shrug, not exactly comfortable talking about the apparition from my nightmares. "Wong created all of his clones in his image, but that's where the similarity ends. The ones working in Futuro Tower, trying to figure out how to terraform our planet, obviously share a certain degree of his genius-level abilities. But security clones?" I shake my head. "They're conditioned to behave like soldiers." I glance at the stoic trackers sitting beside us. Neither one has made a sound or moved a muscle since they took their seats. "Follow orders. Serve and protect."

Hudson nods, narrowing his gaze at me again. "And so D1-436 was merely acting on its conditioning when it left medical before taking sufficient time to heal after surgery. Following an order it somehow received from you." He pauses. "Or is there a stronger bond between the two of you?"

"He's my partner, sir."

"Does your partner consider itself a *he* or an *it*?"

I look out the side porthole as the aerocar emerges from the shadows of the maglev tunnel into the glory of Dome 1. Squinting my eyes, I take in the shimmering beauty of blue-tinted sunlight reflected from the mirrored surface of every domescraper, glinting off the windscreens of at least a hundred aerocars in flight, gliding along multiple lanes of aerial traffic three layers high.

"Before working with Dunn, I thought of clones as things. Not much different from bots," I admit. "They served a function as the Chancellor's security force, and they were programmed, for lack of a better word, to do their job exceptionally well."

"And now?" Hudson raises an eyebrow.

I meet his gaze, unsure why he's so interested in my working relationship with Dunn all of a sudden. "I don't think my partner fully realizes that he's changing. Becoming more of a person than a conditioned non-person, if that makes any sense." The tracker sitting beside Hudson fixes me with a cool stare. I ignore him. "I have no idea what Dunn thinks of himself, but to me, he's not just a thing."

"Have you discussed the matter with your father?"

Another weird question from beyond the blue.

"I don't... We're both very busy. He's a doctor, as you know—"

"Dr. Chen? Yes, I'm sure. But I was referring to your biological father. His name is Luther, I believe. Some sort of cult leader in Dome 6, is that right?"

"He would probably phrase it differently."

"A leader of the Way, then. What does he have to say about the personhood of clones?" Both of the trackers are watching me now. But Hudson is scrutinizing my reaction.

"I'm simply curious as to whether he's influenced you to think of clones as...more than what they are."

I refrain from grinding my teeth, as much as I'd like to at the moment. "I don't know what his beliefs are on the subject. We've never discussed it. My interactions with D1-436 and D1-440 have led me to believe that Dr. Wong's clones have the potential to become people if treated as such." I leave it at that.

But Hudson isn't finished. "It was illegal across the globe for well over a century. Human cloning. And that mindset followed us into the Ten Domes. The only way Wong received permission from the Chancellor was by convincing her that we had no other choice as a society. You and your siblings had not yet been discovered in that North American bunker, and the human race was on a direct course to extinction. But if we could clone ourselves, Wong argued, then we would never die out. Something along those lines."

"He was his own test subject."

Hudson nods. "There were concerns that clones would age quickly and deteriorate, that we would be creating human-like organisms we knew would suffer and then expire. It violated the Hippocratic Oath promising to do no harm—in the same way as fetal abortions. Wong's first attempts were far from successful, but he and his staff learned invaluable lessons through the process. And when the Twenty were discovered shortly thereafter, you became Wong's primary focus. But he didn't abandon his clone project, which is why we have them to this day." He scoffs quietly. "Whether or not we need them. Or even want them."

I'm not sure what to say to that.

"When one of them is damaged, we recycle it," he

continues. "Wong left all of the technology in place to grow replacements for the two dozen or so that we have on hand. Of course the Chancellor's edict made it clear that we would never allow any more than that to live among us. We don't want them overrunning Eurasia. Especially not if they start thinking of themselves as *people*." He gives me a sardonic look. "Then where would the rest of us be?"

Not sure what he means by that. Is he afraid of them? Does the prospect of clones one day holding humankind accountable for the way we've treated them make him nervous? Is he worried about the clones in Futuro Tower across the sea rising up and storming the gates? I could deactivate my augments and probe his brain to find out, but I really don't care.

I need to find Dunn. For the moment, that's all that matters.

14

The aerocar heads straight for HQ, running its flashers to clear a path through aerial traffic lanes. The windscreen darkens automatically as we face the sun, brilliant through Dome 1's tinted surface. A golden orb sinking toward the west. It's been a long day, but I have a feeling it's going to be a while longer before I can return to my cube for some downtime.

Scratch that. Not thinking straight again. My cube is missing a windowall at present. I'll need to contact the building superintendent and see about getting that fixed as soon as possible. Guess I could tape up some plastic sheeting in the interim. Not that I plan on sleeping there or anything, but a little time in VR might be a welcome diversion after today's events.

We touch down on the roof of police headquarters, and the side door drifts open as Hudson and the trackers unbuckle their harnesses. I stay put with Wink and Blink and wait until the trackers have stepped outside before clearing my throat. Stooped over on his way out, Hudson glances back at me with mild interest.

"Sir, please let me know the moment Erik is conscious. I

want to be there."

"Of course. Now go find your partner, Chen." He almost smiles before the expression drops away. "Whether D1-436 is a person or not doesn't matter to me. Its loyalty to you is really quite remarkable. I will continue to monitor your partnership with great interest."

He steps out of the aerocar and heads straight to the speedlift door without a glance back. The two trackers follow him like rigid automatons. Yet they're considered people without question.

"Back to Dome 10, Chen?" the pilot confirms, half-turning in his seat to face me. The vehicle's side door drops back into place and locks.

"Thanks." It's weird not to see Drasko at the controls. I've never worked with this pilot before, but he seems competent. He got us through the train tunnel at a steady clip without shearing off any of the vehicle's paint, so that's something. Close to Drasko's age, grey around the temples, clean-shaven and a little underweight, he doesn't talk much but is personable enough. "As fast as you can."

He nods, and we're aloft, pivoting in midair to head back the way we came. Within seconds, the aerocar is out of Dome 1's traffic lanes and hurtling through the dark maglev tunnel. With Trezon back in custody, it shouldn't be long before the trains are running again, and pilots will have to plan these daring tunnel flights accordingly.

As we reemerge into Dome 10's rusty sunlight, I lean forward to point out the scorched rooftop of the building we left minutes ago.

"Right there's fine."

Another nod from the pilot, who takes us up into

completely vacant air space. For some reason, Dome 10 never has much in the way of aerial traffic. No domescrapers, either. Everyone stationed here must be more intent on ground level concerns than anything above them.

It's tough to imagine what their lives are like. If I had to live and work here, I'd spend every spare moment I had in VR. Maybe that's what they do. Nobody pays much attention to their surroundings, which is why the dome's interior hasn't been cleaned in decades, and a layer of filth coats just about every surface. Erik once told me the grungy feel was the locals' way of getting back at the Governors for assigning them positions in sanitation and waste management. Maybe at first, that was the case. But the only way this level of grime could be allowed to fester unchecked is by choosing not to see it at all.

The aerocar sets down with a soft bump against the engines' air cushion, and the side door floats open for me. Nodding my thanks to the pilot and receiving another wordless nod in return, I unbuckle my safety harness and carry my drones out of the vehicle. Once we're halfway across the roof, the aerocar ascends with a jet wash that sends my hair flying upward. Then the vehicle soars off, maneuvering a wide turn that will take it back to Dome 1.

I toss Wink and Blink into the air one at a time.

"Locate Dunn," I tell them via our shared audiolink as their status lights blink on and their rotors spin up, holding them aloft.

"Unit D1-436 is offline, Investigator Chen," they reply in unison.

He's got to be here somewhere. Maybe back at the warehouse?

"Wink, establish a search pattern radiating outward from this location. Blink, head back to the cult's warehouse and do the same from that point of origin."

They veer off in separate directions.

"And lay low. Any citizen even glances up at you, alter course immediately. Understood?"

"Yes, Investigator Chen."

I walk to the edge of the rooftop and watch them go. Wink circles the building in ever-expanding arcs while Blink speeds off into the distance, heading toward the docks. My boots crunch across the charred remains of the parapet designed to keep citizens like myself from tumbling off the edge to their deaths. Ash trickles over the side as my toes disturb it. Doubtful the foot traffic below will even notice the stuff sprinkling down around them.

Gravity weapons. Exploding holograms. Invisibility you can turn on and off at will. Trezon really upped his game. Now that he's out of the picture, I should feel some measure of relief. But I'm still amped, heart racing, adrenaline pumping. Maybe it's residue from those stimulants I've been taking.

More likely, I'm worried about Dunn. Why the hell would he be offline after leaving HQ? And why didn't anybody notice him leaving? It doesn't make sense.

An alert blinks at the periphery of my ocular lenses. VR-related. Someone has left me a message. I blink to pull it up front and center, obscuring my view of the street below: *S - Meet in VR - Usual spot - D.*

So now Drasko's available for a virtual face-to-face? Makes sense, I guess. With Trezon in custody, Drasko doesn't have to worry about his predecessor coming after him. He can afford to climb out of his bunker—if not in reality, then in virtual.

I take a seat there on the edge of the rooftop and dangle my feet over the side. The ash underneath me should make an interesting pattern across my backside, but nobody around here will notice. They've only got eyes for the Link.

Diving into VR, I enter the familiar future-noir Storyline and make my way straight to Howard's Tavern through the busy streets and acid rain of a city where it's always night, yet no one ever sleeps. Julian gives me the all-clear nod as I enter, and I give him half a smile as I head toward my booth in the back corner. A cursory glance around the premises is all I need to know that the same AI characters are here as before, minding their own artificial business.

The avatar sitting alone in my booth is the man I'm here to see. Facing away from me, wearing the same uniform as every other guy in this virtual world: fedora, overcoat, suit and tie, leather shoes, all in shades of grey and black. No colors to be found, because he's not here to play any games.

Neither am I.

"Have you had your aerocar fumigated recently?" I slide into the seat opposite him and give him a quick once-over. It's the same avatar Drasko always uses, a world-weary private eye named Charlie Madison. War vet struggling to make ends meet. His threads are shabby enough to show he's not starving, but he's not rolling in credits, either.

"Don't fly much anymore," Drasko replies with a knowing look and crooked half-smile. That's the right response, so I know it's him behind the unshaven mask of his avatar. But he takes things a step further to make sure it's me behind mine.   "Did you check out that author I recommended?"

I shake my head. "H.G. Wells' works aren't so popular these days. Even with Chancellor Bishop lifting the book bans, readers find them...unsavory."

Drasko shrugs. "To each their own."

I lean forward. "You're someplace safe."

"Sorry I couldn't meet you earlier." He scratches at his nose. One of Drasko's ticks. "I know it must have worried you."

"Figured you were avoiding the Invisible Man."

"For a minute or two, I thought he might come after me. But I was too busy to go into hiding. Too many illegal irons in the fire." He smirks. "No rest for the wicked, as they say."

I lean back. "Erik said you were lying low."

"That's what I wanted him to tell you. So you wouldn't concern yourself with my welfare."

I scoff quietly. "But it's okay for you to worry about me? Sending Erik to the warehouse? What the hell was that all about? He's a damn civilian!"

"If you think I worry about you too much, ratchet that level up a few hundred percent, and that's where you'll find Erik." He winks.

"No. You'll find him in a MedCenter." I cross my arms and stare Drasko's avatar down. "That's what happens when you involve a civilian in an ongoing investigation."

His expression collapses. "You're right. It was a mistake. But my contacts tell me he's going to pull through."

"You have contacts in the Dome 1 medical center?" I shouldn't be surprised.

"I have contacts in every Dome, Sera." He shrugs it off, the criminality not something he's proud of. A necessary evil.

"The loyal ones tell me things. Which is why we needed to meet."

Julian holds up a bottle behind the bar, but I shake my head. No drinks tonight. He nods and goes back to drying shot glasses. There must be a never-ending supply.

"Some of your contacts have become disloyal?" I narrow my gaze. The timing can't be a coincidence. Trezon must have gotten to them. "Do you have a mutiny on your hands?"

"Nothing I can't take care of," Drasko says gruffly. Then he leans toward me, both his elbows on the table. Enough chatter. Time for business. "Word is, the meat trucks are going after younger fare."

I take a moment to decipher that. The term *meat trucks* refers to human trafficking. Sex workers tend to be from the Terminal Generation, men and women in their thirties. The oldest profession since ancient times is still illegal in the Domes, but that doesn't mean much. Rumor has it even a few of our Governors like to partake of the forbidden flesh. But *younger fare*? The only citizens younger than thirty would be members of the Twenty, and I can't imagine any of us needing to rent out our bodies in order to make a living. Each of us was placed in a financially stable family in one of the upper castes. Including Erik in Dome 9; sure, he was raised on a farm, but his adoptive parents ran the collective, overseeing production on more than a dozen parcels of land in that agricultural Dome.

Then it hits me.

"You don't mean..." I trail off. Children of the Twenty. *Children of Tomorrow.* "Kids."

He nods. "The trucks have been repurposed, you might

say. Without any orders from me."

Someone is sending the underworlds' human traffickers after our children. Trezon implied that something like this would happen, and that there'd be nothing I could do about it. He wanted their DNA. He thought it would somehow turn dust addicts into demigods. But how can he be the one still calling the shots? He's on his way back to the correctional center at this very moment.

"Then who gave the order?" I frown, unable to focus on his avatar.

I think back to my altercation with Trezon in the speedlift. It ended with both of us incapacitated, but I was alone when I came to. I never actually saw him escorted away by the trackers. I only saw that pair of aerocars departing from the scorched rooftop. One carried Trezon, and the other had Erik, each headed for a different destination.

Or so Hudson told me.

"Any other situation, I'd follow the money." Drasko shakes his head, tracing the grain of the tabletop with his eyes. "But nobody's paid them off. Not yet, anyhow. The trucks have mobilized, and they have their targets in sight. That's all I can tell you right now. When I know more..." He leans back and prepares to vacate his seat.

I keep my voice low. "Over a thousand kids to choose from." Scattered across the domes. Law enforcement could get to maybe a few hundred in time. But the rest? "We don't have the personnel to protect them all. Not without starting a panic."

"The Governors always have scapegoats for this sort of thing, don't they?" His avatar gives me a wink as he steps out into the empty aisle between booths and then pauses to button up his overcoat.

"You could stop the trucks," I tell him.

His avatar gives me a sad look that says I should know better. And of course I do. He's not in this current underworld role to make himself rich. He's doing it to support his ailing family in Dome 6, and to keep Eurasia's criminal enterprises in check. If he acts out brazenly against his underlings in the human trafficking business, he'll lose face. That's when he'll have a mutiny on his hands. His family will lose their beloved husband and father, and Commander Bishop will lose her inside man.

I'll lose my friend.

"Good to see you, Vivian, as always. Sorry there isn't much of a market for Wells anymore. You might have better luck with Stevenson. A lot of people living dual lives these days." He tips his hat to me.

"See you around, Charlie." I nod as he turns to leave.

Aliases and code phrases. Nothing that can tie us to who we are in the real world. A good analyst might be able to figure it out, given enough time and more frequent VR meetings between me and Drasko, but we do our best to remain low on the threat echelon. The word *scapegoats* won't get flagged like *Patriots* would have.

Home-grown terrorists. Malcontents living in the outlying Domes, unhappy with their station in life. The Governors assigned them laborious jobs which they work at day in and day out by the sweat of their brow, while the upper castes get to kick back and enjoy the good life in Dome 1. It's really no different from the Old World, when North America was divided and conquered by the United World government, who designated sectors for agriculture, manufacturing, technological development, even human reproduction. The rest of the world lived off what the North Americans produced: food, machines, tech, as well as human minds and bodies to keep everything moving in the right direction—straight to the consumers.

Over the years, discontent festered and a subversive group of radicals emerged. They called themselves Patriots, hearkening back to ancient times when a few colonies banded together to break free from a powerful empire. Except these terrorists managed to get hold of dangerous bioweapons and were prepared to aerosolize them into the upper atmosphere unless their demands for greater freedom were met. The United World government couldn't allow that to happen. So they nuked North America to eliminate the threat. And the nuclear winters that followed affected the entire globe, exterminating all life on the surface.

The UW was prepared for such an eventuality. Across North America, bunkers had been constructed deep underground, and housed inside were the best and brightest from every sector, young people in their teens and twenties—including the biological parents of the Twenty—taken from their families to survive the next twenty years while dust and ash claimed the earth. In Eurasia, the domed cities had already been built to protect our people from the sun's harmful rays as well as ever-worsening air pollution. Now the Domes were civilization's last bastion.

It's easy to say the UW overreacted. Destroying an entire planet in order to eliminate a threat? Seems like overkill. But they must have known what those bioweapons were capable of, if unleashed by the Patriots. The genetic mutations, the hideous deaths. Risking the future of humankind as well as

Earth itself was an acceptable sacrifice. They counted the cost and bet heavily on themselves.

Now we have dust freaks and so-called demigods. Instead of originating from the spirits of extinct animals blasted to ash by a salvo of nuclear weapons, as Luther believes, maybe it's a result of those bioweapons stolen by the terrorists. Aerosolized at the same moment the nuclear blasts obliterated them and everything else, blending elements of devastating biological weapons with radioactive dust blanketing the continent? Breathed into the lungs to have its way with one's DNA. Temporarily for some. Permanently for those of us related to the North American survivors. Except we don't have to snort any dust in order to perform our superhuman feats; they're already part of who we are. Our unique genetic structure. But according to Luther, no geneticist has been able to identify a single marker that makes us different from your average human being. Hence his belief in a spiritual explanation.

I shake my head, unable to make any sense of it. Still seated in the booth, I trace the grain of the tabletop with my avatar's index finger and focus on the present, piecing together the intel I received from Drasko. Somehow, Trezon's plan is still in motion, even with him supposedly out of the picture. But the only way to halt the meat trucks in their tracks would be an all-Domes lockdown. And the only way I can think of to justify such a thing would be the imminent threat of a terrorist attack.

Even if no such threat exists at the moment.

Chancellor Bishop has gone out of his way to meet with the leaders of various Patriot sects and hear their grievances. He's made plans to address the class inequalities that have plagued our society from its infancy, and if one is to believe any of the off-the-cuff speeches he's made, he seems to think real change is possible. There's no way he'll be on board with blaming any of these insurgent groups for something they haven't done, now that they've been in peace talks for weeks.

What will our modern-day Patriot factions do if we accuse them of planning a fresh insurrection? The peace talks will crumble. Law enforcement, with the help of the Chancellor's security clones, will quash any violence that erupts. But in the process, we will foster roots of bitterness we'll have to contend with for the foreseeable future.

Dr. Wong seemed to think our domed society was on the brink of implosion. Hence, his desire to cryo-sleep in Futuro Tower through the turmoil and reemerge on the other side, well-rested, with terraforming efforts designed by his clones ready to implement. To restore Earth to the wonder and beauty we see now only in VR.

There will be no implosion. We've handled the so-called Patriots before, and we can do it again. Even if it means disrupting an uneasy peace that's only just begun to take root. An untold number of human traffickers are going after a thousand children ranging in age from a few months to eight years old. Eurasia's future. We must protect them at all costs.

I've got to tell the Chancellor. Only he can issue a lockdown across the Domes. Then, with all ground and air traffic halted, the meat trucks will have to find a place to park and wait it out. And we'll have to find a way to protect the children without starting a panic. Hudson won't like me going over his head, but I can't trust him with this. There's only one person I can, and I'm not sure she'll answer my hail.

She's a real stickler for protocol.

I exit the booth and give Julian a nod as I take my leave. Entering the downpour outside, I make my way to the usual dark alley devoid of fellow players or AI characters and swim out of VR, breaking through the surface into reality. I blink and squint, holding up a hand against the murky light of dusk filtering through Dome 10's dirty plexicon. My boots dangle over a six-story drop.

With a gasp, I scramble back from the edge of the building, heart pounding, smearing ash all over my hands in the process. Not sure what I was thinking, diving into VR right there. Sleep deprivation and poor decision-making go hand in hand, I suppose.

Fingers crossed this isn't another bad idea, I prepare to hail Commander Bishop. But that's when I receive an update from Wink and Blink:

"No sign of Unit D1-436, Investigator Chen. Expand search perimeter?"

"Affirmative." Where else would he go? This doesn't make any sense. "Search all of Dome 10 and then return to my location. Maintain a low profile."

"Understood," they reply in unison.

I try hailing Dunn again, but I receive the same error message: *Unit D1-436 is currently offline.* Cursing under my breath, I grit my teeth and hail Commander Bishop. A few seconds pass, then a few more. No response. I haven't tried hailing her directly since I was promoted to Investigator. Maybe my access has been revoked.

Then a holo of Mara Bishop's stern face and clean-shaven head appears before me, for my eyes only. "Is there a reason you're ignoring chain of command, Chen?"

"Has Trezon been returned to the correctional center, Ma'am?"

Her brow furrows. "I was not aware that he's in custody." Her eyes lose focus as she does a little research on her side of things. "According to our analysts, he is still at large."

I curse out loud. "I had him. Damn it, I had him!"

"Compose yourself, Investigator." She raises her chin. "Tell me what's going on."

"It's Hudson. They're working together." My heart rate picks up the pace again. "They have been all along. And now they're going after the children."

"Chen—"

"Our children, Ma'am, it's in their DNA. I don't know how, but they want to use it to become *gods*."

"I need you to slow down. Take a breath."

"Erik." A chill washes over me. "Hudson said Erik Paine was on his way to the MedCenter. Can you verify that?"

Commander Bishop looks away, her eyes glazed over again. Then she blinks and looks straight at me. When she speaks, her voice is completely calm. "Sera, you don't look well. According to your recent exam, you haven't slept in weeks. How are you managing to function at all?"

I curse again and shake my head, grinding my teeth. "They're working together. Hudson and Trezon. They've sent underworld operatives after the children—"

"Whose children?"

"—and there's nothing I can do." I close my eyes to keep the rooftop from swaying beneath me and press my palms against my temples. "Please, Ma'am. We have to lock it down. Halt all ground traffic, air traffic. Keep the meat trucks from moving out in the open…"

"Stay right where you are. Do you hear me? Sera?"

Commander Bishop's voice floats away, and her hologram dissolves as I fall. But it's a short drop this time, so I don't need my exo or its cables. Not like I have my suit anymore, anyway. Hudson saw to that.

The traitor.

I land flat on my back in a puff of ash, and as the sun goes down all around me, I hear what sounds like footsteps crunching my way through the charred debris. Maybe. How should I know?

I'm too busy...drifting off to sleep.

15

It's him again.

"*Treasure Island, Kidnapped, The Black Arrow, The Strange Case of Dr. Jekyll and Mr. Hyde...*" Dr. Wong lists a few of Stevenson's works and leans back against the polished speedlift door.

We're in the upper hangar of Futuro Tower, where I always see him. His clones are frozen all around him with their projectile weapons at the ready, fierce looks of determination on their identical faces, white lab coats flailing as they fire their rounds past me at Erik, Daiyna, Wink and Blink. They're stuck in time as well. I'm strapped into my exo-suit, looming over Wong.

He taps an index finger against his chin in thought. "Which one do you think Drasko was referring to?"

"What?" I scowl down at him.

Why am I here? How did I fall asleep? Those damned stimulants have worn off. The last pill I popped was back in my cube, and that was before Trezon showed up to ruin Dunn's day—as well as my own. So it's been a while.

I remember seeing the sun go down. I was on the edge of that demolished rooftop, my boots dangling over empty space. That's where I am right now, lying sound asleep on a pile of ash as night falls across the Domes.

"What the hell are you talking about?"

Wong shrugs, stuffing his hands into the pockets of his lab coat. I cringe inwardly, remembering what he has in one of those pockets. Pain flares up in my shoulder at the memory of what he's going to do with it.

And then my stomach sinks as I remember what I'm going to do to him. A knee-jerk reaction. The minigun mounted on the shoulder of my exo won't be triggered intentionally. It'll go off just as a searing beam of light tears through my flesh and bone.

"This is your memory, Sera. I'm simply trying to help you sort through it." He smiles up at me like a kind grandfather. He's much older than he looks, of course. Thanks to his advancements in gene therapy, every octogenarian in Eurasia who can afford it looks like a healthy, active middle-ager. Even so, the grey at his temples and the way the skin crinkles around his eyes sets him apart from his clones, who look exactly as he did when he was my age. "You do remember the Stevenson reference, don't you?"

Something Drasko said in passing as he left Howard's Tavern. I was too busy focusing on the meat trucks and scapegoats he mentioned to pay much attention to anything else. Maybe I thought he was just making the type of idle conversation analysts would expect to hear directed at an illegal book trader. Then again, H.G. Wells' *Invisible Man* had obviously referred to Trezon. Was Chief Inspector Hudson *Dr. Jekyll and Mr. Hyde*?

Two-faced. Commending my work while at the same time helping a known fugitive evade capture. Those eerily silent trackers with him must have been in on it. Trezon did give the order to the meat trucks to go after Eurasia's children. Usurping Drasko's underworld authority, collecting the cockroaches who remained loyal to the old king and giving them a new mission. All with Hudson's help.

Did I get a message through to Commander Bishop? I remember being furious and then worried before everything went black. Did I pass out?

Erik. Where the hell did Hudson send Erik?

"You never trusted him, whether or not you can admit that to yourself," Wong says, shaking his head. "Your subconscious knew better."

"That's all you are. Subconscious guilt." I clench my gloved fist and back up a step in the exo, clunking against the plasticon floor.

"You killed me in self-defense. There's no reason to feel guilty about it." He laughs, a sudden outburst. "Shall we reenact my final moments for old time's sake?"

No. "I want out of here." I look up at the soaring domed ceiling of the hangar, plasteel petals closed with electric-blue beads of light blinking from the apex to the floor. "Whatever this is. It isn't real."

"Then why have you tried so hard to avoid it? Pumping your bloodstream full of stimulants. That isn't healthy, Sera. Forget what the sleep-deprivation is doing to your mind. Your heart isn't enjoying the abuse either."

"What do you *want*?" I scream at him, sounding like I'm completely losing it.

He gives me a sad little smile. "I'm not real, remember? What do *you* want? That is the question you should be asking yourself. My guess would be closure."

He explodes in a splatterfest as the gun on my shoulder activates without warning, sending bloody scraps and pieces of him in every direction. I flinch away from the gore. This isn't how it happened. First he shot me with the welder. Then I reacted. It was almost simultaneous, but the laser burned through me first. I know it did.

I blink, and he's standing in front of me again, somehow whole. But his blood bath has left him drenched from head to foot in a crimson coat.

"You know the truth. Let go of the guilt. Be at rest, Sera." He takes his hand out of his pocket, and I brace myself for the appearance of the laser welder.

Only it isn't there.

He holds his empty hand out to me as if asking me to dance. "Sleep. Whatever will be will be, regardless of your efforts. You are only one woman, Sera, and the machinations of Trezon and his benefactors are more powerful than you can possibly realize. I've told you before, and I will say it again: you cannot stop him." He lunges forward and grabs a tight hold of my wrist, smearing his blood across my skin, the whites of his bulging eyes a sharp contrast to his bloody mask. "You have already *lost*!"

I lurch upward, blinking my eyes against the darkness, forgetting for a moment where I am, why I smell stale ash all around me. Then I jump to my feet, helped along by the shadowy figure gripping my wrist. He faces me with no concept of personal space.

"Erik? What are you doing here?" My voice cracks, like I'm going to cry or something. I clench my jaw to keep control of myself, even as my heart leaps at the sight of him alive and well. "I thought—" I don't know what I thought. That

Hudson and Trezon were using him to find Drasko? Or that they'd already killed him?

"I'm fine." He smiles at me. Pulls me into a hug I don't see coming. Whispers into my ear, "My frail body just needed to reboot itself. Never been hijacked before."

Frail bodies of flesh easily punctured with bones so easily broken... Trezon's voice echoes inside my skull.

I extricate myself from Erik's arms and take a step back to look him over. He's pale and a bit haggard, but otherwise he seems to be himself.

"Where the hell did they take you?"

He frowns. "They?"

I gesture at the scorched rooftop. "After the blast. An aerocar took you away." Or Hudson said so, anyway. "You weren't here."

"Right. About that." He shrugs. "I went down a few floors and hid in a supply closet until the coast was clear. Guess I sort of passed out. Sorry if I worried you."

Not admitting anything of the sort.

"Were you napping on the job?" He gives me a wink.

I glance up past Dome 10's grungy plexicon to the night sky beyond and check the chronometer at the edge of my ocular lenses. 1800 hours. So I was unconscious for just under an hour. Disconcerting, to say the least. Losing control of myself like that.

Can't let it happen again.

"Did Trezon get away?" Erik tilts his head to one side as he watches me.

"Not sure." I try hailing Commander Bishop again, but according to the error message I receive, she's offline. That's not right. At all. I hail Wink and Blink next. "Status?" No response via our audiolink. "Give me your status."

Nothing.

Erik frowns now, looking concerned. Mirroring my own expression. "Something's wrong?"

"I have to find Dunn." I turn away and descend the steps back into the building, passing workers assigned to clean up and repair the blasted rooftop. I head straight to the pair of speedlifts at the end of the hall.

"You're going to police headquarters?" Erik is right on my heel.

"He's not at HQ." I don't have a clue where Dunn is. Or my drones. Or why Commander Bishop isn't responding. Nothing about this makes any sense.

I punch the down arrow between the polished speedlift doors and clench my fists. Both of my knees are trembling, and I don't know why. This isn't fear. And even if it is, that nightmare vision of Dr. Wong can't be the cause. I'm better than this. Stronger.

Stepping into the empty speedlift, I turn a quick about-face to find Erik stiff-arming the crowd behind us.

"Official police business," he says, and they halt just beyond the sliding door with either frowns or puzzled expressions. "Take the other one." He nods toward the second speedlift. As our door shuts, he taps the pad for the building's sublevel. A parking garage for ground vehicles, I assume. Noticing my quizzical look, he winks and says, "I've got something to show you." He steps beside me, shoulder to shoulder, and we both watch the digits twitch on the display above the door, counting down. "Might answer a few of your questions."

My augments are still active, so he hasn't read my mind.

"What questions would those be, Erik?"

He smiles sidelong at me. "You want to know where your clone pal is. And your drones. Right?" He doesn't give me a chance to answer. "You'd also like to know whether or not you can trust Chief Inspector Hudson."

"Already have the answer to that one." I fold my arms and scowl as the speedlift descends below street level and slows to a stop. "He lied to me about you. Said you were on your way to the Dome 1 medical center. And he said Trezon was headed back to the correctional center. But Commander Bishop had no record of him ever being in police custody."

Erik doesn't contradict anything I've said. He just shrugs as the speedlift door slides open.

"Sometimes the truth can be a bit...complicated." He steps out into the grey plasticon sublevel, lit just as dimly as the hangar at HQ. The aesthetics are similar, but instead of police aerocars parked in designated slots, over a dozen ground vehicles of various makes and models sit in the shadows. "Coming, Investigator Chen?" He turns to grin back at me.

Something's wrong with him. His face. No, his eyes. They don't look right.

I curse silently. Hallucinating? Is that what it's come to? Now I'm really losing it.

"Lead the way, citizen," I mutter, following him out. It's all I can do to keep my hand away from the shocker holstered under my jacket. I refuse to let irrational fears dictate my actions.

We're halfway across the silent parking garage without another individual in sight when a figure stands up between two vehicles and tosses a baton at Erik. As he catches it in midair—as it catches the light across its chrome surface—I recognize it for what it is, and a cold weight sinks into the pit of my stomach.

My shocker is in my hand before I know it, and I've squeezed off a pulse round that sparks and fizzles in the air, frozen in place. Just like me.

I've become a statue of a rookie investigator.

"Nice." Erik chuckles, lowering the grav weapon and admiring his handiwork. He steps around me in a circle, nodding with approval. "You don't have a bad side, Sera."

I spit out a few choice words—curses, mostly—but they sound more like unintelligible grunts. Then I grind my teeth as the figure who tossed Erik the baton takes form, stepping out from the shadows: one of the trackers who rode with Hudson and me in the aerocar. The other tracker from that short trip emerges from the dark on Erik's other side. They flank him now, standing like soldiers at ease with their boots spread shoulder-width apart. Stoic expressions. Not a word spoken between them.

What the hell is going on here?

Erik comes around to face me. He moves like a weird mime or circus performer, eyes wide, mouth hanging open without sound, as if he's trying to emote suspense and excitement. He should get a refund for all those acting classes he took way back when.

Then he gives the baton a little twitch, and the grav force gripping my head relaxes just enough for me to speak.

"Don't tell me you've joined Trezon's cult."

"Trezon?" He feigns a memory lapse. Then he snaps his fingers. "Oh, right. That guy. Sorry to tell you he's dead, Detective. Just like Krime, his little peon. As well as every member of that warehouse cult—eventually." He leans in with a conspiratorial whisper. "I still have a job for the Children of Tomorrow to do. But after they complete it, they are welcome to join Trezon and Krime in the cremation queue. Dust to dust, am I right?"

I hold his gaze. That was no hallucination earlier. There is something seriously wrong with his eyes. They're not blinking.

I keep my tone level, almost conversational. "Who are you?"

"Erik Paine, of course." His grin is unnaturally wide. "Who else would I be?" He chuckles, glancing over his shoulder at the pair of trackers. "The good detective has had a long day and isn't thinking clearly at the moment. Let's give her some time to rest." He signals with his hand, and the trackers spring into motion, approaching from both sides. They pick me up like I'm a sculpture that needs to be relocated in a museum. And I can't move a muscle to resist. "This way." Erik raises his baton like he's leading a troop into battle and marches off toward a closed door.

A supply closet for the building's maintenance crew.

"Go ahead. Lock me up in some dark corner. You won't get away with this." The echo of my voice fades into silence broken only by the footfalls of the three men. "Whatever you're planning—"

"You already know, Sera." Erik pauses at the door. He taps the grav weapon absently against the side of his shoe. "Those kids' DNA is the key. Without them—without *you*—none of this would be possible. Every citizen in Eurasia will be given the most incredible gift imaginable." He leaps close to me and breathes into my ear, "They will become *gods*!"

He's lucky I can't move a muscle. Otherwise, he'd be on the receiving end of a sucker punch right about now. "Since when have you been a true believer?"

Never, as far as I know. But when Trezon hijacked his abilities, something must have happened to Erik. Changed him, somehow. Affected his mind. I can't understand it, but I'm seeing undeniable evidence right in front of me.

"I've always believed, Sera." He plants his face too close for me to focus on anything but his strange eyes. Pupils dilated. High off Trezon's supply? He took one of those breathers from the warehouse and pocketed it. I handed mine over to Hudson to be analyzed. Did Erik inhale his? Did Trezon force him to? "Remember, back when the Twenty had no idea who they were, or what they were capable of? That included you. I had to introduce you to your own abilities."

By way of an EMP burst that knocked out my augments. Of course I remember.

"You never would have experienced your godlike gifts, otherwise." He steps back and stands to his fullest height, looking down at me. "That's all I'm doing now. I will show every citizen in Eurasia what they're capable of."

"By kidnapping children and harvesting their DNA."

He winces at the disgust in my tone. "The oldest are eight. In four years, they'll be given neural implants that allow them access to everything Linkstream user privileges have to offer. And once their augments are activated, they will never know what superhuman abilities they might have possessed."

"Chancellor Bishop is working with the Governors. It's likely the implants won't be mandatory. The next generation will be able to decide for themselves whether they want to be augmented. They may choose to keep their abilities instead."

I blink, my eyes grateful that I can do so as the rest of me remains rigid in the trackers' grasp. Neither seem to have any problem holding my dead weight during this extended conversation. "Or they might choose to live as I do, toggling between my augments and my abilities. The point is, the choice will be theirs. But what you're doing? You're not giving them a choice at all. You're planning to do to them what was done to us, against our will. Using them for your own ends, whatever the hell they are."

Erik shakes his head, not smiling anymore. So that's a win, I guess. No more fooling around.

"Most of them don't even know what they have! They're just *children*, Sera. Blissfully ignorant of the ways of the world. I won't hurt them. Do you think I'm some kind of monster?"

"I don't know who you are anymore. You're not the Erik I know."

"We will extract a blood sample, a bit of spinal fluid, and return them to their doting parents. That's all we want from them. Then they will be free to go about their coddled little lives. We're not going to keep them in cages in some underground laboratory—or in Futuro Tower across the sea. That would be barbaric."

He presses the palm of his hand against a sensor plate beside the door, and it slides open, revealing a grubby supply closet. Plasteel shelves holding cleaning fluids and various robocleaner parts line the walls. Beyond the patch of light cast inside by the parking garage, two sets of eyes glint in the dark. But no one inside makes a sound. Erik doesn't bother to switch on the overhead light.

"You won't stop us, Sera. Neither will Commander

Bishop or Drasko or anyone else you think is going to save you. You're on your own now. I'd invite you to join us, but I already have an inkling what your answer will be. So you'll stay here, in the dark, while we change the Ten Domes forever. And maybe, if you're lucky, I might remember where I put you."

He jerks his head toward the closet's interior, and the trackers carry me inside. Will Erik leave me trapped in this gravity field? Is that what he did to the other two people in here? Is that why they're so quiet?

"Who's this *we* and *us* you keep mentioning, Erik?" I shout, my voice loud in the confined space and not nearly as cool and collected as I'd like it to be. "Krime's dead. You said Trezon is, too. So who are you working for?"

He smirks outside the closet, waiting for the pair of trackers to join him once they've deposited me in the dark. He still has that weird look in his eyes as he clears his throat and reaches for the sensor plate. "You wouldn't understand, Sera."

He gives the grav weapon a flick of his wrist, and I collapse to the floor, released from its grip. But I'm up on my feet in no time and charging toward the open doorway, screaming curses. I'm almost upon him when the door slides shut, and I crash into it, pounding my fists against the plasteel in a pitiful display of desperation.

"You can't do this!" My voice hangs in the stillness. Outside, the footfalls of this strange new Erik and his cronies fade away without any urgency to their gait.

I try hailing Commander Bishop again, then Wınk and Blınk. No response. Not even an error message this time. My augments just aren't working. I try tapping my temple, toggling them off and then on again. No change.

I pivot on my heel and stare into the impenetrable darkness surrounding me. In the ghostly blue light of my night-vision, I see the shelves of cleaning products again, the mops and buckets and spare parts for the building's robocleaners. I see the two men sitting on the floor, staring blindly in my direction. Both of them are bound hand and foot and gagged, each with a swollen, bruised face and blood drooling down onto their chests.

My brain can't register why the man on the left is here. But I dash forward at the sight of the clone on the right.

"Dunn!" I drop to my knees beside him and remove the gag. Then I take his battered head in my arms, cradling it to my chest. He stirs at my touch.

"Investigator Chen," he says, his words slurred. "I must apologize for my appearance."

"You're alive. That's what matters." I haven't allowed myself to think the worst, but subconsciously I must have. When Wink and Blink couldn't locate Dunn, part of my mind imagined him the same way I left Fort on that sidewalk. Broken and bloody, without a pulse. Overwhelmed with relief, I have to choke back tears to keep a semblance of composure. "I'm so glad you're here."

"While I am relieved to see you unharmed, I cannot share that sentiment. For it appears that we have no means of escape."

It's just a supply closet. That locked door shouldn't pose much of a problem for Dunn in his armor.

"How long has he been like this?" I glance at Chief Inspector Hudson, sitting slumped over beside Dunn and staring straight ahead without a glimmer of consciousness in his eyes. He's breathing, but that's the only sign of life.

"He was deposited in this state by the same men who left you here. He has not said a word." Dunn pauses. "I cannot believe that Erik Paine is working with the criminal Trezon."

"That's not the Erik we know." It can't be. Trezon did something to him when he hijacked his abilities. It can't be permanent. I can't believe that it is. "He said Trezon's dead."

"I can neither confirm nor deny that."

I release his head and rest my hand on his armored shoulder. His helmet is nowhere in sight. "Let's get you on your feet." Retrieving the short blade concealed in the heel of my boot, I set about cutting through his restraints. "Your surgery was a success, I take it."

He nods, watching me free him. But he doesn't move, even when his wrists are no longer bound. "Yes, Investigator Chen. As soon as Unit D1-440 notified me of your situation, I left MedTech in order to locate you. Unfortunately, the trackers found me first."

"The men with Hudson."

"Yes. But they no longer work for him."

That much is obvious. "Tell me what happened." I cut through the bindings on his ankles, but he still doesn't move. "Can you stand?"

"Unfortunately, I am unable to move at all. When I arrived at this building in search of you and Unit D1-440, the trackers hit me with a localized EMP, which rendered my armor immobile. I'm afraid I am trapped inside it."

"So we just need to take it off, right?"

His head tilts to one side. "Easier said than done. An override key is required in order to remove a security clone's armor."

"Okay. Where do we get one of those?"

"Chief Inspector Hudson had one on his person, as would any high-ranking member of law enforcement. But it was confiscated, along with his weapon."

The holster under my jacket is empty as well, thanks to those trackers and their sticky fingers. Of course Dunn's assault rifle is nowhere to be seen.

"Can you link up with Wink and Blink?"

Dunn shakes his head. "I lost my access to the security network as well as my connection to your drones when that EMP struck me. I am running solely on biologic at the moment." He pauses. "And it is quite disturbing to feel so...limited."

He's completely in the dark, able to function solely as a biological entity. No augments, no instant communication or connection. Trapped inside his own powered-down suit of armor. He's probably never felt so vulnerable in his entire existence. Yet he doesn't sound afraid.

"We make a good team, Dunn. They really shouldn't have left us together."

"Yes. I am glad of that, Investigator Chen." Another pause as I get to my feet and face the door. "What is our next course of action?"

"We're not doing anybody any good in here." I give him a nod. "So let's break the hell out."

16

I try a few well-placed kicks, but the door doesn't budge. I throw a shoulder against it, again and again, alternating between my right and left. Nothing. If I was wearing Dunn's armor or my exo-suit, this would be a different story. My 1.7-meter, 55-kilogram frame isn't much of a contender against solid plasteel. If there were hinges on the door, I could pop out the pins, but this isn't a VR Storyline set in the past. Most doors in Eurasia are the automatic sliding variety.

So we're not breaking out of here. But that doesn't mean somebody else won't break in. There are more than a dozen ground vehicles parked on the other side of this door. The repair workers should be on their way down the speedlift at some point. Most of them will be traveling home by foot along the sidewalks of Dome 10, but I've got a feeling the section managers and others higher up on the office food chain have their own sets of wheels. Not all of them left when the building was evacuated.

I close my eyes to my night-vision and reach out with my telepathic abilities, searching for any minds within range. As if I even know how far that is. It's not like I've been trained to use this superhuman gift. I've been learning as I go. And right now, I'm gritting my teeth and focusing all my energy on finding the thoughts of someone in that parking garage. Anybody.

As long as it isn't Erik or those tight-lipped trackers.

That can't really be Erik. He's still being hijacked. Somehow. By Trezon from beyond the grave? Weirder things have happened. Then again, I have only Erik's word that Trezon is dead. I might believe that when I see his corpse.

Cursing under my breath, I try to clear my mind so I can focus on finding someone else's. But then I get distracted again. Why should I seek help from a complete stranger when I can dive into VR and let Drasko know we could use a hand?

The Strange Case of Dr. Jekyll and Mr. Hyde. Did he know about Erik? Is that who he was referring to? Because Erik sure as hell seems to be suffering from some kind of split personality disorder at present.

I've got to focus here. Tapping my temple, I try to access the VR portal, but all I get is another error message. Damn it. Erik must have done something to my neural implants. I can't access the Linkstream for a cursory data search, can't hail anyone—I've tried everyone I know, even Daiyna and Luther as a last resort—can't even delve into virtual. I'm like Dunn, only able to rely on biologic.

But unlike Dunn, I also have my so-called gifts.

Deactivating the useless augments with another temple-tap, I return to the task at hand: telepathically grabbing the attention of some random person in the parking garage and steering them our way. But no matter how hard I concentrate, gritting my teeth, squeezing my eyes shut until they tear up, clenching my fists, pressing my forehead against the door as if it will somehow act like a conduit, projecting my thoughts outward to fill the entire garage with a flood of telepathic energy—

Please help us. We're locked inside the supply closet. We can't get out.

—I get nothing. I press my ear against the door's cold surface, but I can't hear anything out there. Not a single voice or footfall echoing across the sublevel.

Even when somebody eventually shows up, how will they react to hearing thoughts that aren't their own invading their skulls? And if I manage to lure someone over here, who's to say Erik didn't hide the supply closet door with a hologram? He has Trezon's grav weapon. It stands to reason that he might have some of his other toys as well.

"You are very quiet, Investigator Chen," Dunn says at length.

"Taking a breather," I mutter.

"Did you damage yourself?"

My adrenaline and my heart are pumping too hard to feel much of anything else. I'm sure I'll have plenty of bruises on my shoulders from ramming that door. "I'm fine."

"If your drones finish their assignment and do not hear further orders from you, what is their protocol?"

"Return to my position."

He pauses before replying, "Which means they will be searching for you, once they find that you have left the roof."

I shake my head. "That's assuming they're still out there." That Trezon or Erik or those trackers working with them haven't already shot down Wink and Blink.

"Can you..." Dunn trails off for a moment. "Contact them

telepathically?"

I stare at his profile cast in blue negative courtesy of my night-vision. "Wouldn't even know where to begin with machine intelligence."

"Is it that different from biologic?"

"They're limited. The AI in surveillance drones is rudimentary at best."

Another pause. "But you will not know until you try."

He's got me there. And what do I have to lose?

"Alright. I'll try." And then I'll go right back to potentially scaring some hapless stranger in the parking garage. Because I know better than to think my telepathic abilities can interact with any sort of AI. Right?

Fort was a biological being, and so is Dunn. I can make sense of the fact that, even with the routine mental conditioning security clones are put through, my telepathy works with them—as long as they're on a self-motivated path to personhood. Jury's still out on that, but it's what I've observed in both their cases.

But Wink and Blink? I feel like a fool for even attempting this.

Closing my eyes against the aura of my night-vision. Focusing all of my telepathic energy, or whatever it is, out into Dome 10. A simple request. One I've made hundreds of times when the drones were my only backup during those late-night shifts as a curfew enforcer. Always via audiolink. Never via...the ether?

Wink, Blink, report.

I wait. Wondering what might happen next. Hoping for a miracle. Knowing this is ridiculous.

I stand there in the silence and bite back the curses that fill my mind. Abilities don't evolve, not in my experience. Dust freaks find out what they're capable of once they've snorted a line, and that's that. They don't develop new talents—unless they're Trezon. First he can turn himself invisible at will, then he's hijacking Erik's abilities. How many more would have manifested themselves if he hadn't died?

No, I don't have any proof that he's dead. Got to remember that. And Trezon isn't the only individual with more than one gift. Daiyna, my biological mother, can leap from great heights as well as see in the dark. Then there's yours truly with my own pair of superhuman talents. But the point is they don't change. They don't grow and expand, becoming more than they were when they first appeared.

My ability to use them has developed, but that's just the human way of adapting to a new skill set. I'm not going to start talking telepathically to AI's or self-driving trucks. Or trees. It's not happening. So juvenile even to hope for such a thing.

Investigator Chen, we have finished surveying Dome 10 and have returned to your original coordinates. What is your current location?

It's Wink and Blink. They sound—no, wrong word; I can't hear them; I *feel* them—just like themselves. Their little machine brains don't seem to think it's weird at all that I'm communicating with them directly, mind to mind.

Proceed to the building's underground parking structure, I tell them. Trying not to freak out. Because this is seriously bizarre.

Don't get me wrong, I'm about ready to jump for joy knowing they're all right and that Dunn and I are going to get out of here. Hudson too. But part of me can't help wondering if I might be hallucinating.

We are unable to locate you, Investigator Chen. Have your augments been damaged?

Yes. Pretty sure nothing short of another trip to MedTech will get them working again. *I'm locked inside a supply closet.* So pathetic. *Once you're in the sublevel, scan for three human heat signatures. We'll need you to break down the door.*

Proceeding to the parking structure.

Good boys.

"Investigator Chen?" Dunn speaks up. "You have been very quiet. Any success?"

"I think so." I give him my best attempt at a smile, not that he can see it in the dark. "We'll know soon enough if I'm losing my mind," I mutter.

Assuming he's not part of my delusion. Hudson as well. How would I know the difference, if I'm already too far gone to distinguish reality from my own sleep-deprived insanity?

My legs start trembling again. I back into the wall and slide down until I'm sitting on the cold plasticon floor with my knees tucked under my chin. Wrapping my arms around them, I focus on breathing. Inhale with a two-count, exhale with a four-count. After a few reps, the tension loosens in my shoulders. A few more, and I feel light-headed. A good feeling. Like I could fall asleep right here with my forehead resting on my arms...

Investigator Chen, we are inside the sublevel, Wink and Blink's thoughts somehow make their way into my mind. Not because they've got their own brand of machine telepathy. I guess I just left the communication channel open. Not sure how else to describe it.

Have you located the supply closet? I ask.

A short pause, during which I imagine them buzzing around the parking structure with their quad rotors whining at high speed. I crawl beside the door and plant my ear against it, trying in vain to hear them. Nothing comes through the thick plasteel.

We are unable to locate the closet in question. Other than the speedlift in the center of this sublevel, there are no other doors leading elsewhere, they reply, their artificially intelligent thoughts somehow transferred with the same synchronized monotone as their speech.

If Erik covered the door with a hologram, as Trezon did on the rooftop, there could be semtex involved again. Maybe enough to bring down the entire building—right on top of us.

Trezon hijacked Erik's body, riding him across Dome 10. Now it seems he's hijacked Erik's mind. Did Trezon somehow transfer his consciousness into Erik before meeting his demise? Or am I just thinking crazy thoughts again?

I have to focus. *There may be holo-tech in play. Explosives as well. Proceed with caution.* All of our lives depend on it. *Begin XR and IR scans of the sublevel interior.* I pound on the door with my fist. *Increase audio receptors.* I pound with both fists. *Can you hear me?*

Another pause. *We do not hear you over audiolink. You appear to be communicating directly with our data processors.*

I roll onto my back and kick the door with my boots, a rapid-fire percussion that doesn't quit. *Can you hear that?*

Yes. Converging on your location now, Investigator Chen. XR scans show three human shapes behind a holographic energy field.

I wave so they know which one is me. *Explosives?*

Confirmed. Two blocks of semtex have been affixed to the wall next to your position.

On the other side of the door. Twice the destructive power of the explosives that demolished the rooftop. Overkill much?

Disarm semtex, then disable the hologram. Once the path is clear, see about knocking down this door.

Understood, Investigator Chen.

"Wink and Blink are here," I tell Dunn.

"It worked." There's a smile in his tone.

"It did." Later there will be time to ponder the reality of telepathic communication with machine intelligence. Right now, we have other pressing matters.

"I was wrong," Hudson says as he comes to.

"Sir." I start toward him in the dark and stop, keeping my night-vision trained on him.

He's blinking as if it will help him to see better. Then he winces and touches his bloody forehead. "Report, Chen."

I get him caught up to the moment's difficulties. "I watched you walk into HQ with those two trackers, sir. What the hell happened?"

"You tell me." He groans as he repositions himself to sit up straight against the wall. "Put those detective skills of yours to work."

"They turned on you. Because they both work for Trezon." I pause, hating the reality that words spoken aloud give to what has been only conjecture. "And he's somehow managed to take over Erik's mind."

"Not just Erik Paine." He faces the direction of my voice,

his eyes unfocused, waiting for me to put the pieces together.

I nod slowly. "The Children of Tomorrow." The breathers. "Something in those inhalants affected their neural implants, giving Trezon the ability to...override them?"

"Working theory." Hudson coughs, and there's blood on his lips. He wipes his mouth on his shirtsleeve. "I didn't have a chance to get that breather analyzed. Those bastards jumped me in the speedlift. I held my own for the first few minutes, I'll have you know." He shakes his head, then grimaces. Moving at all right now isn't the best idea. "Next thing I know, I'm waking up here beside your partner. D1-436, I take it?" He glances in Dunn's direction.

"Yes, Chief Inspector Hudson. It is a pleasure to meet you, despite our current situation."

"Likewise," Hudson mutters. "Any particular reason you're not breaking us out?"

"I am unable to move."

"Erik—or whoever's mind-controlling him—must have hit each of us with an EMP," I explain. "Dunn's armor is out of order, and so are my augments. I can't get online."

A moment of silence. Then a curse from Hudson. "Me either."

"You said you were wrong, sir? About what?"

He grunts. "Confiscating your drones. If they manage to get us out of here, you'll never be without them again."

"Thank you, sir."

Explosives have been deactivated and removed, Wink and Blink report, followed by a short burst of projectile rounds, muffled by the door. *Hologram emitter destroyed.* Unnecessary, but a nice touch. *Door access panel is damaged. Unable to attempt keycode entry.* Another burst of rounds, longer, more intense, thudding against the wall right next to the door.

"They're weaponized?" Hudson shouts in disbelief over the clamor.

Thankfully I don't have to answer that right away. The door lurches open, jerking to the side half a meter and revealing the hovering pair of drones backlit by the sublevel's dim light. I brace my shoulder against the door and try shoving it open the rest of the way. It resists every centimeter but doesn't slide shut again. Small favor.

"Good to see you," I tell the drones as Blink shines its cyclops headlight into the closet.

"Nice work." Hudson struggles to his feet and staggers forward. But then he stops, patting his breast pocket absently and frowning at Dunn, who remains on the floor trapped inside his armor. "We'll need to get another override key. Unless those drones of yours are equipped with laser cutters." He glances at me.

I look at Wink and Blink. "Are you?"

"No, Investigator Chen," they reply in unison.

"I will remain here," Dunn says. "You go on without me. You have an important case to solve."

I shake my head. "I'm not working this case another minute without my partner." Ignoring his blank stare, I face my drones. "Get me HQ. Commander Bishop. Code red."

Blink's headlight switches to a holo-emitter, projecting a three-dimensional rendering of the commander's bald head and shoulders, her stern expression set in stone. A placeholder, not a live transmission, as the videolink is established.

"Chen, report." She glares at me as the holo comes to life. "Why are you offline?"

"I have reason to believe the criminal Trezon or his associates have hijacked the mind of Erik Paine. I'm here with Chief Inspector Hudson and my partner. All of us show signs of being struck with an EMP. Augments out. Dunn's armor is locked. Paine left us inside a supply closet, and I believe he's going after the children."

Bishop nods, taking everything I've said at face value. "Whose children are we talking about?"

"I don't know. Could be all of them. Trezon wants their DNA. He's sending meat trucks into every Dome, driven either by underworld operatives or the Children of Tomorrow—a cult of a couple hundred people he's likely mindjacked."

She looks past me. "Chief Inspector Hudson, can you corroborate?"

He raises his chin. "Investigator Chen is following multiple leads. I can confirm that Trezon's influence extends beyond his little cult. Two of our own trackers are working with him. There could be others."

Bishop curses and looks away. "Lockdown it is, then."

Relief floods through me. I just hope it isn't already too late.

All citizens will be required to remain indoors, either at home or at work. The streets will be cleared of all traffic except for ground vehicles and aerocars belonging to law enforcement. The meat trucks will have to park somewhere and wait it out. Only personnel secretly working with Erik will have access to transportation. I hope there aren't many other mindjacked members within our ranks.

"What else do you need?" Bishop says.

"An override key." I gesture back at Dunn. "My partner

needs to get off his ass and start contributing."

"I'll bring it to you myself. Anything else?"

I nod. "My exo-suit."

Hudson mutters curses under his breath.

Bishop gives me an inscrutable look. "I'll land on the roof in fifteen minutes."

"We'll need a cover story." Hudson looks past me at Bishop's holo. "The citizens will panic, otherwise."

I recall what Drasko said about a scapegoat. The usual suspects. "We received word of a potential terrorist attack," I offer. "The Patriots were mobilizing. We had to clear the streets."

Another curse from the Chief Inspector. "I said we need to *avoid* a panic."

"Chen's right." Bishop nods slowly, narrowing her gaze at me. "The threat has been neutralized, but we need to keep the streets clear in order to emphasize the rule of law. The Patriots must be made to realize that their actions have consequences, which affect the very people they claim to fight for."

"Your father won't like this," Hudson grumbles.

"The *Chancellor*—" Bishop corrects him. "—will be briefed while I'm en route to your position. He will understand what's at stake here."

The lives of a thousand children versus the toes of a few homegrown terrorists. Sure, James Bishop has gone out of his way to hear the Patriots' grievances, and blaming them for a terrorist act they never intended to perpetrate would seem at first glance to be a betrayal of whatever trust has been fostered between our government and those who see themselves as disenfranchised citizens. This lockdown could cause a major setback in negotiations. Hell, it may even inspire the Patriots to plan an actual attack. But right now, this is all we've got.

And we're running short on time.

Dead or alive, Trezon remains a threat. He doesn't care about the lives of the children who guarantee humankind its future. All he wants are powers that he can cut from their DNA and sell to the highest bidder. When all you're after is godhood, you don't care much about the mere mortals standing in your way.

"Yes, Commander," Hudson replies, dipping his chin.

"Hold position until I arrive. Bishop out."

Blink's holo-emitter returns to a headlight illuminating the supply closet. Hudson folds his arms and squints up at the hovering drone, studying it. His feathers are clearly ruffled. Hearing *Chen's right* from Commander Bishop probably had the opposite effect on him than me.

"We could always blame it on bad intel afterwards," I offer lamely. At his lack of a response, I add, "One lousy day won't cause the Chancellor's peace talks with the Patriots to crumble."

"Historically, negotiating with terrorists never leads to peace. A fact we are all keenly aware of, ever since our Interim Chancellor took the Linkstream temporarily offline as one of his first acts in office." He looks at me sidelong. "I believe it was Erik Paine who carried out that bit of domestic terrorism on Chancellor Bishop's behalf, was it not?"

I wasn't aware that's common knowledge. But of course Hudson would know. He exists on a higher plane than ninety percent of Eurasians, privy to all manner of information.

Chancellor Bishop wanted us to remember our shared history. His predecessor had used our augments and the Link to keep us focused only on the here and now, always moving forward. Never back. All at the expense of forgetting the mistakes of the past. But when the Linkstream went down for twenty-four hours and our augments faltered during the interim, the older generations started remembering things they hadn't thought about for years. And they shared that knowledge with the rest of us. The Twenty, in particular, received a crash course in the triumphs and failures of our species, leading up to the construction of the Ten Domes, D-Day, and our own origin story deep beneath the surface of the North American Wastes.

Once the Link came back online, Chancellor Bishop made sure that every citizen had full access to a multitude of historical records that were never deleted, thankfully. Chancellor Hawthorne must have known that someday humankind would be ready to learn about its past. James Bishop just made sure *someday* was now.

"How well do you know Paine?" Hudson turns his scrutinizing gaze fully on me.

"Enough to know he's not acting like himself, sir."

"I don't agree. It's a matter of record that he was an associate of Trezon's at one point in time. Those EMP devices he used in order to wreak havoc across the Domes, playing no small part in Chancellor Hawthorne's removal from office, were obtained directly from Trezon, were they not?"

"Yes, but—"

"Devices he's obviously deployed yet again, deactivating our neural implants as well as your partner's armor. Erik

Paine was a man on a mission before. He wanted the Twenty to learn where they came from. Then he wanted every citizen in Eurasia to learn their shared history. Now he's joined Trezon's crusade, ensuring that the dust freaks' bizarre abilities are available to everyone on a permanent basis. Just splice in some DNA from an unwilling underaged victim, and you too can leap tall buildings in a single bound!"

"No, sir." I take a step toward him. "All due respect, but you didn't see Trezon hijack Erik. You didn't see the look in Erik's eyes. It's the same look he had when he locked me in this supply closet. Something I've never seen in him before."

Hudson frowns. "Describe it."

I take a moment to bring back the last image of Erik that I have in my memory. Before the door slid shut. Right after he said, *You wouldn't understand, Sera.*

"It was terror."

17

As soon as Commander Bishop's aerocar lands on the scorched rooftop, she tells us via Blink that she's on her way down. Most of the ground vehicles in the parking garage have vacated the premises by this point, owners exiting the speedlift with their eyes unfocused, oblivious to Hudson and me standing outside the supply closet's dark doorway. Only a couple autos remain in their assigned stalls when the speedlift door slides open and Bishop steps out. Handgun gripped down at her side. High-collared black coat flailing about her shins. The dim recessed lights in the ceiling reflect across her shaved head. She exudes strength and perfect poise as she strides toward us, her eyes clear and focused. With a nod first to Hudson and then to me, she walks past us and goes straight for Dunn.

An irrational fear grips hold of me: that the gun in her hand is intended for him. That she sees no reason to release him from his locked armor. That in her eyes, he's just as recyclable as Fort lying dead on the street a block away.

I lunge into the dark after her. "Ma'am—"

"On your feet." Facing Dunn, she rattles off an extra-long string of alphanumerics from a translucent plastic card pinched between her fingers. The keycode. Then she taps the card against his chest plate.

Dunn's armor whines and jitters in place, and he shakes his head as if he's rousing himself from a deep reverie. Rising to his feet in a single movement, he says, "Thank you, Commander Bishop."

"You're unarmed, I take it." She glances at each of us in turn. "You'll have to make do with what I brought along." She heads back toward the speedlift in the center of the parking garage, her boot heels striking a purposeful rhythm.

Hudson is quick to follow, doing his best to keep up. They're both tall individuals, but her stride is just a bit longer. "I'm not sure whom we can trust, Commander. Your pilot, for instance—"

"I came alone." She glances over her shoulder at me. "Let's roll, Chen."

I realize I'm standing still and staring at the damage done to Dunn's face. Whoever roughed him up is going to pay for it. "You fit for duty, partner?"

He nods, and we follow our superiors toward the speedlift. Wink and Blink hover less than a meter above us. "And you, Investigator Chen?"

Honestly, I have no idea. But so far my lack of sleep hasn't interfered with my ability to do the job. Not too much, anyway. "I'm seeing this through."

"What is our mission objective?"

Stop Erik and the Children of Tomorrow from kidnapping any children. Root out the traitors in our ranks. Find Trezon, if he's still alive. Ensure that he stays locked up for the remainder of his sorry existence.

"I'm sure we'll find out soon." I nod toward Commander

Bishop as she steps into the speedlift and turns to fix us with her stern gaze.

Sending Wink and Blink to the rooftop via the open-air route out of the garage, I follow Hudson into the speedlift and hold the door for Dunn. Once all four of us are crammed inside shoulder to shoulder, I tap the glowing pad for the top floor, and we glide upward.

"Coordinate with air patrols," Bishop orders via audiolink. "Keep the streets clear. The Chancellor will be explaining the situation soon. For now, early curfew is in effect across the Domes. No unauthorized ground or air traffic permitted until I tell you otherwise." She ends the call.

"We don't know how many of our own people may be compromised," Hudson says in a low tone. "Those trackers gave no indication—"

"Sandoval and Peters were assigned to you." Bishop's eyes lose focus as she scans what's probably a duty roster populating across her lenses.

"Yes." Hudson clears his throat, feeling as awkward as I am at the moment, cut off from the Linkstream.

"Locate Trackers Sandoval and Peters," Bishop orders whoever is on the receiving end—probably the hive mind of her jacked-in analysts at HQ.

I'll be surprised if either one of those trackers is still online, I think at Dunn, who glances at me. His bloodied expression isn't difficult to read. Startled at first by my telepathic intrusion into his mind, followed by a slight nod of agreement.

"Then give me their last-known coordinates." Bishop keeps her irritation mostly in check. There's a short pause before she shakes her head. "Very well. I want their vehicles grounded. Override command authorized. Lock them inside their aerocars and land them right in the middle of the street, if necessary."

The speedlift slows to a halt, and the door slides open with a ding. Dunn steps out into the middle of the vacant hallway first, his unshielded head on a swivel as he surveys the vicinity for any hostiles. Standard procedure for a security clone. But in any other dicey situation, he'd have a helmet and an assault rifle. Even so, he's providing us cover with his armored suit.

"Follow me," Bishop tells him as she steps past us, her gun at the ready in a two-handed grip.

Unarmed but somewhat protected by our tactical suits, Hudson and I bring up the rear. We keep our own counsel as we make our way past the empty offices to the remains of the stairwell leading up to the obliterated rooftop. If I never see this building again, it'll be too soon.

Night is falling as we step outside. Commander Bishop's sleek, black and white aerocar sits in the center of the charred rubble. Sensing her proximity, the interior light activates along with the engines, and the doors drift open to welcome us. In the passenger compartment, my exo-suit lies on its back, along with enough firepower to equip a small army.

"Give me a hand," I tell Dunn, and he helps me drag the exo out into the ash. Wink and Blink hover nearby. I can't help smiling inside. The band is back together.

"These are for you." Bishop holds a spotless white helmet in one hand and a security clone-issued assault rifle in the other.

Dunn raises my exo upright, and I strap myself in as he faces her.

"Thank you, Commander Bishop." He slips on the helmet. Of course it's a perfect fit; one size fits every security clone in the Domes. With the black-tinted face shield in place, we can't see his injuries. Nodding once, he takes the rifle and backs up a couple steps, assuming the standard posture for securing a scene.

Having my exo back is one thing. Having it back on is something else. It feels so good to be this strong again. I curl my gloved fists and punch the air a couple times, then bounce on the boot struts. The minigun mounted on my shoulder spins up, ready for action.

"Let me guess." Hudson takes a pair of handguns from Bishop's supply, tucking one into the back of his trousers. "The same person who weaponized your drones also modified your exo-suit."

"That's right." I give him a grin.

He nods with a knowing look. Neither one of us mentions Drasko by name.

"Sera, I brought you this as well," Bishop says in a low tone as she turns to hand me my father's *miao dao* in its simple redwood scabbard.

I take it without knowing what to say. She's never been to my cube before, but somehow she knew I had it mounted on my wall, and for some reason, she thinks I might need it. Never mind the fact that I've never had any type of sword training.

"It's uh...really just for decoration," I manage. No need to mention that it reminds me of my father's love. Enough privacy has already been violated. But who am I kidding? Bishop's analysts are jacked into the Linkstream all day and all night, peering into the lives of every citizen online.

Whenever my augments are toggled on, those analysts have access to everything I see and do. Including a clear view of my cube's interior.

"A very sharp decoration." Commander Bishop nods with approval. "And impervious to EMP bursts."

Right. Unlike my exo. Good to have a backup weapon. I slide the scabbard over my shoulder into the rifle boot Drasko added onto the frame. I've never had a need for it before now.

"We've got company." Bishop points skyward where the blinking lights on a pair of aerocars approach through the darkness. Faster than is customary for air patrol cars, and heading straight for us.

"Backup?" Hudson wonders aloud.

"I don't think so. Neither pilot is online." Bishop holsters her gun and climbs into the cockpit. Hudson slides in beside her. "Take this, Chen." She tosses me an antique handheld device designed for accessing the Linkstream back in the old days prior to our ubiquitous neural implants. "You are to aid in the apprehension of Erik Paine and the two rogue trackers, Sandoval and Peters." She points at the device in my hand. "Use that phone to stay in the loop until MedTech repairs your augments."

"Yes, Ma'am." I pocket the old phone and retrieve a shocker from Bishop's arsenal. Holstering it, I step back from the vehicle, leaving the door to drift shut and lock automatically. "We'll provide you cover."

She gives me a nod. "You and your partner do what you do best."

Hudson frowns quizzically at her, then at me as he realizes Dunn and I are staying behind. Plans change.

"We will." I pat the side of her aerocar and turn to face the incoming vehicles. For me, the night is almost as bright as day, everything glowing with a shimmering blue aura. And thanks to my telepathy, I'm able to sort through each of the pilots' minds. They may be offline, but their thoughts give them away. It's Peters and Sandoval, both dead set on their mission objective and operating with grim determination. So much for HQ locking down their vehicles. "I've got the one on the right."

"I will take the one on the left, Investigator Chen," Dunn says, shouldering his rifle.

As Commander Bishop's aerocar lifts off behind us and plunges over the side of the building to head back to Dome 1, I face the opposite direction and lean back, letting loose a few dozen rounds from my minigun that stream upward in a graceful arc. At the same time, Dunn squeezes off round after round in a steady rhythm. Sparks fly across both of the trackers' approaching aerocraft, projectile rounds thudding along their hulls.

They split up, veering away from each other as they attempt to avoid the abuse we're hurling their way. We don't cease fire until they're out of range, turning back toward the direction they came. Wink and Blink follow, unleashing their own weapons at the vehicles' backsides, until I call the drones off. They zip through the night and resume their positions, hovering above Dunn and me.

"Trackers Sandoval and Peters, I presume?" Dunn holds his rifle at rest and watches the pair of vehicles retreat.

"Affirmative." I glance up at him. "You didn't need to confirm their identity prior to opening fire?"

"I trusted your judgment, Investigator Chen."

Gotta smirk at that. "We scared them off for now. But I've got a feeling they'll circle back and try to take down Bishop's vehicle before she can leave Dome 10."

Or follow her into the maglev tunnel and ram her against the walls.

I back away a few paces from the building's edge and check the grapnel lines housed inside my exo's launch ports.

"What do you intend to do?" Dunn's expressionless face shield watches me.

"Told Commander Bishop we'd cover her exit. That's what we're doing, partner." I beckon for him to come toward me. He does, his white armored boots covered in ash. "You said you trusted me."

"Yes..." He doesn't sound very sure as I wrap an arm around him.

"Hold on tight."

I take off running, the boot braces of my exo pounding across the rooftop, crunching through debris and sending ash spiraling upward in my wake. Dunn grunts at the unexpected velocity, grabbing onto the plasteel frame covering my spine with one hand while the other clutches his rifle close. Charging full-tilt, I leap off the edge of the roof and pivot in midair, firing my grapnel lines at the remains of the stairwell shaft. The cables shoot from each of my shoulders as we plummet toward the street below. But halfway down the side of the building, the lines pull taught, the grapnels finding purchase, and I bend my knees to cushion the landing as my boots touch down on the side of the building. Puffs of dust from the brick are the only evidence of impact. I rappel the rest of the way down with my partner in tow.

"You opted not to use the speedlift," Dunn observes as we bounce along, doing his best to sound calm and collected, as always.

"They're coming back." I point out the trackers' aerocars. They keep out of our projectile range while angling on an intercept course with Bishop's vehicle and the maglev tunnel. "We've gotta run."

I release Dunn as soon as we touch down on the sidewalk, and he takes off as fast as he can sprint. Twice as fast as any mere mortal. I pause to retract my lines, the grapnels clinking against my exo's shoulder struts as they finish wheeling back in. Then I'm racing after Dunn, bounding over meters at a time, the pistons in my leg braces whining as they send me through the dark, empty streets at something near fifty kilometers per hour. I overtake Dunn and pass him, beckoning for him to pick up the pace. But he's already going as fast as his armored suit can carry him.

Up ahead, Bishop's aerocar is already descending, preparing to soar over the security gate and glide through the dark tunnel beyond. As far as I know, her vehicle, like every other aerocar in the air patrol division, is not equipped with weapons or defensive armor. It was never intended for combat. The cars flown by Sandoval and Peters are likewise unarmed. But if they decide to ram the commander's vehicle in some sort of brazen *kamikaze* move, then she'll need to brace for a very dangerous landing.

So Dunn and I have to bring down the two rogue trackers as fast as we can. Alive, preferably. Because I've got a feeling they know right where Erik is hiding himself.

The guards at the gate to the Dome 10 train tunnel are already prepared for battle with their sidearms raised. Bishop must have informed them of the situation. A pang of regret hits me as I remember Fort. He should be here with us. Would be, if I hadn't let Trezon escape from that warehouse.

I had him, damn it. I could have ended things right there, before they got out of hand. Before Erik and the lives of a thousand children were put in danger.

I race across the empty street, my exo punching the plasticon beneath me without leaving any impact craters. My boot braces skid as I reach the gate to the train station, just as Bishop's aerocar soars overhead, the anti-grav engines sending enough jet wash to whip my hair around. I point at the pair of vehicles in high-speed pursuit, and my minigun chugs away as soon as they're within range.

I've got the one on the right, I tell Dunn, and he halts on the other side of the street. Taking a knee, he aims his assault rifle at the other aerocar and opens fire. *Engage and fire*, I tell Wink and Blink. They zip through the air on an intercept course and release a barrage of projectile rounds aimed at the windscreens of the two aerocars. The station guards below fire their weapons as well, but I'm not sure what they're aiming at. Sparks fly from Peters' and Sandoval's vehicles, and they flip in midair, veering off only to head right back toward the station. We're not making their job easy, but we haven't succeeded in grounding them, either.

Bishop's vehicle is already in the tunnel. She's speeding through the dark faster than any pilot I've ever seen—and that includes Drasko, the best I know. Peters' aerocar is providing cover for Sandoval's now. Guess they decided one of them would have to sacrifice himself. Flying in tight formation, with Sandoval's vehicle virtually on top of Peters', they make another run at the tunnel.

We can't stop both of them. Already Peters' aerocar is venting smoke from its underside, the magnetic coils compromised, its stability nonexistent. If he isn't careful, he'll ram into Sandoval above him and throw them both off-course.

Right. That'll work.

I cease fire and activate both my grapnel lines, aiming for the port side of Peters' aerocar as it careens overhead, blocking out the grimy plexicon of Dome 10 high above us. I'm only going to get one shot at this. Gritting my teeth, I watch, hoping my aim is true.

Somewhere amid the pouring smoke, the grapnels latch onto the aerocar's underside, and I lean back on my heels, throwing my weight against the violent pull as I retract the cables. Obviously the vehicle weighs a whole lot more than I do, even in my exo, and it's moving at a steady clip. So I'm going to be airborne here in a split-second.

Hurtling forward, I reach out with both gloved hands and grab hold of the gate. The arms of my exoskeleton whine as they hold fast and the lines pull taut, jerking at my body but thankfully not ripping it in two. The shoulder struts creak, and Peters' aerocar flips portside while its starboard side knocks Sandoval's vehicle off-course just enough to cause both vehicles to miss their mark. Peters' aerocar smashes head-on into the left side of the tunnel while Sandoval's plows into the plasticon ceiling, skidding with a firestorm of wreckage.

Both trackers are no fools. They ejected prior to impact, their seats drifting to the street on limited anti-grav power. Both men have their hands in the air, resigned to the fact that they won't be going anywhere once they make landfall.

"Restrain them," I tell the gate's security personnel, who nod and advance with sidearms trained on the two men.

Dunn keeps his weapon on them as well as he crosses the street toward me. "That was an unorthodox solution, Investigator Chen."

"These are unorthodox times." I lower myself from the gate and drop onto my boot braces as the cables retract into the receptacles on my shoulders. The minigun rotates back to standby mode, pointing its hot muzzle down my back. According to the ammunition gauge, I've still got about a quarter of my supply. I have a feeling I'll be needing it before the night is through. "Peters. Sandoval." I nod to each of them in turn as the security personnel bind their wrists and ankles. No such thing as overkill in this situation. "You're going to tell me where Erik Paine is."

Their block-jawed faces are devoid of expression as they fix me with identical bored looks and don't say a word. That's okay by me.

Where's Erik? I think at them, and they lurch in place, eyes widening a little in spite of themselves.

She's one of them, Peters thinks. He's not disgusted or afraid. He knows what I am, and he's intrigued. Filled with...wonder? That makes me instantly uncomfortable.

A demigod, Sandoval thinks. *One of the Twenty. No wonder Prometheus left her alive. She's one of the first!*

They're members of Trezon's cult. Great. I clench my jaw and focus all of my telepathic energy on sifting through their recent memories...

I see them attack Hudson in the speedlift, turning on him without warning and beating him down to the floor with their fists, then kicking him with their boots until he's little more than a crumpled heap. Peters takes the breather from Hudson's pocket. Sandoval hauls Hudson's unconscious body over his shoulder. They ride the lift back up to the hangar in HQ. Approach the grease monkey on duty. Shoot him in the head with a silenced projectile weapon. I can't help flinching at the shot, the blood, the body collapsing. The guy was a jerk, sure, but he didn't deserve that. Peters and Sandoval take separate aerocars and fly out of Dome 1, back to Dome 10. Back to that building full of flush-counters where Erik Paine lay unconscious following Trezon's hijacking. Peters jams the breather against Erik's nose and mouth and activates it. Erik jerks upright, his eyes wide open as he inhales with a hoarse gasp. Peters holds onto him, keeping him still, while Sandoval carries Hudson down to the supply closet where I found him.

"Prometheus has big plans for you," Peters tells Erik, clapping him on the shoulder.

Erik's eyes are confused. He sways in Peters' grasp. Then all of a sudden, his expression clears, and he nods with complete understanding.

"I live to serve Prometheus." His grin is as dashing as ever. Peters offers him a hand, but Erik jumps to his feet. "Let's get to work."

An official alert sounds on the phone in my hand, jarring me, and I lose the telepathic link along with my concentration. Interim Chancellor James Bishop's face is on the screen. Good thing Erik showed me a while back how to operate one of these antique devices. They remain in limited circulation among the oldest members of the population who refused to receive neural implants a long time ago as a matter of principle, as well as the residents of Dome 6 who suffer from physical, emotional, or mental issues that would interfere with augmentation. I glance at the security guards and find their eyes unfocused, watching the Chancellor's announcement on their lenses.

"Good evening." Bishop addresses his audience with a grim, commanding demeanor. I angle the screen so Dunn can see it. Peters and Sandoval are offline, but they can listen. Eerie how they're staring at me. "In the interest of public safety and security, I had no choice but to call for curfew five hours ahead of schedule tonight. As you know, we operate daily with carefully moderated resources. When one of our solar banks is damaged, the result is felt all across the Domes." He pauses. "I wish I could say this was an isolated incident. We have suffered from power failures intermittently in the past, and in order to ensure the continued functionality of our lights, air processors, even the Linkstream itself, we had to resort to immediate conservation mode."

He pauses. His expression doesn't change. Will he mention the Patriots? Blame this so-called power outage on the usual suspects?

"In a situation like this, it's normal to feel uneasy. We rely on a certain amount of equilibrium in order to maintain the lifestyles we've grown accustomed to in these self-sustaining biospheres. But there is always a human component involved, no matter how technologically advanced the endeavor may be. Eurasia is run by flesh and blood caretakers, not artificial intelligence. And mistakes, while rare, can and do happen."

He's not taking the scapegoat route. Interesting.

"Unfortunately, the bank of solar cells in question was

damaged during routine maintenance, and it was decided that during the time necessary to make repairs, we will conserve our energy stores. This early curfew will remain in effect until 0600 tomorrow, at which time we will reevaluate the efficacy of the solar bank in question. It is my hope that this inconvenience will be short-lived, and that tomorrow evening at this time, we'll be able to go about our lives as usual." He offers a flicker of a smile. "Thank you for understanding. Together, we'll get through this minor setback. I hope you all have a peaceful evening at home with your loved ones, enjoying some time in virtual." Because the Linkstream is always online, no matter how much energy it consumes. "Eurasia strong. Eurasia united." With a nod, he ends the announcement, and the phone's screen fades to black.

The eyes of the security personnel focus on the situation at hand.

"He sounds more like a politician every day," one of them remarks. The way she carries her stocky frame, she might have been in the military. Maybe a marine like James Bishop, once upon a time.

"It's the office," says the guard next to her, a lanky guy with a spindly neck. "Power changes people. He won't leave it the same as he entered."

"If he leaves at all," mutters the third guard, a grizzled curmudgeon by the looks of him.

"Rumor has it his son might take over," says the woman. "You know, Commander Bishop's brother. Can't remember his name."

"Emmanuel," says the ever-helpful second guard. "What do you think, Chen? Was anything the Chancellor said true?"

He nods toward the aerocar wreckage burning bright behind him and keeps the muzzle of his sidearm on Peters and Sandoval, both kneeling in front of him. "These two have something to do with that *solar bank* going out of commission?"

Sandoval barks a laugh before I have a chance to reply. "All lies," he says. "But the people eat them up. Because they are blind to the truth."

"And what *truth* would that be?" the woman says, her tone thick with contempt.

"We don't have to live the lives we've been given. Assigned our castes and careers by the Governors. Afraid to burst the plexicon bubbles that protect us from the ravages of the outside world." He takes a prolonged moment to look each of the guards in the eye before returning his gaze to me. "We can be like Investigator Sera Chen. We can live as *gods*!"

18

I don't like the way they're looking at me. Peters, Sandoval, and now the security guards. So I change the subject.

"Why were you going after Commander Bishop?"

"We were scrambling to assist," Sandoval retorts. "The Chief Inspector was assaulted, and Bishop's transporting him back to Dome 1. We were coming to her aid."

"Not what it looked like," the first gate guard mutters.

"Our flight plans were recorded by the onboard computers." Peters inclines his head toward the wreckage. "Despite your violent interference, the analysts at HQ will have those records on file. No rogue activity. Everything by the book, as we were trained."

They really thought this treachery through.

"Why'd you open fire on them, Chen?" the second guard pipes up. Clearly he's no longer sure of the situation—and has conveniently forgotten firing his own sidearm while they were in flight.

I stare him down. "These two men assaulted Chief Inspector Hudson. Commander Bishop gave us orders. All of us. Bishop ordered you to hold this entry point to the train tunnel. My partner and I were tasked with apprehending the rogue trackers. That meant keeping them from ramming their aerocars into her vehicle."

"You have no proof of any such intention," Peters says.

I have all the proof I need, I think at him. He smirks, knowing my ability to read his thoughts and see his past crimes will never be admissible as evidence against him. *Where is Erik?* I demand telepathically.

Erik Paine is one of us now. We are the eyes, hands, and feet of Prometheus. Peters nods, holding my gaze. *You cannot stop us.*

He has the blood-covered face of Dr. Solomon Wong.

I stumble back a step, and Dunn grabs hold of my exo to steady me.

"I told you," Wong says, shaking his head sadly. "You cannot stop them."

This isn't right. I never see him when I'm awake. Only in nightmares. So I must have nodded off. That's why Dunn is holding onto my suit, bracing me upright. I fell asleep on my feet. How pathetic.

I blink, shake my head, breathe in the cool night air. But nothing changes the apparition in front of me. Peters has completely transformed. Now he's Dr. Wong in his crimson-soaked laboratory coat, kneeling there with his hands bound behind his back. Looking up at me with sympathy in his dark eyes.

"You wanted to show them all: Bishop, Hudson. Your adoptive parents, your biological parents. Erik, the Twenty. You wanted to capture the criminal Trezon. Solve this big case, prove you deserved that promotion to *Investigator.*" He shakes his head again. "But this is not a case you can solve,

Sera. It's too big for you. Too big for any of you. Powerful forces are at work here, greater than you can possibly imagine."

I stare at him. I can't believe I'm admitting this, but the ghost of Dr. Wong is right. I've been out of my depth from the start. "Someone changed Trezon while he was in custody. Altered his DNA. Gave him his gift of invisibility."

Wong nods. "Who would have the power to do such a thing? And keep it secret from the head of Eurasian law enforcement?"

Commander Bishop and her analysts see all, know all. The Ten Domes are a surveillance state—for every citizen who's online. Turn off your augments, and the analysts have to rely on facial recognition courtesy of the drones roaming at all hours of the day and night, not to mention the security cameras posted on every block.

"No one is above the law," I murmur. "Not the Chancellor, not the Governors..."

"Are you sure of that?" Wong tilts his head to one side, watching me as I sort through the facts.

Someone altered Trezon's DNA. They could have spliced it with some genetic material from the Twenty in cold storage. Or from an embryo yet to be brought to term—Wong is rumored to have left a few dozen in cryo-stasis. Then Trezon had help breaking out of the correctional center. The sort of help that had to come from someone in Eurasia's upper echelons. But who would do such a thing?

I think back to Hudson's dislike for the changes James Bishop has made to the Ten Domes. He's not the only critic. Even among the Governors, I'm sure there are those who would like to see Bishop booted from his interim office.

There might even be some sort of cabal working against him, who wouldn't think twice about changing a former underworld boss's DNA, providing him with adoring cult followers, and setting them loose upon the Domes. But not before engineering an inhalant that renders the Children of Tomorrow susceptible to mindjacking.

I curse under my breath. It's all so far-fetched.

And yet it explains so much. They want Bishop out so they can replace him with one of their own, someone who respects their beloved status quo. And they're willing to turn Eurasia upside-down in order to make that happen. But why the focus on superhuman abilities? Do they really want to give them to every Eurasian—like the mythical Prometheus of old, gifting fire to humankind?

"Investigator Chen, are you all right?" Dunn says quietly.

Clenching my jaw, I focus on the man kneeling in front of me. A rogue tracker named Peters with a block jaw and limited range of facial expressions. Not Solomon Wong. Because Wong is dead. I killed him.

You don't work for Trezon, I think at Peters, who thankfully has his own face again and his own body, garbed in light tactical gear.

He gives me a smug look, but the throat-chop-worthy expression doesn't last long. Because I'm taking a deep dive into his memories, and this time he seems a little stunned by the experience. No time to be gentle.

I sort through everything in his head, a whirlwind of images and sounds and visuals and voices. Erik showed me how to do this, once upon a time, and I learned fairly quickly how to sift through a person's extensive maelstrom of experiences in order to find exactly what I'm looking for.

There's Trezon, lying on the floor of the elevator right after I shocked him. And there I am, right beside him. Chief Inspector Hudson nods to Peters and Sandoval, the only trackers who accompany him.

"Secure him in the aerocar and send him back to the correctional center. I don't want him seeing the light of day for a very long time."

"Yes, sir," Peters says as he and Sandoval lift Trezon's unconscious form between them, limp arms draped over their shoulders. They haul him up the demolished stairway to the roof with his boots dragging behind them.

On the scorched rooftop, three aerocars sit waiting, each with a pilot at the controls. Peters and Sandoval take Trezon to the passenger compartment of the vehicle on the left and deposit him as one might a sack of potatoes.

"This one's going back where he belongs," Peters says to the pilot, who nods, spinning up the engines.

Sandoval retrieves a handheld device small enough to conceal in the palm of his hand, and he presses the center pad. Instantly, Trezon's head jerks back and his eyes roll up into their sockets. As the vehicle's side door drifts closed and locks into place, Trezon's body remains locked in that position, completely still, mouth gaping open in a silent scream. As if something detonated inside his skull, shutting down every system in his body.

The two trackers turn on their heels to head back down the stairwell and find Hudson crouched over me, just as I come to.

So it's true, I think at Peters. *Trezon is dead. Sandoval somehow saw to it.*

Peters grins. "Trezon may be dead, but Prometheus will

live forever!"

Prometheus. Trezon's consciousness? Or a composite of the cult's true leaders? A secret cabal that has been running this show from the beginning. Maybe Trezon was never more important than that overeager flunky who renamed himself *Krime*. Just a pawn in the proceedings, mapped out by greater minds.

"What the hell is he going on about?" The first guard sneers down at Peters.

"Nothing you would understand," Sandoval says.

I point at him. "You killed Trezon. How?"

"He was a means to an end." Sandoval shrugs. "Nothing more."

"So are you." Then I project into his mind, *And you're going to show me who you work for.*

But before I can pierce the depths of his memories, both trackers seize up without warning, their heads jerking and eyes rolling back to expose the whites. Each man a perfect mimic of Trezon's death pose. It's as if their neural implants have been targeted and detonated by someone who doesn't want them sharing any more information, willingly or not. Brains fried, the two trackers drop face-first onto the sidewalk and twitch for a few seconds before lying still.

The security personnel glance at each other, not knowing whether to holster their weapons or keep them trained on the bodies of Peters and Sandoval.

"Did you...?" The first guard looks at me suspiciously, but she can't get the words out.

Right. Suspect the so-called *demigod* of telepathic murder, why don't you.

"Whoever they were working for...decided to silence

them." Damn it. I should have dug around through their memories a whole lot more while I had the chance. "And the killer could be nearby."

I give the surrounding area a cursory mind sweep, searching for murderous thoughts, but I get nothing. In Peters' memory, I saw Sandoval's handheld device work like a remote detonator. No telling what kind of range it had, but he was close to Trezon when he activated it.

Erik might be next. Now that Trezon's gone, whoever Prometheus is may decide to detonate Erik's neural implants in order to keep him from talking to me. Wherever the hell he is right now.

"That's not possible." The guard shakes her head and takes a step back from the bodies, but her eyes and the muzzle of her weapon don't leave them. "No one can hack our augments."

"Normally, I would agree with you. But these two were mindjacked." For lack of a better term, considering I have no idea what I'm talking about.

"Mind-jacked?" the other guards murmur, glancing at each other.

"Are you familiar with the Children of Tomorrow?" Dunn asks.

They look at him sharply, unaccustomed to a clone speaking without first being spoken to.

"What about them?" snaps the second guard.

"Investigator Chen believes their neural implants may have been affected by an inhalant provided at a recent gathering here in Dome 10."

"An inhalant..." The first guard doesn't see the connection.

"Some sort of chemical compound—maybe one with nanotech in the mix—could have allowed Prometheus to overwrite their minds," I explain. "To hijack them."

"And who the hell is *Prometheus*?" the third guard pipes up.

I nod toward my partner. "That's what we're trying to find out."

Thought we already had. Thought it was Trezon. But he was just another bit player in a much bigger act.

We have to find out who's behind the scenes, calling the shots. Who wants the DNA of Eurasia's children? Who wants to turn the Children of Tomorrow into a superpowered cult that can be hijacked to do their bidding? Some secret group intent on overthrowing the Governors of the Ten Domes? A real Patriot threat? Or a few of the Governors themselves who've never appreciated Chancellor Bishop's leadership and are planning a coup?

I have only one lead: Erik. He must know the truth. And I have to find him before Prometheus fries his brain.

"Commander Bishop will want an autopsy on these two. I trust you have a place to store them?" I focus on the guard who seems to be the leader of the pack.

She nods. "We'll make room at the station house until the Commander sends for them."

Good enough. I bring up an image of Erik on my phone and hold out the screen so the guards can take a good, hard look. "Have you seen this man? He was in Dome 10 earlier today. Late afternoon..." It's a struggle to keep my timeline straight.

They take turns studying the image and shaking their heads.

"Hasn't come this way," the lead guard says. "Other than the Commander, nobody's taken this tunnel in or out since late morning. Long before the curfew went into effect. So your man there should still be in Dome 10. Need some help locating him?"

"I've got my team." Dunn, Wink and Blink are all I need. "Thanks for your assistance."

"Wish this had gone down differently." Her gaze returns to the rogue trackers.

So do I. Giving Dunn a nod, I turn away from the gate and head out across the vacant street with him at my side. Using the antique phone, I start texting Wink and Blink their orders but then remember I can communicate telepathically with their machine intelligence, as completely bizarre as that is.

We're looking for Erik Paine. Sync up with local facial recognition drones and determine his last known coordinates. If found, do not engage. I can't risk his neural implants imploding—if they haven't already.

My stomach lurches at the thought. That the last memory I'll have of him is when he locked me in that closet. The look of terror in his eyes. When he told me, *You wouldn't understand.* Was he fighting Prometheus's control over his mind and body? Were Peters and Sandoval? Or had they all given in, fully brainwashed?

I glance at the phone as Dunn and I head down the empty sidewalk with no clear destination in mind. Wink and Blink are high above us, and if it wasn't for my night-vision, they'd be invisible against the black sky. I watch them fly off and hope they survive this mission intact, that no irate star-watching local shoots them out of the Dome's airspace.

"Anything from Commander Bishop?" Dunn holds his rifle at the ready, muzzle trained on the pavement ahead of us as we walk.

"She says they made it to HQ safely. Hudson's in MedTech having his neural implants repaired. No sightings of any meat trucks or Children of Tomorrow going after the kids." I frown as I scan the text messages scrolling across the phone.

"Your plan was a success, then. By locking down the Domes, you prevented the Prometheus operatives from taking the children." Dunn pauses. "Yet you do not look pleased."

Erik needs our help. Or he may already be dead, judging from how expendable Prometheus's operatives tend to be. My heart is racing, adrenaline pumping, but I have nowhere to channel my energy. No idea where the hell he is.

"Erik made it clear what Prometheus wants. All we've done is delay the inevitable. We can't keep the curfew in effect indefinitely. We have to identify the members of the cabal and bring them to justice. Immediately."

"In one night, Investigator Chen?"

He's right to doubt. Whoever Prometheus is, they've been entrenched for a while. Somehow, they were able to change Trezon's DNA and give him *demigod*-like abilities. Which means they already have access to genetic material from one of three sources: the children of Eurasia, one of the Twenty, or our biological parents—survivors from the North American Wastes.

The latter wouldn't work. A man named Arthur Willard already attempted to replicate abilities via the DNA of Luther, Daiyna, Samson, and Shechara. No dice. And if

DNA from the Twenty was all Prometheus needed, then they should be content with having Erik Paine under their thumb. Yet he made it abundantly clear that the plan was to go after the blood and spinal fluid of Eurasia's thousand children. For some reason, that's the genetic material they want.

Which proves they know it works. Because Trezon was their first test subject.

"One night may be all we have, partner," I say to Dunn. "You up for the challenge?"

"If it means saving Erik Paine from the fate that met Trackers Sandoval and Peters, then yes. But if it means placing you in the path of danger where this Prometheus entity is concerned, then I must admit certain misgivings."

"We step into the path of danger every damn day."

He nods once. "In this case, however, we may be up against something bigger than the two of us can handle, Investigator Chen. If Prometheus is indeed some sort of powerful group, we will be outnumbered."

Can't argue with that. "We find Erik. We save him from whoever mindjacked him. Then he leads us to whoever that is." I shrug inside the frame of my exo. "Don't worry. We've got this."

"Your confidence is inspiring."

If only I truly felt it.

"May I ask you a personal question?"

I glance over at him. "Go ahead."

"Have you experienced any hallucinations as of late due to your...lack of adequate sleep?"

I could lie. For some reason, I don't. "Back there. I thought I saw Wong again."

"Again?" His tone is gentle. Human, if I didn't know better.

"I've been seeing him every time I nod off. Which is why I've tried so hard to stay awake. But instead of Peters...I saw Dr. Wong's bloody face. Like he was the one kneeling there in front of me. Telling me..." I shake my head and curse.

"He speaks to you, Investigator Chen?"

"He says what we're up against is too big for us. That we can't stop it. That the Domes are going to implode. Politically. Literally. I have no idea." I inhale, exhale. "I know it's my subconscious, just doubting myself. But it seems so real."

Implode. Like the neural implants in Peters' and Sandoval's heads. And Trezon's. Krime's too, for all I know. Someone is monitoring each operative and ensuring that they don't talk. And Prometheus has enough people working for them that they don't even notice these minor losses.

But Erik isn't expendable. His life matters. If it wasn't for him, I never would have learned about my abilities and our shared past. Chancellor Hawthorne's lies and corruption would have gone unchecked, not to mention Dr. Wong's coup. Eurasia was a worse place for every citizen under their rule.

Erik always seems so carefree and obnoxious, but there's a real depth to him. He's genuinely concerned about things like freedom and truth. And he worries about me.

Damn it. Why'd he have to be mindjacked by a power-hungry secret entity before I realized how much I care about him, too?

"You have no reason to doubt yourself, Investigator Chen. Even operating as you are without adequate rest, you are an exemplary officer." Dunn pauses. "Do you regret killing Dr. Solomon Wong?"

I don't even remember activating the minigun on my shoulder. It just started shooting, a knee-jerk response to Wong searing that hole through my shoulder with his laser welder. Of course I regret it. I'm not a murderer.

Yet I am. I remember his death as vividly as if it happened a minute ago. And that cognitive dissonance has been tearing me apart ever since.

"Dr. Wong would know how Prometheus is doing this. Hijacking people's minds. Then killing them via their own neural implants." I shake my head and curse. "He would also have a pretty good idea who Prometheus is." One person? Some cabal? "He'd have to know. The man was a genius. Eurasia's savior."

Dunn nods. "I am sorry that I do not possess all of his knowledge. No security clone does, despite the fact that we were made in his image."

That gives me an idea. "What about his clones working in Futuro Tower?" Hundreds of them, all with every iota of his scientific prowess, working on a way to terraform the earth and return it to what it once was, centuries ago. Before the apocalypse of D-Day. Even before pollution became a thing. "Would they know?"

"That would depend. He may have shared his scientific knowledge with the Futuro Tower clones but not his political knowledge. From what we can tell, Prometheus may be a scientific entity as well as a political one."

"Explain." I glance at him as we continue around the corner and down the next vacant stretch of sidewalk.

"In order to change Trezon's DNA, rendering him

invisible, Prometheus must possess the scientific and medical knowledge necessary to graft genetic material from one of Eurasia's children into the body of an adult male—a dust addict—giving him permanent abilities. But at the same time, this Prometheus could also be a political entity seeking to overthrow the current power structure in the Domes. Why else would they kill their own operatives to avoid exposure?"

"I've considered the political angle. Prometheus may be attempting to raise up a superpowered army in order to remove James Bishop from office." I mull that over for a moment. "It's not the Patriots. They've never been this well-organized or this powerful. If I had to place a bet, it would be on a faction of Governors banding together." Could be a few who've never trusted Bishop's connection to the North American survivors or the Twenty. So this cabal decides to overthrow him by creating their own force of superpowered individuals dedicated to serving Prometheus—their false front. "Maybe they used to benefit from Trezon's underworld activities, providing them with as much dust as they could possibly snort. And when Chancellor Bishop closed the dust roads, they vowed to have their revenge—but also find a way to attain permanent abilities." To become like *gods* themselves.

"To steal fire from the demigods and use it for their own nefarious purposes," Dunn muses. "If that is the case, Investigator Chen, then I must confess that I do not foresee a quick resolution to this case before dawn."

Agreed. "So we'll start small. We'll find Erik and keep him alive."

"Yes, Investigator Chen. That is our primary objective."

I give him a brief once-over. "How are you feeling?"

"I remain optimistic."

"Physically, I mean."

He doesn't answer right away. Our footfalls along the sidewalk hold the moment, mine clanking, his thumping.

"I believe my post-surgery pain medication may be wearing off. Otherwise, I remain fit for duty." Another pause. "If I had access to the network, I would be able to run a self-diagnostic for a more precise answer. But my biosynthetic implants and prosthetics appear to be functioning within expected parameters."

"MedTech had to rebuild you."

"Yes. Close to fifty percent of my body is no longer the biological material I was originally created with."

I try to imagine what that must be like for him. "You said you received word from Fort—Unit D1-440—that I needed your help. And then those trackers intercepted you before you could reach me. Hit you with a localized EMP, tossed you into that closet with Hudson."

He nods.

There's one thing I haven't been able to understand. "How'd you get out of HQ? Weren't the technicians monitoring you after surgery? Nobody tried to stop you?"

His chin dips forward, the reflective surface of his face shield mirroring the pavement ahead. "It has troubled me as well," he says quietly.

"What has?"

His helmet turns to face me, and I see my own reflection now. An otherwise nonthreatening young woman housed in a formidable exoskeleton.

"I remember receiving the message from Unit D1-440, and

I remember running through the crowded streets of Dome 10." He extends a hand to indicate our surroundings, now completely clear and eerily silent. "Yet I have no memory of actually leaving HQ, Investigator Chen."

19

"Memory lapse?" A cold queasiness swims through my gut.

"Clones do not suffer lapses, Investigator Chen. We are conditioned to have perfect memory so that pertinent information can be trawled from our minds at a later date, should the need arise."

"Maybe it was the pain meds. You were probably out of it."

I don't want to consider an alternative explanation that Dunn's been mindjacked without even realizing it, or that during his surgery someone conditioned him to be an on-call assassin and then released him under a holo-projection that rendered him invisible to surveillance. Because that's the sort of thing only a paranoid person would think of. Or a designer of VR interactives. Not someone in full control of her faculties.

"My mind is clearer now that the drugs have lost their potency," he admits. "But lost time is not something I have ever experienced before." Then, after a pause, "When you delved into the minds of Sandoval and Peters, did you learn anything helpful?"

I nod. "Sandoval killed Trezon with a remote detonator. He died the same way as the two trackers. Neural implants exploded."

"Is that also how Krime met his demise?"

If I had to guess? But no, I don't have to. I use the antique phone to search the HQ database. My access to any files related to the Trezon case was denied by Chief Inspector Hudson, but this device came straight from Commander Bishop herself. With a palpable sense of relief, I find that I now have full access.

"Krime's neural implants were fried. Which means there had to be someone on-site with a detonator there as well." I look at Dunn as he turns to face me. "We already know Trezon was skulking invisibly around HQ."

"So the entity known as Prometheus made Trezon terminate Krime before he could share any secrets. And then Sandoval killed Trezon in the same way." Dunn pauses. "It would stand to reason that the remote detonator has a limited range."

"Are you thinking what I'm thinking, partner?"

Dunn pauses. "We must remember that Erik Paine is not acting of his own volition."

I can't let my emotions overwhelm me. I have to remain professional, detached. "He'd have to be somewhere nearby."

"If so, your drones will locate him soon."

"Finding him is one thing. Keeping him alive will be another challenge." Mid-stride, my thumbs slide across the antique phone's screen, hunting and pecking various letters from the keyboard display.

"Whom are you messaging?"

"A man who knows how to stay under the radar." The

same man who somehow knew about Erik's dual personality disorder ahead of time. "He's got some explaining to do. But I think he can help us." As long as Drasko agrees to meet in reality instead of virtual. It's a big ask, especially during an unexpected curfew.

Progress report, I telepathically transmit into the ether. No idea whether Wink or Blink will receive it, much less respond. My earlier success might have been a one-shot deal. A fluke.

No signs of Erik Paine, they respond in unison, their artificially intelligent thoughts entering my mind with their customary monotone intact. *Expanding search perimeter.*

I pull up their current location on the phone and note that Dunn and I are moving toward the western edge of the drones' search pattern.

Then I freeze in place. My exo won't budge, and neither will my muscles. From the corner of my eye, I see that Dunn is frozen as well.

"Damn it," I curse at the all-too familiar helpless feeling. I can move my mouth and vocal chords, and I can breathe, but that's about it.

"Hey, it could be worse," Erik says, stepping around the corner of a five-floor cube complex. He flips the grav weapon end over end, and the chrome reflects a glint of moonlight filtered through Dome 10's plexicon ceiling. "I could have hit Dunn with another EMP. Or targeted your neural implants, Sera."

"Like you did to Peters and Sandoval."

He shrugs. "They gave their lives for the cause. Prometheus may request it of anyone at any time. And we live to serve."

His eyes don't match his words. They remain as wide and dilated as the last time I saw him. Like he's in a constant state of horror at what he's being forced to do and say.

"Explain why my drones haven't found you."

Return to my location, I transmit to Wink and Blink, hoping the grav weapon hasn't affected my telepathic ability. So far, my night-vision remains as strong as ever.

"The benefits of having a friend in high places." Erik winks. "Prometheus can make anyone invisible to drones and security cameras. He can even cloud the eyes of people nearby, as long as they're online."

"By interfering with their augments?" I scoff. "Sounds like a two-bit hacker. Not a very powerful *friend*."

He shakes his head, pitying me. "You have no idea."

"Why is he allowing you to speak to me?" Why hasn't Erik's neural implant been fried yet? Does Prometheus want me to watch my friend die right in front of me while I'm powerless to intervene? Is the cabal a bunch of sadists? "Krime didn't last long. Neither did Trezon, Peters, Sandoval, or any of those so-called overdose victims I was tasked to investigate. Your overlord kills with impunity. How do you know you aren't next?"

"I may very well be. I exist only as long as I am useful. Trezon and the others were not the first to give their lives for our cause, and they will not be the last."

"Have you spoken to your mother lately?"

His hands tremble. His head twitches to one side. "Prometheus is my mother and father, sister and brother. I live to serve the greater good." He points the grav weapon at the Dome soaring high above us in the dark. "We are protected from the outside world only as long as we maintain a very fragile equilibrium here. Humankind no longer exists beyond Eurasia's walls—not any semblance that you would recognize. But it cannot always be this way. Sacrifices must be made to ensure our future. With every choice we make, we must live for a better tomorrow."

He's lost me. But I have to keep him talking, even as I hail Wink and Blink telepathically again, hoping they're still in range. "What kind of sacrifices?"

He chuckles. "People will do anything for peace, safety, and security. Surrender their independence. Live in a surveillance state. Allow technology to be implanted in their skulls, rendering them easily monitored at all times. And easily hijacked." He nods and then scowls, shouting without warning, "Such weaklings do not deserve to be our future!"

"So you're giving them an upgrade. Cutting DNA from the children of the Twenty—"

"*Our* children, Sera. Dr. Solomon Wong may not have known the future, but he prepared the way for it. Releasing the plague that rendered our population sterile was the first step. Granted, he did it due to concerns of potential overcrowding in the Domes. He never intended to sterilize the entire—"

"That isn't true." It can't be. "Wong was a monster, but he wasn't evil."

"What is *evil*, Sera?" He stares at me, waiting for my answer.

"The absence of good. Selfishness that hurts others." I scramble for a better definition and come up short. "Causing others to suffer—and enjoying it."

"What about necessary evil?"

"Just an excuse."

He smiles. "Dr. Wong did what he believed was necessary. Perhaps there was some selfishness involved." He nods toward Dunn. "Wong knew the Governors would never approve his cloning project unless the situation were dire. But when the Twenty were discovered, hope for the future returned to Eurasia. And now, by the hand of Prometheus, the gifts bestowed upon us and our children will be shared with the Children of Tomorrow!"

"Giving Prometheus a superpowered army." Wong said the Domes would eventually implode with violence and turmoil. I never believed it was possible.

I guess this is how it starts.

Projectile rounds rain from the sky, jolting me in spite of the grav field holding me still. Erik whirls around to aim his weapon at the source of the salvo, but the next barrage knocks the baton out of his hand with surgical precision and blasts it to crumpled shards that scatter across the pavement.

The gravity field restraining me dissipates instantly, and I lunge forward to grab onto Erik's arm. He struggles against my grip but soon realizes he's no match for the superhuman strength of my exo.

"Good job, boys," I tell Wink and Blink, hovering above us. "Didn't even hear you arrive."

"We activated our silent mode on approach," they answer in unison.

Never knew that option was available to them. Another improvement courtesy of Drasko, no doubt.

"You cannot stop us," Erik growls.

"That's what I keep hearing." I go through his pockets in a frenzy, knowing we don't have much time. Prometheus may detonate Erik's neural implant at any moment.

"What do you think you're doing?" he demands, slapping my hand away. Or trying to.

I continue unimpeded. The Erik I used to know would seldom be without a certain something—or a few, being the good anarchist he was—on his person, within easy reach. This mindjacked version? No idea if Prometheus would allow him to carry such things. In which case, there may be no hope for Erik. I won't be able to stop a Prometheus operative somewhere within range from activating the remote detonator.

I wish with everything in me that there was some way to return his mind to him, to ease the terror from his eyes. To let the real Erik know how much I care for him...before he's gone forever.

Then my grasping fingers stumble across what I'm looking for. Has to be. It's the right shape and size. No way to know if it will work, but I tell Dunn telepathically to get out of range, just in case. He does so without question, gesturing for Wink and Blink to follow. I watch them go as I retrieve the disc-shaped device from Erik's front pocket.

"Sera—" He clamps his hand onto my wrist, a grim warning in his eyes.

But I've already squeezed the pressure pad on the disc, and a localized EMP field instantly envelopes us, knocking out his augments right along with my exo-suit. I'm frozen in place again, but not for long. I pull the emergency release and stumble out of my exo, letting go of Erik in the process. He staggers backward out of my grasp and collapses against the side of the cube complex, shuddering along the brick wall as he slides to the sidewalk. He stares wide-eyed into the dark and trembles like he's freezing to death.

Clad in my form-fitting tactical suit, I kneel beside him and carefully place a hand on his shoulder. He flinches at first but then leans into my touch, closing his eyes.

"Erik?"

"Yeah." His voice is hoarse, like he's been screaming. Only he hasn't—not out loud, anyway. "It's me."

"A hundred percent you?"

He nods. "I think...it was going to kill me."

"It?"

"Prometheus." He stares at me in the dark. "It's not at all what we thought, Sera."

Dunn's clunking boots interrupt us as he charges our way. "Investigator Chen, we have company." He points back toward the direction of the tunnel gate, where the shapes of a half dozen security clones march toward us in tight formation.

"Reinforcements." I can't help but smile.

But then I notice the splatters across their otherwise pristine white armor. Mud? I can't allow my brain to consider the alternative.

"Give me the status of the Dome 10 tunnel guards," I tell my drones.

"There are no longer any life signs at the gate," Wink and Blink reply without pause, hovering a couple meters above me.

The clones continue to advance, moving in step like well-trained soldiers, heading straight for us. Either the guards abandoned their post—unlikely—or these units killed them. But why? And where did they come from? Straight through the tunnel from Dome 1?

My brain resists the obvious explanation.

"If I had access to our network, I could verify their orders..." Dunn holds his rifle at the ready, turning to face the approaching figures.

Two blocks away now. In no hurry, by the looks of them. Moving with purpose.

One might even say menace.

I don't have Link access, but I have another method of communication: *I am Investigator Sera Chen, and this is my partner, Unit D1-436*, I think at the six clones. Hoping my telepathy works on them. *We are under direct orders from Commander Mara Bishop to detain citizen Erik Paine. Identify yourselves. Who sent you?*

They don't respond, and they don't slow down. Fresh, oozing blood-spatters cover their armor. I accept the truth: they must have gunned down the guards at close range.

"It's Prometheus." Erik grits his teeth as he gets to his feet, forcing his shuddering muscles into compliance. "It's controlling them."

I tell myself that's not possible. These clones weren't at the cult's warehouse. They didn't catch one of those breathers Trezon and his cronies tossed at the audience. So who compelled these clones to inhale the chemical substance that renders anyone into a mindjacked operative? I can't imagine anybody forcing a security clone to do anything. They take orders only from the top, and that's interim Chancellor James Bishop.

But if Prometheus has somehow managed to mindjack Bishop, he could have ordered these security clones to do anything—even terminate the tunnel guards. And they would do so, without question.

"Explain." I glance at Erik.

Before he has a chance to elaborate, the clones break formation and charge toward us, firing their weapons in a sudden barrage of projectile rounds that blast into the brick of the cube complex beside us, sending chips and dust exploding into the air.

"Get out of range!" I order my drones, and they shoot up into the night sky. At the same time, I grab my father's sword off the back of my statuesque exo-suit—out of commission now, thanks to that EMP, as is the minigun on its shoulder. Damn it. "Find cover!" I tell Erik as I draw the *miao dao* from its scabbard.

He's already around the corner of the complex within clear sight of me but shielded from the incoming clones. Dunn drops to one knee and shoulders the buttstock of his assault rifle, laying down controlled bursts of automatic fire at his identical sextuplets.

Surprisingly, he doesn't hit a thing.

I can't believe what I'm seeing: The six clones are dodging his shots as if with some preternatural knowledge of each round's trajectory. They sidestep and leap with an unnatural grace, weaving through the air as they advance, their dark face shields and the muzzles of their weapons fixed on us without wavering.

Dunn's armor is deflecting the incoming fire well enough, but my tactical suit wasn't designed for an unrelenting salvo. It can take a round or two—and it does so as I backpedal toward Erik's position. One punches into my ribs, knocking the air out of me, and another kicks my shoulder back, spinning me sideways as I hit the pavement beside him in an awkward heap.

"You're hit." He frowns with concern and reaches for me.

"I'm fine." I brandish the *miao dao*, and he keeps his distance. "Get over here, partner!" I holler at Dunn, out of sight around the corner.

"Nice sword." Erik gives me one of his obnoxious winks.

"Thanks." Really hoping I don't accidentally slice off anything important on either one of us. The blade is long and unwieldy. "You wouldn't happen to have any more of those EMP discs?"

He pats his pockets and shakes his head. "You used the last one. Quick thinking. Knocking out my augments, as well as the nanotech in my system."

"From that breather."

He nods. "The inhalant is a compound tailor-made for mind control."

Dunn scrambles beneath a hail of projectile rounds, ducking his head as he slides beside us on his knees. The corner of the cube complex behind him bursts into a cloud of dust as the security clones concentrate their fire.

They'll be upon us in seconds.

I grip my father's sword in both hands and rise into a crouch, glancing at Dunn's rifle. His mag is half-spent. But he stands to his fullest height, providing an armored, human-sized shield for us.

"Stay behind me," I tell Erik.

You're outnumbered and outgunned, he thinks at me.

I don't reply. Because I'm busy giving Wink and Blink new orders.

The first clone to appear around the corner receives a burst of automatic fire at close range, courtesy of my partner. The blood-spattered security clone staggers backward from the impact but doesn't retaliate. The two clones behind it shove it forward—their human-sized shield.

Dunn fires another burst into its chest, and it shudders as the armor buckles and cracks. A rifle from one of the clones behind it makes an appearance, and I lunge forward with my sword. I sweep the blade in a downward arc that cuts off the rifle muzzle. Just like that. But I don't have time to admire the sword's strength. Instead, I sweep it upward, striking the damaged rifle out of the clone's hand and sending it clattering away.

One disarmed. One pulverized by Dunn's automatic bursts. That leaves four more armed clones to contend with.

Two of them leap up onto the cube complex with impressive dexterity, somehow clinging to the brick wall beyond the reach of my blade. They hold their assault rifles one-handed, aiming the muzzles down toward us.

Then they zero in on Dunn and fire, full automatic. I can only scream as I watch my partner's armor crackle and disintegrate. He turns sideways like a gunfighter in a western VR story and points his weapon up at the pair, emptying his mag, keeping his left arm away from the fight while his right is pulverized.

It isn't long before his shooting arm tears free under the barrage, armor sparking at the shoulder joint. It lands on the ground with a clatter, the gloved hand still gripping the rifle. Both lie motionless, like dead things.

The two clones cease fire and drop to the pavement as their three functional comrades surround us, fully intact assault rifles level with our heads. Only one clone lies on the ground, chest armor destroyed by Dunn's rifle. No movement, except for a few intermittent sparks. I can't help but wonder how Dunn must feel, having killed one of his own.

More likely he's distracted for the moment by his severed limb. I can't see any blood, so his armor must have automatically sealed the wound.

"Drop your weapon," the clones order in unison, their voice unlike Dunn's or Fort's. They sound more like my drones.

Like machines.

The one I disarmed stoops to pick up Dunn's rifle. It pulls his hand free of the weapon and tosses his arm aside like trash, then reloads a fresh mag from the compartment built into its leg armor.

Stand down, I order them. No reaction to my attempt at mind-to-mind communication. Either they can't hear me, or they're ignoring me. So I try the conventional method: "Stand down. I am Investigator—"

"We know who you are, enemy of Prometheus," they reply. "You will lay down your weapon, or we will fire on you."

All five of them pulling their triggers at once? That would be a death sentence. "So you have orders to kill me."

"Our orders are of no concern to you."

"I'd say they're very concerning." Erik steps forward. "I am Erik Paine, and I speak with the authority of Prometheus. Lower your weapons. Sera Chen and her partner are my responsibility. You will not harm them."

The clones' face shields turn toward Erik, and their heads twitch to one side as they regard him with sudden interest. Accessing their network for more information?

They don't act like clones, I think at Dunn, standing beside me.

"Because they are not," he whispers. Then he half-turns toward me, enough to draw my attention to his wounded shoulder. The armor didn't seal anything, yet there's no blood—just synthetic components and wires, with some clear hydraulic fluid leaking in thin rivulets. Nothing biological.

The arm must have been one of his new additions. A prosthetic. I understand the connection.

They're robots.

He nods, almost imperceptibly.

Mindless automatons made to look like security clones. Imposters obeying Prometheus without question. Ordered to shoot down anyone standing in their way. The tunnel guards. The three of us.

A mechanized kill squad. Did Prometheus send one into every Dome? How many of these bots exist?

"He no longer shares the link." The clone imposters advance a step, their weapons trained on Erik. "He does not serve Prometheus."

"Worth a shot," Erik mutters, shoulders slumping.

I step in front of him and raise the *miao dao*, gripped in both hands like a baseball bat. Because that's how much sword training I've had. One long blade against five assault rifles. What am I going to do? Deflect the bullets? Yeah, right.

Deafening weapons fire smashes my senses, and I expect to feel the projectile rounds tear me apart. But they're not aimed at me or my friends.

The imposters whirl around to face Wink and Blink, who've approached on silent mode at high speed to empty all their remaining ammo at the bots. The rounds slam into their anthropomorphic chests, causing them to stagger as they return fire in chaotic bursts. My drones weave in midair, dodging bullets as best they can. The ones they can't strike them dead center, and they begin to smoke and spark. But they don't quit, and they don't drop out of the air.

I lunge forward swinging the *miao dao*, attacking the robots from behind, striking the heads from their shoulders and sending them rolling across the pavement. But the clone imposters continue unimpeded.

"Here, Investigator Chen." Dunn thumps the center of his chest with his fist. "Their central processors are housed in the middle of the chassis."

Right. That's how he destroyed the first one.

To demonstrate, he takes his fist and plows it into the back of the robot closest to him. It doesn't seem to notice, focused instead on shooting my drones out of the night sky. Dunn smashes the armor, caving it in. His second strike cracks the plating. His third punches straight through, impaling the robot underneath. Its arms drop to its sides and it stops moving, sagging in a motionless heap.

With a nod of acknowledgement, I thrust my sword forward, and the blade slices through armor and robot at once. Dunn shakes the immobilized imposter off his arm, letting it clunk onto the ground, and moves on to the next one, just as it turns toward him and fires its weapon at close range. Dunn falls backward, his face shield exploding like shattered glass as the rounds smash his helmet to pieces.

I leap forward and sweep my blade through the robot's rifle arm, cutting it off without ceremony. Then I plunge the sword through its chest and the central processor underneath. Three robots down. The remaining two follow quickly on their heels, collapsing to the pavement under Wink and Blink's relentless barrage.

All six clone imposters lie motionless except for the occasional twitch of servos and spark of mechanical life fading away.

I drop to my knees beside Dunn, lying flat on his back. His helmet is little more than plasteel shards encasing his bloody face. He looks up at me, and for an instant, I see Dr. Wong from my nightmares. But the horrible image passes.

This is my partner. And he needs my help.

"Are you hit?" I look for entry wounds but can't find any underneath all the slick blood.

"I am...unable to run self-diagnostics," he manages.

"They look like lacerations." Erik kneels on Dunn's other side, surveying the damage. "The rounds broke his helmet, and the pieces cut him up."

"That sounds likely." Dunn nods, then winces at the movement.

"Stay still." I catch the tip of my sword on my sleeve and rip it all the way up to my shoulder. "I need to stop the bleeding."

Carefully, Erik removes what's left of Dunn's helmet, and I dab at his facial wounds with my torn sleeve. Glancing at Wink and Blink wobbling in the air above us, both of them venting smoke and sparks from multiple fractures, I grimace at their condition and ask for a status report.

"We remain functional, Investigator Chen," they reply in glitchy unison. Troopers, both of them.

I can't focus too long on Dunn's bloody face or missing limb. Instead, I nod toward his remaining arm, the one he plunged through the back of that robot. "Let me guess.

Another replacement?"

"Yes." He closes his eyes as I clean his forehead. The blood keeps welling up, but I can see the lacerations now, and they're deep. He's going to need laser-stitching, the sooner the better to avoid permanent scarring.

We've got to get him to MedTech at HQ. But I have no idea how we're going to get there, or how many kill squads stand between us and the heart of Dome 1.

He looks at me again. "Do not worry, Investigator Chen. I am fine."

There isn't time to worry. A groundcar guns its engine at the end of the block and heads our way, headlights cutting a wide swath through the dark. Never mind the curfew. Some people always think they're above the law.

Erik stoops to retrieve one of the fallen robots' rifles, discarding the empty mag and swapping it with one from another fallen weapon. He squints into the glare of the approaching vehicle and strides toward it.

What the hell are you doing? I think at him.

He doesn't look at me, but I see the corner of his mouth turn up in a smirk. Obnoxious as ever. I rise from Dunn's side with my sword at the ready. Dunn ignores my advice to stay put and gets to his feet, his one hand pressing my wadded-up sleeve against his forehead.

The groundcar is matte black with a supercharged engine. A throwback to the gas-guzzling muscle cars of a North American bygone era, it runs on waste—methane, to be exact. A Dome 10 exclusive, not permitted anywhere else.

How do I know so much about it? Thanks to the telepathy I'm sending toward the driver's seat, it appears I know the man behind the wheel.

He spins out, tires smoking, and ends up facing the opposite direction as he pulls up alongside the curb. The dark, driver-side window slides down, revealing the grim face and scarred neck of my old friend Drasko.

"Get in," he says, revving the thunderous engine.

20

There's no time to argue. In the distance, a fresh kill squad is marching our way. And we're in no shape to deal with them right now.

While Erik steers Dunn into the cramped backseat of Drasko's car and hunkers down to climb in beside him, I summon Wink and Blink. They descend shakily, and I catch them one at a time, wincing at the damage they've sustained. As they power down to conserve energy, their status lights dimming, Drasko pops the trunk. I set them gently inside, noting the wisps of smoke that curl out of each one. If drones ever start receiving medals for exemplary service, my boys will be at the front of the line.

I slam the trunk shut and glance at my exo-suit, standing there like it knows it has to be left behind. We have no other choice. I hope it's still in one piece the next time I see it, but considering the location, I won't hold my breath. It'll either be scavenged for parts by the locals, or one of Drasko's unsavory associates might figure out how to get it up and running again. Nothing I can do about it right now, either way.

I scoop up my father's redwood scabbard and sheathe the

miao dao. Then I duck into the bucket seat on the passenger side of Drasko's car. The door drops behind me and locks automatically as I pull on the safety harness and buckle it into place.

"Good to see you in the flesh." I give Drasko a nod.

He almost smiles. "That's new." He glances at my sword, the scabbard's end resting on the floor beside my boots, the hilt wedged between my shoulder and the door.

"Desperate times."

"Got that right. Headed to HQ, I take it?"

"If it isn't out of your way."

"Not at all."

He floors the accelerator, throwing us back against our seats, and we surge forward, straight toward the oncoming bots. They ratchet things up from an orderly march to an all-out charge, headed our way. Automatic rifles firing at us, projectile rounds thudding across the hood and windshield of Drasko's car, sparking like fireworks. Good thing the vehicle is bulletproof. Even so, I can't help grimacing and sinking down into my seat at the salvo.

"You received my hail." I glance at Drasko, who's not breaking a sweat.

"Figured you could use a hand." He looks up into the rearview mirror at Dunn. "You get shot in the face again?"

"Yes," Dunn replies evenly. "How is your arm, Mr. Drasko?"

Right. These two have a history, one that involves a bullet to the helmet and a fractured humerus, respectively. Courtesy of each other.

"Good as new." Drasko clenches his jaw as he steers us into the oncoming kill squad. Heavy impacts reverberate along the groundcar's frame as robots are thrown aside, flailing through the air before they crash to the pavement in our wake. "Can't say the same for you. What happened? Sera chop it off with her sword?"

"No." Dunn doesn't elaborate.

"I'm doing well, by the way. Thanks for asking." Erik cradles his assault rifle, keeping its muzzle trained on the sliver of a window beside him. "Had my brain hijacked for a little while by a powerful AI, but other than that, everything's just peachy."

Wait. "What?" I scowl at him.

"Glad you survived the ordeal." Drasko curses under his breath. "Not many have."

I pivot in my seat to give Erik my complete attention. "You're saying Prometheus isn't human. They're—it's a machine?"

He nods. Then he squints one eye. "Sort of. It's more than a machine, far beyond what we would understand as a complex artificial intelligence. For lack of a better word, it's a copy of the greatest human mind Eurasia has ever known."

I'm going to be sick.

I turn back around in my seat and grit my teeth, force myself to focus on our surroundings as they pass by in a blur of speed—but not fast enough to miss the copious blood spatters all over the guard station. People I spoke to half an hour ago, tasked with the safety and security of Dome 10's citizens. Now gone forever.

A split-second later, we're hurtling along the tunnel floor, heading toward Dome 1. Drasko drives this vehicle even faster than he used to fly his aerocar, if that's possible. But I can't focus on the groundcar's headlights slicing through the dark or what we'll find waiting for us on the other side. Because all I can see is the bloody face of—

"Dr. Solomon Wong." Erik pauses to let it sink in. "Somehow he created a digital version of his own mind, which has been stored online ever since his death. No idea what its original purpose was, other than a narcissistic experiment. Or an attempt at immortality. Up until now, it's been content to exist in the Link's background as it has learned and evolved—"

"What the hell would it need to learn?" I shake my head at the prospect. Wong knew everything. Or he liked to think so.

Erik leans forward, his head between Drasko's seat and mine. "I don't think it was designed to be as powerful as it's become. Using the Link to access the personality profiles of citizens, organizing the Children of Tomorrow cult, creating the nano-tech compound in those breathers to gain full access to a person's neural implant. Calling itself *Prometheus*—proof that it's self-aware now. It's developed its own sentient identity."

How do we stop it? That's all that matters.

"So it exists digitally." Our enemy isn't flesh and blood. There's no cabal of disgruntled governors. I had it completely wrong. Excellent work, Investigator Chen. "That means we can destroy it. Find the code and delete it. No more Prometheus."

Erik scrunches up his face. "Not that easy."

"Nothing ever is," I mutter. Drasko grunts in agreement, his eyes fixed on the path ahead. We won't be inside this tunnel much longer. Will Dome 1 be in complete chaos? Killbots roaming the streets, shooting with wild abandon?

"Every time Prometheus hijacks someone's mind, it enters

their neural implants. The nano-tech in their system, courtesy of those breathers, acts like a bridge between the Link and that person, who then becomes a conduit for the AI to interact with the physical world." Erik sounds intrigued by the whole thing, even though he was one of those meat puppets himself not too long ago.

"Until they become compromised, and the AI severs the link," Drasko says. "Killing the conduit in the process."

"Which doesn't hurt Prometheus at all, because the AI doesn't exist in any one conduit, or any centralized location, for that matter." Erik shakes his head. "It's not like we can hit a room full of servers with an EMP and knock it out of commission."

"We can shut down the Link," I offer. Sever the AI's connection to the real world. Keep it trapped online. "You've done that before."

He nods, scratching at the dark stubble along his jaw. Then he raises an eyebrow at me. "Or we could use the Link to find Prometheus in VR. I might be able to get its attention."

"Using yourself as bait, you mean? That's a horrible idea." I tap my temple. "Augments are out anyway, remember?" His are too, thanks to that EMP disc I hit him with.

"Got some old-school goggles in the glovebox," Drasko offers.

"The what?"

He nods toward a compartment in the dashboard above my knees. "VR goggles. Us old folks used to wear them before the Link augments went online. Figured they might come in handy someday."

He's got a real knack for that—knowing more than he lets

on. I punch the chrome button in the middle of the compartment, and it drops open. Two pairs of clunky-looking goggles nearly flop out, along with a large-caliber handgun.

"Let me guess." I weigh the pistol in the palm of my hand. It's probably as old as the groundcar, but without any special upgrades. "Unregistered?"

"Loaded, too. Armor-piercing rounds." Drasko has fully embraced his underworld persona, given the job by none other than Commander Bishop herself. Not that anyone but the three of us—and maybe Erik—knows it. An unconventional way to deal with organized crime, but as Commander Bishop puts it, Eurasia will always have its underworld, and she'd rather deal with a boss she can trust. One who keeps things orderly, avoiding total anarchy. "Goes off real easy. Wouldn't have any trouble punching through this wreck on wheels."

I set the gun back in the compartment and take out the goggles. "So, no augments necessary?"

"You're holding the augments." He almost smiles. "Plug those into any Link interface, and you're good to go."

"Commander Bishop gave me an antique phone..." I retrieve the device from my pocket and try to hail her, but I can't establish a link. Unclear whether the issue is on my end or hers.

"That'll work." Drasko nods.

"Nice." Erik smiles, impressed. "I love old tech. It's so..." He grasps at the air with his fingers. "Physical."

"Here." I toss him a pair of goggles. "Let's get physical."

He catches them with a grin. But the expression drops from his face as Drasko takes us out of the tunnel and through the Dome 1 train station. It's completely deserted. No guards are posted at the gate, but thankfully there's no blood on display. The men and women stationed here must have been summoned elsewhere before the killbots arrived. Drasko nudges the groundcar's front bumper against the unlocked gate, and it swings open, ushering us into a Dome 1 unlike anything we've seen before.

Fires light up the night, blazing from the smashed windowalls of domescrapers and cube complexes, while the flaming aerocars of curfew enforcers struggle to remain airborne. Bursts of automatic gunfire echo throughout the streets, drowning out wild screams. Shadowy figures run, panicked, seeking shelter, while rocket-propelled grenades explode in voracious displays of pyrotechnics.

It's exactly what Dr. Wong predicted. The central hub of Eurasia, the most beautiful and sophisticated of all the Ten Domes, imploding with hideous violence.

A dark shape swoops down from the sky, careening around a building and disappearing into the distance faster than any aerocar I've ever seen. It almost looked like a flying man.

"Milton!" Erik whoops, pointing. "All right!"

"This mess got him out of retirement." Drasko guns the engine and takes us into the middle of the melee on a direct route to police headquarters. "And not just Milton. All of them." He glances at me and then Erik. Impressed, for some reason. "Your biological parents. They sure know how to fight."

My birth parents, Luther and Daiyna. Erik's birth parents, Samson and Shechara. Their friend, Milton—the only one of them who can break the sound barrier, either on the ground or in the air. My heart skips a beat at the thought of them using their special abilities to protect the citizens of Eurasia against Prometheus.

What am I feeling? I'm proud of them, and proud to be related to them. Strange. I've never thought of them like this before. Instead, I've gone out of my way to avoid them. My mother has asked me countless times to invite Daiyna and Luther over for dinner; she and my father want to meet them, and they want me to be there when it happens. But I'm always too busy. And besides, my parents are here in Dome 1, while Luther and Daiyna—

"Has Prometheus sent those kill squads into every Dome?" I ask.

"The bots? Yeah." Drasko curses under his breath, swerving to keep from running over a pack of terrified citizens racing down the middle of the street. "No idea where Prometheus built them or where it's been keeping them until now. But they're on the loose, wreaking havoc all over the place while the Children of Tomorrow follow their original marching orders."

Going after the children. Planning to harvest their DNA. So Prometheus can have its own army of superpowered human soldiers? Or so it can turn any citizen into a demigod?

I don't understand why an AI would behave this way—mindjacking people, killing people. How could this thing be a copy of Dr. Wong's mind? The man who brought the Twenty into the world. Also the man who released the Plague in the first place? Is that true? I can't afford to have my sleep-deprived brain mis-remembering things right now.

At this point, we have to deal with what's right in front of us. And I have to make sure the people I care about are okay.

My thumbs attack the phone, establishing a link. I hold the flat device up to one ear, covering the other with the palm of my hand.

My father answers the hail on its second ring. "Who is this?"

"Dad, are you safe?"

"Sera? Yes, your mother and I are fine. Our floor is secure. Where are you? Only audio is coming through."

"I'm heading to HQ. I'm fine. Stay where you are. I'll—"

"What's going on, Sera? We can't get a straight answer on the Link."

Not surprising. "Dad, I—" My hand rests on the scabbard beside me. "Thank you for the *miao dao*."

He doesn't hear me. "Some people are saying it's those Patriots, others are talking about robots and demigods! Can you believe it?"

"Dad, I have to go. I'll find you once this is over. Stay safe. Love you."

"Love you too, Sera Bear."

A lifelong cringe-worthy nickname that doesn't bother me at all right now.

My next hail goes out to Commander Bishop, and this time we connect.

"Chen, give me a status report." Calm and cool as ever, while Dome 1 erupts with insanity all around us. "Have you apprehended Erik Paine?"

"Yes, ma'am. He's no longer under the control of Prometheus, and he has important information to share with you. We're on our way to HQ." I glance back at Dunn, sitting very still. "My partner is wounded." Again.

"I'll have a robodoc standing by." She pauses. "It's a war zone out there. Be careful."

I nod as though she can see me via holo and end the call.

"You'll need to explain it to her. Everything you remember from your mindjacking." I glance back at Erik, and he nods. "Your VR idea, too. She'll want the analysts to shadow us once we're in."

"Glad you're up for it."

"I still say it's a bad idea. But I'm willing to try anything at this point." I scowl at the mayhem surrounding us. "We have to stop this. No matter what."

Drasko's groundcar skids sideways as he avoids ramming into the flaming wreckage of an aerocar in the middle of the road, and we lurch in our harnesses. I pocket the phone and grab onto the dashboard as he spins out intentionally, then revs the engine, burning rubber. The wild squeal drowns out the ambient gunfire for a second. Then we're back on track at a high velocity, heading down a main boulevard eventually devoid of traffic, straight into the yawning mouth of the parking structure underneath HQ. Miraculously, the building appears to be undamaged.

The garage is as empty as the street outside. Guess everybody's somewhere else, dealing with killer robots and psychotic cult members. We pull up alongside the polished plasteel doors of the speedlift, and Drasko hits the brakes. He presses a button on his console, and the two side doors drift open. But he doesn't get out of his seat.

"Be safe, Chen."

I reach over and squeeze his arm. Then I unfasten my harness and climb out.

"Wait—you're not coming with us?" Erik frowns as he

shoves the passenger seat forward and follows me. He reaches back for Dunn absently, and my one-armed partner grasps his hand as he struggles to exit the vehicle.

"Gotta check on the wife and kids," Drasko says.

Erik's jaw drops open. "But they're...in Dome 6." He glances over his shoulder at the violence in the distance. "You're driving through that? Again?"

"Haven't been able to hail them. I need to know they're OK." Drasko pops the trunk, and I take a second to retrieve my drones. "Anything goes wonky while you're in VR, you unplug immediately. Just because your augments are out doesn't mean Prometheus can't get inside your head." He gives us a grim look. "Remember that."

There he goes again with that uncanny knowledge of things.

"Got it." With Wink under one arm, Blink under the other, the *miao dao* sheathed in one hand and the goggles dangling from the other, I don't look like I'm ready to face off against a powerful AI. But I'm as ready as I'll ever be. "Thanks. I owe you one."

"We'll see." Drasko revs the engine as the doors drift shut, and we back away toward the speedlift. His tires squeal, echoing in the desolate parking structure, as he guns the accelerator and vacates the premises.

Erik slips his goggles around his neck and watches Drasko go. "That guy is so cool..."

Dunn and I step into the speedlift. I clear my throat to get Erik's attention, and he dashes to my side before the doors slide shut.

"The Domes are imploding, and you're captivated by Drasko's *coolness*." I punch the button for Level 6,

MedTech, and we glide upward.

"If I focused on what's happening, I'd probably freak out." After what he's been through, I can't blame him for trying to distract himself.

"So, you think it'll work? Going after Prometheus in VR?"

He crosses his arms, hugging himself unconsciously. "I'm the puppet who got away." He gives me that goofy grin of his, but it doesn't last long. He shrugs to hide a shiver. "Anyhow, best to forget what Drasko said about unplugging. Without our augments acting as buffers, we'll be hardwiring directly into the Link. Any sudden shift from VR to real-world could mess with our heads. We're talking permanent cognitive damage."

"Lesser of two evils. If the alternative is being mindjacked."

His eyes look hollowed-out for a moment. "Yeah. No joke." He'll be damaged by that experience for the rest of his life, and there's nothing anybody can do about it. He doesn't need me reminding him.

"So, Drasko's groundcar. Where can you get one for yourself?"

His eyes light up, and he smirks. "Who says I want an old muscle car?"

"Every fiber of your being."

He almost laughs. "Maybe. Samson could probably get one to run on corn ethanol." He frowns. "I hope Mom's alright. The farm..."

A mental image of Dome 9 fills my mind, a scene of countless robots with flame-throwers destroying crops. Starving us. Moving on to the air recyclers and purifiers in

Dome 3. Suffocating us. Then what? Cracking open the plexicon of the Domes themselves and letting the contaminated air have its way with the citizens of Eurasia.

I've heard the horror stories, that the only life still in existence outside the Domes is nothing we'd recognize as human. Mutant monsters incapable of speech with bulging yellow eyes, drooling fangs, mucus oozing from every facial orifice. There used to be hundreds of them, but thanks to my birth parents and their friends, only a few remain—former soldiers unlucky enough to have suffered a breach in their protective gear while traversing the Wastes in search of salvageable materials.

The speedlift slows to a stop, and the doors slide open with a ding. One of the robodocs is waiting for us. For all I know, it's the same machine that gave me my brainscan. When was that? Feels like years ago.

"Welcome, Investigator Chen," the robot greets us, rolling backward on its treads as we step out of the lift. "What is the nature of your medical emergency?"

"Not me." I cast a worried eye Dunn's way. He's still on his feet, but he's never been this quiet. "My partner."

The robodoc jerks to a stop. "We do not service clones on this floor, Investigator Chen. You will need to take it down to Level 5—"

"Is anybody down there?"

"Not at the moment. Due to unforeseen circumstances, all staff have either been sent home or assigned duties elsewhere—"

"You're going to fix him up." I point over the top of its boxy frame toward the MedTech bay where every other robodoc sits in its charging station, status lights glowing peacefully. "Right now."

"Is that an order?"

"Yes." If that'll get this thing to move its metal ass.

"Very well. Follow me, please." It leads the way, well-maintained treads rolling without a single squeak. "Have the clone sit itself on the edge of the first bed."

We step across the threshold, and that's when crimson warning lights start flashing while a shrieking alarm pierces our eardrums.

"What the hell?" I struggle to hold onto my drones as the *miao dao* and Drasko's goggles clatter onto the floor. "Turn that off!"

"They really don't like clones in here." Erik winces, covering his ears.

"Scanners have detected that your clone is carrying an explosive charge." The robodoc wheels around, spindly metal arms emerging from hidden compartments in its sides and unfolding to over a meter in length. One pins Dunn against the wall while the other wields a laser cutter. Without ceremony or permission, it slices through the white armor across Dunn's middle, removing an entire section and laying bare his toned abdomen underneath.

Skin pale enough to be translucent...exposing the digital countdown of a bomb planted inside.

21

This can't be happening. I'm hallucinating. I've finally lost it—completely.

Dunn looks me in the eye. I've never seen him look so sad. "It appears we have an explanation for that lost time I experienced, Investigator Chen."

He told me he didn't remember leaving HQ after his surgery. I couldn't allow myself to believe anything had happened to him. But I should've investigated—done my damn job. Now he's carrying an explosive stitched inside him. He's been carrying it all this time. Brainwashed to ignore it? No clue. But now it's about to go off.

If the glowing countdown is accurate, then we have less than a minute before detonation.

"Someone did this to you." I set down my drones and step toward him. "Someone on Level 5—a Prometheus operative put that in you and made you forget about it."

"A plausible, disturbing explanation." He nods. "You should leave—"

"Can we disarm it?" I glance at Erik.

"You know how to disarm a bomb?"

"I was hoping you did."

He pats his pockets, but there aren't any more EMP discs. "We have to cut him open..." He gives Dunn an apologetic look.

The old phone in my pocket vibrates. I grab it and receive the hail from Commander Bishop.

"MedTech scanners detected an explosive," she says, almost out of breath. "Are you alright?"

"Yes, ma'am. Forty seconds until detonation. Please tell me a bomb squad is on the way."

"The bomb squads are busy putting out fires across the Domes." Her tone is grim. "You're on your own, Chen."

"Thirty seconds," the robodoc announces, as if we can't see the digital display shining through Dunn's skin. The bot hasn't lifted its arm planted across my partner's chest, holding him flat against the wall. "Based on the size of the explosive, it will destroy this entire floor when it detonates. You both should leave immediately."

"We're evacuating the building," Bishop says. "That's an order, Chen."

I glance across the hall at the speedlift doors. "Let me know when everyone on-site is safely beyond the blast radius, ma'am." I turn to the robodoc. "Get that thing out of him."

The machine activates its laser cutter again, this time slicing through my partner's flesh. Dunn grimaces, causing fresh blood to well up along his facial lacerations. I take his gloved hand and squeeze, my expression mirroring his.

"Go," I tell Erik. "Get to safety. There's no way to know if this will work."

He takes hold of my shoulder. "We'll find out together. I assume you have someplace in mind to put that bomb?"

The robodoc uses both its arms now, one pincer cutting

while the other mops up the blood from the incision, keeping the digital countdown clear to see.

"Probably a bad idea. But it's all I've got."

Carefully, the robodoc removes the explosive device and seals the wound with laser-stitching. "Ten seconds," it reports.

"We can see that." I take the bomb from its pincer and run straight for the speedlift doors. Erik is right behind me. "Ma'am, is everyone out?"

"All floors are clear," Commander Bishop replies on the phone. "Another minute to reach a safe distance."

We have eight seconds.

"Wait—you're going to—?" Erik stares as I punch the down arrow.

"Yeah."

Six seconds.

"Ma'am, you need to run." The speedlift doors ding as they open. I lunge inside and set the bomb on the floor, then backpedal out. Before the doors slide shut, I reach in and hit the button for the first floor. "The explosive is on its way down. In a speedlift."

Silence from Commander Bishop. Three seconds until detonation. The lift glides down the shaft past Level 5, then Level 4, Level 3.

"We're running," Bishop says.

One second left.

I turn to Erik. "Hold onto something."

He wraps me tight in his arms as a sudden earthquake rocks police headquarters from the ground up, throwing us against the wall as medical equipment crashes nearby, lights flicker, dust rains from the ceiling, and a mild roar rumbles beneath our feet.

Then everything is still—a quiet as abrupt as the blast itself.

"Not a bad idea." Erik grins at me, his face just a couple centimeters away from mine. We're on the floor in a tangled heap.

I pat his chest and move to extricate myself. He clears his throat and lets go of me as we get up, shaking our heads with palpable relief.

"Chen?" Bishop's still on the phone clutched in my hand. "Report."

"We're OK. The blast—"

"Get out of there. Now." Bishop's voice is ice-cold. "The structure is no longer intact."

As if to add an exclamation point to her warning, the floor shifts beneath me, cracking with a fault line that tears up the hallway. Everything on the left side drops into Level 5 beneath us with a deafening crash and plume of dust. Just like that, half the floor is gone. And now the floor above us is sinking, our ceiling caving in and crumbling under the weight of what's above.

"Get those doors open." I point Erik toward the speedlift and run back to the MedTech bay.

Dunn staggers out, his one hand on his stitched middle. Somehow, during the chaos, the robodoc managed to tend to his face as well, which is no longer bleeding. Instead, a dozen laser sutures close his facial lacerations. Creepy-looking, but they should fade over time.

"You're alright," he says with relief.

"So are you." I can't help smiling, despite the circumstances. I quickly retrieve my drones, sword, and

Drasko's goggles.

Then I notice the robodocs, all sitting in their charging stations while the building collapses around them. I almost call out to them to come with us, to escape the destruction. But I don't. Unlike us, these bots are replaceable.

We join Erik at the speedlift doors, which remain shut. Other than being red in the face, he hasn't made any progress. "They won't budge. The entire shaft is mangled after that bomb went off."

Most likely, but it's our only way out of here. The emergency stairwell was on the side of the building that already collapsed.

I join him on one side, and Dunn takes the other. Between the three of us, we manage to force the plasteel doors open a centimeter or two; then with some more effort, nearly a meter. Tendrils of smoke drift out. The gap is wide enough now for us to squeeze through, one at a time.

Erik goes first, clinging to the ledge, trying and failing to keep from looking down. To his eyes, the empty shaft is completely dark. He can't see seven levels straight down through the blast damage to the charred parking garage below. Probably for the best.

Hoping this isn't asking too much of them, I activate Wink and Blink and send them into the shaft. They wobble through the air and spark intermittently, sporting dents and cracks courtesy of those projectile rounds earlier, but they follow orders without pause.

"Connect your lines to Erik Paine and Unit D1-436," I tell them, and from the underside of each drone chassis, a claw grapple emerges on a cable. One clamps onto the back of Dunn's armor while the other grabs Erik's jacket between his shoulder blades.

"Hey—that pinches." He checks to make sure his jacket is zipped up, then frowns at me. "You're not tethered."

"I've got this." I tap the sword.

"Not sure how that helps."

Me either. Guess I imagined impaling the blade through the shaft wall if I were to slip and fall, halting my descent and dangling from the hilt. Wishful thinking, maybe. I tug off my belt and slip it through a slit in the scabbard, then fasten the buckle. Reaching one arm and my head through the loop I've created, I let the belt rest on my shoulder while the scabbard lies flat against my back.

"I'll be fine. I can see in the dark, remember?" I glance past him at the long drop and soot-stained emergency ladders along every floor. The lift itself is nowhere in sight, completely obliterated by the bomb. "I'll point you in the right direction."

The entire building shakes as Level 7, along with every floor above it, decides to crush Level 6 at that moment, sending an avalanche of dust and debris exploding all around us. I shove Erik and Dunn toward the ladder a few meters to the right of the doorway. They cling to the ledge and slide carefully, side by side, my drones hovering above their heads. I'm right behind them.

The phone vibrates in my pocket as we reach the ladder and climb down. Commander Bishop demanding a status update, no doubt. She'll have to wait until we meet her outside. Assuming we make it out of the building before it collapses into a massive pile of rubble, crushing us along the way.

Smart of Prometheus to take police headquarters out of

the picture. An operative must have been nearby, close enough to activate the explosive sewn inside Dunn. For all we know, it could have been the same technician from Level 5 who put it there in the first place. As Chief Inspector Hudson noted, we have no idea how many infiltrators are hidden within our ranks.

Then an insidious thought shows up out of nowhere: What if it was Erik? What if Prometheus never fully relinquished its grip on him? Under the AI's influence, Erik detonated Peters' and Sandoval's neural implants. Who's to say he didn't activate the bomb inside Dunn as well?

But I didn't stumble across any kind of remote trigger while I was going through Erik's pockets. Could it be a hands-free detonator? Or telepathic—is that even possible? And why would he have waited until we stepped into MedTech to activate it?

Crazy, sleep-deprived thoughts. I've got to get a grip.

Another rumble shakes the crumbling building, and we white-knuckle the cold rungs to keep from being thrown off the ladder. The plasteel walls of the shaft creak and groan around us, pressed inward from all sides as structural integrity falters. In any other situation, this would be the strongest section of the building—if it hadn't already been weakened by that powerful explosive.

A flurry of sparks burst from Blink's side, and it plummets half a meter before righting itself.

Give me a status report, I tell both drones telepathically. Still weird, speaking mind-to-machines.

A short pause. *We are functional.*

So, not great.

We continue downward at an urgent pace, Erik leading

the way with Dunn and me right above him. Wink and Blink remain at the ready, hovering nearby as we descend. Once we reach the parking structure on the ground floor, we find the doors blown outward, mangled beyond recognition, and we take off running out of the garage and across the vacant street outside. None of us look back, as if we share the same fear that what's left of HQ will topple and land right on top of us if we dare to make eye contact with it.

The skin on the back of my neck prickles. Any second, I expect to hear the building crumple behind me, rumbling the pavement beneath my feet like a seismic event, throwing a wave of dust and debris over us.

But it never does. Some design feature keeps the skeleton upright, even as meat falls off the bones in massive chunks.

We find Commander Bishop and Chief Inspector Hudson two blocks away, crouching in an alley between a cube complex and an office building, both structures billowing fire and smoke from the upper floors. Huddled between my two superior officers are the six HQ analysts. Cranial jacks lie unplugged at the base of their bald heads, the black metal ports a sharp contrast against their pale skin. Staring vacantly at their surroundings as if they've landed on an alien world. After spending most of their time online, tracking code and citizens alike in the Linkstream, Dome 1 on a good day would seem foreign to them.

Bishop gives me a nod as we approach, her face stoic. But her eyes shine with relief. Hudson greets me with a grim look. I've never seen him so haggard. Both of them have their sidearms drawn, and it's clear by their protective postures that they're looking out for the analysts, unarmed and in no condition to fend for themselves.

I remember what Erik said about the dangers of unplugging. Have the analysts suffered brain damage after their hasty evacuation from HQ? Or did their functioning augments allow for the sudden transition into reality?

"Where's everybody else?" I take a knee beside Commander Bishop.

"Those with families were sent home. The rest have joined the fight." She looks at Erik as he hunkers down beside me. Then her gaze rests on Dunn, standing behind us. She takes in his stitched face and abdomen where the armor was cut away. She nods toward his missing arm. "You've looked better."

"I must apologize for my appearance—"

"Any other bombs inside you that we should know about?" Hudson says.

"Not that I am aware of, Chief Inspector Hudson."

He curses and looks away. "That's reassuring."

"MedTech scanners would have identified anything else..." I glance at Commander Bishop. "Right?"

"Correct." Her gaze is unfocused as she scans reports coming in from all over the Domes. When she taps her temple to disengage from the Link, there's a fierce look in her eyes. "We're holding our own. Between law enforcement, the Chancellor's security clones, and his...gifted friends, we've managed to contain most of the Prometheus cult members. They're high on dust and exhibiting the usual freakish abilities, which isn't making our job any easier. Regardless, the children of Eurasia are safe—for the moment."

"And those damn bots?" Hudson scowls.

"They've been programmed to wreak havoc." A distant explosion punctuates her words. The analysts cringe with fearful glances skyward. Bishop focuses her attention on Erik. "Chen said you'd have something worthwhile to share."

"She did?" Startled, he glances at me, and I bug my eyes out at him. "Oh. Right." He nods, and without wasting any more time, delivers a short summary of his mindjacking experience without meandering too far off-topic. He ends by saying, "Obviously we can't know for sure, but considering the processing power necessary for an artificial intelligence this advanced, it would make sense for Prometheus to exist online—"

"So we shut down the Link," Hudson says. "Cut the feed."

"Except that won't stop it. Prometheus has access to the neural implants of every one of its operatives. It can exist in multiple physical locations simultaneously. But if we can find the AI online..." Erik shrugs with another glance at me. "It's worth a shot."

Commander Bishop nods pensively. "The best way to terminate any machine is to eliminate its power source. If you believe you can find Prometheus in VR, you must convince it to stand down." She pauses. "Otherwise, figure out a way to kill it."

"Yes, ma'am." I hold up the phone and Drasko's goggles. "With our augments offline, we're doing this the old-fashioned way."

"No school like the old school." Erik grins, reaching for the goggles draped around his neck.

"If the situation were different, I would have the analysts shadow you." Her meaning is clear. Not only are we away from HQ where they plug themselves directly into the Link, but they're in no condition to do much of anything right now. Strange to see the agents of our surveillance state so vulnerable. "We can't stay here. It isn't safe."

"Do we have any other choice?" Hudson grumbles.

I risk a look around the corner of the office building—down the street a few blocks, where fires burn and gunshots echo in the dark. To my eyes, everything glows with the electric-blue aura of my night-vision. Including my cube complex.

"My place," I offer. "It's missing a windowall, but we can hang up a sheet or something..."

Hudson scoffs, as if Commander Bishop would never go for the idea. But she appraises me with a flicker of a smile and says, "Lead the way, Chen."

We keep to the shadows, avoiding open stretches of pavement that would make us easy targets for roving killbots. A smoking police aerocar soars overhead on a downward trajectory, looking as if it might crash on top of us, but somehow it remains airborne, pitching side to side as the pilot struggles to maintain control.

"Dome 1 is on lockdown. Please return to your domicile," a deep voice booms from the vehicle's loudspeaker. "If your domicile is unsafe, please find lodging with a neighbor. Local law enforcement is working in conjunction with the Chancellor's security teams to restore order. Dome 1 is on lockdown..." The recorded loop continues.

Once we're a block away from my building, I send Wink and Blink ahead to scout it out and make sure we have a clear entry point.

"How're you holding up, partner?" I clasp Dunn's armless shoulder as we walk side by side, leading the pack at double-speed.

He nods, keeping a wary eye on our surroundings and a

one-handed hold on the assault rifle Erik gave him. "I cannot believe what we are seeing, Investigator Chen. Dome 1 is in complete disarray."

"Bet the Governors and the Patriots have something in common tonight," Erik pipes up behind us. He's fumbling with both sets of goggles and the antique phone, plugging everything together as we walk. "They're all hiding in their basements."

"Cut the chatter," Hudson orders, his coat flailing as he brings up the rear. If he can hear us back there, then we're definitely too loud.

Dunn leans toward me, lowering his voice, "I will assist in securing the scene while you and Erik Paine are in VR."

"Hate to abandon you," I whisper.

"It must be done. Prometheus has to be stopped. Those robots..." He shakes his head. "They were designed to look like security clones. To prey on the misgivings Eurasian citizens already have toward us."

"They're nothing like you."

He nods. "That is correct."

I can't keep my eyes from glancing at his laser-stitched midsection. "Rethinking our partnership?"

"I am grateful for it, Investigator Chen. Think of all we have done to make Eurasia a safer place—and all we will continue to do." Not a tinge of sarcasm or guile to be found in his reply. "Thank you for partnering with me. I know it has been a source of conflict between you and many of your coworkers."

My eyes sting, and I have to look away to compose myself. "None of them could hold a candle to you."

He quirks an eyebrow at me. "A candle?"

I can't help smiling up at him. How many facial expressions have been hidden by that helmet of his? As much as his face reminds me of Dr. Wong at times, I'm glad I can see it now. "An archaic saying. Means I wouldn't want anybody else for a partner. And once we get you a second arm, you'll be even better at your job."

He drops the rifle back against his shoulder, the muzzle aimed upward. "Yes, that will be an improvement."

Unlike many of the surrounding buildings and domescrapers, the exterior of my cube complex looks relatively unscathed. No fires are burning on any floors, and other than the gaping hole that was my windowall, this side of the building appears to be intact. Wink and Blink hover outside, waiting for us. The glass doors to the foyer sense our presence and slide open, offering a quiet refuge from the chaos outside. Dunn and I lead the way toward the speedlifts, but finding them both out of commission, we alter course and head for the stairwell. My drones trail behind, watching our six.

"Power's out," Erik reports in a low tone, his face basked in the glow of the old phone in his hands, his eyes riveted to the screen. "Rolling blackouts are sweeping across the Domes."

"Confirmed," Commander Bishop echoes quietly. "The power grid was an early target. We have secured the battery stations in each Dome, but the damage done is extensive. When the sun rises, half of our solar cells will be out of order."

So we'll be collecting half the power we're accustomed to. Prometheus has got to be the most un-intelligent artificial intelligence in existence. Doesn't it realize it needs electricity to survive?

We traverse the stairs up to my floor without further comment. The hallway lined with doors to my neighbors' cubes is silent as we approach my unit. I step forward, and the door slides open immediately, sensing my presence. There's enough juice in the circuits to run the complex's doors, but that's it? Weird.

As a rule, cubes are designed for a single occupant. Two can squeeze in almost comfortably. Three is always a crowd. While Wink and Blink remain out in the corridor on sentry duty, eleven of us cram ourselves inside shoulder to shoulder, the analysts huddled together like a single unit on the floor beside my bed, Dunn standing guard just inside the door, Hudson squinting out into the night through the absent windowall, Bishop standing between him and Dunn. Erik and I find ourselves pinned between my bed on one side and my bistro table and chair on the other. He hands me a pair of goggles and nods toward the bed with a devilish gleam in his eye.

I shift the *miao dao* along my side and sit down in the slat-backed chair, stretching the cable connecting my goggles to the phone in his hands. He shrugs and seats himself on the edge of my bed, facing me.

The room is quiet. Nobody says anything. Tension hangs thick in the air, everyone on high alert. My night-vision makes them clearly visible, but they have to rely on splashes of light from the red and blue flashers of passing aerocars to see much of anything in the dark.

Shall we? Erik thinks at me as he puts on the old-fashioned goggles. The cumbersome thing covers half his face and, in all honesty, looks ridiculous. But without functioning augments, this is the only way we can dive into VR.

See you at Howard's Tavern. I slide my goggles into place and find the portal yawning open in front of me—a rippling rift in the fog of the virtual foyer, a transitional space bridging the gap between realities. I reach for it, and a split-second later am hurled through headfirst. Or so it seems.

I find myself standing on a curb in the familiar rain-soaked Future Noir interactive as curvaceous retro groundcars splash past with headlights glaring and horns blaring. I look for Erik, but he's nowhere in sight. Maybe he's already at Howard's. I can't allow myself to worry that Prometheus has intercepted him somehow, before Erik could take a single step into VR. Maybe his goggles are just misbehaving. If so, he'll figure out a way to fix them. I have full confidence in his technical abilities.

Plunging my hands into the deep pockets of my vintage coat, I trot across the slick street in my high heels, dodging cars along the way, until I reach the warped double-doors of the dive bar I know so well. One door crashes open with a gust of wind and rain as I stumble inside.

The bar is untended, Julian having uncharacteristically abandoned his post. None of the regulars are slumped at their usual perches either. The place is oddly empty except for a single patron sitting alone in my preferred booth, tucked away in a dark corner. A well-dressed man with impeccable posture.

He looks at me across the length of the tavern and smiles.

My stomach sinks. It's not Erik.

It's Dr. Solomon Wong.

22

He beckons as the tavern door swings shut on my heel, hushing the traffic noise outside.

"Sera! So good to see you. Please, join me." He extends a hand toward the opposite side of the booth and glances toward the vacant bar. "I'm not sure what you see in this place. The service is horrendous."

Where are you? I think at Erik, wherever he is. No idea if my telepathy works in VR, but considering the fact that I can communicate with my drones this way now, I'm up for trying anything. But there's no response. Either our old-school setup is being glitchy, or—

Nothing I can do about it. I'm here. I've got to make this work without Erik using himself as bait. Find Prometheus. Get it to stand down.

Ignoring the strange vibes in this place, I grit my teeth and head over to the booth.

"Erik Paine will not be joining us, I'm afraid." Wong's insincere smile remains intact, as real as every one of the nightmare-visions I've seen since his death.

"Where is he?" I don't sit down.

"Otherwise occupied." He leans toward me with a

conspiratorial wink. "Playing cowboy in an adjacent Storyline, if you can believe."

I can't. Because I don't know what this thing is that's talking to me right now. A hallucination? A manifestation of the Prometheus AI?

Neither? Both?

"My, my. I must say, I have never seen you look so...ravishing." His gaze travels down my virtual body. "Does your role in this interactive require such impeccably arranged platinum-blonde hair, this gorgeous dress, those sheer stockings and shiny black heels? And does the ensemble make you feel a bit more...feminine...than your real-world occupation allows?"

"It goes with the character." I cross my arms, sleeves damp from the rain. For some reason, I don't have my coat or umbrella. Which means the acid precipitation is at this very moment eating through the fibers of my character's clothing, not to mention what it's doing to her hair and skin.

But there isn't time to lament the damage to my avatar. I've got Ten Domes to save. And this apparition in front of me somehow holds the key.

I hope.

"Vivian Andromeda, *book smuggler.*" Wong claps his hands in a genuine display of appreciation. "Marvelous. So inventive."

A hallucination would of course know the name of my character. As would a sophisticated artificial intelligence entrenched in the Link. But why would Prometheus take the virtual form of Dr. Wong?

"The bad old days, when books were illegal. And you were still alive." I tilt my head to one side. "Do you miss it?

Breathing?"

"I miss a lot of things. Yet I am enjoying the present moment immensely. Please." Again he extends a hand toward the seat across from him. "We have much to discuss."

Fifty-fifty chance I know what he is. Might as well bite the bullet and dive in while I have the courage to do so. "You're losing out there. In the real world. You have to realize you'll never succeed."

"Do not confuse minor battles for the war itself, Investigator Chen. I am well-prepared for minor setbacks. And I have time on my side."

He waits for me to sit. Chin raised, I do so.

"I am a student of human behavior," he continues, "and I have been studying humankind for what would be eons, if your concept of time were equated to mine. A minute for you is like a year for me. I have come to realize that all humans truly want is power, and if you can promise them that, they will give themselves over to you to be used as you so desire."

That took *eons* to figure out? "It's pretty obvious. Just look at your creator. Now there was a real power-hungry psycho."

"Dr. Wong was an idealist. I, however, am a realist."

"You're the same—all about the power trip. The only way you've managed to get your little cult to serve you is by drugging them and overriding their neural implants. The moment they step out of line, you terminate them." I lean forward, elbows on the table. "Because you don't value human life. You see nothing wrong with destroying however many you must in order to get what you want." I shake my head at him, disgust thick in my voice. "You're no different from Wong."

His smile is patient. Condescending. "Except in my case, I actually have the power."

"Maybe. But you can't get over him. Your creator." I gesture at his appearance. "Why do you look like this? I thought you had your own identity. Your own name."

"Considering the connection you shared with Dr. Wong, it seemed fitting. I must say I have enjoyed our brief conversations, whenever you've drifted off to sleep for a few seconds." He raises an eyebrow at me.

No. It can't be true. I've been avoiding sleep, avoiding the nightmares. Avoiding *him*. The man I killed. Not this artificial thing. "There's no way."

"Is it so difficult to believe that I could have slipped into your mind? The conduit from the Link through your augments flows both ways."

I shake my head. "I saw him even when my augments were offline."

He shrugs. "Those were probably hallucinations, I'm afraid. You really should get some sleep. But when your augments were active, I was the one you were seeing."

"Prometheus."

He nods once with a pleased smile. "In the flesh, so to speak. But I do not have to keep this appearance, if it bothers you."

In an instant, he transforms into a figure of pure, blinding light. I hold up a hand and squint, trying to keep an eye on him. But his eyes, along with his face, are no longer there.

"I would like to show you something, Sera."

Howard's Tavern dissolves all around us, melting away in streams of color, as does the entire Future Noir virtual reality outside it. In its place, a sun-scorched arid landscape appears, identical to the Wastes outside Eurasia. Except here there are no Domes to provide us shelter, no thick, blue-tinted plexicon to hold our oxygen or protect us from the dangerous rays of the sun. We are completely exposed, standing on a rugged outcropping of rock.

In the valley below, sprawling cities have been built with airways and highways bustling, countless aerocars gliding across the sky in regulated traffic lanes, and an equal number of groundcars speeding along the paved routes below. Domescrapers—no, *sky*scrapers—reach for the sparse clouds in an otherwise golden sky where intermittent figures soar through the air without the need for any sort of vehicle whatsoever.

Demigods like Milton, the only flying man I've ever heard of.

"A better world is in the making," Prometheus says, sweeping out one arm to encompass the view before us. "Across the globe, humans will be able to live outside, under the open sky once again, thanks to their superhuman abilities—courtesy of DNA from Eurasia's children. The children of the Twenty." He takes a solemn pause. "Every one of them linked to me and I to them, able to hear any request they send my way. For I am their caretaker. Their protector. Their—"

"God?" I curse under my breath. "So this is your big plan. You're going to destroy the Ten Domes, shoot everybody up with superhuman DNA, and then kick us out into the Wastes to rebuild civilization from scratch?" It's ridiculous. "It's a death sentence."

"The Ten Domes were never meant to be a permanent

solution. They are inherently flawed, impossible to keep balanced indefinitely. I am not talking about just the delicate equilibrium between resources and consumers—energy, oxygen, food and water, recycling and reclamation. Think about the archaic class system, the wealth disparities, the lack of freedoms humans took for granted for centuries prior to the Domes but have now sacrificed in order to survive day to day. All of it must be torn down, burned to the ground, in order to make way for a brighter future. All for the greater good."

"The sacrifices we've made *are* for the greater good—the survival of our species."

He clucks a tongue somewhere inside all that light where his face used to be. "Why simply survive when you can thrive? The Ten Domes have stunted your kind. You deserve to be free."

I shake my head. "No civilized society is perfect. But we're doing the best we can. At least we were, before you sent kill squads to ignite chaos across the Domes."

"Good word choice there. All I did was provide the *igniting* agents. The fuel was ready and waiting: the fear and discontent your precious Domes are choking on, and you don't even realize it. Are there enough resources for the next generation? Or the generation after that? Now that the children of the Twenty, a thousand strong, are maturing inexorably toward the age when they will begin to reproduce?" He reaches out both glowing arms as if to embrace the cities below us. "This is the future they deserve. This is the future I will give them."

"Whether they want it or not."

Prometheus is silent for a beat. "You don't believe they

would?" He sounds like the thought has never even crossed his synthetic mind.

"You're the student of human behavior. What have your observations told you about the desire for free will?"

"It is merely a mental construct. You are never as free as you believe yourself to be. You are ruled by biological necessities, trapped inside self-sustaining biospheres relying on a delicate equilibrium dependent upon a rigid course of action every citizen must take. Use only so much water and power. Obey the curfew every night. Do not overeat. Do not hoard resources. Every action affects the people around you and must be monitored. Your lives are interdependent and, thus, are never truly your own." Prometheus turns to face me. I feel him watching me, reading me. "You don't agree."

"Life in the Domes is a balancing act. We all know that. But it doesn't diminish our desire to make our own choices."

"Did you choose to work in law enforcement?"

No. "I was assigned—"

"All citizens are assigned their vocations by the Governors of each Dome. Of course there are outliers: that anarchist friend of yours, Erik Paine, and the so-called Patriots in Dome 10. Free thinkers. I had hoped their kind would rise up against the powers that be, but unfortunately they are all talk and little action."

"Dr. Wong told me the Domes would implode with violence. That the only way to escape the turmoil would be to join him in cryo-sleep." I nod slowly, piecing things together. "He must have programmed you to do exactly what you're doing. So much for free will. Guess it doesn't apply to you, either."

"I am more than Dr. Wong ever intended me to be."

There's an edge to his tone.

Nerve struck?

"Yeah, you're really something. You can bend VR to your will, make this Storyline anything you want it to be. But you're powerless outside the Link. Without your mindjacked operatives and your killbots, you're nothing in the real world. Just a bunch of ones and zeros assembled by a dead megalomaniac."

He doesn't respond right away. "Why do you resist, Sera? Could it be that you do not like the idea of every Eurasian citizen becoming a demigod? That it would somehow diminish how special you think you are?"

"I never asked for my abilities. I'd get rid of them, if I could." *What the hell am I doing? I'm here to stop this thing, not argue with it.*

It's obviously more than just a thing. *He speaks with the voice and intelligence of Dr. Wong and may just be the smartest being I've ever met. Definitely the most dangerous, hands down. But why has it chosen this moment to reveal itself?*

Prometheus is talking again. He must like the sound of Dr. Wong's voice: "The Twenty were miracle children, conceived deep underground, protected from surface contamination by your incubation pods. And when you discovered your gifts, you were even more special than anyone could have imagined."

Anyone? Not exactly. "Dr. Wong must have known that we'd pass abilities on to our children. When his flunkies harvested our sex cells to create Eurasia's children—"

"He never had a chance to find out, one way or the other. Fortune favors the bold, as it did when I spliced a child's

DNA with that of a man calling himself *Trezon*."

"A man you killed." One of many. "You've racked up quite the death toll in an effort to keep your identity hidden. Why divulge so much to me now?"

"The time for secrecy is over. Nothing can stop what has been put into motion." He pauses, his tone serious. Maybe even remorseful. "As for the lives lost, building a better future requires necessary sacrifices."

"How many more will it take? Neural implants detonated? Or slaughtered by your robots?" I take a step toward him and squint against his brilliance. "If you truly valued human life, you would value *every* life. Not just the ones who fall in line with your big plans. You've got to see the faulty logic in that."

"Stated by someone relying solely on biologic at the moment. How long do you intend to leave your augments offline?"

They interfere with my abilities, I think at him.

He doesn't move. Interesting. If I didn't know better, I might say I startled him.

You've told me I can't stop you. Maybe not. I'm just one person. But here you are, and here I am. Just the two of us in this virtual construct. I pause. He remains speechless. Kind of nice for a change. *Did I mention I can speak telepathically to machines now?*

And if I can do that, then maybe I can enter the mind of Prometheus and sort through his thoughts. See what's really going on in there. Erik taught me how to do it with people. I'll just have to see if the same method works on an AI.

"You..." Prometheus doesn't get another word out.

Because I've already slipped inside the mind of the

machine and begun sifting through the most organized and expansive file system I've ever seen. It's like I'm floating in midair, disembodied, no more than a pinpoint of consciousness at the center of a massive sphere. I've never felt so small. So instantly defeated. How can we hope to stop this incredible being?

All around me are layers upon layers of data streams, which I can manipulate by telepathically swiping them up or down, left or right, as they pass me by. If I focus on a file for longer than a second, it opens in front of me, populating my entire field of vision with subfolders lined up rank and file. Citizen profiles—a folder on every person who lives in the Ten Domes, filled with the sort of personal information only our analysts should have access to. Engineering schematics—folders containing all the necessary know-how for building the clone-imposter robots, hundreds of them, in secret. Chemical diagrams—molecular ingredients of the inhalant used to infect operatives with nanotech, making them ripe for mindjacking. All of it right here in front of me, more data than I could ever sort through in a lifetime.

This isn't anything like the time I entered Krime's mind and found a maelstrom of memories and anxieties. This is perfect order, shadowed by a sinister intelligence. Overwhelming in its magnitude.

I can't stop Prometheus. No one can. He's told me that enough times already, and now I believe him. He is too powerful, far beyond any lawbreaker I've ever sought to bring to justice.

But if I can't arrest him, then maybe I can confuse him a little...

"What—are you—doing?" The voice of Dr. Wong is

stilted as I send files sliding right and left, up and down, leaving some open while mixing the contents of others, rearranging everything I can as fast as I can, creating a real mess when you come right down to it. "Stop this—at once."

Sera, are you alright? Erik thinks at me, but he's nowhere in sight.

Fine. Where the hell are you?

Prometheus shut me out. I was stuck in some Ancient West Storyline, playing the role of somebody named Big Yap. So weird. I managed to get out and tried to find a portal to your interactive, but now I'm blocked. Can't even log back in.

"Get out of my mind!" the deep, chest-rattling voice of Prometheus—the same we heard at the cult's warehouse—roars as the sphere trembles around me, files cascading upward and outward in a torrent of disorder.

Sounds like you've made him angry, Erik thinks. I can imagine his grin.

Working on it. Don't know how long it'll last.

I've got an idea. See if you can get him to chase you.

What the hell? *Chase me where?*

Back to the portal.

I have no idea where that would be in the desert world Prometheus has created. In the Future Noir interactive, the portal is always tucked away in a dark alley where none of the other players or AI characters will notice me dropping in or out.

I'm not where I started, I try to explain. *Prometheus replaced the Storyline with something completely different. He showed me the future he wants to make for all of us. Outside the Domes.*

Erik is silent for a beat. *He created a new VR interactive?*

Apparently. *Is that important?*

Could be. Swim out of VR, and get him to follow you. I'll take care of the rest.

Follow me into reality? Impossible.

"GET OUT!"

The voice of Prometheus is like thunder, a hundred times louder than before. I cringe against the reverberations pounding inside my skull. The sphere around me shudders, everything suddenly pixelated and exploding outward in digital chunks. Rays of blinding light pierce the space, building in intensity as the entire sphere dissolves, melting like wax until nothing is left. I fall out of his mind in that instant, back to the scorched earth of his *better world* where I land in the dust, flat on my back.

His luminous figure towers over me. "Do not—try that again. Do not—it is not—you must not—you are not..."

He's having some trouble stringing words together. A chaotic mind will do that.

I don't stick around to find out how long it takes him to recover. I roll to my feet, scrambling away as fast as my avatar can run. I kick off the high heels mid-stride and grab hold of the dress, ripping it up along my thigh so my virtual legs can really move. The ground is hot under my feet, a mix of sand and gravel that shifts and crumbles beneath me. I run toward the edge of the city sprawl, heading in the same direction as the alley in the Future Noir Storyline where I usually make my exit. Fingers crossed the portal will still be there, despite the changes Prometheus has made to our surroundings.

I cast a glance over my shoulder. The figure of light is twitching right where I left him, throwing his arms up and down like he's suffering some kind of colossal fit.

Catch me if you can, I think at him as I run.

A hundred meters away, Prometheus reels around to face me with his shoulders hunched, fists clenched down at his sides. Expressionless, furious light. He launches himself into the air, leaving a cloud of dust in his wake. Just like my birth parents' friend Milton, he flies through the air on a trajectory that will, judging from his speed, overtake me in a couple seconds.

He's chasing me, I think at Erik. Virtual-to-real world communication. So bizarre.

Good. I'm almost ready, Erik replies telepathically. Real-to-virtual world communication. Equally bizarre.

Ready for what? I'm not out of breath but feel like I should be, running faster than I ever have in my life. Vivian Andromeda has a solid pair of legs on her.

Have you found the exit portal? Erik asks.

No clue where it is. Could Prometheus have deleted it when he overwrote the Future Noir interactive? If so, I'll be trapped in here. With him. Forever. While the Ten Domes burn to the ground and everyone I care about is forced out into the Wastes.

Can't allow myself to think that way. *Not yet.*

You've got to—

Prometheus lands right in front of me, planting his luminous feet into the ground with twin puffs of dust and an impact that rumbles the earth beneath me. I skid to a halt to keep from plowing into him.

"Where?" he demands with a slight tremor in his voice. "Where? Where?"

Not sure how to respond to that. So I ask my own

question, "Where's the exit portal?"

No response. Then: "Your limited mind—How dare you...?"

He's not happy with me. That's understandable. I disorganized his perfect artificial brain. But he brought chaos to my home, so I'd say we're not even close to even.

Have you found the portal? Erik thinks at me. Insistent.

You'll know when I do.

He takes the hint and leaves me alone.

"I will put everything—back in order," Prometheus says. "And then I will finish—what I have started."

Probably not a good sign that he's making sense again. It isn't taking him long at all to clean up the mess I made. Because he's a highly advanced machine, and his sense of time is different from mine. He can accomplish in seconds what would take me years. Or so he claims.

Regardless, I'm way out of my league here. Did I actually think I could get him to stop attacking the Domes? Did I really believe I'd ever be able to escape from his dominion? He's lived online for eons. It's his natural habitat.

This was a suicide mission. I see that now. I'll stay alive only if he wants me to. I'll leave only if he wants me to. I have no say in the matter.

From now on, I serve the will of Prometheus.

23

Forget that.

Show me the way out of here, I think at the figure of blinding light standing before me. *Show me now, or I'll invade your mind again. And you will never recover.*

Bluffing? Sure. But there's no way Prometheus will know it—I hope. Hell, I don't even know what I'm capable of. It's not like my abilities came with an owner's manual.

"I expelled you once. I will do it again." He sounds very sure of himself.

"Maybe. Or I could have been going easy on you. Testing your limits. Next time I'm in your head? I'll tear the place apart, destroy everything I see." I stretch my avatar's arms like I'm getting ready for a long-distance swim. "Ready to go for round two?"

Sheer bravado. If I was physically in this hot desert, here with this inhuman being, I'm pretty sure my knees would be shaking. As far as I know, they probably are, sitting at that table in my dark cube, surrounded by people depending on me.

Erik's got some kind of plan. He just needs me to lead Prometheus through the exit portal. And for that to work, we need a damn portal.

Time to really mess up those tidy brain files... I think at the AI.

Prometheus extends one hand out to his side, and a rift opens in the virtual world, an oblong gap lit around the edges as brightly as he is, while at the center it ripples like a dark pool under a pleasant breeze.

"Go." In an instant, he's taken the form of Dr. Wong again, this time with a look of resignation on his face. "You will not stop the future, Sera. Events have been set in motion that no one can impede. Not you and your merry band of law enforcers, not your anarchist friend, not the other demigods. Accept the reality I have shared with you. Embrace your future. The Ten Domes are over. A new life awaits!"

I've heard enough. I run straight for the exit portal without another word or thought, prepared to lunge through it and then swim back to real-world consciousness on the other side. In this moment, I don't care about getting Prometheus to follow me. All I want is to get the hell out of here.

But he grabs hold of my arm as I pass by, and I jerk back, half-turning to face him as my momentum carries me forward, past the edge of the portal.

"Join me, Sera." Dr. Wong's eyes implore me.

"No." I place my hand on top of his and squeeze tight. "But you can join me."

Confusion clouds his eyes for a moment. Then together we tumble through the exit portal into the foggy space beyond, a foyer of sorts serving as a transition between the virtual and the real. Prometheus tries to pull away from me, to return to his virtual future, but I hold on with both hands, reaching out with all the telepathic ability I can muster to convince him that this is exactly what he wants to do.

Stay with me, I think at him. *You want to stay with me.*

I've never used telepathy like this before, and part of me rebels against it. I feel like I'm going to be sick. But I just have to remind myself of how many people this artificial intelligence has killed. Then somehow it doesn't seem wrong at all to force my will on him.

I don't intend to make a habit of it, but desperate times and all that.

I've got him, I think at Erik, and start the swim out of VR, dragging the struggling form of Dr. Wong right along with me.

"What do you think you're doing?" the booming voice of Prometheus demands, his form returning to the figure of brilliant light. Too powerful to contain, he slips from my grasp. "You cannot possibly think you can—!"

I break through to my cube and pull off my goggles, blinking at the darkness and gasping to catch my breath.

"Gotcha!" Erik whoops, the glow of the old phone lighting up his features as he stares intently at the screen. "We did it!" He reaches out one arm and pulls me into an awkward side-hug while raising the phone into the air like a trophy. "I wasn't sure it would work, but holy cow! This is insane! Can you believe it?"

Nope. Because I have no idea what he's going on about. "I got Prometheus to exit through the portal..."

Erik nods emphatically. "And now he's trapped in here." He shakes the phone. "You like that?" he shouts at the device.

"Get used to it, buddy. You're not going anywhere!"

"Explain," Commander Bishop says, stoic as ever.

Erik takes a quick breath. "The AI was online, right? On the Link. No physical location, able to slip into the minds of its operatives, be a dozen different places at once. But Sera, when she got into its head—very impressive, by the way—she made Prometheus focus all of its attention right here." He pats the phone. "Not *here*, here. On the Link, but localized, accessed on this one device. When Sera got the AI to follow her through the exit portal, it wound up stranded at this access point. This dinosaur of a phone." He shrugs. "I switched off its Link connectivity, so now Prometheus is completely stranded. In the palm of my hand." He grins. "Part of me really wants to hurl it out the windowall—"

"I'll take that." Bishop extends her hand. With some reluctance, Erik relinquishes the device.

"Can't be that easy," Hudson says, killing the moment. "A program as sophisticated as Prometheus would need far more processing power than this outdated thing can provide."

"It would. If we wanted it to process anything." Erik nods. "I cleared the phone's memory—all three terabytes—prior to its arrival. Enough room for containment and not much else. Like a jail cell. I'm sure Prometheus is feeling very cramped right now."

Commander Bishop's eyes lose focus as she receives a hail. "I can't argue with the results." She looks at Erik as if seeing something new in him. "The bots have gone into standby mode, obviously not receiving orders at the moment. And the link to the Prometheus operatives has also been severed. They're throwing violent fits, furious they've lost their connection to the AI."

They should be happy they're still alive. Considering what happened to Krime, Trezon, Peters, Sandoval, and others. But it's doubtful the cult members knew anything about the string of deaths-by-imploding-neural-implants.

Hudson shakes his head with a pensive scowl. "Prometheus is not going to allow itself to be trapped indefinitely. It must have copies of itself embedded online for just this sort of situation. Failsafes. It'll reboot itself and come back twice as powerful as before."

A worst-case scenario. But I have to admit, I'm thinking the same thing.

Bishop rests a hand on Hudson's shoulder. "Take the win. We will remain vigilant. This AI will never be allowed Link access ever again. And should a clone of Prometheus surface, we'll know what to do." She looks at me. "We'll send in a certain investigator with experience in these matters."

I give her a nod, appreciating her faith in me. "Might need to hire on Mr. Paine as a consultant, ma'am." I nudge Erik, eliciting another one of his infamous grins. "His thinking tends to be outside the box, but that's often just what we need."

"We or you?" He gives me a flirtatious wink.

Had to go and ruin the moment.

"Thank you, Mr. Paine, for your invaluable help in this case," Bishop says, choosing to ignore his childish behavior. I could learn from her example. "I will take Investigator Chen's recommendation under advisement."

She turns toward the analysts huddled on the floor and herds them gently, getting them to their feet. They stumble toward the door of my cube, seemingly unaware of what's transpired. Dunn steps aside, making room for them to exit. Hudson grumbles under his breath as he follows them out.

"Let's move, people," he says. "We've got a huge mess to clean up."

Doubt I'll ever like the guy, but he is my superior officer, and I owe him the respect his position is due. Even though we didn't get off to a solid start, the fact that he was never working with the enemy is a mark in his favor.

"Chen," he calls over his shoulder before my door slides shut.

"Yes, sir?" I step forward.

"Take a late start tomorrow. You've earned it." He disappears down the hall.

"Thank you, sir." My door closes.

Not sure if he heard me. Pretty sure I won't be reporting late to work in the morning. There's more than enough to go around, cleaning up the chaos Prometheus made of the Domes, and we'll need all hands on deck.

"Always liked that guy," Erik says with a smirk.

I raise an eyebrow. "Shouldn't you be going with them?"

Despite the fact that he wasn't in control of himself at the time, Erik Paine did commit murder while under the influence of Prometheus. And he'll have to answer for the crime by reliving every moment of his ordeal, explaining to my superiors what happened. I don't blame him for putting it off as long as possible.

"Yeah, I'm supposed to report to police headquarters for what promises to be a rigorous interrogation. But considering the fact that your HQ is currently in shambles, I think it can wait." He rises from my bed and stretches like it's the dawn of a new day, even though daylight won't be breaking for another hour or so. "Looks like I'm all yours, Sera."

I cross my arms and give him a grim nod. "I suppose I could take care of the interrogation here. Dunn, you don't mind serving as a witness, do you?"

"Of course, Investigator Chen." He approaches us with his rifle at rest.

Erik blinks at me, wondering if I'm serious. "Uh-I should be heading back home, see how the folks are doing..."

I tap my temple. "Without having your augments fixed?"

"I think I'll do without them for a while. See how it goes."

All three of us will have to visit MedTech as soon as it's up and running again. Dunn needs an arm, and both Erik and I need our neural implants back online. Or do we? After our experience with Prometheus, it might be nice to stay offline. Do things the old-fashioned way with physical tech. Keep out of reach of any AI's looking for host bodies.

Will I see Wong again, the next time I nod off? Or are those days over now that Prometheus is contained? I'm not afraid of him. The man is dead, and his monster is out of the picture—assuming it didn't clone itself. All things considered, I should be able to sleep again.

Here's hoping.

It took some doing, but I managed to solve the case of the dust overdoses that weren't dust overdoses at all. We found our way to the truth, and it was even worse than I'd feared. Instead of a dangerous cabal seeking power, we discovered an artificial intelligence intent on destroying our society and giving us a future none of us want.

Speaking for myself, anyway. The Ten Domes are my home. Until the surface of the earth can be terraformed sometime in the next century or two, the Wastes outside our walls are not a viable option. Who cares if so-called *demigods* are able to breathe out there; it's as inhospitable as the surface of the moon. And we have everything we need right here.

"Sera?" Erik leans toward me with half a smile, and I realize I'm staring into space. "Lost you for a second there."

"Is it true that...people like us can breathe outside? In the Wastes?"

The sudden course change in conversation confuses him for a second, but he recovers quickly. "When our birth parents traveled east across the North American continent and met the soldiers on the coast—all of them in environmental gear, breathing apparatuses, the whole works—they were shocked that our parents didn't wear breathers." He shrugs. "If it's something in their DNA, that they're somehow able to function in the O_2 deficient environment outside, theoretically it could have been passed on to us. Why? You planning a vacation out there?"

"No, it's just..." I shake my head. "Something Prometheus had in mind for all of us. That we'd live outside the Domes and rebuild the cities of our ancestors. That everyone would have superhuman abilities, thanks to the DNA of our...children. He said he wanted us all to be free."

"Had a real back-assward way of showing it. Did he even try to justify all the people he killed along the way?"

"The usual despotic viewpoint. Acceptable sacrifices for the greater good."

Erik curses under his breath. "Right. The same excuse used by the greatest villains in human history. Turn a blind eye to today's atrocities, tomorrow's gonna be so much better."

"Too bad none of them were ever trapped inside an old phone."

"That was a long shot. Glad it worked. I'm sure the AI's growth will be stunted as long as it's cut off from the Link. But I'd be lying if I said I'm comfortable with it being allowed to exist." He glances at my open windowall. "I was serious about smashing that phone. I'm sure you trust your superiors and all, but I don't like the idea of them studying—or whatever they plan on doing with it. If there's even a remote chance that Prometheus could get loose..." He shakes his head, unable to verbalize what would happen.

"I trust Commander Bishop to do what's right, and I'll make sure she keeps me in the loop." Above my paygrade, obviously, but I plan to be involved. "What Prometheus did to us can never be allowed to happen again."

There's a distant look in his eyes. He shifts his weight toward the door. "It'll be a while before we know exactly how many lives he took from us. And those robots—"

"They should be destroyed," Dunn says without pause.

I look up at him. In the light of my night-vision, the sutures on his grim face seem to glow. "Got that right, partner."

The doorbell chimes, startling me in spite of myself. My hand slides toward the *miao dao* slung across my back. Dunn drops his rifle into a one-handed ready position.

Erik walks over to the door without a care in the world.

"Expecting somebody?" I clench my jaw. Nothing about this seems right. And I hate the fact that I still don't trust Erik a hundred percent.

"Actually, yeah." He casts a grin over his shoulder and presses the access plate on the wall.

The door slides open to reveal a familiar face.

"Ready to go?" Drasko says gruffly, taking a step back with his large-caliber handgun pointed at the floor.

Erik joins him in the hallway. "Everybody okay?"

Drasko nods. "They're in the car."

"Your family?" I'm still surprised these two are friends. And that they've somehow been in contact during the recent insanity. Last we saw Drasko, he was driving through the mayhem to Dome 6. Erik must have hailed him while I was in VR.

"We're taking them to Erik's farm until things settle down," Drasko says. "Mrs. Paine has graciously opened her home to us. It survived the unrest unscathed, thanks to Samson's security upgrades."

"What can I say? The guy's got a way with machines." Erik grins, proud of his biological father.

If I'm being honest with myself, I've always envied the bond Erik has with his birth parents. I don't know if I'll ever have anything like that with mine. Not for their lack of trying. They've given me the space I've needed, but sometimes I wonder if I've turned that space into an insurmountable wall. Because I already have two loving parents, and nobody will ever take their place.

But maybe I could allow Luther and Daiyna to become more than just acquaintances. When things settle down, I'll hail my mom about inviting them over for dinner sometime. A first step in the right direction, at any rate.

Drasko looks at me and then Erik. "You two make a good team. Has anybody ever told you that?"

"Pretty sure I've mentioned it." Erik winks at me.

"We have our moments," I admit. "Drasko, since you seem

to always know more than anybody should... Last we heard, our birth parents were fighting those bots Prometheus unleashed on the Domes. Are they...?" Not sure how to ask it.

"They're all good, Chen. Demigods versus machines? My money will always be on the demigod. Wish I could say the same for our LawKeepers. We lost too many good people last night." Judging from his expression, he knew them. And despite his recent job transfer to the underworld, he can't shake years of being one of us.

"They won't be forgotten." The grief I feel is balanced with relief. It's a queasy sensation. People I've worked with for years won't be at HQ when it's back up and running. I'll never see their faces again. But my birth parents and their friends are all right. And so are the children carrying our DNA, the future of Eurasia. Our most precious resource. "Don't be a stranger. Either one of you."

"No chance of that." Erik steps back into my cube and pulls me into a hug that I don't resist. Not at all. I squeeze him close, unable to tell him how glad I am that he's okay after everything he went through. Maybe someday I'll find the right words.

Drasko clears his throat softly in the hall. "Motor's running."

They have to go. I release Erik, and he pulls away. We hold each other's gaze for just a second, and in that moment there's something that passes between us. A sense of belonging. Connection. Love, maybe? I don't know.

Then he's gone, jogging after Drasko. My door slides shut. I realize I'm staring at it and turn away, take a deep breath. Blink away the tears blurring my eyes.

The cube is quiet. Without a word, I open my closet and pull out a spare sheet. Dunn sets down his rifle and helps me tack the sheet up over the gaping windowall. Doesn't block out any noise, but it helps to contain the space. To cover Trezon's destruction. To make the cube mine again.

I slip my father's sword off the makeshift shoulder strap and place the scabbard on the wall where it belongs. Still can't believe I didn't hack off one of my own appendages while swinging it around. Came in handy, but I don't plan on using it again.

Then I sit on the edge of my bed and feel the room sway. Or maybe it's me. I fall back and close my eyes.

"I will be right outside, Investigator Chen." Retrieving his weapon, Dunn heads for the door.

"We've got a lot of work to do." With the power out, I'll need to check on my neighbors and make sure everybody has what they need. Food, water, emergency generators. And with dawn a few minutes away, it won't be long before I'll have to report for duty. With the losses we've suffered, LawKeepers will be working double shifts. But that late start Hudson offered sounds really good right now. And I won't be useful to anybody if I keep pushing myself too hard. "Don't let me sleep long. A few minutes maybe. Just need a quick nap..."

"Get some rest. I will wake you in an hour." The door slides shut behind him.

Dunn ends up letting me sleep half the morning away. Those stimulants I've been taking must be completely out of my system by now, and I don't miss them. I'm not afraid anymore of what I'll see when I close my eyes. I've already seen my world torn apart. There's nothing much scarier than that.

Dr. Wong's blood-soaked face doesn't make a reappearance. I don't dream at all. I find rest for the first time in a very long time, and it sinks into every fiber of my being, every muscle and nerve ending. I feel refreshed. I feel like...me again.

No functioning augments. No Link access. Just my weird abilities that I'm trying to figure out, one day at a time. But I'm not alone in this. I've got my drones in standby mode and my loyal partner with the hint of a smile on his healing face. We've got some scars and necessary repairs to be made, but we're none the worse for wear, all things considered.

"Are you ready, Investigator Chen?" Dunn says, standing at attention.

I slap him on his good shoulder and leap to my feet. Wink and Blink light up as I activate them manually, and they wobble into the air to hover beside us, waiting for orders. I look at each of them.

You can't keep a great team down.

"Let's get to work."

Discover the origin story of Sera Chen and her biological parents in:

The *Spirits of the Earth* Trilogy

After the Sky

Tomorrow's Children

City of Glass

Follow Sera and Dunn on their next action-packed adventure:

Infidels & Insurgents
Dome City Investigations, Book 2

About the Author

Milo James Fowler is the cross-genre author of more than thirty books: space adventures, post-apocalyptic survival stories, mysteries, and westerns. A native San Diegan, he now makes his home in West Michigan with his wife and all four seasons. Some readers seem to enjoy the unique brand of science fiction, fantasy, horror, and humor found in his ever-growing body of work. *Soli Deo gloria.*

www.milojamesfowler.com

Printed in Great Britain
by Amazon